Praise for *Hot Dish*

"With her contemporary debut, C_____ modern times with her rapier _____ tact. Regardless of the ti_____ sheer magic. I'd say, 'Welcome _____ Connie!' but, quite frankly, I'm not su_____ tion."
—Elizabeth Bevarly

"A dazzling contemporary debut!" —Christina Dodd

"A hilarious, bittersweet look at going home. Connie Brockway proves she's got the contemporary chops to go the distance."
—Eloisa James

"Connie Brockway's contemporary debut is wry, witty, and wonderful! This cast of unforgettable characters will tickle your funny bone and your heartstrings."
—*New York Times* bestselling author Teresa Medeiros

"How best to describe *New York Times* bestseller Brockway's leap from historicals into the contemporary genre? It's a little bit bitter, quite sweet, but mainly hilarious. This combination caper and comedy-of-errors story is just wacky enough to keep you giggling. Brava!" —*Romantic Times*

"A smart and funny page-turner featuring a cast of small-town characters who never seem anything less than real. Season it all with Ms. Brockway's rapier wit and you have a winner on virtually every level." —All About Romance

"Splendidly satisfying. With its surfeit of realistically quirky characters and sharp wit, *Hot Dish* is simply superb."
—*Booklist*

continued . . .

SKINNY DIPPING

Connie Brockway

AN ONYX BOOK

ONYX
Published by New American Library, a division of
Penguin Group (USA) Inc., 375 Hudson Street,
New York, New York 10014, USA
Penguin Group (Canada), 90 Eglinton Avenue East, Suite 700, Toronto,
Ontario M4P 2Y3, Canada (a division of Pearson Penguin Canada Inc.)
Penguin Books Ltd., 80 Strand, London WC2R 0RL, England
Penguin Ireland, 25 St. Stephen's Green, Dublin 2,
Ireland (a division of Penguin Books Ltd.)
Penguin Group (Australia), 250 Camberwell Road, Camberwell, Victoria 3124,
Australia (a division of Pearson Australia Group Pty. Ltd.)
Penguin Books India Pvt. Ltd., 11 Community Centre, Panchsheel Park,
New Delhi - 110 017, India
Penguin Group (NZ), 67 Apollo Drive, Rosedale, North Shore 0632,
New Zealand (a division of Pearson New Zealand Ltd.)
Penguin Books (South Africa) (Pty.) Ltd., 24 Sturdee Avenue,
Rosebank, Johannesburg 2196, South Africa

Penguin Books Ltd., Registered Offices:
80 Strand, London WC2R 0RL, England

First published by Onyx, an imprint of New American Library,
a division of Penguin Group (USA) Inc.

First Printing, January 2008
10 9 8 7 6 5 4 3 2 1

This one is for all you crazy McKinleys.

Prologue

"This came in the mail last week." Mignonette Charbonneau Olson, aka Mimi, slid the greasy, mangled postcard across the gray metal office desk to the detective.

Otell Weber didn't look like a private detective to Mimi; he looked like a retired Nate's Men's Clothing Store salesman, a little stodgy, a little tired, a little worn down at the heels. But Mimi's employer, the great and all-knowing Oz, had vouched for him, and Mimi trusted Oz, who had many reasons to know Minneapolis's most inexpensive yet reliable private detectives.

Otell peered through his reading glasses at the note scribbled on the postcard:

> *Hi, kiddo. Montana's great!!! Enjoy the summer and don't think about school. Life's too short! Love, Dad*

The sight of her father's once familiar scrawl no longer had the effect of sucking the air from Mimi's lungs. Like a lot of things over the three decades since his disappearance, she'd grown used to it.

"Wish my daddy had held a similar view," Otell muttered,

turning the postcard over. The picture side featured a giant rabbit sporting antlers and sitting in front of a distant blue mountain. The caption below it read, "The Rare Montana Jackalope."

"Quite the yuckster, your old man."

"He was being ironic, Mr. Weber," Mimi said. She leaned forward and flipped the postcard back over, pointing at the cancelation mark covering the stamp. "That's what I wanted you to see."

It was postmarked June 22, 1979.

Otell's interest finally woke up. "You just got it?"

Mimi nodded.

"You know, you hear of things like this. A wallet left by some long-dead carpenter in a wall and found during remodeling, a letter wedged in a PO mailbox delivered decades after it was sent."

"Yeah, and this would fall into the latter category."

"So, what exactly do you want me to do with it?"

"I want you to find out what happened to my father." Just saying the words out loud made Mimi uncomfortable. After years of learning to ignore the question of what had happened to her father as being unanswerable, the unexpected reminder that he was still out there somewhere (or at least parts of him were) rattled Mimi far more than she would have expected.

Since receiving that postcard, Mimi had lain awake at night. Mimi disliked anything interfering with her sleep. She had long ago embraced a serene, uncomplicated lifestyle founded on a refusal to reflect on the past or predict the future. But this postcard had nibbled at her tranquility until, with a sense of dismay, Mimi had concluded that *something* would have to be done. Which is why she was here.

"Ah-huh," Otell said, nodding tiredly. "He skipped out on you?"

"No," Mimi said, offended. "He disappeared. Thirty years ago. He dropped me off up north with my relatives for the summer and said he'd be back before Labor Day. He never showed up."

"Any child-support issues? Court orders, lawsuits, that sort of thing? Any . . . habits?"

"No." Mimi shook her head. "Look, Mr. Weber. There's no reason my dad would want to disappear. My mother had all the money. Dad didn't pay alimony or child support. He didn't have a worry in the world."

"Ms. Olson"—Otell Weber leaned across his desk—"if he had a kid, take my word for it, he had worries. I got five. I got a *world* of worries."

"You don't know my dad," Mimi said confidently.

Otell regarded her disbelievingly. "Huh."

Mimi didn't care whether he believed her or not. It was true. John Olson didn't owe anyone anything. He had no debts of any kind. He never made waves. He didn't tell people what to do or how to live. He didn't expect things from anyone. He wasn't materialistic or envious. And if Mimi's mother, Solange, had passed down the rather severe indictment that John Olson was defined more by what he wasn't than by what he was, it worked for him. He'd been the happiest guy Mimi had ever known.

Otell finally began using the pad of yellow legal paper he'd placed on his desk. "Has anyone else ever made any attempt to find him? Was a missing person's report ever filed?"

"Yes and yes. My grandfather hired someone. The police in North Dakota were notified." At Otell's questioning look she elaborated. "He was in North Dakota the last time we heard from him. He called us from a public phone."

"Do you happen to remember the date of that call?"

Mimi didn't have to think. "June seventh."

"Well, that's something," Otell said, leaning back in his chair. "How about Canada? Mexico? Anyone look there?"

"I think so," Mimi said. "My grandfather contacted just about everyone he could think of, and he must have done a pretty good job, because the courts didn't have any trouble declaring my dad legally dead in 'eighty-six."

"Hm. But you don't think so."

"His death was only declared because of his absence, not because they found him or anything that suggested he was dead. Maybe he's in a jail in Irkutsk or something. I don't know. That's why I'm hiring you."

Otell tapped the end of his pen against the yellow pad. "Well, let me give you my spiel first, Ms. Olson. Then, if you decide to hire me, I'll tell you what I'm going to do and what it's likely to cost you."

He sat back in his chair. "After thirty years, there's not much of a chance I'll find anything. Most people wouldn't remember what their next-door neighbor looked like after thirty years let alone some guy they passed at a gas station. But we do have the information that he was in Montana, and the police didn't have that back then. I'm just warning you that you're likely not to get much satisfaction for what it's going to end up costing you."

She nodded. "I don't have a lot of money."

He sighed in disappointment. "Well, the good news is that a lot of searching can be done online now. So that'll keep the bill down. The bad news is that other pieces of information could come dribbling in for months. Is there any hurry?"

"After thirty years? No. None at all."

"Okay, then what I propose is this: I'll do what I can from the computer in my spare time and, barring that, through the good old U.S. postal system. Anyway, that way I can charge you a cut rate. Then, if I find anything interesting, we'll decide if it's worth pursuing. It could take months," he warned her. "Probably will."

"I understand." She hadn't expected anything else. She just wanted to fall asleep. And the money didn't matter to her. She didn't have anything else to spend it on. Not herself and not anyone else.

She truly was John Olson's daughter.

• • •

When Mimi got home she decided she might as well get the other chore on her list out of the way, so she called her doctor's office about what she assumed was a missent lab report. The records clerk put her on hold a few minutes, and when the phone picked up again, Mimi was surprised to hear her doctor's voice.

"I am *so* sorry, Mignonette. We *never* mail out positive lab results without first talking to the patient."

"No skin off my nose," Mimi said. "But you do have my test results there, don't you?"

"Yes. Of course."

"Anything interesting?" Mimi asked. "Anything I should know about?"

There was a longish pause.

"Doc?"

"You mean aside from your pregnancy?" her doctor asked.

Mimi authored the next long silence. "I'm pregnant?"

"Well, yes," the doctor said, clearly confused; then, "Oh. Oh, god. I'm sorry. I assumed you knew. I thought the report was pretty straightforward—"

After that, Mimi didn't remember anything too clearly. She had a vague recollection of mumbling affirmatives for a while, then being shunted back to the front desk. It was all kind of a blur.

At least she'd spared herself the ignominy of shouting, "I can't be!" Fact was, she could. True, the candidates for her baby's father were limited to one, a hot-air balloonist, and the possible times of conception limited to the three hours after he'd told her he was moving and after asking her to come with him and after she'd told him she'd no intention of moving to Arizona. And after laughing.

She hadn't meant to hurt his feelings. He'd surprised her, and she frankly had thought he was joking. They just didn't have that sort of relationship. She didn't have those sorts of relationships. When she saw that her amusement had hurt him, she'd deviated from a long-established rule of no unprotected intercourse as a way to make up for her gaffe. She hated bad feelings to ruin the memories of a perfectly fun and pleasant relationship. And so there she was, forty-one and knocked up.

She'd never wondered whether she'd be a good mother. She didn't do so now. Wondering about things, trying to anticipate what was coming, what was going . . . she'd never had particular success in these areas. To be truly content you simply had to let life happen without interfering. Her dad had taught her that. "Just let it slide, honey, until it slides right on by."

That afternoon, she returned to her apartment and ordered in pad thai. She did not get around to addressing the practical matters of her pregnancy. She didn't get around to it the next day either. Or the next week. Or the next.

She would, she decided, just wait and see what happened. Except . . . she found herself speculating about who the baby would be like, what bits of DNA would show up that marked her or him as an Olson, or even a member of her mother's Charbonneau family, or the hot-air balloonist's. Images filled her brain like champagne bubbles, phosphorous and fragile, of herself holding a baby, or handing an infant to a faceless young woman, or lying on a table with her legs in stirrups.

For six weeks her restlessness grew, until in surprise she realized that this time waiting was not going to work. She made an appointment with an obstetrician.

The night before her appointment, she miscarried. It was a small event as events go. If she hadn't read the initial lab report in the first place, she would have assumed she'd simply been late, like lots of women her age, and never known she'd been pregnant.

But she did know.

It subtly changed things, skewed her in some fundamental way. She'd assumed that with the end of the pregnancy, she would return to her carefree ways. It didn't work that way. She'd still felt that uncomfortable sense of anticipation, like she was being prodded by some internal mechanism to *do* something. She just didn't know what.

She sure wasn't waking up shouting, "My God, I *need* to be a mother!" She was actually pretty certain she didn't. But Possibility, in all its vague and chimerical forms, had reared its ugly head.

SUMMER

Chapter One

Early September

Splat!

"For Chrissakes!" Eighty-two-year-old Birgie Olson lurched upright on the derelict swimming raft she occupied, setting it teetering precariously.

She looked around. Inches from her feet lay a broken blue balloon amidst a bright sunburst of orange tempura paint.

"What is it?" her great-niece Mimi asked from somewhere alongside the raft.

"Some little shit launched a water balloon filled with orange paint at me."

"Splotchball," Mimi said.

"Huh?" Birgie rolled over onto her stomach, dipping her side of the raft a good six inches lower into Fowl Lake than its opposite. She was a large woman.

Below her, Mimi lay spread out atop an ancient, much-patched tractor tire's inner tube, her twin pigtails of dark hair floating amongst the duckweed. She wore a shapeless, faded Speedo swimsuit, much like the ones she'd worn when she was sixteen. Her eyes were shut.

"Splotchball," Mimi repeated calmly. "The kids made it up. It's like paintball, except no one here can afford the special guns and ammo, so they adapted slingshots and water balloons. Really, it's pretty enterprising."

Birgie ignored Mimi's admiration. "There he is!" She spotted a furtive figure plastered tight against the side of one of the six cottages that comprised the Olson family's ancestral vacation retreat, Chez Ducky. He looked like an albino spider monkey, all arms and legs, his towhead gleaming like a beacon. "Who is he? There. By Cottage Six!"

Mimi craned her neck to look around. "I think it's Carl Junior," she said after a minute. "Maybe Emmit. Could be Hal. Young Scandinavian males all look pretty much the same."

Birgie stuck out her arm and pointed at the kid, shouting, "You hit me with one of those things again and I will hunt you down and skin you alive, you odious example of unprotected intercourse!"

With a shriek of delight, the kid darted into the woods, a small motley dog dashing after him. Having dealt with the interloper, Birgie settled back and folded her hands over the field of blue hibiscuses printed on her bathing suit, a Lands' End double-wide, and stared at the beach.

"Who the hell are all those people?" she grumbled.

"What people?"

"Those kids. Emmits and Carls and Hals and God knows who all."

"Those would be the people staying at Chez Ducky," Mimi replied. Birgie could hear the smile in her voice.

"It's not funny."

"Well, it is sort of funny. Now that Great-Aunt Ardis has passed on, you're the matriarch of Chez Ducky. You oughta know the names of your loyal subjects."

Birgie sourly surveyed the domain that tradition was attempting to dump in her lap. At the edge of an old white pine forest, a series of derelict cabins spread out equidistant from one another, leading to the Big House, a white clapboard construction rising two stories high, its fieldstone foundation padded with moss and its oft-patched roof wearing a Jacob's coat of different-colored asphalt. A few scraps of the original gingerbreading still clung tenaciously to the upper eaves, but other than this initial stab at gentrification, no attempts had ever been made to gussy the place up. Named Chez Ducky by some wit, the compound had been built over a hundred years ago on eighty acres abutting a third-rate lake situated five hours north of the Twin Cities and half an hour west of the nearest town, Fawn Creek.

"Some kingdom," Birgie muttered, though in truth she was very fond of the place. She was fonder still of the fact that she could escape the summertime heat of her principal residency in Florida and spend the season up here for free. "If nominated I will not run, if elected I will not serve."

"No one's asking your permission. It's a hereditary position," Mimi replied. "Chez Ducky has always been run by the oldest Olson female."

Easy for Mimi to say, Birgie thought sourly. With a few silver strands just starting to appear in her dark pigtails, her peeling nose tip tilted and freckled, and faint smile lines permanently stamped at the corners of her mouth, Mimi reminded Birgie of a superannuated Pippi Longstocking. At forty-one, Mimi still occasionally showed up in mismatched socks or oversized sweatshirts turned inside out.

No doubt about it, Mimi had it good: no responsibilities, no obligations, no one to answer to. Birgie had it good, too—or at least she did before her big sister, Ardis, had up and died.

"Mimi," Birgie said, "I'm eighty-two years old, and I've learned as many new names in my life as I want to. Besides, most of the people here aren't even related to me."

She nodded toward Chez Ducky's beach. Little figures chugged up and down the shoreline, toting folding chairs, blankets, ancient TV trays, portable Weber grills, bags of charcoal, and cans of lighter fluid in preparation for the picnic later that afternoon. Birgie didn't know two-thirds of them.

Chez Ducky was like some petri dish experiment run amuck.

Seeded more than a hundred years ago with a few grains of expansive, indiscriminating, and congenial Olson DNA, the Chez Ducky population had exploded over the decades, devouring anyone with the slimmest association to an Olson. There were ex-wives and ex-husbands and new wives of ex-husbands and children of new husbands from former marriages and half brothers and sisters and their friends and . . . gawd! It made her head hurt thinking about it. She knew none of this was necessarily a bad thing, but it wasn't the same Chez Ducky she'd known growing up. And Birgie wasn't the only one expressing discontent with what Chez Ducky had become.

"Oh, I imagine you still have room in your old gray head for a few more names," Mimi said.

Birgie wondered whether Mimi would be so calm if she knew that certain family members, some of them the legal heirs to the property, were discussing selling the Chez.

If Chez Ducky got sold, that would be that. On the up side for Birgie, there'd be no family enclave to be the head of; on the downside, she'd be stuck in Everglades City year-round because she didn't have enough money to rent a place up here and she couldn't stay with one of her Minnesota relatives for more than a few days.

And where would Mimi go? As far as Birgie knew, this place was the only constant in Mimi's life. No doubt about it, they'd be screwed. But what could either of them do about it? Still, she supposed she ought to say something to Mimi . . . just let her know people were talking . . . but . . .

Beneath her blunt and blustery facade, Birgie knew herself to be a coward. She'd been too cowardly to get married, to have kids, to move into the head surgical nurse position at the hospital where she'd worked for forty years, or to tell someone bad news. She'd long ago come to terms with this failing in her character. She could, she reasoned, have had worse flaws. For instance, she could have been a Republican.

It wasn't that she thought Mimi would break down and bawl. Even when Mimi had been eighteen and the courts had declared her father legally dead, she hadn't blubbered. But Birgie never wanted to see that stricken look on Mimi's face again.

"What would you do with your summers if you didn't spend them here?" she asked as casually as she could.

One of Mimi's gimlet dark eyes opened. "But, I *do* spend them here," she said. "And I intend to spend them here. Always. Until they wrench the key to Cottage Six from my cold, dead hand. And who knows?" Mimi mused, closing her eyes again and grinning. "I might not even go then."

"What? You're going to haunt the place?"

"Maybe."

Birgie snorted. Mimi was a tele-spiritualist . . . or was it tele-medium? Birgie never could remember what the operators of Uff-Dead—Birgie's pet name for Straight Talk from Beyond, the paranormal hotline Mimi worked for and which catered to Minnesota's Scandinavian population—called themselves. Unlike the rest of the Olson clan, who, uncertain whether they should be concerned, conciliatory, or amused about Mimi's career and so opted to take the traditional Scandinavian route of ignoring it, Birgie wasn't above open scoffing. Not that she had many opportunities to do so.

The only time Mimi referred to her job was when someone suggested aloud that Mimi's father, John Olson, who'd disappeared when Mimi was eleven, was dead. Mimi would look the offender straight in the eye and reply, "If my dad was dead, I'd be able to contact his spirit, wouldn't I? But I can't, so he isn't." That generally shut down any further conversation.

Birgie didn't know what Mimi's mom, Solange, thought of her daughter's refusal to entertain the possibility that her ex-husband was dead, but she'd guess Solange didn't ignore it. No, sirree. Mimi's mom, Solange, was the anti-Olson, focused, insistent, and relentless. Not that Birgie considered Solange a bad person. It must have about killed her to return Mimi to the midst of her indolent former in-laws every summer after the divorce. But she had. And she'd continued to do so even after John's disappearance.

Solange and John had met in college at a University of Minnesota job fair—she was there for a job; John Olson was there for the free hotdog. Solange hadn't seen the carefree, wanderlust-prone young man as her polar opposite. She'd seen a gorgeous Gordian knot of potential she itched to unravel. John saw a pretty, starry-eyed girl who hung on his every word and enjoyed sex. No one had ever hung on any of John's words before. They married.

When Solange finished unraveling John, a process that took an embarrassingly short time, she realized he wasn't ever going to amount to anything, big or otherwise, and that was exactly the way he wanted it. Sadder but wiser, Solange divorced John and swept their black-haired baby girl off to her parents' palatial home (Solange's great-granddad being Jacque Charbonneau, the depilatory king, creator of Hair Today, Gone Tomorrow). There, Solange wasted no time trying to root from Baby Mimi any suspected slacker tendencies she might have inherited from her dad. Her fears, Birgie conceded, were not without justification. As it turned out, Mimi was a slacker of the first order. Unfortunately for Mimi, it also turned out she had a sky-high IQ.

Solange, not one to suffer waste gladly, set about "encouraging" Mimi with extracurricular activities, handpicked playgroups, accelerated this and fast-tracked that—at least that's what Mimi's dad, John, had said. This encouragement met with mild success and probably would have escalated had not Solange remarried a decade later and forthwith produced two more bright little girls who, unlike their older half sister, not only *wanted* Solange's encouragement but actually seemed to benefit from it. And substantially, too. Mary and Sarah, Birgie recalled the girls' names.

Not that Mimi talked much about them. She kept her relationship with her Charbonneau relatives strictly separate from that with the Olsons. Or more specifically, her relationship with Chez Ducky. Since her dad had disappeared, Mimi had been living pretty much like she had a terminal disease. She had no responsibilities to anyone but herself and didn't owe anyone anything. Owning nothing of value, she had nothing to protect.

Except Chez Ducky.

That, Birgie thought sadly, was the hell of it. You couldn't get out of life without at least a few things sinking their hooks into you. And the fewer things that got to you, the deeper they set their hooks. For Mimi it was Chez Ducky. For Birgie, too, damn it.

She cleared her throat. "Mimi. You . . . ah, you got anything going on in your life?"

"Nope. I'm free as a bird. What do you want and when?"

"That's not what I meant. I meant, do you have a boyfriend? Or a girlfriend? Or anyone?"

"You are acting *so* weird today," Mimi said, wiggling her way up onto her elbows to peer at Birgie. "You feeling all right?"

"I just . . . you know. I want to you to be happy," Birgie muttered uncomfortably. Mimi's peer turned into a stare. Birgie understood. She was a little surprised to hear such maudlin crap coming out of her mouth herself.

"The thing is, things are changing so fast," she said, carefully feeling her way. "And, ah, they could change even faster."

"Birgie, I realize this is rough for you," Mimi replied, looking nauseatingly sympathetic, "but no one expects you to replace Ardis."

"Good. Because I'm not going to."

"And no one wants you to. You know that, right?"

"Right." She took a deep breath. "Look, Mimi, there's something you maybe ought to know—"

"No, there isn't," Mimi said quickly. Mimi had always seemed to have a sixth sense when it came to uncomfortable subjects and a successful tactic in dealing with them; she simply blew right past them.

"Really. I think—"

"I think we should go skinny-dipping!"

"Ah, geez, Mimi," Birgie burst out in strenuous objection, secretly relieved. At least she could tell herself she'd tried to warn Mimi of the way things looked to be heading. "You'd think you were a goddamn nudist. Look at the sky. It's broad daylight."

"So what?" Mimi said, dropping off the side of the inner tube into the water. "I'm suggesting skinny-dipping not nude sunbathing. We're a hundred yards from shore and our lady parts will be discreetly hidden by the water. Come on. You can strip underwater."

Suiting action to words, Mimi disappeared beneath the surface of the lake, a circle of bubbles marking her descent. A minute later her fist popped out of the water clutching her blue Speedo. Mimi's head followed, water streaming down her face.

"See?" she said, flinging her sodden suit at the pontoon. It caught on the corner with a wet *thwack*. "Easy."

"Easy for you. Honey, I'd need a crowbar to get me out of this suit when it's wet." Birgie looked down. Shame. She liked skinny-dipping, too. It was a Chez Ducky ritual. Usually enjoyed after dark and for excellent reasons.

"That sucks," Mimi said.

"Yeah, well—"

She caught sight of the missile a second before it hit the side of the pontoon and exploded green tempura paint all over her. "Damn it!"

Birgie heaved herself to her knees and lurched to her feet, setting the raft rocking.

"What are you going to do?" Mimi asked.

"I'm gonna go find those little bastards," Birgie said grimly.

"I'm in," Mimi said. "Just let me get my suit back on."

"No. You stay. You'd only cramp my style by trying to keep me from killing those kids. I'm gonna put a moratorium on teenage boys at Chez Ducky. If I gotta be the goddamn head of this goddamn place I might as well get some satisfaction out of it. Unless you want to be the head of the place?"

"Ha. Ha. No, thank you."

She hadn't thought so. It was too bad. "Can I take the inner tube?" she asked. "I'm not as strong a swimmer as I used to be."

"Sure," Mimi said. "You sure you don't want me to come with you?"

"Nah," Birgie replied absently. She was thinking. What she needed was a replacement. But who? The Olsons of Chez Ducky had always been led by a matriarch, and the only other old ladies around were Birgie's dead brothers' widows, Naomi and Johanna. Neither would work. Naomi had been halfway round the bend for years and Johanna was so frantic trying to keep hidden the fact that she'd lately started shacking up with Charlie, her long-dead husband's twin, that she was on the verge of a nervous breakdown. But there was no reason *Mimi* couldn't head the family.

True, Birgie couldn't think of anyone more ill suited for the job, but she also couldn't think of anyone better equipped. Ill suited by virtue of her temperament, well equipped by virtue of her abilities. Mimi might deny it with her dying breath, but the fact was that everyone knew that during Ardis's last few years it had been Mimi who'd been the glue that had held Chez Ducky together. She'd sent in the taxes, arranged to have the septic tank sucked, kept track of . . . whatever needed to be kept track of.

True, Mimi might hate it, but she *could* do it. Hell, she

might even keep Chez Ducky from being sold, and that would be good for her. Okay, *them*. Two birds, one stone.

True, Mimi would never agree, and she couldn't be pressed into service. Mimi had withstood her mother's demands to apply herself and do something—anything—for three decades.

But if Birgie was really good, really careful, and played this right, Mimi *might* be slipped into the position. Like an oyster slips down your throat.

Hell, Birgie thought as she dipped up and down on the corner of the raft, sending the pontoon rocking violently, it was worth a shot. She dove into the lake, causing barely a ripple.

Chapter Two

Birgie was wrong, Mimi thought, studying the family holdings. Chez Ducky hadn't changed. The same shorn-off boulder on which a half-dozen generations of Olsons had tanned still basked in the same bulrush-choked waters where, Mimi was quite certain, the same family of leeches still waited patiently to attach themselves to the next crop of Olson bottoms.

True, the cottages had faded to gray and their gutters sprouted seedlings. And the slide some forgotten Olsons had pilfered from some long-closed school yard had rusted and now listed sideways in the water as though attempting to struggle out of the lake and return to the playground. But other than those small signs of passing time, things were the same now as they'd been when Mimi was born. Or her father was born. Or her grandfather.

A single electrical wire connected them to the outside world. No telephone lines, no gas lines, no sewage lines. Here, the past and present not so much coexisted as existed parallel to each other.

It was too bad Birgie wasn't enjoying the last few days of summer before they shut the place down for the season. But Mimi would be acting weird, too, if she had a bunch of people expecting things of her. Thank God, she didn't. And wouldn't. If Birgie did squirm out of this—and it looked like she might—her sister-in-law, Mimi's great-aunt Johanna, was heir apparent, then Mimi's grandfather's second wife and widow, Naomi. Okay, maybe Mimi's step-grandmother Naomi would need a regent. After Naomi came Debbie, who was married to Naomi's son and Mimi's half-uncle, Bill.

Debbie. Always doing things, fixing things, organizing things. Though she didn't *seriously* think Debbie could single-handedly run Chez Ducky into the ground, Mimi would still prefer to be dead before Debbie took over. But since Debbie was only ten years older than Mimi, she didn't hold out much hope for this. Maybe she'd be demented by then? The thought cheered Mimi considerably.

She turned on her back and floated. She was immersed in blue: the jade-speckled indigo of the blooming lake beneath, the cobalt sky above, the blue-green of pine trees drifting by on the shore. She closed her eyes and drank the soft air, a hint of autumn crispness teasing her exposed skin into goose-flesh.

It was late summer, almost autumn.

And so are you.

She jackknifed in half, dropping beneath the lake's surface and coming up sputtering. *Where the hell had that come from?*

She was only forty-one. The only difference between early summer and late summer was a few less hours of daylight. And all that meant was that there might not be quite as much time to get things done.

Or get things going.

Jesus! What had gotten into her lately?

Lately? She could pin down the exact date: March fourteenth, around four o'clock in the afternoon, when the mail arrived with the lab results for a pregnancy test she hadn't even realized she'd taken.

This year when she'd packed her borrowed car to come to Chez Ducky, she'd come with a motive: she was determined to recapture her lovely soporific bliss. For the most part it worked. But even here she sometimes grew fidgety, her unoccupied thoughts seesawing between her father's postcard and a computer-generated lab report. Frank Sinatra kept crooning, "It Was a Very Good Year" in her head, and she'd taken to captioning her experiences with Hallmark card sentiments like "It was late summer, almost autumn, and so was she."

"Mimi!"

With a sense of relief, Mimi swam around the raft to see who was yelling. The beach was filling up with people arriving for the picnic. Birgie was nowhere to be seen, but Mimi spied Debbie holding court near the fire pit in the middle of the beach. Naomi perched atop Chez Ducky's other pontoon where it had been beached three years ago as unusable.

"Mimi!" Naomi hollered again. She'd draped herself in a white bedsheet, which she'd hitched up around her waist, revealing a pair of bright pink polka-dot pedal pushers underneath. Above her head she waved the claw hammer with which she'd spent the last two days pounding together some sort of scaffolding on top of the pontoon.

To Mimi's knowledge no one had bothered to ask Naomi what she was doing. Few people did anymore. The answers might lead to uncomfortable conclusions about Naomi's mental state. It wasn't that Naomi was incapable of taking care of herself, or wasn't aware of what was going on, or who was who. Not at all. She just reveled in being odd.

"What?" Mimi called back.

"You're going to turn into a prune!" Naomi shouted. "How long you planning on staying out there? People are starting to arrive."

Naomi had always taken her step-grandmother duties seriously.

"I'm coming in now!" Mimi shouted back.

"Good!" Naomi stooped down and recommenced thwacking at some boards.

Mimi paddled to the pontoon to retrieve her swimsuit. It was gone. She frowned, gripped the edge of the raft, and was about to hoist herself up to peer over the pontoon to the other side when she realized she'd be hoisting herself out of the water in full view of the picnickers on the beach. She moved to the other side and looked around. It was empty.

In a flash, she realized what had happened. Her suit, caught on the corner of the pontoon, had fallen into the water when Birgie had jumped up and down before diving into the lake. Mimi dove under the raft, squinting as she tried to see through the soft green veils of suspended algae. No good. She couldn't make out a thing. She swept her arms around, hoping her suit had gotten tangled in the weeds as it drifted to the bottom twenty feet below. She came up after about a minute—sans suit.

Damn. She scanned the beach, looking for some place she could make shore and scoot straight into some bushes. There was none. A hundred years of pulling up brush had made the Chez Ducky beach, if not the cleanest one in the county, at least one of the more open ones.

The closest any bush came to shore was fifty feet past the Big House, where a swamp elder thicket marked the border of Olson land. Better still, the shoreline there was thick with water lily pads. If she could slither to shore, then duck into the brush, she might be able to sneak through the woods to the other side of the property, where arriving guests would park their cars. Someone was bound to have left a door open, and every Minnesotan carries a blanket in the trunk. Even in the summer.

Besides, she didn't see that she had much of a choice. The option, marching out of the lake naked in front of a hundred people, didn't hold much appeal. Naomi might think Mimi had finally seen the light and was going Druid, but the rest of them ... well, Mimi wouldn't mind their amusement as much as Debbie's assessment. Nope. Mimi did not think she wanted svelte, liposucked, gym-toned, spray-tanned Debbie giving her body a pitying once-over.

Mimi waited until everyone on the beach was occupied, then began nonchalantly breaststroking her way to shore. As she got closer, she sank lower in the water, submerging until only her eyes and nostrils were above the smooth surface of the lake. Sort of like a Nile crocodile approaching a wildebeest herd, she thought. She imagined launching herself out of the water, grabbing Debbie, and dragging her back into the lake. She grinned as she drew closer to shore, making a mental note to share this vignette with her cousin Gerry's wife, Vida, who held similar views regarding Debbie.

She took a deep breath and sank seamlessly beneath the water. Once under, she shot forward, porpoise kicking for all she was worth. The water grew warmer as it got shallower. The wild celery swept along her sides and brushed her stomach and thighs and breasts, as silky as feather boas. Her lungs had just started to burn when her hand hit the mucky lake bottom.

She planted her knees and carefully raised her head. Bingo. She was in the lily pads, only yards away from the beach and bushes. She yanked up a thick handful of the tuberous lilies and festooned herself with them just in case someone did spot her—she didn't want to be responsible for some little old man dropping dead at the sight of her in all her feminine glory. Then, trailing her legs in the mud, Mimi crept forward on her elbows and forearms until she felt the kiss of cool air on her ass. She tucked her feet beneath her in a runner's crouch, took one last glance at the people on the beach, and shot out of the water, diving headfirst into the bushes, shedding weeds and muck as she went. She rolled and squatted, listening. Nothing.

She smiled. From here she could stay in the brush all the way out to the dirt road that led to the lake, cross that, then continue through the woods to where the cars would be parked.

"Ow!" Her smile faded. A posse of mosquitoes was humming excitedly around her, alerting their brethren to the bounty of exposed flesh that the mosquito gods had sent them. It was going to be a long hike.

Fifty yards up the beach, Naomi stopped pounding nails and looked down into the upturned face of the little boy tugging at her bedsheet.

"What is it, Emil?"

It would have surprised Naomi to hear that the kid's name wasn't Emil, and in fact, the little boy wasn't even an Olson. His name was George. But as he was only three, it didn't really matter to either of them what Naomi called him.

"Did you see the monster?" he demanded.

Naomi, who loved children, put down her hammer and patted Emil-George's head. "What monster?"

"The monster that came out of the lake." He pointed down the beach.

"What did this monster look like?" Naomi asked.

"Smelly."

Naomi regarded the child in delight. "What else?"

Emil-George nodded. "Dirty."

"Ah," Naomi breathed, nodding sagely. "That wasn't a monster, dear. That was your aunt Mimi."

This apparently made sense to Emil-George, for he said, "Oh," and wandered off.

Naomi went back to her hammering.

Chapter Three

Joe Tierney squatted next to the front tire of his rental car, staring at the lug nuts he'd tightened. He'd been squatting for five minutes, his shirtsleeves rolled up, one arm resting on his thigh, a wrench hanging loosely in his hand. He wasn't staring because he didn't trust the job he'd done—it wasn't rocket science—but because as soon as he got up he would be forced to continue the journey that ended at Prescott's new vacation house.

It was an obligatory visit, just as it had been an obligatory invitation. Joe could have found a hundred excuses not to go, and most of them would have been valid, but Joe Tierney was nothing if not persevering, and he had not yet reached the point where he was willing to give up on this relationship— despite Prescott's obvious wishes to the contrary. Joe was unused to failure.

As a richly endowed venture capital group's chief field executive, Joe's job was to go into recently acquired companies, assess, evaluate, and then make a recommendation on the future of those companies. As such, he was used to resentment. He didn't take it personally. But Prescott's dislike was of the most personal variety, and Joe had no idea what to do about it. Doubtless, it might help if he understood it. He didn't. Most people liked Joe. He was poised, polished, and

amiable. A little compulsive, perhaps. For example, some
people might say his fastidiousness bordered on the obsessive. But Joe preferred to think of himself as tidy. And committed. Which was why he was here on a dirt road in the
middle of northern Minnesota; he was committed to connect-
ing with Prescott.

Commitment, however, did not require enjoyment. The
early Christians had probably not been rubbing their hands in
anticipation as they stumbled into the Colosseum to face the
lions. He had just added "fire jumpers diving out of airplanes
into infernos" to his list of the Unhappily Committed when
he heard branches snapping in the woods on the other side of
his car.

Joe had no idea what sorts of animals roamed the woods
three hundred miles north of Minneapolis and within spitting
distance of the Canadian border. Bears? Moose? Wolves? For
all he knew, Sasquatch was standing on the other side of the
car. He waited. A few seconds later he heard the unmistakable sound of whatever it was moving closer. He quietly bent
lower and peered under the car.

On the other side was a pair of dirty, sand-encrusted,
scratched, feminine feet. He knew they were feminine because the nails had been painted a hideous neon pink. They
shuffled a bit, and Joe heard his car door open. Joe, much reassured (no one who wore that color nail polish could possibly be a danger to anyone—except possibly the standards of
good taste), stood up. "May I . . ."

A naked female was on her knees on the front seat of the
car, dripping mud and gunk all over it. Weeds caped her
shoulders, and twigs and leaves stuck out of curly dark pigtails. Mud caked her from elbow to ankle. For an instant she
froze, a pair of wide, startled eyes gleaming up at him
through a tangle of wet, dank hair.

"Jesus Christ," Joe whispered. "A Wolf Girl."

Whoever it was jumped like she'd been hit with a Taser,

banging her head on the car roof. She grabbed the top of her head. "Holy Mother! Sonofabitch—"

She caught the direction of his gaze and looked down. With a sound halfway between a shriek and a squeak, she turned and bolted, crashing headlong into the undergrowth.

Joe stared, uncertain whether to follow her or call the cops. Obviously she was running away from something, but she hadn't appeared scared; rather, she seemed flustered and, after she hit her head, pissed off. Followed by extremely embarrassed.

She'd probably strayed off the grounds of some sort of local cult, a cult that worshipped nudity and mud and . . . twigs.

Crap.

If there was a cult up here he hoped to God Prescott wasn't involved in it, but that hope was faint. No one was riper for cult picking than Prescott: wealthy, socially awkward, defensive, and pathetically eager for admission to any group. Even twig worshippers. Joe was prepared to do a lot for the sake of their relationship, but he drew the line at twig worship.

All these thoughts zipped through Joe's mind in a matter of seconds and were interrupted by a female cry rising above the sound of crashing in the underbrush. This was followed by a string of colorful and anatomically specific invectives. She must have hurt herself and might need help. Joe, as incapable of leaving a situation that needed attending unattended as he was of breathing underwater, walked to the edge of the woods. "Are you all right?"

There was a long pause, then a grudgingly relayed, "I've got a mother of a thorn in my foot."

Joe carefully parted the top of the shrub in front of him. Ten feet into the woods he saw the woman hunkered amidst a thick undergrowth of plants that hid most of her bottom half. She was holding her foot in both hands.

"Want me to take a look?" he asked.

"No!" She hunched down further in the weed patch. "You scared me," she went on accusingly. "I didn't think there was anyone near that car— Hey! Do *not* look at me! I'm naked. Geez!"

He turned around and considered asking her why, if she didn't want anyone to see her naked, she had shed all her clothing, but something in her tone argued against this.

Perhaps she wasn't part of a cult, simply mentally unbalanced. She didn't sound particularly loony, but his experience was admittedly limited.

"I'm sorry," he said soothingly, just in case she was crazy. "I was changing a tire."

"Oh."

"Are you in some sort of difficulty?" he asked, keeping his voice mild.

"I would think that's pretty obvious," she snapped. "Yes, I am. I don't have any clothes and I am supposed to be at a picnic on the beach down there."

He assumed she was pointing. He waited.

"I was skinny-dipping and my suit fell into the lake and I couldn't find it so I swam to shore where there were no people hanging around and came up through the woods."

"I see."

"I was *hoping*," she went on accusingly, "that I'd find a blanket in your car so I wouldn't have to march through a crowd like this."

"That's certainly reasonable." He supposed. "And all the muck and weeds and things stuck to you?"

"It's a mucky lake," she replied coolly.

Okay, maybe she wasn't nutty. "How can I help?"

"*Do* you have a blanket in your car?"

"It's not my car; it's a rental, so I don't know."

"A northern Minnesota rental," she said. "It'll have a blanket in the trunk. If you could get it for me?"

"Of course." He suited action to words, returning to the car and popping the trunk open. Sure enough, folded neatly behind the rear seats was an old polyester stadium blanket. He shook it out, grimacing as dust exploded from it and wondering what antique bacteria was at that moment taking root in his lungs. Joe admitted that at times he was a little overly "health conscious." Now was not one of those times.

He returned to the woods in time to hear another sharp yelp, some sniffs, and then— She was crying. Concerned, he pushed his way through the brush toward her. "What is it? What's wrong?"

"Don't look!"

He snatched the blanket up in front of his face, silently consigning her back to the unbalanced side of the population. "Listen," he said, losing patience. "I've seen naked women before. You're hurt and you need help. Given the circumstances, the modesty bit is a little out of place, don't you think? Believe me, I am not interested in leering at you. Frankly, in your current condition I can't even tell if you are leer worthy."

"I know that!" she shouted. "God! Do you think I don't *know* that? It's just that I . . . I . . . don't think I can walk!"

Joe realized he would never understand what her inability to walk had to do with her not wanting him to look at her. Stress had evidently short-wired her thought processes. She possibly even *knew* she wasn't making sense, but she was caught in some sort of mental loop. He'd seen it before. Mostly in political debates. There would be no reasoning with her until the shock had worn off.

"Okay. Okay," he said. "You tell me what you want me to do."

She snuffled loudly. "Could you please bring me the blanket? Without looking?"

"I can try." He started cautiously forward, sweeping his foot out in front of him as he went.

"A little more to the left."

He went left.

"Not that much. There. Good. A few more feet. Straight. Almost . . . Stop."

He stopped, the blanket still held up between them. "Now what?"

"Just, ah, throw it over me. Really gently. I'm right in front of you about three feet away."

"Okay." He held the blanket at arm's length and tossed. It landed on her head and draped itself over her. "I'm looking now. You're covered. Mostly."

"It's not big enough to cover all of me," her muffled voice announced. "It's the size of a shawl and it stinks of mildew."

He considered. "Hold on. I have an idea."

He reached into his pocket and took out the silver penknife he carried. Then he put one hand on top of her head.

"What are you doing?" she asked.

"I'm going to cut a hole for your head," he said. "Hold still."

Gingerly, he plucked the blanket up a few inches above her head and slipped the pointed end of the blade into the material. The polyester didn't offer any resistance; it sliced open like butter to a hot knife. He sawed a foot-long slit in the blanket and pocketed the knife. Then he reached down and tugged on the blanket until her head popped through the slit. She blinked up at him. She had pretty eyes, dark and luminous. Other than that, it would be hard to say what she looked like until someone turned a hose on her.

"Thanks," she said and smiled. Okay, he thought. A very nice smile, too, even with the caked mud cracking on her cheeks.

"No problem," he replied. "Now what?"

"If you could find me a nice sturdy stick I could use to walk, I'll be fine."

He looked at her, small and bedraggled and filthy, her legs scratched and bug bitten, barely covered by a GO VIKINGS lap rug. His shoulders slumped with the certainty of what he would have to do. He would have to touch her. It was so clearly his duty. Before she could protest, he bent down and, with what he considered a heroic disregard for his clothing, picked her up. She wiggled.

"Please stop writhing about," he said as the aroma of lake bottom met his nose. "My shirt is a lost cause, but I still hold out a slim hope that my pants can be saved."

She gave a little offended gasp but stopped wiggling.

"Now, I'm going to take you to the car and drive you wherever you want to go." His tone brooked no argument and he got none. He straightened. Slowly. She was heavier than she looked.

"How much do you weigh?" he asked, fervently hoping his back didn't go out.

"I'm dense," she said coldly. "My specific gravity is higher than other people's. And I didn't *ask* you to pick me up."

"You're welcome." He made it upright without feeling any back muscles give and bounced her into a more comfortable position. Thank God, the car was only twenty feet away.

He stumbled out of the brush toward the car. He did play it up (a bit) because she was so noticeably lacking in the gratitude department. He stopped halfway to the car, panting noisily. "I'm okay. I'm . . . fine. I'm just glad . . . I could . . . be . . . of service."

"Look, if you're going to have a heart attack, I can hop." Her tone was stiff, but her expression was worried.

"No," he gulped.

"Listen, I can't drag you into that car, and even if I could, the hospital is half an hour away. Let me down."

"I got it." He staggered the last ten feet and lowered (dropped) her to the ground.

She lifted her injured foot, bracing herself against the car as Joe opened the back door. She pivoted, plunked down, and pulled her legs in after her. He shut the door and got into the driver's side, glancing into the rearview mirror as he slid behind the wheel.

"So, where to?" he asked. "Hospital? Home?"

She met his gaze in the mirror and her eyes narrowed. "How come you're not panting anymore?"

"The doctors tell me I have a really impressive recovery rate," he said, eyes on the road as he turned over the engine and shifted the car into gear.

"You were faking the groans."

"Not faking. Exaggerating," he said. "I did consider faking an attack and letting you perform CPR, but I have delicate ribs."

She laughed. He looked up into the mirror in surprise.

"I suppose I would have deserved it," she said. "Let me try to redeem myself." She cleared her throat. "Thank you very much for rescuing me. You're a true white knight and I've been acting more like the dragon than the damsel. Looking more like the dragon, too. Scales and all."

He smiled back. "Ah, damsels are overrated. How often do you get to pick up a woman with a higher-than-average specific gravity?"

"True," she said without missing a beat.

He grinned, enjoying himself in a way he hadn't for a long time. He'd never really thought much about it, but right now he was struck by the fact that for all its ostensible glamour—the exotic locales, the various cultures, power and wealth—the life he led might be a bit, well, boring. Most of his time was pretty tightly scheduled, he met few people in a strictly social way, and he had few experiences either socially or work related that he didn't fully anticipate. This place, this situation, but most of all this woman were completely unanticipated.

He turned his head. "I'm Joe."

"Hello, Joe." She trailed the name out à la Lauren Bacall. "I'm Mimi."

"Mimi." He liked it. "Where can I take you, Mimi?"

"If you just follow this road another quarter mile you'll

come to a Y. Keep to the right and in another few hundred feet I'll be home."

"You sure you shouldn't have a doctor take out that thorn? It might get infected." You could never be too careful about open wounds.

"Oh, there'll be some docs at the picnic. True, they'll be veterinarians, but a thorn's a thorn, right? Everyone on the lake and half the people from Fawn Creek'll be there."

Joe wondered whether Prescott would be there, too. From what Mimi described, this picnic had to be very close to his house.

"Sure?"

"Absolutely. Believe me, I won't lack for attention."

No, he shouldn't think so, he mused as he drove the short distance. As the mud and weeds began to flake off, a nice set of features was emerging. Not classically beautiful, not cute, but oddly attractive.

He followed the Y she described to a narrow, rutted drive lined on both sides with cars and pickups and a few SUVs. Groups of people and flocks of children were passing back and forth through a row of little, dilapidated cabins.

"Told you everyone would be here," Mimi said. "Pull off here. See the cottage at the far end? The one with the striped beach towel hanging outside the front window? If you could pull your car up really, really close to the door, I can dash in before anyone sees me."

"You got it," Joe said, bumping over tree roots and hummocks until the back door of the car was parallel to the screened door on the cabin Mimi had pointed out. He put his arm over the back of the seat and turned to look at her. "There you go."

"Thanks, Joe," she said. He wondered what her hair would look like without the shrubbery. "You saved the day. I owe you."

"My pleasure, Mimi." Surprisingly, he wasn't overstating

the matter. Sure, he could have done without the dirt, but he had been richly diverted for a short while.

She pushed the car door open and swung her legs out, putting her injured foot gingerly on the ground. She winced.

"Do you need some help getting in?" Joe asked.

"No. I'll be fine as soon as I get a pair of tweezers in my hand." She smiled. "I appreciate the offer this time, though."

She prepared to bolt, but then stopped. She turned her head to look at him.

"Are you hungry?" she asked.

"Ah . . . I . . . Sure."

"If you'll wait here while I get this two-by-four out of my foot and clean up a little, I can promise you the best homemade picnic fare you're ever likely to have. How about letting me repay you a little for your kindness?"

Joe looked down at his shirt. "I'm not company ready. I'm a mess."

"No one will notice," Mimi promised. "Not here. Besides, most of the dark splotches were just water and it's almost dried now."

Joe considered, which in itself was surprising. Joe was not the sort of man who appeared in public in a dirty shirt. But the shirt wasn't really *that* dirty, and as Mimi had pointed out, as it dried the stains *were* less noticeable, and he *was* hungry. He'd just be very careful of which home-prepared foods he chose.

Besides, it wasn't as if Prescott were waiting for him with bated breath. Most likely he'd forgotten Joe was coming. Prescott might not even be there himself. Once Joe had visited Prescott at MIT, where Prescott taught, only to be greeted by a note on his apartment door that said Prescott had gone to New York for the weekend. Prescott had neglected to leave a key.

"What do you say?" Mimi asked.

"Is there somewhere I can wash my hands?"

"You bet."

Chapter Four

After digging a half-inch-long thorn from her heel, washing her hair, and scrubbing herself clean, Mimi looked for something to wear. Unfortunately, she hadn't driven into Fawn Creek to do laundry in more than a week. She tried on the sweatshirt and pants she'd worn while scraping the grills that morning, but even by her admittedly relaxed standards the greasy streaks were off-putting. The rest of her clothes were in no better shape. It had been that kind of week.

Finally, in desperation, she'd searched the crawl space above the cottage and hit pay dirt: a long-forgotten beach bag filled with teenagers' beach wear. The girl who'd worn the clothes might well be a grandmother by now, but Mimi didn't care. They didn't smell, they weren't dirty, ergo they were fit for a picnic. She held up a violently blue terry cloth beach robe with orange starfish embroidered along the yoke and slipped it over her head, then hobbled out in search of her rescuer. She found him standing a short distance from the picnic tables, eyeing the feast spread out on them.

She eyed Joe.

He was absolutely gorgeous in a Fortune 500 sort of way, handsome, sophisticated, and *really* well-groomed. His dark hair gleamed; his blue eyes gleamed; his square jaw, shaved as smooth as a river stone, gleamed; even his blue dress shirt gleamed with the soft sheen of really expensive Egyptian cotton—where it wasn't splotched with faintly damp green marks.

In the Land of Ten Thousand Cabela's catalogues, by dress alone he stood out like a rainbow trout amongst bullheads. His shirt cuffs were rolled up over nice masculine forearms in what she suspected was his nod to "casual," his camel-colored slacks had a crease in them, and his loafers—doubtless made by some Italian in a little workshop in Florence—looked as soft as butter. She guessed him to be in his early forties, a solid, broad-shouldered man who not only made Armani look good, but even stripped of his couture, she suspected, wouldn't be anyone you'd be in a hurry to throw a stadium blanket over, either.

Not only did he look good, but he oozed confidence, sophistication, and composure. Lots of composure. In other words, the guy was Cary Grant. Cary Grant on the set of *The Beverly Hillbillies.* Which, she supposed, made her Ellie Mae—with a few more years behind her.

She must have looked like a complete madwoman, popping up like the creature from the black lagoon on the other side of the poor man's car and then running away like an idiot. Luckily, she'd never been burdened with much self-consciousness.

"Hi."

He looked around and smiled. He had a killer smile. It reached right up into his eyes.

"Hi. You're clean."

"Soap'll do that."

She'd always had a thing for a really good male voice, and Joe had one of the sexiest she'd heard, the sort of voice that affected your body at the cellular level, like twenty-year-old Scotch: smoky, smooth, and intoxicating.

"Someone left it here," Mimi said, seeing his gaze slip to the smiling starfish romping across her chest. "Mid-seventies, I'd say."

He looked down at her feet encased in worn, cheap pink flip-flops. She'd wrapped her foot in gauze and secured it with sticky tape. Both foot and gauze were already a little grimy.

"Is your foot okay?" he asked.

"Fine. I popped that thorn out like a pit from a ripe cherry. You know how those things are: the instant they're gone, you feel better."

A look of alarm crossed his face. "You didn't use your fingers, did you? I mean you *did* sterilize a needle or something?"

She looked at him with amusement. Joe was a germaphobe? Cute. "Don't worry," she said. "I fired up the Bic and put flame to metal until it was so hot I dropped the damn tweezers on the floor."

At his involuntary wince, she laughed. "I'm messing with you," she admitted, succeeding in making Joe look even more disconcerted. She suspected not many people "messed" with Joe. "How about I take you on a culinary tour of the place?"

She led him between the picnic tables, their faded red-and-white-checkered tablecloths billowing around their legs. At least a hundred people milled around the grounds, strolling along the paths, settled in cheap lawn chairs in front of the cabins, or ensconced within their small screened porches. A group was playing volleyball on the beach, swearing and laughing as those on the sidelines cheered.

Mimi's favorite cousin, a blond giant named Gerald who'd been tormenting her since childhood, hollered at her to join them, and she hollered back good-naturedly, "Can't you see I'm limping? There's a reason I'm limping! I'm injured! Geesh!"

She looked over her shoulder at Joe. "I can't spike, but I can dig."

"Me, too."

She glanced at him sharply, uncertain whether he was now

messing with her. He didn't look like the pickup-game sort. The type who had a personal trainer, yes. Maybe polo. Not beach volleyball.

She brought him to a halt in front of a fragrant, rubicund pile of thinly sliced, garlicky-smelling meat. "I suggest starting with a sandwich."

Joe regarded her with an oddly uncomfortable expression before carefully surveying the bounty in front of him. Then, just as cautiously, he picked up a plate and speared a slice of spiral-cut ham. Mimi regarded him with pity. With all the spectacular homemade cuisine staring him in the face, he would have to choose that.

"Ah, just so you aren't disappointed, that ham is"—she glanced swiftly left and right, looking for eavesdroppers, then leaned over the tray of deviled eggs between them and whispered—"water packed."

"Water packed," he repeated.

"Yup. Johanna's been sticking cloves in commercial hams for years and passing them off as her own."

"Johanna?"

"One of my great-aunts," she said. "Everyone knows, but no one says anything. No, no," she said as he withdrew his poised fork. "You can't put it back! She's watching. You don't want to hurt her feelings, do you? Put it on the plate. Good. Now cut off a piece as if you can't wait. Now smack your lips. Go on, smack them!" she whispered urgently.

He smacked, eyeing Mimi cautiously as she nodded approvingly.

"There. You've made her happy. Now let me make you a real sandwich." She slapped down two slices of rye bread on a Chinette plate and heaped the homemade corned beef on one slice before handing the plate to Joe.

A movement at her feet drew her attention. She looked down in time to see a small, hairy, dirty brown face poke out from under the table. It was the same ugly little dog she and Birgie had spied earlier chasing the splotchball assassin. Joe tore a piece of corned beef from the edge of his sandwich and dropped it. The dog snatched it out of the air and disappeared.

"Your dog?" Joe asked.

"No, I don't know whose it is," she said, casually uncovering the top of his sandwich and ladling on a creamy sauce. "Horseradish," she said in answer to his questioning look. "Homemade. Really good."

"Ah-huh." He smiled and took a tentative bite. The uneasy expression disappeared, replaced by one of rapture. "I can't tell you the last time I had anything homemade," he said. "This is . . . It's . . ."

"Just eat," she said.

He ate.

"So, is this a yearly ritual?" he asked curiously after finishing the sandwich.

"God, I hope not," she answered, laughing.

"Why?"

"Because this is a wake."

Chapter Five

"A wake?" Joe asked, pointedly eyeing the manically grinning orange starfish. "Interesting wake-wear you have on there. Most people just go the easy route and opt for black."

She laughed. "It's not supposed to be a solemn occasion. Ardis would have hated that."

She cleaned up well, Joe thought. Really well. "Who is Ardis?" he asked.

"One of my great-aunts, Ardis Olson." Some fond memory awoke a fleeting smile. "She would have been eighty-five today."

"That's a pretty long life."

"It would have been a longer life still if she hadn't tried to squeeze in another nine holes of golf."

"Stroke?" he asked quietly.

"Nine iron," she replied. "Her partner nailed her with a Titleist on the fourteenth hole of the Pelican Strand golf course while she was in the rough, searching for her ball."

"Ouch."

"Thank God, no," she said. "The doctor has assured us Ardis literally never knew what hit her."

"That's nice," while appropriate, just didn't seem tactful, so Joe said, "That must be a comfort."

"For most of us, yes. But her golf partner, Morris, has

sworn never to play again. That's Morris over there." She gestured toward an affable-looking bald guy in canary yellow golf pants taking a practice swing with an imaginary golf club. He was surrounded by a critique group of similarly attired men.

"Just between us, I do not hold out much hope of that particular vow being honored for very long," Mimi said.

"Maybe I should leave," Joe suggested. "If this is some sort of memorial I'm crashing . . ."

"Please don't," Mimi answered. "Ardis has been blowing in the wind over the Mexican gulf since May. At least her ashes have, as per her request. We decided to have the memorial at Chez Ducky because everyone would be here and we thought it would be nice to have it on her birthday."

"Chez Ducky? What's Chez Ducky?"

"This"—she swept her arm out—"is Chez Ducky. Eighty acres of weedy lakeshore, scrub alder, and pine trees."

"And all of these people are Olsons?" he asked.

"In one way or the other. The Olsons take the 'end' out of 'extended.' Once you're part of this family, there's no going back. Not because of divorce, remarriage, adoption, religious conversion, or sex reassignment," she said. "If you've been declared 'family,' the only way out is death."

He couldn't imagine a family so large and inclusive and unplanned. He and Karen had had only one child. Even before Karen had died a dozen years ago, they'd never been the classic nuclear family. He'd been working overseas most of the ten years they'd been married, while Karen had stayed in Chicago and raised their son. It wasn't what Joe had necessarily wanted; it had just worked out that way. Karen took pride and pleasure in being a stay-at-home mom, and Joe had done his part by making it possible for her to be one.

"But even that's just an assumption. Or wishful thinking," Mimi went on. "Actually, there's hoards of Olsons on the Other Side just waiting to give the newly departed a big group hug."

Joe regarded her narrowly. She returned his gaze with un-blinking sincerity. He *didn't* think she was putting him on, but he wasn't entirely sure, and that knocked him a little off balance. Joe read most people as easily as Superman reads an eye chart.

She smiled. He relaxed. Of course she was kidding.

She waved her hand around the compound. "And every-one else you see here who isn't related to the Olsons has long ties to Fowl Lake. Why, the Sbodas over there"—she pointed to a group of redheads with a predilection for plaid—"*may* have been the first family to build on the lake, though we Olsons fervently resist that notion. Besides," she said smugly, "*we* have our original buildings. Those cottages over there? They've been here since before World War One."

Unable to hide her pride, she continued. "Note the sim-plicity of the design, the clapboard exterior, the narrow porch, the length of the facade. Inside are twin rooms on ei-ther side of a central hall, a feature, you may be interested in knowing, that makes them the dictionary definition of 'cot-tage.' So do not make the outlanders' mistake of calling them 'cabins.'"

"Go on," he said, actually interested.

"Well, the Olsons and the Sbodas were the first on the lake, and, as you can see, we are all still well represented. In fact"—she looked around—"excluding you, there isn't any-one here without a pedigree going back at least three gener-ations. The community around Fowl Lake is notoriously exclusive. We think of ourselves as sort of the Hamptons of the Bogs. Sans the money— Oh!" Mimi abruptly exclaimed, grabbing his elbow.

"You simply cannot miss these cashew bars," she said, picking up a battered pan of gooey-looking stuff and prying a roughly rectangular-shaped piece out with her fingers. Joe winced.

"Susie must have just set these out," she mumbled around

a mouthful of bar. "They won't last ten minutes once they've been discovered."

She bumped the pan against his chest. Thus encouraged, he used a plastic fork to pry another square from the opposite corner. One bite told him all he had to know. Some things were worth risking your health for. In quick order, he'd stockpiled several more before moving out of the way of the incoming crowds swarming toward them like yellow jackets at a barbeque, alerted by some sixth sense to the cashew bars' presence. Together, he and Mimi retreated, carefully shielding their bootie with paper napkins.

She led him to a bench completely encircling the trunk of an old ironwood tree and motioned for him to take a seat. She finished two more cashew bars before she spoke again.

"What's your story, Joe? How did you come to these strange shores? Who are your people and are they waiting in the woods for your signal to attack? Do we stand in imminent danger of having our picnic raided and our cashew bars plundered?"

"Nope. I'm just visiting."

"Oh? One of the new places?" Her friendliness faded a bit. "Which one?"

"I'm not exactly sure. It's somewhere around here. I was on my way when I got the flat. Maybe you know—"

"Nah," she clipped out before he could finish. "We don't rub elbows with the McMansioners."

Ouch.

"How long are you staying?" she asked.

"If I don't get kicked out, the weekend."

"Do you get kicked out of a lot of places?" Her face tilted up toward his. It was a piquant face. Definitely used to being au natural. Scrubbed and tanned and a little weathered. Unlike any of the few women he'd dated in the last decade, she didn't have a bit of style to her.

He shrugged. "It's the karaoke machine. People go crazy jealous when I break it out."

She snickered. "Michael Bublé?"

"Paul Anka."

She laughed, a full-throated and infectious sound, and glanced at him from beneath a fringe of dark lashes. They didn't need any mascara to exaggerate their length. She was flirting, he realized. And so was he. When had he last casually flirted? But she was so distracting, and the circumstances of their meeting so bizarre, and the whole wake setting so odd, it seemed completely natural.

"Tell me more about your family," he asked.

"What do you wanta know?" she replied around another mouthful of bar. "They're just . . . family."

She was wrong. There was no such thing as *just* family. "Who is who?" He angled his head toward the crowded picnic area. "How are you related?"

She blew out her cheeks and looked around. "Really?"

"Really."

"Okay. Ardis, the deceased, was the oldest of six sibs. The next oldest is Birgie, another maiden lady. That's Birgie over there, the one that looks like a truck driver."

He followed Mimi's gaze to where a square figure with short white hair sat splay-legged across the table from a tall, raw-boned woman with a single long gray braid streaming down her back.

"I thought she *was* a truck driver."

Mimi pursed her lips and ignored this comment. "Believe me, the fact that neither of the girls married and that both spent their childhoods—and I use the term loosely—taking care of four younger brothers has not been lost on anyone. After Birgie came Emil, who is dead but survived by half a dozen grandchildren. The oldest one of his grandchildren is Gerry, the big guy who wanted me to play volleyball. He's married to—forget it. Let's stick with the principals."

"Okay."

"After Emil were the twins, Charles and Calvin. Calvin, too, is dead, but Charlie is one of the guys trying to improve

Morris's never-again-to-see-a-fairway swing." She pointed to a tall, skinny old man wearing mirrored aviators, his hands on his hips as he stood silently watching Morris take another imaginary swing. "Charlie is a bachelor."

Mimi then nodded to the woman with the long gray braid. "Sitting across from Birgie is Calvin's widow, Johanna. Johanna of the water-packed ham? Charlie and Johanna have lately become an item. They think none of us know.

"After the twins came my grandpa John. He died a while back after marrying twice. The first one produced my father, John, and the second marriage, to Naomi . . ." She looked around. "She's the one wearing a bedsheet." She shrugged. "Anyway, the second marriage to Naomi produced my half-uncle, Bill."

"Is your father here?" Joe asked, curious.

Her expression didn't change an iota, but suddenly where there had been a relaxed, easy candor, there was a distance. "Nope. My parents were divorced when I was a baby."

"I'm sorry."

"Yeah. Happens a lot," she said brusquely.

"Anyway, my grandmother passed on early, and after a couple decades, Grandpa married Naomi and promptly got her pregnant with Half-Uncle Bill."

"Which one is your half-uncle Bill?"

She looked around again. "Not here. But there's his wife." She pointed at a well-packaged brunette in a dark, short-sleeved dress. *"Debbie."* Her upper lip curled as she said the name. "She'd be the one in obligatory black," she said. "I suppose we should be thankful someone in the family has a sense of decorum."

"You don't like Debbie."

"I don't like her or dislike her. She alarms me."

"Why's that?"

"She always looks like she's wondering what good use she can put me to and suspicious there might not be one," Mimi confided.

"And you're worried she might be right?" Joe asked, quietly sympathetic. He could imagine how unpleasant it would be to have someone question your value. Not that anyone had ever questioned his.

"God, no!" Mimi rocked back. "I'm worried that she'll never figure out that she *is* right about me and leave me the hell alone! It's exhausting just knowing she's out there planning something or arranging something or fixing something. Just look at her." Mimi jerked her head in the direction of the picnic tables where Debbie bustled about, older people scattering before her approach.

Joe studied Debbie. She didn't seem so bad to him. A woman who saw confusion and imposed order; what was wrong with that?

"Is Bill also an organizer?"

"Nah," she said. "Olson men are utterly and blissfully undesirous of heading anything. Especially anything that has to do with Chez Ducky. I suspect it began when Great-Great-Great-Grandfather Günter wrote in his Chez Ducky journal, 'I make decisions all the time but here, in this place of retreat and refuge, I refuse to make any.'"

The notion was as foreign to Joe as ritual disfigurement. He couldn't imagine not *heading* things. Control was too important a thing to cede to the less capable. Not to mention irresponsible.

"Ever since then, the Chez has been strictly a matriarchy," Mimi continued. "There are six legal heirs to the place, but everyone's kids and spouses and whoever else wants to gets a say in what happens here. Every year, just before we close up the cottages, we have a family meeting to decide if anything needs to be decided. Ardis used to oversee that, and before her my great-grandmother Lena."

It sounded to Joe like a criminally inefficient way of dealing with things. "What does this matriarch do?"

"Besides look wise at the end-of-the-year powwow? Just stuff related to Chez Ducky. Poll the family on things like whether we should get a phone line in here or just hope the microwave tower in Bemidji gets a stronger signal. Keep the golf scores for the family tournament. Make sure the inner tubes are patched." She said this last with a solemnity that suggested it was one of the more important duties.

"You don't have phone service?"

"Not a land line. We get cell on and off."

"Who'll be the matriarch now?"

"Birgie," Mimi said. "She has large shoes to fill."

"What if Birgie doesn't want to fill Ardis's shoes?" he asked conversationally.

"Oh, she doesn't," she said. "But it's one of the last traditions the Olsons have. The oldest Olson woman has been here ruling the roost at Chez Ducky ever since Olsons bought the land."

"If Birgie doesn't want to do it, why not you?" he asked. It seemed a reasonable suggestion. She obviously cared about the place, and she was just as obviously intelligent. "Ever think of initiating a coup d'état?"

She burst into laughter. "*Me?* Ha! Nope. If Birgie doesn't take the honors, someone else will, and we'll just carry on like we've been carrying forever."

She glanced toward the burr oaks at the far end of the compound. "Except for the view."

He shifted. "The McMansions?"

She gave him a sharp glance. "Bingo."

"I take it you're not too happy about the, ah, recent lakeshore development."

"*Lakeshore?*" She eyed him narrowly. "Look, I may be fond of this place, but it's like being fond of a ditzy relative who farts in public. You like 'em in spite of their shortcomings, not because of them. The only reason the Sbodas and Olsons and everyone else here have a place on Fowl Lake is because none of their families, even way back when prime lakeshore was cheap, could afford better."

"But you've stayed for generations."

"Well, it's better than nothing," she said practically. "None of us are wealthy enough to trade up. But now people like your friend have run out of premium lakeshore to exploit and are starting to take over the smaller lakes. Crappy lakes. Like this lake. Only they call 'em 'wilderness lakes.'" She snorted derisively. "They're running off the locals. Putting up monstrosities and eating up acreage and raising the property taxes until people who've been here for decades can't afford to stay."

"I suspect I'm going to regret saying this, but aren't you overreacting?" he asked.

She regarded him sadly a few seconds, then slapped her thigh and stood up. She reached down for his hand. He didn't hesitate to take hers. "Come on, Doubting Joe," she said. "Let me show you something."

Chapter Six

Mimi was limping purposefully past Cottage Two when her great-aunt Johanna literally popped out of the bushes.

"Geez!" Mimi gasped. "You scared the crap out of me, Johanna!"

"Sorry, Mimi," she said, regarding Joe with interest. "I'm hiding from Naomi. She keeps trying to hang a bedsheet on me."

"It's a tunic," Mimi said. "She wants us to celebrate Ardis's passing in a traditional Viking manner."

"And that means a toga? I thought togas were Roman."

"It's not a toga, it's a tunic," Mimi repeated patiently. "And just be glad she didn't pound breastplates out of garbage-can lids."

Johanna's gaze shifted to Joe. "And who might this be?"

"This is Joe."

"How do you do, Joe? You must have just gotten in. Staying the night? The week? The cabins are awfully cozy, aren't they? I hope Mimi's taking good care of you?"

Mimi waited. Johanna was the romantic in the family and fancied herself a matchmaker. The fact that she'd never actually had any success in this area did not deter her.

"I couldn't hope to be in better hands," Joe was saying, "Miss . . . ?"

Johanna fluttered. "Olson. *Mrs*. Olson, actually. Johanna Olson."

"Ah, lucky Mr. Olson."

Smooth, Mimi thought admiringly. He'd even managed to say it without sounding smarmy. Which was quite a feat since it was a highly smarmy comment.

"Oh, he died," Johanna volunteered. "Thirty-five years ago come November."

"I'm sorry to hear that," Joe said, dialing down the charm.

Johanna nodded, lowered her eyes respectfully, then said, "So. How did you meet our Mimi, Joe? Did you call her eight hundred number? She meets a lot of men that way. Of course, most of them are losers, not to put a shine on it. I can't imagine *you* calling."

Mimi looked at Joe to see how he handled these decidedly provocative comments. Unsurprisingly, he looked nonplussed. How else would he look? Johanna had made it sound like she worked on a phone sex line.

Mimi took pity on him. "Gotta go, Johanna. Taking Joe on the grand tour. Back later." She hooked an arm through his, steering him away from Johanna and onto the footpath leading through the woods.

"What did she mean?" Joe asked.

Now, Mimi wasn't embarrassed by her occupation, but experience had taught her that most people considered phone sex purveyors marginally more principled than mediums. So generally when she met people, she tried to keep from revealing her unusual career until after she'd hopefully established herself as a sound, reasonable, and principled woman. But even if Joe was the handsomest man she'd met in ages, he was just somebody's temporary houseguest, and she was just filling up a few hours before the toasts to Ardis began. There was no reason to equivocate.

"I'm a tele-medium," she said, hobbling along. "People call the eight hundred number I work for and I contact the Other Side for them."

He slowed down. She kept moving.

"Really?"

"Yup. We work out of an office and everything."

"Huh. Then . . . you weren't kidding when you said there's no escape from your family even after death? I mean, you think you really know this for a fact?"

"I just calls 'em like I sees 'em," Mimi said. She could almost hear Joe mentally floundering for the right tone, some rejoinder that would be neutral. She'd been here before.

"Interesting," he finally said. "How does that work? Do you charge by the minute?"

As a neutral gambit, it wasn't half bad. He didn't even sound flustered. "Mostly, but we have All You Can Talk weekly and monthly payment plans available, too. Look," she said, happy to leave the subject of her work behind. "We're here."

They'd come out of the woods and stopped cold. They'd had to. The other option was to walk into a wall of logs.

"Behold the Next Generation!" Mimi declared, pointing. Standing three-plus stories high, its massive "logs" gleaming gold with some sort of sealant, topped by a small forest worth of cedar shake roofing channeled with copper flashing, was what looked like a resort but was in fact what someone apparently considered a "weekend place."

Down a ways from where they stood, Mimi's cousin Gerry and a group of his pals stalked along the edge of a tiny strip of manicured lawn. They reminded her of something. . . . She had it. They looked like the primates confronting the obelisk in the beginning of *2001: A Space Odyssey.*

They grumbled and gestured as they walked, in particular her big, blond, Thor-lookalike cousin Gerald, who kept flinging his arms out in an apelike show of aggression. For the sake of the family's dignity, she hoped he didn't start throwing tufts of grass at the place.

Only Half-Uncle Bill, aka Mr. Debbie, stood motionless, his naturally benign face corrugated in lines of concentration as he chewed on a piece of grass. Poor Half-Uncle Bill; the years of marriage to Debbie were taking their toll. For one, he was wearing a salmon-colored polo shirt, salmon-colored polo shirts being this summer's uniform for upper-middle-class, fiftysomething men. For two, a neat little bouclé rug of dark hair covered his balding head.

Mimi followed his unblinking gaze. He was probably admiring the monstrosity. All indicators suggested he'd been brainwashed by Debbie into that perpetual state of misery known as "wanting more."

"Isn't it the most obscene thing you have ever seen?" Mimi asked Joe, feeling perversely proud.

Joe didn't answer. He was watching her narrowly, like he half expected her to start chanting a spell. Oh, yeah. She'd told him about Uff-Dead. She ignored his speculative look and tried again to get his mind off her job. "I talked to the builder when it was going up this spring. Do you know what it is?" She didn't wait for his answer. "It's a replica of an Adirondack's *camp* built in the 1880s. Of course, it has a few modern embellishments. Those would be the home theater, a three-thousand-dollar built-in cappuccino machine, and a four-car garage," she said. "Want to hear the best part?"

"Do I?"

"You do. It's not even real. I mean logs. They're made out of recycled newspapers and cocoa-bean hulls. Very environmentally correct." She glanced at him to see whether he appreciated the irony of this. "Yup, you're looking at over ten thousand square feet of environmental correctness. I wonder what his heating bill is."

"Ah, hell. I'll bet the guy heats the whole damn place with wood. Look out, Superior National Forest! The environmentalists are coming!" While she'd been talking, Cousin Gerald and little grizzled Hank Sboda, who owned the cottage on the other side of the monolith, had detached themselves from their companions and wandered over.

"Gerry, Hank, this is a friend of mine, Joe," she introduced the men. "Joe, my cousin Gerry, and this is Hank Sboda."

"Friend, huh?" Gerry said, looking Joe over. Mimi had followed her older cousin around Chez Ducky throughout her childhood. Consequently, he still felt a certain responsibility toward her. "Mimi doesn't have many— I mean, she doesn't bring many friends up here. You must be special. How'd you meet?"

Joe clasped Gerry's proffered hand. "I helped her out of a bit of a mess."

Gerry shot a concerned glance at Mimi. "You in trouble?"

"No. He meant a literal mess. I was covered in mud and he offered me a ride."

"Oh." That she'd been covered in mud obviously didn't surprise Gerry. His gaze fell on the stains on Joe's shirt. He opened his mouth, caught Mimi's eye, closed his mouth, and turned back to the mansion. "So, whaddya think of 'er, Joe?"

"What do you think?" Joe rejoined.

"I think," Gerry replied, "that is the biggest pile of crap to hit the North Woods since Babe the Blue Ox took a dump. I mean, look at it, Joe. It's a good ten feet taller than any building within fifty miles."

"We call it Prescott's Erection, after its owner," Hank Sboda put in, coloring and glancing sheepishly at Mimi, who, despite not only having heard the tag before but having been the one who'd coined it, demurely lowered her eyes.

"Prescott's—" Joe choked. Men were so sensitive.

"Aw, come on," Mimi said. "You don't think maybe there's a little compensation going on here?"

"Can you imagine what it'll be like at the Big House this winter after the trees drop their leaves and you look out and instead of a winter wonderland all you see is that thing looming up into the sky?" Gerry muttered.

"Unpleasant?" Joe asked.

"And look at *that*." Mimi pointed up at the octagonal

tower perched at the corner nearest them. "There are fire towers up here that aren't as high."

"You're exaggerating," Gerry said.

"Okay," Mimi conceded. "But the point is I come up here in the fall sometimes and with that thing towering over me I'm going to feel like I'm in a prison camp waiting for the guards to open fire."

"Chez Ducky doesn't look much like a prison camp," Joe said uncomfortably.

She peered at him. "Say, you don't actually *like* this thing, do you?"

"No." His response was immediate and sincere.

"*We* hate it," she said, looking to Hank and Gerald for confirmation. Both men nodded.

"Hate it," echoed Gerry's wife, Vida, emerging from the wood's path.

Mimi approved of Vida, a wiry redhead who had gone back to school a few years ago in a felicitous move to become a massage therapist—felicitous because she often practiced on Mimi.

"Hi," Joe said. "I'm Joe."

"I'm Vida. Wouldn't you hate it if you were us, Joe?"

"Absolutely," he said. "In fact, I'd probably consider selling because of it."

Mimi waited for someone to point out the error in his reasoning. No one did.

"And go where?" she finally asked, exasperated with her relatives. "It would only be a temporary reprieve. Sooner or later every pothole in the state is going to be cheek to jowl with places like that." She jerked her head toward the faux-log monstrosity.

"Besides, we could never replace Chez Ducky. It's paid for, and spreading the cost of upkeep makes it affordable for all of us. Plus, some of us couldn't afford any vacation at all if we didn't have here to come to," she finished pitiably.

Gerry shot her a bemused glance. She ignored him. No

need to tell Joe her "vacations" usually lasted from May through September. She was aiming for sympathy here, not full disclosure.

"We're selling."

Mimi's, Gerry's, and Vida's heads snapped toward Hank Sboda.

"Huh?" Gerry asked, his lanternlike jaw dropping open.

"We decided to sell," Hank said, his tone defensive. "Fowl Lake in't what it used to be and never will be again. We can't afford to stay and we can't afford not to sell. Just like Mimi here said."

"I never said that!" Mimi protested.

Gerry stared at Hank in horror. "You can't be serious. The Sbodas have been on Fowl Lake almost as long as the Olsons."

"Longer," Hank said primly, "but that in't the point. Point is, a . . . realtor tells us she can sell our land for enough that we can buy a condo in Fort Myers."

Gerry snorted, his expression contemptuous.

"Don't look at me like that, Olson. You're a young man," Hank said.

Actually Gerry was pushing fifty, but now wasn't the time to point this out.

"And you got lots of folks to help with all the stuff needs doing," Hank went on heatedly. "My kids got their own kids now and don't get up here more than a couple times a year. That leaves all the maintenance to me and Mary. Damn near got a hernia getting the dock in this spring."

"You're selling 'cause it's *too much work*?" Gerry asked. Despite plenty of evidence to the contrary, like most line-bred Minnesotans Gerry liked to think he represented the apex of a staunch work ethic. Hank Sboda enjoyed the same fantasy.

The woolly caterpillar of Hank's brows dipped toward the bridge of his nose. "Course not," he exclaimed. "That's just part of it. Hell and damn, Gerry! It's fine for you to talk. You got eight *thousand* feet of lakeshore and a whole forest standing between you and what's happening out here. "I got two hundred feet with this, this—*hotel* on my east, and now Svenstrom's sold on my other side and I hear the guy what's bought it is going to start excavating next spring and it's gonna be another one of them!" Hank stabbed a finger at the log wall. His face had gone an alarming shade of fuchsia. "Hell, I'll be hemmed in with nothing to look at but fake log siding."

Aha, thought Mimi, the Svenstroms' inexplicable absence from the party was thus explained. Turncoats. She gazed sadly at Hank, uncertain what to say and guiltily aware that deep within she was giddy with relief that such considerations didn't affect Chez Ducky. Still, Fowl Lake wouldn't be the same without the Sbodas puttering around it in their old twelve-foot Alumacraft.

"Might as well sell now before someone wakes up and realizes this is nothing but a glorified slough." The air seemed to have gone out of Hank, because he said this last on a forlorn whisper.

"How much do you expect to make?"

Mimi wheeled around to discover Debbie beside her.

"Debbie," Hank said, "you know—"

"Two thousand a lake-frontage foot," she answered for him. She reached across Hank, shoving her hand toward Joe. "Debbie Olson. Nice to meet you."

He held out his hand to shake hers and instead she slapped a small printed card into his palm.

"What's that?" Mimi asked.

"My business card. As soon as I pass my realtor's test, I'll be licensed."

Everything started to make sense. "*You're* the realtor who Hank here has been talking to?" she asked, shocked at this open betrayal of family and friends and . . . Chez Ducky.

"I'm not a realtor yet. But yes, Hank and I have had a few talks." She didn't look in the least bit embarrassed. The woman had no shame.

Mimi rolled her eyes, disgusted.

"That *is* a lot of money," Vida conceded. She caught Mimi's dagger glance. "I mean, this isn't Gull Lake or Vermillion. Why'd anyone be willing to pay that for land here?"

"The 'where' don't matter to people like Prescott," Hank said sourly. "He just wants to build a big, new, showy place to prove how successful he is to his friends. Though there don't seem to be too many of *them* crawling around."

"You know Prescott?" Joe asked, breaking his silence.

"Nah-uh," Hank said. "One of the local guys doing the landscaping—and, *come on*! This is the North Woods, for the love of God. Who landscapes the *North Woods*?—told us his name."

Joe turned to Gerry. "Have you met him?"

"Nope. The guy's a hermit," Gerry said.

"I think he may be agoraphobic," Mimi put in, turning her shoulder to Debbie. Birgie would deal with her later. "He's a computer genius, a professor on sabbatical from Berkeley or MIT, I think. He invented some sort of Web application he gets millions in royalties for and decided to build that place as a retreat. There he is now." She pointed up at the third-story turret window, where a pale, pudgy face looked down at them.

"He looks so young," Joe murmured.

"Yeah," Mimi said. "He can't be much more than twenty-three or twenty-two. Probably one of those kids who graduated from college at twelve. He's always up there looking down like some weird little male Rapunzel. I'd feel sorry for him if I didn't have to look at this eyesore every day. Kind of kills the sympathy reflex, you know?"

"He's pathetic," Gerry agreed. "I mean, what kind of guy pays God-knows-what to build a house as big as most resorts, then never has anyone up to visit and never comes outside?"

Joe sighed, his gaze fixed on the face in the window high above. He lifted a hand in a weak salute. "My son."

Chapter Seven

Prescott Tierney looked down as his father gave him a brief two-fingered salute. He flushed with embarrassment and attempted to melt back into the room and out of sight. Unfortunately, Prescott's was not a physique given to melting.

What the hell was Joe doing down there amongst *his* neighbors? Joe was *supposed* to be visiting him. Not that Prescott gave a damn if or when Joe visited, but it was just common courtesy to show up when you said you were going to show up. Seeing Joe down there, ecstatically not with Prescott, brought back all his adolescent anger. God knew, it was an old pattern.

Even before his mother's death, Joe hadn't been around much. He was always somewhere else, becoming rich, worldly, and important. Oh, he showed up during holidays and birthdays, always toting some wildly inappropriate gift. The man apparently never talked to his wife or looked at his son, or he would have known that Prescott had no discernable athletic ability.

Why couldn't Joe have just celebrated the fact that Prescott was a genius? He wasn't bragging; it was fact. He'd been a boy genius who liked math and physics and *The Lord of the Rings* and would have preferred his own computer to some stupid hockey stick. Besides, who was supposed to show him how to use a hockey stick? Not Joe, not in the five minutes every few months he was around. And it sure as hell wasn't going to be his mom. She, like him, was an academic. She, like him, was a genius (IQ 165). She, like him, lived a cerebral life.

And *she* was proud of Prescott.

Proud of *them*, he amended. His mother's single-minded dedication to his welfare had seen that he'd had the best possible educations. Since that obviously meant home-schooling—for, as she'd often said, who better to teach a genius than a genius?—it also meant constantly preparing herself for what she'd called "the sacred task of molding a brilliant mind." Her faith in herself was not misplaced, either. At nine, he'd nailed the SATs.

Then she'd died, hit by a bus as she was crossing the street talking on her cell phone in a heated debate with the chancellor of Harvard University over whether or not Prescott would be admitted as a full-time student at age ten. Prescott had never forgiven Harvard. He'd done his undergraduate work at Princeton.

Joe had shown up in time for the funeral looking confused—the only time in Prescott's memory he could recall Joe looking so. After a week of staring at each other, Joe had come up with the outrageous suggestion that Prescott tag after him when he returned to work and attend schools in other countries. Prescott had wasted no time in shooting down that halfhearted proposal. And it was halfhearted. Even at ten Prescott recognized relief when he saw it.

Prescott proposed instead that he go to the elite boarding school he and his mother had occasionally toyed with the idea of his attending while they waited for him to reach the chronological age supposedly erudite institutions required of their students. He didn't so much propose as insist.

Thank God, Joe had let him go. The only mildly surprising part was that Joe had actually continued showing up on holidays and birthdays, and persisted in taking him out of school for a month each summer to live in whatever luxurious short-term rental he was then currently occupying. It must have become an ingrained habit, because Joe was still showing up periodically even when it should have been clear to him that Prescott did not need Joe to play daddy. He didn't *need* Joe at all.

He supposed Joe's ego could not stand the idea that his only child didn't care for his company. Especially when everyone else did. After all, Joe was handsome, debonair, and charismatic.

Prescott's lip began to twitch. He banged his forehead once against the wall next to the window—but not too hard, as he bruised easily. Plus it had taken him hours to get his Diane Arbus originals perfectly aligned. He looked down.

How *had* Joe come to be there?

Knowing Joe, by now the Olsons had discovered he was some sort of prodigal son or better yet, the uncrowned king of the Olsons and invited him to be guest of honor at their little shindig. That was typical of Joe. Somehow, he always managed to fit in. Despite looking like he just stepped out of *GQ,* he seemed perfectly comfortable amongst the Nordic types standing around admiring Bombadil House.

Okay, he knew it was a little sketchy, but Tolkien had been his hero since he'd been five. And so it was fitting that he should name this place, which he'd designed, with some help from *Architectural Digest* and *Adirondack Home,* to be his refuge from the outside world, after *The Lord of the Rings'* famous happy hermit. He briefly wondered whether anyone at MIT realized he'd gone into self-imposed exile. He doubted it.

Except for some of his students at MIT, no one had even asked where he was going on the year sabbatical he'd taken following the college's sale of his Internet security program. Fine with him. He didn't feel any compulsion to share his personal life with the school's second-gen Silicon Valley greedmeisters and relentlessly ambitious grad students. They could jockey all they wanted for the second rung on the genius ladder. He knew he stood at the top. Still, it was hard standing alone at the top of the heap. He needed a break; he needed to find himself a simple place where a man could contemplate whatever it was he wanted to contemplate and not be made to feel like an outcast by even so little as a walk across the campus grounds.

Here, at Fowl Lake, he felt he more or less belonged. No one expected anything of him. They didn't ask him stupid questions like what his favorite football team was, or what he was working on that would make his next million. Here, he just was part of the scenery. Like the Olsons. Oh, he realized he wasn't here as a part of the Olson milieu—he wasn't delusional. They were more like sea lions and penguins in the South Pole, cohabiting on a rock atoll, separate but equal.

Prescott's eye caught a motion below and he looked down at the scrawny red-haired woman who'd joined the group below. He wondered whether Joe had told the Olsons he was his son. He leaned sideways and peered closer. Nope. Prescott knew this because no one's face betrayed the startled expression people always got upon hearing this news. He'd seen the look countless times before.

Cool it, he told himself, all this alpha male bullshit was understandable when he was a teenager, but Prescott was twenty-three. He was independently wealthy due to the sale of a revolutionary Internet application he'd invented, he had a higher IQ than anyone he knew and a fabulous house, and he didn't make a living screwing with people's lives like Joe did.

"Damn."

None of those things could cancel out the fact that Joe stood beside Mignonette Olson. Prescott pivoted his head against the wall and gazed forlornly down at them.

When Prescott had moved in three months ago, he'd asked one of the workmen about the abandoned resort next door.

He'd assumed it was a resort because of the old sign with a wood-burned Daffy Duck–like creature squatting at the bottom of the drive. It read CHEZ DUCKY. To his surprise, he'd learned it wasn't a resort at all, and despite appearances, not abandoned. It was apparently some sort of enclave belonging to a family named Olson, a huge extended family whose members drifted in and out all summer long as the spirit moved them.

Prescott, who had never done anything without adequate preparation and plenty of forethought, and whose only relatives consisted of a set of ancient maternal grandparents, an elderly second cousin he'd never met, and Joe, was enchanted. Watching them from his tower—something he admitted he maybe spent a *little* too much time doing—was as good as reading a Dickens novel. Not the maudlin ending, but the cheery, warming middle part describing all the good and decent people who would soon be snatched away from whatever pathetic little lisper Mr. Dickens was tormenting. The only constant, the only fixture in the ever-changing cast of characters populating that tumbledown compound, was *her*.

The first time Prescott had seen her, she'd been sitting under one of the big pine trees cutting her toenails and singing an Abba tune. Loudly.

He'd cracked the window open to hear better, even though he knew it would play hell with the state-of-the-art HEPA filtration system he'd installed in the house's ductwork. Not to mention the havoc it would play with his allergies. She didn't have a very good voice.

As Prescott had listened, wincing, a teenage kid came up to her. Prescott hadn't been able to hear what he'd said, but he'd assumed it was a question about life or love or some other weighty matter because the woman had taken the kid's hand, looked soulfully up into his eyes, and said, "Oh, honey, just let it slide."

Prescott could see the tension seep out of the kid, and, as

weird as he knew it sounded, he felt some of his own melt away. The woman had smiled her Madonna-like smile and gone back to trimming her toenails.

He was smitten.

Here was a woman who didn't care that her voice was lousy or the song she warbled even lousier. She apparently didn't care that she would never be young again or that she must have no money because she spent her summers in what was little more than a shack. He didn't know how he knew these things, but he did. She was a little disheveled, she didn't have much of a wardrobe, but she obviously didn't care about those things, either. *This* woman had it all figured out.

She spent hours (and there were a lot of them) floating on the lake in an inner tube, likely contemplating some bottomless well of inner tranquility. She was probably some sort of Zen yoga master. That she was the center point around which the Chez Ducky world revolved was evident. She was the only one who'd been up here every day since he'd moved in.

"Let it slide." To someone who had dedicated his short life to excelling, no words had ever resonated so loudly. He saw her constant presence here as a beacon, guiding the way home for all her family. The only constant Prescott had known in his life had been his 4.0 grade point average. Joe's seasonal visits didn't count because they were merely duty calls.

Joe was big on duty. But as far as Prescott was concerned, Joe's visits were a waste of time. He and Joe had nothing in common. Prescott *did* have a lot in common with the woman at Chez Ducky. They were both conscientious, both environmentalists (Prescott had decided this was a likely reason she wore vintage clothing), and both spiritual rather than physical beings.

Prescott had discovered that her name was Mignonette Olson. *Mrs.* Olson, he assumed because, first of all, being short and dark, she didn't look anything like the big blond

Olsons, and second, he couldn't imagine her not sharing her
life with someone. She was a sharing sort. He could only
conclude by the absence of a Mr. Olson worshipping at her
feet that she was a widow. A childless widow.

And he was an orphan. Or as good as one.

He released a gusty sigh and pushed away from the wall.
He wondered what she was saying to Joe. Were they talking
about his house? Was Joe trying to charm her? She didn't
look charmed. She looked frankly disgusted.

Take that, Joe, Prescott thought, mentally pumping his
arm. *Your sleep-aid-commercial voice and used-car-
salesman charm aren't going to cut it with a woman like Mrs.
Olson. She's not so easily bamboozled.*

A shout drew his attention back outside. He looked down
to see a teenage boy racing out of the woods, gesticulating
wildly.

Prescott gnawed his thumbnail. He wanted to hear what
was going on but he didn't want the Olsons to think he was
eavesdropping, and he was afraid they might see him if he
lifted the window sash. On the other hand, everyone had
turned their attention to the kid.

Prescott dropped to all fours and crawled under the window, reaching up and shoving the sash up an inch or so. He
was going to pay for this tonight when his allergies kicked in,
but it was worth it. Observing the Olsons had become more
than an idle pastime. He'd invested so many hours watching
them, he felt he'd adopted them.

"—a funeral pyre!" the giant blond male was bellowing.

Prescott curled his fingers over the lip of the sill and
peeked over. The people had circled around the kid.

"Yes, sir! She's down at the dock right now pouring
kerosene over a stack of kindling in the center of the pontoon."

Prescott snatched the binoculars he kept by the window
and rose to his knees. He trained the lenses on the small area
of the beach visible in front of the blistered old two-story

house at Chez Ducky. Sure enough, an older woman wearing some sort of white drapery stood knee-deep in the water, up-ending a red gallon can of liquid on top of a pile of branches in the middle of some sort of raft. He lowered the binoculars and pressed his ear to the window opening.

"That doesn't make any sense," the skinny redheaded woman next to Mrs. Olson was saying. "There isn't any Ardis to burn."

"She's got a poster of Ardis on top of the wood," the kid exclaimed.

"Aw, geez," the blond guy muttered.

Prescott adjusted the focus on the raft. Yup. A life-sized, grainy picture of an old woman carrying a golf bag stuck out of the branches. As Prescott watched, the woman in the water struck a match and threw it onto the twigs. Fire flared up, followed by a black belch of smoke.

He wasn't the only one to see the smoke. Mrs. Olson spied it, too. "Holy shit," she said. "We better get over there before she burns the whole place down."

She struck off into the woods with the others close behind.

Including, Prescott noted with a hollow sensation, Joe. But then, what did he expect? That Joe would have preferred his company?

Not likely.

Chapter Eight

Birgie plopped down on the plastic lawn chair she'd dragged down to the beach and watched the spectacle unfold.

As Viking funerary boats went, Naomi's was a piss-poor example, but none of the crowd gathered round to watch seemed disappointed. Friends and neighbors and whoever the hell else these people were stood three deep on the beach, watching the pontoon bobbing gently twenty feet offshore, the poster of Ardis jouncing so gaily it seemed like Ardis was doing a little victory dance.

Maybe she was, Birgie thought. She should ask Mimi.

After the initial belch of smoke erupting from beneath the scaffolding Naomi had constructed, the fire had petered down to a few flames. Naomi, who'd pushed the pontoon out from the shore and was still standing knee-deep in the lake with the hem of her bedsheet floating around her, turned around in disgust and slogged to shore.

"This sucks," she said to Birgie, who happened to be the closest to her. "I knew I shouldn't have used a match. You're supposed to shoot a flaming arrow into the pyre."

"Ah-huh," Birgie muttered before upending the last swigs of a can of Diet Coke into her mouth.

"I don't understand it," Naomi went on. "I used a gal—"

A sudden whooshing sound spun Naomi around. Birgie

was already staring. The flames had found the gas. The fire shot eight feet into the air, embracing the Ardis poster in glowing orange and blue. Birgie could hear the Styrofoam backing popping as the picture slowly melted, reminding her of the Wicked Witch of the West after Dorothy had doused her in water. Ardis would have appreciated the comparison.

"Hot damn!" Naomi said gleefully, rubbing her hands. "Wait here. I'll say my piece and be right back."

"Wasn't going anywhere, Naomi," Birgie said, crossing her ankles. She liked Naomi. She wasn't nearly as crazy as the younger generations thought. Except for Mimi, of course. But then most of the younger generations thought Mimi was a little odd herself, what with the medium thing and living like a gypsy. Birgie suspected Mimi dragged eighty percent of her worldly possessions with her up to the lake each year and she still didn't fill up the trunk of a midsized car.

"Oh, Viking Maiden, may your journey to Valhalla be swift!" Naomi waded back out toward the burning pontoon, her arms raised above her head. A rising wind whipped the bedsheet around her. Birgie had to admit it, Naomi looked pretty impressive.

"May you soon reach the distant shores of eternity!"

Impressive, too, was the way that same wind was whipping the fire higher.

"May your proud spirit find rest in the halls of your great ancestors!"

And really impressive was the way the wind had turned around the pontoon with its roaring fire and was pushing it back toward shore.

"May you— Aw, shit!" Naomi hoisted up her bedsheet and lurched toward the pontoon, obviously intending to push it back out into the lake.

"Don't do that, Naomi!" Birgie called, a little concerned. "You'll get your hair all burned off!"

Birgie had just lumbered to her feet when a group of people burst from the woods next to the Big House and raced toward the shore. Gerry, his kid Frank, and the guy who'd been following Mimi around the picnic were in the lead, but Vida and Bill were close behind, followed by Debbie and Hank Sboda. Mimi was last, but not by much; she was hop-skipping on one leg like a madwoman.

The well-dressed guy waded into the water next to Naomi and with a clipped, "Sorry," tore the bedsheet off her, dunked it in the lake, and flung it across the pontoon.

"Well, crap," Naomi muttered, looking down at her Playtex Eighteen Hour bra. She turned sullenly away from the burning pontoon, now being covered with all manner of sodden bed dressing, and struggled up out of the water to Birgie's side.

"It wasn't going to get close enough to set anything on fire," she grumbled. "I had it anchored offshore."

Birgie couldn't say she was surprised. Naomi might be colorful, but she wasn't incautious.

"Should I tell them?" Naomi asked.

Birgie considered. The crowd on the beach had shifted its dynamic from spectators at a funeral pyre to active partici-pants at a five-alarm fire. They'd apparently decided to con-centrate their efforts on sinking the pontoon under as many sodden blankets, sheets, towels, and even one mattress, as they could pile on it.

"Nah," Birgie finally advised. "Let 'em be. They're hav-ing fun."

They were, too. Now that it was apparent that the forest wasn't going to catch fire, and only a few wisps of black smoke were left curling up from the pontoon, the fire fight had become a water fight. People were dunking each other, the kids were splashing, and someone had broken into the Chez Ducky water pistol armory and pulled out the guns.

Mimi had sunk down to her knees on the sand, her arms limp in her lap as she stared at the pontoon. Her shoulders slumped with relief. As Birgie watched, the handsome guy who'd stripped the sheet from Naomi came up to Mimi and said something. She smiled up at him. He reached his hand out and she took it. For a heartbeat they froze; then he was pulling her to her feet and letting go of her hand. It didn't matter. Birgie, who'd had half a dozen lovers, knew what she'd seen.

Sparks. Real sparks, too. Not just sex sparks—though God knew, those weren't anything to turn your nose up at.

"Will you look at that?" Naomi murmured. She was watching the pair, too.

"Yup," Birgie said. After being someone's sister-in-law for fifty-some years, some communication didn't need speech. "Know who he is?"

"Johanna said Mimi was toting around some good-looking man named Joe."

"Joe," Birgie said nostalgically. "I had a boyfriend named Joe once—"

"That crazy old woman."

Birgie and Naomi looked around to see Naomi's daughter-in-law Debbie stomping through the sand toward Naomi's son, and Debbie's husband, Bill. Little spits of sand punctuated each one of her angry steps.

"She could have burned this place to the ground!" Debbie declared angrily. A few of those closest looked away uncomfortably. "You've got to do something about her, Bill. Before one of these fool antics of hers results in a lawsuit."

Birgie looked at Naomi. Naomi shrugged.

Debbie looked really shaken. And really mad.

"Now, Debbie. She's my mother—"

"And I'm your wife, and those"—Debbie pointed at a pair of boys wrestling in the surf—"are your sons. And she put *us* in danger. When are you going to grow a spine and do what needs to be done?"

"Why don't you just shut up, Debbie?" Mimi's voice rose above the hubbub. Birgie looked around and saw Mimi hobbling toward Debbie. Joe was gone. Mimi's expression was stony. Almost . . . angry. And her tone was . . . imperious.

It was about time someone had told Debbie to shut up,
Birgie thought. Past time. It was only amazing that it had
been Mimi who'd done the telling. Mimi never took the lead.
She was never imperious. She always claimed she was too
lazy to command anything, but Birgie had always suspected
the real reason was that she didn't want to care so much
about something or someone that she'd felt compelled to act.
She hadn't cared about anything very much since her dad had
disappeared.

Birgie applauded. Gerry joined in. Then Johanna and then
someone else. Not everyone clapped, but enough people did
that Debbie knew where she stood in relation to Naomi. Her
face suffused with color.

"Well, excuse me for not wanting anyone to get hurt," she
sniffed and stomped off, nose high.

Naomi, inured to Debbie's pain-in-the-assness by seven-
teen years as her mother-in-law, sighed. "Poor Bill."

Chapter Nine

As soon as he got back to the rental car, Joe pulled off his waterlogged loafers and tossed them into the backseat. He felt a little as though he'd just popped back up out of the rabbit's hole.

No forty-year-old women of Joe's acquaintance would go skinny-dipping in a lake at the same time a picnic was under way a few hundred feet away. Nor would they run naked through the woods. And if bizarre circumstances should force them to do so, they'd definitely be at least a little nonplussed by the experience.

As soon as Mimi Olson had gotten the ratty stadium blanket over her, every bit of embarrassment had evaporated. It hadn't returned, not even when she'd shown up wearing a kiddy beach robe. Nor when she'd blithely informed him that she spoke to ghosts for a living. On a ghost hotline.

Mimi Olson, he had come to the sad conclusion, was quirky.

That should have been it for Joe, whose few interactions with quirky women had led to no particular desire for more. In his experience, "quirky" people were either "affected" or possibly "mentally lacking." But he decided that Mimi Olson deserved special dispensation. She was obviously the product of her upbringing—as evidenced by her family's peculiar pontoon-burning ritual. Small wonder Mimi was a little odd.

Hell, spend enough time with the Olsons and anyone would be odd. Why, he'd been drawn into odd behavior after just a short time in their company. Should anyone have told him this morning that by afternoon he would be standing fully clad knee-deep in a boggy lake ripping a sheet off an old lady, he would have laid very large odds against it.

He stripped off his sodden socks and wrung the sandy lake water out of them.

Besides, Mimi wasn't *just* quirky. He'd been impressed by the lucid, unsentimental argument she'd forwarded in favor of keeping Chez Ducky in the family. Joe found lucid thinking incredibly sexy. It was one of the chief reasons he'd been attracted to Karen.

He'd met Karen as a senior at Miami Ohio, where she'd just started her freshman year. They'd sat next to each other in an advanced stats class. She'd shown him her class notes and he'd fallen like a ton of bricks. Her notes were a paean to organization and precise detail. Soon they were studying together, then sleeping together.

He knew his frat brothers couldn't figure out what the attraction was on either part, but he knew exactly why he'd fallen for Karen. He'd been the only child of a variously employed couple dedicated to melodrama. For a kid whose home life was in perennial disarray, nothing was as beautiful as meticulousness, order, and reason. Karen was the high priestess of all these traits.

Joe reached down and turned his pant cuffs inside out, upending a pile of sand onto the ground.

No one could have been more surprised than him when Karen had agreed to marry him after they'd gotten pregnant, but Karen, a devout Catholic, wanted to keep the baby. What should have been a Nobel Prize–winning career had been derailed. Joe had landed a good job straight out of college and threw himself into work, determined to earn enough money to send Karen, who'd selflessly opted to stay at home with Prescott, back to college. Soon Joe was making a name for himself as the go-to guy. Unfortunately, that invariably meant "going-to" another city, another state, another country, sometimes for weeks, often for months.

Five years later, he'd taken Karen out to dinner for her twenty-fourth birthday. After dessert, he'd slid a blank check and an application to the University of Chicago across the table toward her.

"What is this?" she'd asked, her face knotted with surprise.

"It's a check. And an application. To the University of Chicago. But that's just for show. You can go anywhere you want to go to school."

"Huh?"

"It's true. You can finally become a nuclear research physicist."

"I have a job," she'd replied coldly.

Mortified by his clumsy misstep, Joe had attempted to backpedal. "I know you do. And you are an exceptional mother." She'd preened a little. "I meant your dream job."

"What about Prescott?"

"Prescott is nearly five. Ready for school himself."

"School?" Karen's voice had risen, drawing glances from nearby diners. "Where do you intend to find a preschool appropriate for a child with an IQ in excess of 150?"

Joe had heard it before, how important Prescott's environment was in order for their son to reach his full potential. "I'm sure there are Montessori schools—"

"*Montessori?* Montessori is for the terminally B-plus child." She'd shaken her head. "No. Thank you for thinking of me, but I have a career, Joe. Not just a job, a full-time *career*. As Prescott's teacher. He is blooming under my guidance. *Blooming.*"

"But what about you?"

"I'm blooming, too. Can't you tell?" She'd smiled, and

he'd had to admit, she seemed happy. "I cannot imagine doing anything more rewarding. Or fascinating. The models for developing cognitive skill sets in gifted children are changing daily. I have so much to learn and so many things I want to try with Prescott."

"I didn't realize . . ."

"You're gone a lot," she'd said, and then, upon seeing his expression, she added, "I'm not complaining. It's an observation."

"You've raised Prescott almost single-handedly," Joe had said. "At least get some help."

"I don't need any help," she'd said tightly.

"Then tell me what I can do to make your life a little easier. That promotion I was telling you about? I'll turn it down so at least I won't be around even less than I already am."

"No!" She'd frowned heavily. "No, don't do that. Prescott's education is going to be expensive, and I'm not just talking about undergraduate school. I want all the resources he might need made available to him as soon as he needs them, no matter what the cost."

"Then I'll only take it if they promise to let me cut back on the travel."

She'd met his gaze. She'd looked frightened, and abruptly Joe had realized why. She'd been afraid he was going to take away some part of the career she found so fulfilling. She'd given up everything, and this, being Prescott's mother, was all she had by which to define herself.

"Please, Joe," she said, substantiating his suspicion. "Don't. Don't interfere. Don't take this away from me."

That sealed the deal. He'd agreed.

I kept my word, Joe thought, swinging his damp pant legs into the car and starting the engine. *What an idiot.*

Joe parked the car in front of the four-car garage and got out. Prescott's place looked like something out of Disney

World, and with about as much North Woods ambience as a pine-scented car deodorizer.

He wanted to like it. He really did. Because he could tell Prescott was proud of it. But . . . it was so damn big. And bogus. And . . . *big*.

Small wonder Mimi loathed it and Prescott. He couldn't say he blamed her. Poor Mimi. She'd looked so mortified when he'd said Prescott was his son. She'd gulped something and been about to launch into unnecessary apologizes when the kid had arrived with the news about the pontoon-cum-pyre. Later she'd tried to apologize again but he'd cut her off, telling her not to worry about it. He'd wanted to say more—he wasn't sure what—but her attention had moved on to—what was her name? Debbie?—stomping over the sand shouting.

Joe reached into the backseat, got his tote and picked his way carefully to the front door on tender bare feet. A little red electronic eye, discreetly nestled in a pinecone above the front door, stared down at him. There was no doorbell, just a small, brass-plated intercom speaker.

He looked up at the red eye and smiled weakly. He hated surveillance cameras and webcams. "Hi, Pres. It's me. Joe." He would have said, "Dad," except Prescott referred to him only as Joe. "I made it. But you already know that."

There was no response.

"This is really some place you have here." Silence.

"Pres? You there?" If Prescott had left there was no saying when he'd be back. Maybe days. "How am I supposed to get into this fortress, anyway?" he muttered, trying the front door knob. It was locked.

"Go around the back," Prescott's disembodied voice answered. "The French doors leading to the deck are unlocked."

I should have known, Joe thought. *He's been watching me, waiting for me to say something incriminating. Let the games begin!*

He headed around to the back of the lodge—what was it Prescott called it? Bum Deal House?— and climbed onto an enormous, prow-shaped cedar deck furnished with expensive cushioned loungers and chairs. Unfortunately, they would never know the imprint of a human butt because the only one who would have used them would be Prescott, and his many unhappily sequential seasonal allergies prohibited his spending any leisure time outdoors.

Prescott refused to take shots. Karen had been suspicious of introducing any chemical into Prescott's body, as it might somehow migrate to his brain. She'd often said, "You don't mess with perfection."

Joe, who'd seen what allergies did to Prescott, would have traded a few IQ points to stop his nose from running. But that was him.

He pushed open the French doors, breaching the purity of Prescott's hermetically sealed house, and looked around. He was standing in a room the size of a gymnasium that stretched in one vast open expanse from one end of the house to the other. Though no walls divided this room, function separated it into three main areas: a great room (though Joe was tempted to call it a Great Big Room) sparsely but attractively furnished with a sofa and some chairs; a dining area; and a kitchen so large it could have serviced a small hotel.

In a far corner of the living area, Joe could see into a hall and from there through an open door and into a bedroom. Apparently the north side of the house was the bedroom wing. Who knew what the rooms on the second and third floors were for.

Prescott was nowhere in sight.

"Pres?" Nothing. He walked into the kitchen and removed the caramel cashew bar he'd carefully wrapped in a napkin from his pocket. He set it out on the corner of a granite-topped island the size of an Egyptian sarcophagus.

The only sound was the softest susurration of a high-tech air-filtration system. Few noises made it in from outside, no bird calls, not the wind moving through the upper branches of the trees, not even the sound of the Olsons partying next door. Joe looked up above the huge dining room table, where the antlers from an entire herd of deer formed a chandelier the size of a tractor tire.

Now, Joe liked nice things. He enjoyed excellence in every way—well-tailored clothing, good music, beautiful artwork, and fine food. But he disliked waste just as much. And this place was an enormous waste of space and materials.

"Prescott! I'm in the kitchen! I brought you a cookie!"

"You don't have to yell, Joe." Prescott's voice, marked by the faintly tinny sound of one speaking from inside a drum, came calmly through a series of speakers neatly concealed in the kitchen's coffered ceiling. He sounded eerily like HAL from *2001: A Space Odyssey.* "I can hear you quite clearly."

Joe looked at the ceiling, trying to spy another red-eyed camera lens. He didn't see any. Thank God. He didn't think he could sleep knowing his REM cycles were being recorded. "Why do you need an intercom system, anyway? You're alone here."

"When the cleaning people come, I like to be able to tell them what needs doing without following after them. Or shouting," Prescott replied without intonation.

"How often do you have cleaning people?" Joe asked curiously. How much clutter could one man create? Not that he disapproved. He appreciated cleanliness as much as the next man. Okay. More.

Prescott didn't bother to reply, but the message was clear. It was the same message Joe had been receiving since Prescott had started emitting sound: *Joe wouldn't understand.*

Still, Joe gave it another shot. "I brought you a caramel cashew bar from next door. These things are amazing—"

"Perhaps sometime in the past you noticed my weight. I'm fat," the disembodied voice broke in. "Perhaps then you will not be surprised when you hear that henceforth I would appreciate it if you could refrain from bringing food such as caramel cashew cookie bars into the house."

"You're not fat. Hefty." Joe considered the word. "No. Large." That wasn't it either. "Sol—"

"Please stop."

Joe stopped and stood there, staring at the ceiling like an idiot and imagining Prescott, in whatever room he was in, similarly staring. Why, Joe wondered, was he still making a pilgrimage to Prescott's door every year, when Prescott clearly saw him as an inconvenience and a nuisance?

He didn't have a good answer. The fact was he'd never felt much like a father.

He recalled the first time he'd seen Prescott in the hospital. Joe had been in the hospital corridor avoiding the accusing glares of Karen's already elderly parents when the nurse had come out of the delivery room, pushing what looked like a motorized cake cart. Inside had been this tiny, scrawny creature wearing minuscule black swimmer's goggles. It had looked like an alien space monkey after crash landing, worried, wiggling, and making squalling sounds.

"He's a little jaundiced, so we had him under the bilirubin lights and had to put goggles on him," the nurse had explained as she maneuvered the cart in such a way that she'd hemmed Joe in next to the water fountain. "But otherwise, he's healthy. Do you want to hold him?"

"Not really." He'd drop him.

The nurse didn't look surprised. "Okay, then. I'll take him in to see his grandparents."

She started to pull the cart back, but something made Joe put out his hand and stop it. He leaned over the Plexiglas cubicle. The little space oddity had disks taped to his tiny dark hide, connected by wires to a machine embedded in the cart. A monitor read out numbers. Joe had looked at those numbers and that helpless creature and felt an avalanche of responsibility sliding down over his shoulders.

He still felt it. As much as he would have sometimes liked to, he could not give himself permission to quit trying to work out this paternal riddle that refused to give up its secrets.

He picked up the caramel cashew bar and took a bite. On the other hand, he'd been standing here like an idiot for almost five minutes with not a word from above.

"You know what? I saw a liquor store in this little town I came through," he said to the ceiling. "Maybe I'll drive up there and pick us up a bottle of wine."

When Prescott spoke, he didn't bother to hide his relief. "Yes," he said. "You do that."

Chapter Ten

"Scootch your shirt up so I can work on your back," Vida said.

Mimi willingly complied, settling on her stomach atop a stack of beach towels on the picnic table, her chin resting on her forearms. Tension drained out of her like sand out of an overstuffed levy bag. Not that there was that much tension to begin with, a fact Vida never hesitated to point out.

"You're unnatural," Vida said, disgusted. "I don't have to do much more than look at you and you release like one of those finger puppets that collapse when you push up on the bottom."

"Consider me a testimony to your skill," Mimi murmured.

The memorial had been two days earlier, and most people had returned from whence they'd come, leaving behind a handful of diehards.

"Go on with your story," Vida said, drumming the heels of her hands on either side of Mimi's spine.

"Where was I? Oh, yeah. So I said, 'Oops.' "

"No!"

"Well, what would you say to a guy you've just told has a son who's a geek, a hermit, agoraphobic, friendless, and probably deservedly so since he has just ruined a perfectly decent view with his hideous attempt to compensate for his undoubtedly inadequate masculinity?"

"Oops?"

"Oops," Mimi confirmed.

"*Then* what did you say?"

"Nothing. Naomi chose that minute to send Ardis to Valhalla." She corrected herself, "Though technically I guess it was Ardis's picture that was being sent to Valhalla."

"It's too bad you made such an ass of yourself. He was a fine-looking man."

"Yup," Mimi replied sadly. She hadn't seen him since the party, though she had wandered along the footpath a couple times, hoping he might be out. Out doing what? Chopping wood? Hardly.

"I don't suppose there's any way you could smooth things over? I know!" Vida paused in her massaging to snap her fingers. "You go over there and say, 'I'm sorry, I didn't realize Prescott was your son.' Just don't mention you're a psychic."

"How many times do I have to tell you guys? I'm not a psychic; I'm a medium. I only talk to the dead, which, now that I think of it, Prescott looks like he might be, so I suppose technically I might have been in communication with him," Mimi said; then her face twisted in self-contempt. "Forget I said that. Way too harsh. I just get so pissed off every time I look at that monstrosity. Besides, you have to admit, he does look like a zombie. A chunky zombie. A goth Peter Pan. It's that black hair and white face. He's gotta dye it."

"His dad has black hair," Vida said, hands working on autopilot. "Maybe Prescott is better-looking in person. It's hard to tell from a few glimpses. He'd almost have to be, wouldn't he? I mean, look at the dad. Yum."

Mimi half turned over to look Vida in the eye. "You're not even trying to be subtle, are you?"

"We love you. We're interested. Where's the harm?"

"You guys need to get a life."

"Gee, and that's just what we say about you. Listen—"

Mimi was saved from having to listen by the arrival of fourteen-year-old Frank, Vida's son. He came loping around the corner of the cottage and skidded to a halt.

"Geez!" He slapped a hand over his eyes and stretched out his other scrawny arm, pantomiming groping for the cottage. "I think I'm blind!"

"Smart-ass," Mimi mumbled, reaching behind to flip down the hem of her oversized T-shirt.

"I'm at an impressionable age," Frank said, splitting his index and middle fingers and peering at her out of one eye. "You could scar me for life. I think I saw something. I'm not sure exactly what it was."

"Ha. You should be so lucky," Mimi said. "What do you want, anyway?"

Frank dropped his hand. "There's something going on over at the Big House. Some sort of conference. Birgie said I better come and get you cause you're involved."

"Involved how?" Mimi asked, more bothered than interested. Mimi understood that Birgie didn't want to be at the family powwow any more than Mimi, but she'd expected more from her great-aunt than an arbitrary "misery loves company" summons.

Frank shrugged. "Dunno. Birgie said it was important, and I should make sure that you come and to tell you that if you duck this meeting, you'll regret it."

"Crud." Mimi scooted off the picnic table. "Are they still fussing about Naomi and the pontoon? Good riddance to the damn thing. It's not like it was even seaworthy. And I said I was sorry to Debbie."

"Did you *really* tell Debbie to shut up?" Vida asked, her mouth falling open. "I thought they were kidding. I can't imagine you doing something like that."

"Me, neither," Mimi said uncomfortably. "I don't know what got into me. I must have been channeling Ardis."

"Even Ardis never told Debbie to shut up. Honestly, Mimi, you have untapped depths."

"Birgie said something about a vote," Frank persisted, obviously taking his job as messenger seriously.

If someone was calling for a vote, that could only mean that people were disagreeing about whatever it was they were voting on. Mimi didn't want to spend any of her valuable free time (just because a thing was plentiful didn't make it less valuable) listening to her relatives debate the merits of a yearly snowplow service contract versus a flat per diem rate.

"Can't your mom go in my place?" she asked, looking at Vida. "I don't care enough about whatever they're voting on to make a decent decision, and Vida here—"

"How could you possibly know that?" Vida asked.

"I sense it," Mimi said, fixing Vida with a level stare. "Hello? Medium! I *sense* things."

"I thought you only spoke to the dead."

"Sometimes I sense things, too."

"Hm."

"Can you really sense things?" Frank asked. "Because Dad says he thinks you really believe you can talk to dead people but you're embarrassed about it and Mom says it doesn't matter what we think, it's what you know that counts," Frank said. "Birgie says she isn't saying what she thinks and Chuck says it's a pile of crap and that you are nothing but a swindler who makes a living out of conning people."

"Really," Mimi said.

"Yup."

"Which one is Chuck?" Mimi asked.

"You don't know?" Frank asked.

"Are you kidding? There's only been about twenty teenage boys around here this summer, all blond, all tall, all built like scarecrows."

"Well, can't you *sense* it?" Frank smirked.

She didn't reply. She simply rolled her eyes back in their sockets and shivered dramatically. "Chuck is the one with the cracked front tooth and . . . and a scar on his right knee he got playing soccer this spring. He did make the goal, though . . ." Her voice drifted off.

The smug smile slipped from Frank's face. But he wasn't an adolescent boy for nothing. "Lucky guess."

Mimi shrugged. "Think what you want. You still haven't answered my question. Can Vida be my proxy? Wait. I sense she can. I hereby declare your mom my proxy."

At this point, Vida, who'd been listening to the prior exchange with a long-suffering look, said, "And I hereby decline. You're the legal heir; you're the one with the vote, not me."

"One of six."

"I don't care. It's your duty."

"Crap," Mimi said. Her gaze fell on young Frank, still assessing her closely. "Hey, Frank. How'd you like to be my proxy?"

Frank's blue eyes blazed with teenage empowerment. "Can I, Mom?"

"No, he cannot," Vida said firmly. "You have to go, Mimi. It's a small enough responsibility. Not nearly as big as keeping up the e-mail list or doing the tax property reports."

"I didn't do those," Mimi said, honestly surprised. "Ardis did."

"Yeah," Vida said. "Sure. With your 'help.' Ardis told Birgie you'd done it all for years."

"What a load." Mimi didn't like having her role embellished. More important, she sure as hell didn't want people expecting her to do stuff. She just often happened to be around at the same time as Ardis because she liked it up here and Ardis happened to like it up here, too. Only a complete ass wouldn't offer to look through some papers or maybe add up a couple columns of numbers to help someone out. She wasn't a complete ass. "I just did what Ardis told me to do once in a while."

"How long? Ten years? Fifteen?"

"What difference does that make?" Mimi asked, exasperated. "It wasn't a big deal."

"Debbie says Great-Aunt Ardis had supernatural powers, too. No, wait. I think she just said she was a witch," Frank piped in apropos of nothing. Both Mimi and Vida looked at him silently before they turned back to each other.

"Big deal or not," Vida went on, "the bottom line is that you know more about this property than anyone else and if a decision needs to be made about it, your input might be valuable. Might save time. Might save money."

Clearly, Mimi was not going to get the rest of her massage. "Okay, okay. I'm going."

Chapter Eleven

Frank accompanied Mimi to the Big House, casting furtive looks at her, which she ignored. She decided to let him stew in his own juices, the little smart-ass. Besides, she didn't want it leaking out that she not only knew the names of all her little second, third, and God-knew-how-many-times removed cousins but could identify them, too. It was important to keep the mystery alive in a relationship, especially a relationship in which she wanted to keep the upper hand, as she did with all Olson adolescent males.

She knew her "second sight" was a matter of some speculation amongst in-laws and shirttail relations. But generally once a new addition to the family realized Mimi wasn't going to fall into a twitching fit and speak with a male voice, the murmuring passed. The older Olsons never had seemed too impressed. Of course, Ardis had purportedly been blessed with "powers," too, and could be counted on to make vague and unsettling predictions like, "Gonna be a lot of mosquitoes this spring," or "Septic's gonna need pumpin' next year."

Mimi used to wonder why no one ever asked her to chat up the Olson dead until she recognized that for the Olsons, calling up the dead was on par with arriving unannounced on an acquaintance's doorstep during the dinner hour. Minnesotans just weren't that forward. Or at one time hadn't been.

More and more, her clientele, once stolid, God-fearing, no-nonsense Scandinavians, were forsaking their grim Ingmar Bergman roots for New Age feel-goodism. What self-respecting Lutheran wants to feel "good" all the time?

Mimi mourned the passing of that dour, stone-faced generation. The world was becoming homogenous, nothing left to set one person or family apart from another. Nothing to link one generation to another. No common traits, no shared traditions, no cultural identity.

Take, for instance, Chez Ducky. How many average, run-of-the-mill, middle-class families had something like Chez Ducky, a place haunted by hundreds of Olsons and rank with genetic memory? Not many. What would happen when there were no Chez Duckys, just once-a-decade family reunions at some interchangeable resort on an interchangeable beach that was as without flavor as it was without history? That's the point Hank Sboda was missing. He might be able to drag his family to Cabo San Lucas with the money he'd make, but he wouldn't be able to drag the memories of a dozen generations of Sbodas with him.

"Do you, like, see things?" Frank asked, interrupting her thoughts.

"All the time." She stopped and touched his arm, her eyes wide with feigned concern. "Don't you? Does your mother know?"

Frank snickered. "Forget it."

"Okay."

A few yards from the house, Frank spotted a trio of his male cousins sneaking off into the woods and with a mumbled, "Ah, I gotta go," shot off after them.

Making it to the Big House, Mimi slipped through the back door and into the long corridor that divided the place in half. The room to her left, a sort of parlor, ran the entire width of the house, while its twin on her right had been divided into two rooms, a back kitchen and a front dining hall, "dining room" being too formal a term for something Mimi imagined

might have been found in a lumber camp. It was here the
Olsons had assembled, some sitting on the benches, others
on overstuffed armchairs dragged over from the parlor, and a
few perched on the padded vinyl kitchen chairs dating from
the fifties.

Debbie stood at the end of the table, talking. Everyone appeared to be listening to her. What was Debbie doing talking?
Naomi was the Olson from that branch of the family with a
vote, not Debbie. Mimi slipped along the side of the room
and took a seat behind Johanna and Charlie.

"What's going on?" she whispered.

"Well, if you'd moved your butt a little quicker, you'd
know," Johanna whispered back over her shoulder, tugging
anxiously at her long braid. Charlie grumbled.

"Well, I didn't, so I don't. Just tell me this, what am I
going to vote on?"

There was a pause, a distinct hesitation as Johanna's fingers stilled on her braid. "Whether or not we're going to sell
Chez Ducky."

Mimi laughed softly. "Okay, I'm a slacker and I don't take
my Chez Ducky voting responsibilities seriously enough.
Point taken. Now, what's this about?"

Johanna turned. Her eyes were grave. "Whether or not
we're going to sell Chez Ducky."

Mimi's gaze shot to the back of her great-uncle Charles's
head. "Charlie?"

He didn't turn around, just gave one terse nod of his head.

And just like that, all of Mimi's breath left her. She didn't
remember exhaling, she was sure she hadn't made a sound,
and yet abruptly, violently, her lungs were empty, her chest
muscles paralyzed.

"Debbie is telling us how much we could get for the place
and what kind of percentage she'd be willing to take to sell
it. She's getting her realtor's license, you know. Soon as she
takes some sort of test."

"So I heard," Mimi said numbly, her gaze locking on

Debbie, standing now in the middle of the group like a hostess in an infomercial. They couldn't seriously be listening to her? To *Debbie*. Debbie was, well, she was *Debbie*. Perennially looking for things and people to fix, better, integrate, improve. Olsons didn't want *improvement* or *bettering*. They wanted things to stay the way they were, without anyone messing with them . . . didn't they?

Mimi's gaze traveled around the room. Some people were nodding, others looked skeptical, some looked unhappy, but all of them looked interested.

This couldn't be happening. They couldn't *really* be considering selling Chez Ducky. Not now. When Mimi was dead, fine. Frank and his cousins could subdivide the whole thing and become millionaires, but she wasn't dead, and neither was Birgie or Johanna or Naomi or Charlie.

Or Half-Uncle Bill, whispered the insidious voice of common sense. Or Gerry and Vida, with two boys heading to college. Or Elsie, who needed a new car. Or Hal, who'd talked about starting up a fishing-guide business. Or half a dozen other grandchildren and grandnephews, half sisters and stepkids in the room. Being unmaterialistic was one thing; being a fool was another.

Mimi's heart began to pound, fear spiking her system with adrenaline. Fight . . . or flight? No contest. Mimi did what she usually did when her emotions threatened to get the upper hand. She decided to run.

She started to get up, but Johanna snagged her wrist, pulling her back down. "No one's decided anything yet," she murmured. "Just listen."

Mimi tried hard not to listen, but Debbie's voice was like a scalpel, cutting through whatever defensive images she threw up: floating on the lake, playing canasta with Ardis at the Formica kitchen table, the pumpkin malts at the Malt Shop in Minneapolis. Even her hitherto unvanquishable daydream about George Clooney disappeared under the onslaught of numbers Debbie heaped one atop the other. Huge amounts of money. Unimaginably huge amounts.

Debbie laid it all out for them: how they could sell the land to a developer, netting close to three million dollars; how the money, according to the terms of the partnership drawn up by the grandsons of Abel Olson nearly a hundred years ago, would be divided amongst the original partners' heirs per stirpes, which meant that an equal share would follow any remaining branches of the original family members.

Debbie then proceeded to outline her part in the proposed sale. As soon as she received her realtor's license she would represent the property, taking only half the usual broker's fee. *Should* the heirs decide to sell. A stern look told them what fools they'd be not to.

At this point, someone asked Debbie just when she would get her realtor's license. Debbie cleared her throat and told them she was certain she would pass her realtor's exam this next time round and have her license by Thanksgiving.

Everyone fell silent. Then Birgie cleared her throat and Mimi nearly swooned with relief. Birgie loved Chez Ducky, too. She was the head of the family now. She'd put them back on track.

Except she didn't. Instead, Birgie looked around, spied her sitting in the back of the room, and said loudly, "What do you think, Mimi?"

Mimi, caught smirking at Debbie, blinked. "Huh?"

"What do you think about this deal Debbie here is proposing?" Birgie asked, planting one hand, elbow akimbo, on her thigh and pivoting on her seat.

What did *Mimi* think? She thought it was horrible, ludicrous, logical, blasphemous, and sensible. But she wasn't going to say that. Not until someone else said it first. She was an audience member. She always had been. Audience members didn't have speaking parts. "I dunno."

Birgie held her gaze a second, then blew out a gusty sigh. "Me, neither."

Birgie rose and made her way through the crowd of people, heading for the door. Conversation started up again, faces puckering thoughtfully, questions addressed to Debbie rising from the group. Mimi couldn't believe her eyes. The new Queen Bee was heading for the hive door, and no one was taking note.

Mimi started to speak, but her protest caught in her throat. She'd lived her entire life by a philosophy of letting things happen. Sure, some things just demanded that someone do something, and in this case that someone was Birgie. But Birgie was at the door, her hand on the knob. And now she had opened it. And now she had left.

In a daze, Mimi got up, vaguely aware of curious gazes following her, voices quieting. She caught up with Birgie as she lumbered down to the beach, the little dog Mimi had noted earlier frolicking behind her like a pilot fish dancing after an orca.

"Where are you going?" Mimi asked, trying to subdue the panic in her voice.

"To look at the lake," Birgie said. "Don't know if I'll see it this time of year again."

Mimi refused to accept the implication. "Why didn't you *say* something? Do something?"

Birgie stopped at the end of the dock, squinting out over the black, mirror-still surface of the lake toward where the old raft floated, barely visible. A loon piped mournfully in the distance.

Birgie tipped her head back, scanning the sky above. It was thick and dark, clouds obliterating everything but an occasional fleeting window into the starred sky above. The light from the hurricane lanterns inside the cottages behind them did little to illuminate the thin strip of beach.

"The new places'll all have yard lights," Birgie said. "People are awful scared of the dark these days." She sat down on the end of the dock, grunting as she bent over, and started untying her Reeboks. She yanked off a shoe and began tugging at her sock.

"Birgie?" Mimi prompted.

"What did you want me to say?" Birgie asked, carefully tucking her sock into her shoe and starting on the other foot.

"Tell them selling is a stupid idea."

"Well, I'm not so sure it is," Birgie said, standing back up and beginning to unbutton her shirt.

"Of course it is!" Mimi said. "We can't re-create this." She waved her arm toward the blackness.

"You're right. In fact, maybe we can't re-create it next year."

"What do you mean?"

"Next year Fowl Lake will be ringed with houses. Not cabins. Not cottages. Big old houses with three-car garages and security systems and satellite TV dishes."

"So? Who cares?" Mimi asked. "We own the entire southeast corner of the lake. The only house near us is Prescott's. I've been thinking maybe we could burn that down after he leaves."

Birgie's hands stilled at her bottom shirt button. "You're kidding, right?"

Sort of. "Of course I am. Besides. He'd only rebuild. But that's not the point. Down here we can pretend the other stuff, the houses and all, aren't happening. We can ignore the north end."

"And the west side?" Birgie asked nodding across the lake.

Two hundred yards away in the dark, you couldn't even see the other side. "We can ignore them, too."

"Really?" Birgie grunted. "You shoulda said that, if that's how you feel."

"I thought *you* were going to say it."

Birgie shrugged off her shirt, folded it, and set it atop her shoes. She reached behind and unhooked her bra, a magnificently anachronistic double-D-cup Maidenform. Her breasts fell toward her waistband.

"I'm not sure I agree," she finally said.

"What?" Mimi's voice rose.

Birgie pushed her shorts and panties down simultaneously past her knees and stepped out of them, adding them to the pile of clothes. "Sometimes it's tough to figure out if what you're trying to hold on to is already gone."

"This is *not* gone," Mimi said firmly.

"Next year there'll be yard lights," Birgie repeated kindly, her compassionate gaze holding Mimi.

This was flat-out bizarre. Birgie was neither compassionate nor kind. She was phlegmatic. Mimi waited for her to say something else, her heart still racing, and hers was not a heart that raced easily or with little provocation.

Birgie turned and waded into the water.

"Wait!" Mimi called. "We still have to talk!"

"Feels warm," Birgie called back. "Come on in."

Crap. Mimi kicked off her flip-flops and yanked her T-shirt over her head. She didn't have a bra on underneath. She jerked down her sweatpants, almost tipping over as she hopped one-legged in the sand trying to disentangle herself.

"Hey!" a voice called from back by the Big House. A porch door swung open on squeaking hinges. "Hey, Mimi and Birgie are going skinny-dipping!"

Excited female voices answered this announcement from deep in the house. Someone else let out a whoop of pleasure. "Last one in!"

Mimi kicked free of her sweats and splashed noisily in after Birgie. She had to talk Birgie into taking her place as leader and leading these dear idiots back to the land of sanity. Once the women were convinced, that would pretty much be that. Birgie was already shoulder deep in the water, moving with the slow, intractable force of a migrating mammoth. On the beach, the little dog bounced in anxiety.

"Wait up!" Mimi called. "You're worrying the dog."

"Not my dog," Birgie said, rolling over and commencing a slow backstroke. "I'm gonna miss skinny-dipping."

Chapter Twelve

The goth look, or whatever its current incarnation was called, was not doing much for Prescott, Joe decided. In spite of the lank, jet-black, dyed hair hanging in his eyes, the steel bolt through his eyebrow, and the chains hanging from the various belt loops of the black, oversized jeans that clanked every time he shifted, rather than dangerous Prescott simply looked uncomfortable. The setting probably didn't help. Joe suspected not many goths had Italian handcrafted furniture.

Of course, Joe wouldn't express this opinion to Prescott. Hell, he had a hard enough time finding something neutral to say. Prescott searched every vowel and consonant for some implied criticism or slight.

"What did she say?"

Joe jerked at the unexpected sound of Prescott's voice.

"What did who say?" he asked.

"Mrs. Olson."

"Mrs. Olson?"

Prescott set the book he'd been reading facedown in his lap. "You were talking to her on Friday. Mrs. Olson."

"Pres, there's about a dozen Mrs. Olsons next door, and I spoke to many of them on Friday. That was two days ago. You're going to have to be a little more specific."

"Please don't call me 'Pres,'" Prescott said in the HAL

monotone. "I am speaking about the middle-aged woman. She's short. Kind of frumpy, I guess. But in a nice way."

A *short*, nicely frumpy middle-aged woman? Huh. He couldn't think who Prescott was talking about. "Keep it coming."

"Dark, curly hair. She was wearing a blue robe with starfish."

"Mimi?" Joe asked. Middle-aged? Joe supposed to Prescott she must seem so. But frumpy?

Prescott's mouth drew together like it had been threaded with a drawstring. "I believe her Christian name is 'Mignonette.'"

"*Mrs.* Olson, you said? She didn't mention a husband." The way she'd spoken about the older Olson women, Joe had assumed Mimi was a blood relation, not an in-law.

"She's a widow."

How would Prescott know that? He never left this place.

"What did she say to you?" At Prescott's persistence, it occurred to Joe that his son's interest in a frumpy, albeit "in a nice way," middle-aged woman was a little unusual.

"I don't know. Things about the lake. The neighbors. Small talk."

"Like what?" Prescott asked, determinedly nonchalant. "I saw her point at the house. Was she admiring it? I mean, her and her family? Did she realize it was an exact replica of the Astors' grandson's Adirondack hunting lodge?"

"You know, she did," Joe replied to keep Prescott talking. This was as engaged as he and Prescott had been since his arrival.

A look of consternation appeared on Prescott's face. "Did you tell her the name of the house?"

The name of the house . . . the name of the house. Shit. He couldn't remember the name of Prescott's house. Bum something? This was probably another one of Prescott's "daddy tests," like, "What sport did I win a medal in when I was thirteen?"

"Ah. No."

Prescott looked disappointed but didn't pursue it. "What else did she say?"

"Well." Joe thought quickly, filtering the truth through a kinder lens. "She was impressed. She mentioned the cocoa-bean-hull logs and the environmental considerations you put into building the place."

"She did?"

"Yes." What was going on here? Did Prescott have a crush on Mimi? Not that Mimi wasn't crush-worthy, but in Joe's experience most men didn't think of the objects of their lust as "frumpy." On the other hand, Prescott wasn't like most men of his acquaintance.

"Anything else?"

"She said you were a genius."

Prescott smiled, and then as if recalling himself, said, "Of course, she would know all about her neighbors. And care about them. She's very nurturing. Very tenderhearted and sweet."

Prescott made her sound like a candidate for sainthood or a well-qualified nanny, neither of which matched the impression Joe had gotten when he'd met her. But Joe wouldn't have called her frumpy and middle-aged, either. Based on first impressions, he would have called her a grimy lunatic. His second impression, he thought, recalling her amused dark eyes and easy manner and, oddly enough, the delicate arch of her sandy feet with their brightly polished toes, had been much better. He smiled.

"Why are you smiling?" Prescott demanded.

"What? Oh. I was thinking I wouldn't call her frumpy."

"Oh, really?" Prescott said, angling his pierced brow derisively.

"Informal, maybe?" Joe squinted, recalling her bare feet, clouds of hair coming out of a rubber band, and ratty beach robe. "Okay, maybe a little frumpy."

"You only met her once. I see her all the time," Prescott said, looking irritated. He picked up his book again.

And things had just been starting to go well—though "well" might be stretching the point. "Say, Prescott," Joe said in his friendliest voice. "Let's play some Ping-Pong."

"It's called table tennis," Prescott replied coldly.

"Right. How about a game or two?"

"I don't have a table."

"Why not? You won a medal in it. It was your sport."

"But it's not a 'real' sport, remember?" Prescott sneered.

Joe turned his hands palm up. "I never said it wasn't a real sport. I said I didn't *know* it was a sport. What can I say, Prescott? I don't watch the Winter Olympics. I apologized. I apologize again because I've watched since, and there is really quite a bit of physical coordination and finesse involved at the higher levels."

"Do *not* patronize me."

He wasn't, but try to convince Prescott of that.

"Just because a sport isn't based on steroid-pumped mutants lumbering after a ball like in football doesn't mean it's not a sport."

Point for Prescott. "I know."

Prescott lifted the book. Maybe they could talk about books. Joe tilted his head to try and read the title. *Ringwraithes: My Metaphysical Journey to the Modern Mordor.* Nope. Not books.

Joe racked his brain for another topic. Something innocuous. Something guys everywhere talk about. "So, Prescott, do you have a girlfriend?"

Prescott carefully set the book facedown on his lap. "No," he said. "I'm gay."

Gay? This was unexpected, Joe thought, but okay. They were getting somewhere. Perhaps Prescott's animosity stemmed from the fact that Joe hadn't recognized his gayness. That would be understandable. But why hadn't he? Far less understandable.

"You're sure?" he asked.

"Do you think I'm lying?" Prescott asked. "Would it be such an embarrassment if your son was gay?"

"Of course not." He leaned forward in his chair, smiling engagingly. "So, you're gay. Do you have a boyfriend?"

"No," Prescott said flatly, picking up his book again. "I'm not gay."

"Then why—" Joe broke off. He already knew why. It had been another test designed for him to fail. The reason why Prescott designed these tests was the only real mystery. What were they supposed to prove? That Joe was an ass? Joe wasn't an ass. Prescott, now *Prescott* was an ass. With an effort, Joe tamped down his irritation. Things needed lightening up, badly.

"Okay," he said. "You're not gay and you don't have a girlfriend. What do you do for fun? You like music?"

"Not really."

"Chess?"

"No."

"Poker?"

"Hardly."

The kid had to do something. "Come on, Prescott. You don't ponce around with a light saber at *Star Wars* conventions, do you?" He laughed, expecting Prescott to at least smile.

His laughter faded. Prescott wasn't laughing. Oh, fuck.

"Not that there's anything wrong with that," he said quickly. "They sound like fun. Really."

"I haven't been to a convention in three years!" Prescott shouted, surging to his feet and stomping heavily out of the room.

Joe rose. "Prescott, please. I was trying to make a joke. It was stupid."

He was talking to dead air. He shoved his hands deep in his pockets. This was senseless. He was only torturing them both by staying here. He'd leave tomorrow. Maybe next year things would be different.

He wandered to the bank of windows overlooking the lake. Intermittent glints of starlight peeked out from between the drifts of clouds, flirting with the lake's surface. Far out, a large, indistinct shape rocked like an anchored ship, shadowy figures moving across its surface. Probably the teenage boys from Chez Ducky.

He hoped none of the young fools decided to go diving. He didn't know how deep the lake was but conscientiousness goaded him into picking up the binoculars Prescott used for bird-watching. The blurry figures remained dark as they grew larger, their outlines taking on shapes . . . older female shapes.

Joe snatched the binoculars from his eyes, then abruptly grinned. The older women from Chez Ducky were skinny-dipping. Just then, on the opposite side of the lake at one of the building sites, a series of floodlights suddenly turned on. Joe blinked at the brilliance, shielding his eyes with his hand as the figures on the raft silently fled, slipping over the side and entering the water without a splash. Within minutes they were gone. No one was left, just an empty pontoon and an empty night. His mood sank.

He turned away, glancing at the doorway through which Prescott had disappeared.

"Prescott," he said. "I know you can hear me. I'm really sorry about the light saber comment."

"And I really don't give a shit." Prescott's voice came out of the overhead speakers, flat and unemotional.

Joe heard the distinct click of the system turning off. He took a deep breath. He needed a walk.

Chapter Thirteen

Mimi trod water next to the raft. Around her, the other skinny-dippers had begun trading stories passed down through the generations. Like when Great-Great-Grandfather Sven had taken his soon-to-be bride, Ita, out in a canoe on the lake to propose, only to drop the ring in the lake. Ita, a frugal woman if ever there was one, had dived right in after it and kept diving until she finally came back up with it. Or the time Great-Aunt Ruth had been driving a bunch of kids back from town in the Model T when the brakes had failed at the top of the hill. The car had careered down the hill straight toward the big drop-off and sank in a stew of bubbles. The Model T, legend had it, was still down there, mired in the muck ten feet below the surface.

Usually Mimi loved these stories, but tonight she heard them not as anecdotes but as a eulogy. Her mood plummeted.

A generator on the other side of the lake hummed to life and a blaze of floodlights erupted on the far shore. With girlish giggles, the women vacated the raft. Mimi followed more slowly. Not giggling.

By the time she got to shore, the others had already dressed and gone up to the Big House. Mimi wrung the water out of her hair, then donned an oversized sweatshirt and sweatpants. She was three-quarters of the way up to the Big

House when she heard Birgie and Vida speaking. They sounded like they were at the back door.

"Of course she's unhappy," Vida was saying. "Mimi loves this place."

Mimi halted, shamelessly eavesdropping.

"If this place is so important to her, she'd say something," Birgie said.

"No, she wouldn't," Vida insisted.

No, she wouldn't, Mimi silently echoed. Then, *Good old Vida. Who'd have guessed she'd champion not only Chez Ducky but me?* Mimi was touched.

"She's not the proactive type," Vida continued, "but that doesn't mean she doesn't feel things deeply, profoundly."

Let's not get carried away, Vida.

"Let's not get carried away, there, Vida," Birgie said.

"I'm not," Vida insisted. "What does Mimi have besides this place? Nothing. Nada. Zilch."

Mimi frowned. "Zilch" seemed an unnecessarily severe way of stating matters.

"The only family life Mimi knows is here, and then only during the summer."

"She *does* have a mother," Birgie pointed out.

Vida made a derisive sound but let it stand. "From what I've heard, Solange Charbonneau Olson Werner doesn't have a family as much as a corporation with herself as CEO. Poor Mimi doesn't have a boyfriend. As far as I can tell, she doesn't even have any close friends. Has she ever brought someone up to Chez Ducky with her? All the rest of us have. Frequently."

Mimi was a little taken aback. Just because she didn't overly invest in other people's lives didn't mean she was friendless. She was simply content with her own company.

"Mimi doesn't own a house, a car, or a pet," Vida went on. "For all I know she doesn't even have a houseplant."

So?

"She doesn't have anything else in her life that she owns. And she only owns a part of this."

Okay, Vida, you've made your point, Mimi thought, feeling somewhat less friendly toward her favorite cousin's wife.

"I blame her dad," Birgie muttered.

Her dad? Mimi's attention snapped back into sharp focus.

"Damn John, anyway," Birgie went on, "wandering off like some old hound to die. Least he coulda done if he was going to die when she was so young was leave a body to bury. Him disappearing like that stunted her."

Mimi's mouth dropped open, first and foremost because she was *not* stunted. She was a whole lot more mentally healthy than almost any one or combination of Olsons or Olson-esques. No trouble sleeping (until recently), no problems getting up in the morning (when she had to get up, which was infrequently), no temper tantrums, no mood swings. She moved through life on the most even of keels. She was fine, thank you very much.

Second, she was amazed that after all this time anyone still insisted on making unfounded assumptions. There was no certainty that her dad wasn't still using his body, which would make burying it something of an inconvenience. Who knew her father better than she did? No one. He could have been hit on the head and have amnesia. He could be in a prison in the gulag somewhere. Or shipwrecked. He could still simply not be ready to come home. Wherever he was, he wasn't here. In any form. Which meant that he was out there somewhere.

Mimi had heard enough of Vida's championing her. She started to slip back toward the beach when she heard a new voice: Debbie's. She stopped, listening warily. She hadn't realized Debbie was with them.

"Fine," Debbie said in exasperated tones. "I get it. And I agree. Mimi's life *is* pathetic."

Pathetic? No one had used the word "pathetic." Mimi waited for someone to refute this. No one did. Is that how

they saw her? As lonely, pathetic . . . she stopped herself
from piling on more unpleasant words.

"But whose fault is that?" Debbie went on. "Not mine.
Not either of yours. Not your kids, Vida. Do you want to explain to them that they can't go to a good college without you
or them going into debt because you felt sorry for some
cousin so many times removed that you would need a calcu-
lator to figure it out?"

Mimi's mouth tightened. Only enormous self-restraint
kept her from shouting, "Third cousin twice removed, asshole!"

But then her anger disappeared. From Vida's perspective,
selling Chez Ducky made good sense. From a lot of Olsons'
perspectives it made good sense. Just think of all the things
they could give one another and their kids with a financial
windfall. Mimi, as it had so recently been pointed out, didn't
have anyone to give anything to. There was no one depending on her for an education, a new car, a wedding, retirement
or . . . or anything.

She didn't have the right to tell the rest of her family what
they should or should not do. If the majority wanted to sell
Chez Ducky, then that's what ought to happen. And if the
thought made her feel as though she'd spun around blind-
folded and was groping toward an abyss, she'd get over it.
She headed back toward the beach, all thought of joining the
others gone. Tomorrow, when she'd found her footing again,
when things had begun to slide into whatever pattern the future held, she'd be fine. But tonight Chez Ducky, always un-
changeable, felt like it was disappearing. And her along with
it.

She wandered along the beach, her footprints in the sand
dissolving in the lick of water. Crickets and night peepers
serenaded her passing, and a glamour of fireflies threaded
themselves amongst the brush like fairy lights.

It should have made her happy. She should have been able
to enjoy the moment for whatever it was, cut it out of its

timeline and live it. She should have been able to look around in pleasure and smile. It was beautiful. Instead, she folded up like an accordion, dropped down on the sand, and bawled.

"Ahem."

She ignored whatever guy was clearing his throat. She didn't want to answer any of Gerry's or Charlie's questions.

"Ahem."

She wiped her nose on her forearm and lifted bleary eyes. "What—"

Joe Tierney stood a few feet in front of her, his hands stuck in the pockets of his perfectly pressed slacks. He was still gleaming. Only now he was gleaming in moonlight. And she was once more coated with sand and soaking wet. Plus her nose was running and she was hiccuping.

She wrapped her arms tightly around her legs and waited for him to remark on her appearance, but he only sighed, a deep, heartfelt echo of her own feelings.

"What happened to you?" he asked.

Her lower lip began to tremble. "They . . . they . . ." She gulped and tried again. "They're going to sell Chez Ducky."

He nodded sadly. He didn't tell her it would be all right. He didn't suggest she could be wrong. He didn't console her. For all these things, she was grateful. He simply lowered himself down onto the sand beside her and stared out over the lake.

"What's wrong with you?" she asked.

Without looking at her, he said, "My son's a dick."

She nodded. For a long while they sat beside each other in silent and companionable misery. She didn't want to talk about Chez Ducky and she suspected Joe wasn't eager to discuss Prescott. They were both, she intuited, private people, uncomfortable with sharing things. But it would be nice to feel someone was close, to share a little warmth, to touch and be touched. *Unlikely,* she thought, looking down at her wet shirt and sand-splattered legs and arms.

"I'm not always covered with dirt and sand, you know," she murmured.

He turned his head to look at her. "No? I thought it might be some sort of Northern fashion."

She smiled wanly. "It is, but sometimes I go metro. A slick little urban alley look."

He laughed.

"And you," she countered. "Are you always so Calvin Klein? All polished and polo looking? And"—she sniffed— "is that aftershave you're wearing?"

"Would that be bad?" he asked, looking amused.

"Well, at least it's not pine scented."

"Too obvious. And no, it's just soap."

"Really expensive soap."

"But manly?" he asked.

"Manly enough." They were flirting, both wanting the distraction. It wasn't anything more. Or was it? She thought she glimpsed in Joe an unexpected kinship of feeling as well as physical attraction, an attraction not unexpected on her part, him being gorgeous and all, but she'd bet his attraction to her had caught him off guard.

"Can I ask you a question?" he asked.

"Shoot."

"Has there ever been a Mr. Olson?"

Whatever she'd been expecting, it hadn't been that. "Ah, lots of them. You must have met about half a dozen on Saturday."

"No. I mean are *you* a Mrs. Olson?"

"Oh. No. Never. Not even close." Clearly, he was going to make a move. But before he did he wanted to ascertain her availability. Was this an honorable guy or what?

He shook his head. "Poor Prescott."

Poor *Prescott*? "Huh?"

"My son thinks you're a widow."

Apparently they weren't in as much accord as she'd thought. He hadn't been contemplating a little diversionary lip action. She shifted away, feeling foolish, and climbed to her knees on the sand. He looked up at her.

"You're going?" He sounded disappointed.

"Yeah. We're closing the place up for the winter tomorrow. I should get a good night's sleep."

"I guess I better get back, too." He got to his knees and they knelt like that, facing each other for a long moment. "I'm glad I met you, Mimi Olson."

"Me, too. Thanks again for the ride. And the lug to the car. And for letting me mess up your nice shirt." She stuck out her hand. He took it and then just held on. She smiled tentatively and tugged gently. He didn't let go. Instead, he pulled her slowly closer to him, bending his head, and, his quizzical gaze never leaving her, he lowered his mouth to hers.

She relaxed, lifting her arms and draping them lightly around his shoulders. He cupped her face between his palms, kissing her slowly and thoroughly, his lips firm and talented. He tasted minty clean. She reciprocated, funneling her fingers through that perfectly clipped head of hair, thick and cool, his scalp beneath slightly warm. He pulled her even closer, one hand gently tilting her head beneath her chin, the other skating down to her hips, looping around her waist, pressing her closer, hip to hip, thigh to thigh, breast to breast.

Her wet shirt soaked his, and the moisture heated up between them. His chest felt solid and heavy and his heart beat a slow, steady tattoo against hers. He deepened their kiss, his tongue sliding between her lips. She opened her mouth, tangling her tongue with his, pulling his head closer. He widened his knees on the sand, bringing her into the lee he created and pulling her sideways off balance. She clutched at him, but her mouth had no intention of giving up its place. He eased her onto the sand, following her down, their mouths locked together.

His hand stroked a path along her ribs to her waist to her hip. He slipped his hand beneath the hem of her sweatshirt and with his thumb slowly drew small ascending circles up her stomach, stopping when he reached the nascent swell of her breast. He brushed his knuckles against her, testing the texture and weight. She arched slightly, purring with pleasure.

He lifted his head and looked down at her. His breath was a little ragged. Hers was definitely ragged.

"Are we going to have sex?" he asked. He sounded like he already knew the answer.

"No," she said, aware she sounded as forlorn about it as him.

"I suppose that's best." He didn't sound certain, though, and she felt perversely pleased.

She waited for him to roll away from her, but he didn't. He studied her with what she could only describe as an odd combination of bewilderment and fascination. He smoothed her damp—and now sandy—hair away from her face, leaning forward to sip a kiss from her lips. Her eyelids drifted shut. Her heartbeat, recently returned to a steadier pace, kicked back into a gallop.

He pulled his head back. "Do you think we could just make out?" he asked.

He looked hopeful and young and a little sad, not at all like a supercompetent captain of industry or high-priced tax lawyer or national-network news anchor or whatever he was. He looked like she felt. Like he needed her like she needed him.

"Yes," she said. "I would like that."

Chapter Fourteen

Mimi piled the wool blankets into the attic bedroom's cedar closet. She'd already brought in the last sun-dried linens of the summer and folded them into trunks. She'd emptied all the "vases"—wine bottles and peanut-butter jars—of their wood asters and coneflowers and cleaned out and unplugged the old refrigerator, sticking an open box of baking soda in the back before clamping on the lock, because you never knew how much stupidity a kid on a snowmobile was capable of but you could be sure it was a lot. Johanna and Charlie were draining all the water pipes for the winter, and Vida, Gerry, and young Frank were pulling in the dock.

They were closing the Big House for the season. Maybe forever.

Maybe next year someone else would own the key to the front door and be backing into the kitchen with a crate full of canned goods and toilet paper. Or maybe no one would enter the house at all. Maybe a big front loader would tear it down, scoop up its bones, and pile them into a Dumpster.

She could live with that. Hell, she thought, she didn't have a choice.

She'd been right to stay away from the rest of the Olsons last night; she felt a hundred times better today. More herself. Not friendless, just happily independent; not poor, but unburdened by possessions. What was pathetic about that? Nothing. She didn't know whether a night's sleep, her own resilient nature, or the mood-enhancing qualities of a good old-fashioned, torrid make-out session had returned her to her former carefree self. She suspected all had played a part.

She wondered whether Joe had left yet. She wondered whether she'd ever see him again. Probably not. Her romantic relationships with men tended to be short-lived, ending pleasantly and without regret. Leave 'em wanting more. Or, in this case, *leave* wanting more. That's the way it had always worked for her. Sure, she'd told him her phone number last night when he'd mentioned something about being in Minneapolis for a while this winter, but frankly, at the time they'd been more interested in nonverbal forms of communication.

She sat down on Ardis's old bed, her gaze wandering about the room. No one had ever figured out why Ardis had chosen as her own the attic bedroom at the top of a flight of steep, knee-devastating stairs, with its sloped ceiling and gabled windows, hotter in the summer and colder in the winter than any of the other rooms in the house. No one except Mimi.

You only had to look through the windows nested under the eaves to understand. Out the north window, the treetops shivered at her feet, while overhead the sky emptied itself into forever. Facing east, she looked down into the grassy area at the side of the house where generations of children had tossed horseshoes, set off bottle rockets on the Fourth of July, and toasted marshmallows. From the south window, she could see most of Fowl Lake.

Mimi closed her eyes and pictured Ardis sinking to her knees in front of the window, her chin cupped in her hand like a little girl as she watched a deer picking its way across the ice on an early March morning. Through Ardis's eyes she spied a pair of otters playing tag amongst the bulrushes.

From here they—*Ardis*—had witnessed a hundred first swimming lessons and the launch of dozens of doomed rafts.

Oh, Mimi understood. She opened her eyes and looked around for some last memento of Ardis: a golf tee, a paperback novel sprouting a bookmark, a nail file. But there was nothing. The drawers in the battered dresser were empty, the hand-braided rugs rolled and stowed beneath the bed, the hangers in the closet naked. Only memories remained, and memories needed conduits to exist.

"Mimi!" Vida called from outside.

Mimi got up and went to the window. Below, at the corner of the house, Vida and the others stood between Charlie's beloved El Camino and Gerry's battered old Toyota Land Cruiser, its back open. Frank was throwing black plastic garbage bags in the Land Cruiser preparatory to the ritual Last Stop at the Dump on the Way Out. Life on Fowl Lake was filled with such little ceremonies. *Had* been full, Mimi corrected herself. She pushed open the window sash and leaned out. "What?"

"We're ready to lock up," Vida called up. "You done in there?"

No. "Yup. Just making sure all the windows are latched."

Mimi closed the window and descended the dark, narrow back stairs to the kitchen. She glanced at the sash locks to make sure they were secure, then, lightly brushing a talisman touch on the old Formica-clad kitchen table, went out the back door.

" 'Bout time," Charlie grumbled, stepping forward with a ring of keys and locking the back door. He straightened, looked down at the keys like he was wondering what to do with them, and tossed them to her. She fumbled them against her chest.

"What's this?" she asked.

"You might as well keep 'em," he said. "I'm going to spend the winter in Phoenix and Johanna's coming, too."

"We're driving down," Johanna said with a prim pressing

of her lips that dared anyone to comment on their relationship going public. "And since neither of us has the best night
vision anymore, we thought we'd take it slow."

"Just how slow were you planning on going? It's
September," Mimi said.

"Just take the damn keys, Mimi," Charlie said.

"Why don't you give them to Gerry?" Mimi asked. She
disliked being responsible for things, particularly important
things. You might lose them.

"Oh, come on, Mimi!" Vida exclaimed irritably. "We live
two hundred miles farther from here than you. Just hold on
to 'em so they're convenient."

They weren't asking her to take care of the place, just
keep the keys. She could do that. She might even drive up
some weekend. Not many people had seen Chez Ducky in
the winter—and with good reason, too. It was bloody cold
and the house was not well insulated—but Mimi had and
considered it their loss.

"Okay," she said, pocketing the keys in her jeans.

"Need any help loading up your car?" Gerry asked.

"Like, when have I ever had enough stuff I needed help
packing it?"

"People change," Gerry said.

"Not me. Travel light, travel fast."

"He who travels the fastest travels alone," Gerry returned.

"Home, the weary traveler," Vida piped in.

"I took the road less traveled," Mimi countered.

"From whose bourn no traveler returns," Charlie added.

"We'll travel along, singing a song, side by side," Johanna
shot back.

They might have gone on like this indefinitely except that
the small dog Mimi had noticed at least half a dozen times
over the past week suddenly shot out of the nearby bushes. It
hurled itself into the back of the Land Cruiser, tore into a
plastic garbage bag, grabbed something loathsome, leapt
back out with its spoils, and dashed away as the Olsons

stared in slack-jawed fascination. It had been like watching an Elite Canine Corps operation.

"Whose mutt is that, anyway?" Charlie asked.

"I thought it was Halverd's," Frank said.

"I thought it was Naomi's," Vida said.

"I thought it was Debbie's," Gerry said.

Mimi clicked her tongue. "Like Debbie would own a mutt."

"Fine," said Gerry. "Then it doesn't belong to anyone here?"

"I guess not." Charlie began easing toward the El Camino, his hand under Johanna's elbow. "Look at the time! We gotta hit the road, Joey, if we're gonna—"

"Oh, no, you don't," Vida said, grabbing the old man by the wrist. "You're going to help us catch that dog. There's not one cabin or cottage on the lake that hasn't been shut down for the season if you don't count Prescott, which I don't because the guy never comes outside. The only other people around are the workmen on the opposite side of the lake. If we leave the poor creature here, he'll starve. If we can stay when we got a nine-hour drive ahead of us, you can stay." Her gaze shot to Mimi, who'd been doing her own retreat to where her borrowed Honda waited. "You too, Mimi."

"Shit," Charlie said.

"Come on, Charlie. It'll be fun," Johanna said, and Charlie, who was as irascible an old coot as nature allowed, pinked up and grumbled and obliged. That was what love did to you.

"Okay, damn it. What do you want me to do?"

"We'll spread out into the woods and push him onto the beach."

"Yeah? And what'll we do then?" Charlie asked. "That thing'll probably attack us. Probably rabid."

Vida thought. They watched. "Damned if I know," Vida finally said. "Poor little bugger. I guess maybe we will just have to leave him . . ."

"We could get some blankets," Mimi suggested gruffly. She hated the idea of that little bedraggled mutt being left behind. "You know. Big blankets. We can toss them over him."

"And if he starts into the water," Johanna stuck in, "Mimi can wade in after him."

"Why does Mimi have to grab the dirty mutt if it gets wet?" Mimi asked.

"Because everyone else has clean clothes on," Johanna answered reasonably, with a telling look at Mimi's chinos.

As Mimi had no reply to this unassailable logic, they dug the blankets from the trunks of the two vehicles and, arming themselves with them, started into the woods. Almost at once, the dog appeared on the footpath, something stringy hanging from its mouth.

"Here, puppy!" Vida called. "There's a nice boy. Girl. Whatever. Come here, sweetie!"

The dog stayed where it was, matted tail wagging warily.

"Okay," Vida said in a low voice, "we gotta circle it. Gerry and Mimi, go left. Frank and I'll go right. Johanna and Charlie walk real slowly toward it. Pretend you have something for it to eat."

Mimi and Gerry sidled nonchalantly to one side, while Vida and Frank sidled just as nonchalantly to the other and Johanna and Charlie moseyed forth, making loud nummy sounds. They spread out, forming a ten-foot perimeter around the dog. Mimi happened to be closest.

"Hey there, little guy," Mimi said, crouching down with her hands on her knees, trying to look dog friendly. "What's that you've got— *Oh, dear God, that's disgusting!*"

At Mimi's unintentional but perfectly understandable cry of revulsion, the dog, fearing his treasure was about to be wrested from him, bolted between Mimi and Gerry. Too late, Gerry hurled his wadded up blanket at the little bugger. Too late, Frank lunged for it, ending up face flat in the dirt. Charlie cackled with laughter, Johanna smacked him in the arm, and Vida cursed. Mimi took off in hot pursuit. If she could corner it, she could toss her blanket over it and nab it.

Ten minutes later, red faced and sucking wind, Mimi realized the error of this reasoning: it is hard to trap something in a corner when you didn't have a corner to trap it in. Still, she trotted gamely on, the Dog in Dreads always a few yards ahead of her, looking over its shoulder and pausing occasionally to let her catch up, like this was some sort of really fun game.

Johanna and Charlie were far behind by now, but she caught glimpses of Vida and Frank pacing her. Gerry was nowhere to be seen. Maybe she should quit, too. Her side was starting to hurt and her lungs sounded like a kid's broken squeeze box. She'd tried. Her intentions had been noble, but now she was getting a stitch in her side. That was it for her. Game over—

She stopped, realizing that the dog was leading her toward Prescott's Erection. The place had more angles and corners than an Escher print. Perfect for her purposes.

"He's heading toward Prescott's!" she called to Frank and Vida. "You guys drive him down that chute between the house and the garage. I'll go 'round the other side of the garage and when he comes out the end I'll grab him. Give me a couple minutes."

"Got it!" Vida called back.

Mimi took off, running as fast as the tangle of brush, her burning lungs, and, okay, yeah, her age allowed. She made it to the side of the garage and collapsed against the exterior wall, gasping for breath, just as she heard Vida and Frank clapping their hands and shouting. "It's coming, Mimi! We're almost there! Yee-ha! Hup! Hup!"

Mimi held the blanket out in front of her, plastering herself at the corner of the garage, holding her breath so she could hear the pitter-pat of little paws. There they were, right on cue.

"Five!" Vida hollered. "Four! Oh, shit. *Now!*"

Mimi leapt into the narrow opening a second before the dog. Caught off guard, the dog tried to pivot but it was going too fast. Its back end fishtailed, sending it piling into Mimi's legs. Quick little bastard that it was, it somersaulted to the side and was just poised to bound away when Mimi acted. She launched herself at it, her blanket sailing before her, her body for one split second parallel to Mother Earth, before hitting the ground with a bone-jarring thud. Beneath the blanket, the dog howled.

Mimi hauled it to her like a fisherman with his net, the wriggling lump screeching in doggy protest. "Oh, fer Chrissake, cut it out," she panted as she clamored gracelessly to her feet, triumphant. "You're just lucky I didn't land on you, Fido."

Frank arrived first, skittering to a halt when he saw her. "She's got the dog!" Frank yelled and grinned at her. "Nice tackle, Mimi. You ever consider going pro?"

"Shut up, Frank," Mimi said, grinning back.

Vida came next, followed by Charlie and Johanna, and a few seconds later, Gerry. He was eating a candy bar, and he did *not* look winded.

"Gee. Thanks for all the help, Ger," Mimi said. The dog continued to howl, not so much anxious as offended.

"No problemo, Mimi," he said, stashing the wrapper in his pocket. "So, now you got the dog, what are you going to do with it?"

She regarded him blankly, still wheezing. "Huh?"

"What are you—"

"I heard you, and why do *I* have to do something with it?" She held up the bundled dog and commanded firmly, "Be quiet." The dog quieted.

"Maybe it wants to breathe?" Johanna suggested.

"Oh." Mimi peeled back the blanket. A malodorous, matted fur face with two black shark eyes stared up at her. It smelled like it had rolled in rotting fish. She glanced down at its crusty little head. By God, she believed it *had* rolled in rotting fish.

"Listen," she said. "*I* caught the dog; therefore, *my* part is done. So one of you is going to have to find some place to drop it off."

"Not us," Charlie said, shifting toward Johanna to present a united front. "I can smell that thing from here, and there is no way it's getting into the El Camino."

"You could wash it—"

"And there's even less chance he's getting into the El Camino wet, and we are *not* sticking around until he dries off. In case you hadn't heard, we got a long haul ahead as it is. In fact"—he checked his wristwatch—"we gotta go now. Come on, Johanna."

With an apologetic shrug that conveyed more relief than apology, Johanna allowed Charlie to take her arm and lead her away.

"And we're not taking it back with us," Gerry said firmly. "We're heading to the UP to visit Vida's mother. If you want, I'll take it as far as the police station in Fawn Creek, but that's as far as he goes."

"Whaddaya mean? You can't take him to the Fawn Creek police. They'll just hold him for a couple days and then they'll take him to a vet and—" She looked down at the mangy mutt. He gazed back at her in canine concern. "*You know.*"

"No, they won't."

"Yes, they will."

"Well, then, drive him down to the Humane Society in Golden Valley."

"I can't take him in the Honda. I rented it from Oz's kid for the summer," Mimi said, a tickle of anxiety rising in her. She did *not* want to be responsible for this mangy little reject from the pound. "It'll scratch the leather. It'll stink up the car so bad they'll never get the stench out. It'll shed."

"Then I guess it'll have to be Fawn Creek," Gerry said.

Crap. "Come on, guys," she implored, shifting the dog higher in her arms. As though suddenly realizing its fate hung in the balance, it had gone slack. Mimi glanced down. Its hair was ropey and dull and his breath was fetid and damp. His teeth didn't look that good, either. It was not a young dog. Double crap.

"Look," she said reasonably. "You've been talking about getting Frankie here a dog for years and now fate has given you one. Look at him. Or her. He's not a puppy, so you don't have to worry about puppy stuff. I bet he's housebroken. Why, with a bath he's probably as cute as a bug's ear."

Vida's gaze shifted unwillingly to Gerry.

Mimi leapt on this faint glimmer of hope. "This little guy needs someone. He needs someone to love him and someone he can love back. A dog is just a gift that keeps giving. He'll watch out for you. I bet he's a great little guard dog, and hey, we know he's smart," Mimi went on in her softest, most earnest tones. She pressed her free hand to her heart. "He or she'd have to be to survive out here alone in the wilderness."

"Ha," Gerry scoffed, unswayed by this gross appeal to sentimentality. "He's survived on grilled chicken and steak for the last week. Just last night Naomi was tossing him hot dogs."

"He needs a family, Gerry," Mimi said. "Vida?" Despite a strong instinct to do otherwise, she lifted the dog close to her face so they could both gaze soulfully at Vida.

"Great. Congratulations on your new dog," Gerry said.

"Yeah. You could take him, Mimi," Vida said, suddenly and, to Mimi's mind, traitorously aligning herself with her husband.

"What? And disturb the sepulcher emptiness of my pathetic little domicile? Why, I don't even have a plant," she said, noting with satisfaction Vida's startled—and guilty—expression. Good. Vida should feel like a worm. *And* she should also take the dog.

"Oh, Mimi." Vida took a step toward her, her arms rising. "I am *so* sor—"

"Fine. You're not taking it. We're not taking it," Gerry cut in just in the nick of time. A few seconds more and Vida would be hurling herself into Mimi's arms, begging for forgiveness and offering to do whatever necessary to make amends. Vida tended toward overt shows of emotion. "What's it gonna be, Mimi?" Gerry went on. "Are we taking him to the police station or not?"

Shit. Vida's guilt would have allowed Mimi to dump a dozen dirty mutts in her lap. And just a glance at young Frank's interested expression revealed he was already more than half on board. But Gerry . . . Drat Gerry, anyway. Olson men were *supposed* to be malleable, to go with the flow, to accept whatever fate tossed their way, to be more like . . . well, Mimi. Why couldn't Gerry be more like her? She had a premonition of her stuff in the Honda stinking like dead musk ox rolled in fish innards. But what choice did she have?

She looked down at the unappetizing little dog. It looked back up at her with an equally unimpressed gaze. She sighed heavily. She might as well haul it down to the lake and give them both a bath before they—

"I'll take him."

The unexpected voice sent the Olson clan spinning around. Standing behind them, hands dug deep in the pockets of big, black, oversized dungarees was a big, oversized kid with lank black hair and a pasty complexion. His shoulders slumped beneath a baggy black T-shirt and he kept his gaze fixed on the toes of his black work boots. He had some kind of bolt through one eyebrow.

My God, Mimi realized, it was Prescott. Prescott Tierney. It was like Boo Radley had suddenly appeared amongst them. Wow.

He didn't look like a millionaire genius. In spite of his size, he looked somehow little. Young. Definitely uncomfortable. It was this last that struck Mimi most. This painfully awkward-looking kid was sophisticated, ultragroomed Joe Tierney's son?

"Ah." Mimi fumbled for her words. "Ah, what did you say?"

"I said I'll take the little dog. I'll keep him."

"Cool," Gerry said and grabbed Vida's arm. "Okay. We're outta here. Let's move!"

He hustled Vida ahead of him, Frank trailing behind. Just before they disappeared into the woods, Vida looked back, her expression still guilt stricken. She held her fist, thumb and little finger extended, up to her ear and mouthed the words, "Call me."

Mimi turned back to Prescott. "You're serious?"

"Yeah."

"You'll treat him well?"

The kid flushed, nodding vigorously.

"Promise?" she asked, mentally kicking herself. If she continued to act this way, he was going to become offended and withdraw his offer.

"Yeah."

Shut up, Mimi. "And you're not going to do anything weird . . ."

"Weird?"

She stared pointedly at his bolt. "Like piercings?"

The kid's head kicked back. "No!" he exclaimed, appalled. "God . . . *no.* That's sick."

"Just asking."

He scowled, thinking. "I'll send digitals to your e-mail if you want."

"Geez. That's not necessary—"

"No. I want to. I insist." His manner was oddly formal, his tone stilted.

"Okay. I'll hold you to it." She recited her e-mail address. "Got that?"

"Yeah."

Mimi gazed down at the mutt. It was looking around

without any apparent anxiety. She'd heard dogs sensed things about people. This dog was obviously not sensing anything bad about Prescott, and she decided that was good enough for her. She'd been delivered. She held the little dog out and dumped it into Prescott's waiting arms. "Thanks."

The mutt really was filthy. He probably carried all sorts of diseases. A sliver of conscience pricked her. She tried to ignore it, but to no avail.

"Look," she said, "I don't know whether he's rabid or not—" *Shut up, Mimi!* "I mean, he's not frothing at the mouth or anything," she hastily added. "I'm sure he's fine, but you know, you might want to get him to a vet. Like, today. Just to make sure he hasn't got fl—" She bit off the word just in time. "Anything you should know about."

Like there was any possibility the dog *didn't* have fleas. Still, no use rubbing Prescott's nose in it. And speaking of noses . . . She caught a whiff of the animal. "In fact, if I were you, I'd run out and get some doggy shampoo right now. You know?"

Prescott regarded her blankly.

"Might even make it medicated shampoo. Or, like . . . flea shampoo. Just to be extra safe."

"Okay."

Shut up, Mimi. Turn around and leave. She took a deep breath. Another. Started to turn. Turned back. "He might be a runner." The words came out in a rush. "So, don't let him go out without being on a leash."

"Okay."

"I really wish I could take him." *Liar.* "But my landlord—" Why the hell was she offering excuses when he hadn't asked for any? "So, I guess that's that."

She started to leave, but his voice stopped her.

"Ah . . . ! Ah . . . You . . ." he began, flushing even deeper.

"What?"

"Are you okay?"

Huh? She touched her nose. Sometimes she got nose-bleeds. Nope. She frowned. "Yeah. Why?"

He was now the color of a Thanksgiving cranberry mold. "You just seem real winded, you know. And your face is really red. And you keep holding your side. You're not having a heart attack are you? I mean . . . are you okay to drive?"

That did it. She was going to start jogging as soon as she got back to Minneapolis. If this overgrown, overweight kid was worrying about her health, she must really look like hell. "I'm holding my side because I have a stitch in it." She didn't feel she had to explain anything more. Besides, clearly sympathy had played a role in his offering to take the dog. She wasn't about to mess with it. "I'm sure I'll be fine in a few minutes. Thanks. Send me those pictures, all right? I'll be looking for them."

She didn't waste any time leaving.

Chapter Fifteen

Prescott watched Mignonette Olson disappear back into the woods. It was obvious she didn't want to leave the little dog behind. Bravely, she didn't even look back. Not once.

He tucked the little animal closer, his eyes already starting to itch and water. Despite his mother's long-remembered admonition not to introduce chemicals into his system, he would have to risk the potential side effects of antiallergens, because he was not going to give the little dog up. His mother would have been appalled at his being so cavalier with his health, but he couldn't let Mrs. Olson down.

Prescott had been up in the tower room, gazing a little forlornly out of the window. Over the last few days all the Olsons had slowly been trickling away, and each night fewer of the little cabins were lit from within. This morning most of the rest of the clan had left. Soon, everyone would be gone, and she'd leave, too. And he'd be alone.

Why this should bother him was a mystery. It had never bugged him before. But ever since Joe had taken off last Monday, he'd been feeling a little low. Not because he missed Joe's company, but because he had an unpleasant inkling he'd been unfair to Joe and an even worse inkling that Joe hadn't noticed he'd been unfair to him, which was the ultimate patronization, wasn't it? When a man was being unreasonable someone ought to at least notice it. Especially his family.

Family. Ha.

As he'd been thinking about this, Mrs. Olson had stumbled out of the woods hot on the heels of some creature. He'd moved to the other window just in time to see her hurl herself and a blanket at it. She stumbled to her feet, gasping and choking, one hand pressed to her heart, the other clinging with a mother's fierce protectiveness to the little bundle.

She was so valiant. But Prescott, who'd watched her for weeks, could tell she was in pain. She was, after all, a sensitive and fragile woman, clearly unwell and just as clearly bravely hiding her distress from her family. He worried about this, wondered whether he should call down and ask if she needed any help. But a moment later other Olsons arrived, though they were not as winded and were soon to prove themselves not nearly as compassionate as Mignonette— Prescott allowed himself the familiarity of thinking of her by her Christian name. He knew this because he'd cracked open the window to listen.

"He needs someone to love him and someone he can love back. A dog is a gift that keeps giving. He'll watch out for you," she'd been telling the others.

The blond giant had scoffed at her next words before saying something more to her. What, Prescott couldn't say; he wasn't paying attention. He was watching Mrs. Olson, hearing her words, feeling her anguish. And an idea was forming.

"He needs a family," Mrs. Olson had gone on.

A family. Prescott hadn't needed to hear any more. He was already moving down the stairs, trying to figure out what to say and how to say it.

He'd take the dog. He'd give it a family. He understood his decision wasn't based solely on helping Mrs. Olson. It didn't take a genius to figure out motives as obvious as his. If he took the dog, he'd have a connection to her and the rest of the Olsons. In a limited way—okay, a *really* limited way—he'd be part of their extended family. Because he'd have her dog.

True, he'd never owned a dog. He'd never owned any living creature. He was allergic to most of them, and those he wasn't tended to be cold-blooded. But that had changed the moment he'd arrived on the scene, a white knight saving the damsel—okay, the damsel's dog—from the Fawn Creek lockup.

And now he had a dog.

He looked down at it; it looked up at him. He sneezed. Now he had a dog he was horribly allergic to but that he could already tell was going to bring a lot to his life. He never would have believed he would voluntarily touch what was without a doubt a tremendously germ-infested creature, but the potential for great rewards often called for great sacrifices. Besides, he had lots of disinfectants in the house.

In the meantime, he felt better than he had in days, weeks, maybe even months. He had things to do, a series of dog-related tasks to perform, *a family*. The thought brought with it a flopping sensation in the pit of his stomach.

Prescott didn't have many friends. He didn't belong to any groups. For all practical purposes, he didn't even have peers. Even among his fellow professors at MIT he was an outsider. Mostly because they were all a good deal older than him but also because they were completely immersed in their research. They lived and breathed their work. Which was fine. But Prescott didn't. He didn't live and breathe anything other than, okay, a perhaps marginally obsessive interest in the works of J. R. R. Tolkien, and that had garnered only snickers or looks of amused superiority from his coworkers. He'd once overheard an eminent researcher tell another that if Prescott could just make it through adolescence, he might not be so annoying. Of course, it was just jealousy speaking. Still, it hurt. Because, damn it, he *was* a kid. Kind of. But then again, he'd never *really* been a kid, not like the other kids in his neighborhood.

Within a year of having written and MIT having copyrighted his Internet security code, the royalties had made him outstandingly wealthy. It hadn't made him any friends, however, and Prescott had spent a long weekend assessing his life. It wasn't the life he wanted. He wasn't sure what he wanted, but he thought it might be belonging somewhere. Or, barring that, being somewhere it wasn't obvious he didn't belong. Like an out-of-the-way hermitage of sorts. A Walden Pond. His Walden Pond.

A few days later a student of his had been showing his classmates pictures his parents had sent of their new lake home. It was near a place called Fawn Creek, Minnesota. It was perfect. And Minnesota? Now there, had thought Prescott, was a state that embraced the different. Why, one of their governors had been an all-star wrestler.

A month later, viewing online digitals, he'd signed the papers buying his bit of the dream. Now, he thought, looking down at the little dog, he had another piece. Soon he might have it all. Prescott made for the garage, cradling the dog in one arm as he punched in the security code and the door slid silently open, revealing the Prius inside. He'd drive straight to town and get the little dog cleaned up. Afterward, he'd buy a digital camera and send Mrs. Olson the pictures he'd promised to prove he was worthy of the unique trust she'd placed in him. He sneezed again.

Then he'd make an appointment with an allergist in Bemidji.

Birgie sat in the Sun Country check-in area in the Hubert Humphrey terminal, waiting to board the flight to Fort Myers, Florida. She had already snagged the last tee time this afternoon at Eagle's Ridge, and she had a friend picking her up at the airport with her clubs. Life, for the next nine months, would be good. After that . . . well, crap. She'd done what she could; she'd tried to push Mimi into taking a stand—and, no, she didn't feel bad about it because from what she gathered from that little conversation they'd had last night before the skinny-dipping commenced, Mimi had been trying to do the same to her.

It was too bad she hadn't been successful. But then, she'd known this wasn't going to be easy. It would just take perseverance, some nudging, and a little emotional string pulling (or jerking, as the case may be) before (if) Mimi did the right thing and accepted the role of guardian and matriarch of Chez Ducky, leaving Birgie to enjoy her last days in peace. Or decades, she amended. She didn't wanta jump the gun here.

In the spirit of string pulling, early, early this morning before she'd hopped in her car and left Chez Ducky, Birgie had set a trip wire at the old place. Now she just had to make sure Mimi sprung it.

All in good time, she thought as the desk attendant announced that flight 451 to Fort Myers was now boarding. All in good time.

Just north of Brainerd, Mimi's cell phone kicked in again and Bette Midler's "Friends" alerted her that she had voice mail waiting. She stuck the phone in the speaker dock—Oz's kid loved his tech toys—and hit her access code.

"You have three new messages. To play your new messages, push one," the digitalized voice announced.

Three messages in what? A month? Yup, a month, because the last couple times she'd been in Fawn Creek to do laundry she'd forgotten to bring her cell phone. She was getting more popular. She punched number one on the cell.

"Message number one delivered August third at five fifteen p.m."

"Hello! . . . Mignonette . . . Olson," an excited male voice greeted her. "You've been chosen to receive a special gift from—" She hit the DELETE key.

"Message number two delivered August fifth at 1:03 p.m."

"Why don't you get a land line installed in that place?"

Oz's voice asked. "When are you coming back to work? I miss your winsome ways. Plus Nordstrom's is having a shoe clearance in September. And my kid wants his car back."

It would be hard for Oz to say which of those two was most important.

"Message number three delivered August twenty-second at ten forty-five a.m."

"This is Otell Weber, Ms. Olson. I'm going to be out of the country on other business for the remainder of the year beginning September tenth. I'll be in touch when I get back. Nothing new to report."

Mimi flipped the top down on the cell phone. Otell never had much to report. But then, his bills, sent monthly, were never very high. She tossed around the idea of telling him to forget the whole thing. But how? He'd left the country a week ago, and anyways, what was the hurry?

There was none. For the time being, she'd just let it slide.

FALL

Chapter Sixteen

"Listen, Ester"—Mimi spoke into the headset's mike—"you oughta buy a Camry through a lease program reseller. That way it'll still be under warranty and you won't be paying three thousand just to drive it off the lot."

"Three thousand dollars?"

Mimi tipped her head, holding a hand over the headset's mouthpiece as she rifled through the Blue Book car appraisals. "Yeah. That's what the initial depreciation is. That's what Einar says."

"Oh, fer cryin'—" The voice on the other end broke off in a gusty sigh. "I s'pose he's right. I'd been feeling sorta down, you know, since Einar passed. Thought I'd cheer myself up with a new car. But that's maybe not such a good idea, I guess."

"Not a brand-new car," Mimi agreed, looking at the image on her open laptop on her desk. She'd been checking her e-mail when Ester called in, and the image she'd been looking at was still on the screen.

There wasn't any text. Just another picture of Bill that Prescott had sent, Bill being the dog she'd dumped on him

(and who named a dog "Bill," anyway?) and whose image
Prescott sent her at least once a week. Sometimes three or
four. Mimi didn't mind. She'd actually grown to look forward to the doggy pictorial. Prescott never seemed to expect
a reply. There was usually little or no text involved, other
than the obligatory, "Bill on the sofa," "Bill sleeping," or
"Bill eating." There were many amongst the last two cate-
gories.

In this particular picture, Bill was sitting on an expensive-
looking low-backed scarlet-colored sofa. He would never be
a good-looking dog, but there was something about his attitude as he gazed disinterestedly away from the camera that
spoke to Mimi. He'd accepted his change in circumstances
without missing a stride, as content on a red sofa as rolling in
a pile of fish guts.

Mimi wondered vaguely what Joe felt about the mutt.
She'd thought about Joe often since she'd returned to
Minneapolis but not with the nostalgic "that was nice" glow
she was accustomed to experiencing when reflecting on a romantic interlude.

Instead, she'd wondered what sort of career he had, if he
and Prescott had patched things up, what they would have
done on a second date (*if* they'd had a first one), if he'd strike
her as meticulously handsome in an urban setting as he had
at Chez Ducky. In short, she'd wished she'd see him again,
and as that was a waste of time, she'd resolved to put him out
of her mind. But Joe refused to be put. Much like the digital
pictures of Bill, his image popped into her mind unannounced and unexpected and with uncomfortable regularity.

She thought of Joe more often than she was used to thinking of people from the past. Even the recent past. And as he
definitely was from the past, she reminded herself, why
waste time dwelling on him?

"I appreciate Einar's concern and all," Ester was saying,
"but it woulda been nice if Einar had been as smart about cars

and such when he was alive as he is now that he's, you know, gone. I don't understand it."

"The thing you gotta realize, Ester, is that being dead tends to make you reexamine your priorities," Mimi said, scrutinizing the century plant perched on the windowsill. It looked unwell. Ridiculous. Nobody could kill a century plant. The guy at Stems and Roses had *sworn* to her that they *thrived* on neglect. "Einar has your best interest at heart."

She rolled her desk chair toward the window and stuck her finger into the century plant's pot. It was as dry as a bone. Which was good, right? The damn thing was a cactus, after all.

Below her second-story window, Starbucks had returned its outdoor tables to upright summer position so people could sip their lattes while enjoying the perfect mid-October Indian summer day. In the small park across the street, some college kids were playing ultimate football while an old guy with a fat dog lounged on a bench and watched.

"Yeah," Ester answered. "I suppose so. Well, you tell Einar I said bye, okay? And make sure you charge me for the full fifteen minutes this time."

"Will do. On both counts," Mimi said, stretching for the bottle of Geyser Spring on her desk and emptying it into the century plant's pot.

"Okay, then. Bye."

Mimi depressed the END CALL button and unplugged her headset. She stood up and stretched to her tiptoes, looking over her cubicle's well-insulated wall into the neighboring one. Her boss, Oswald Otten, aka Oz the Magnificent, founder and owner of Uff-Dead, lay nearly prone on a reclining desk chair, his feet up on the desk in front of him, a Hermès silk scarf covering his face.

"I am in contact." The silk over his mouth fluttered. "He is at peace."

For a moment, Oz listened to whoever was on the other end, then said, "I didn't say he started out his afterlife peaceful. He had to make amends before reaching his present state." Another pause. "Oh, yes. Indeed. It was *very* uncomfortable. And he's very sorry."

There followed long minutes during which the silk above Oz's mouth fluttered ever-more rhythmically, until Mimi wondered whether Oz hadn't fallen asleep. But a few seconds later, his feet swung down off the desk and the scarf slid from his face, revealing a set of neat features just starting to show the effects of gravity.

"I understand," Oz said. "He does, too. Who wouldn't be upset? Sure, you call back whenever. He'll be here. Ah, I mean there." Oz hung up.

"Not a happy reunion between temporal planes, I gather?" Mimi asked, crossing her arms atop the cubby wall and resting her chin on them. "What are you doing in Brooke's cubby, anyway? And what's with the scarf? I thought you didn't need props to make contact."

"Responding in the order in which you asked: First, not particularly. Second, Brooke called in sick." When he wasn't talking to clients, Oz reverted to the clipped tones of the East Coast CPA he'd once been. "Third, I am not using props. I am shielding my eyes. I have a mother of a headache." He pinched the skin on the bridge of his nose.

"The dead will do that to you. Or the living."

A light on Oz's phone console started blinking. "Damn. Can I transfer this one to you?"

"Sure, but I might lose business for you. Brooke's clients tended to want more 'Beyond' than 'Straight Talk.' Lots of tears and 'I'm sorrys,' and 'Does he forgive me?' Not my thing."

"I don't care," Oz said. "Betty's not getting here until after lunch. Parent-teacher conferences. It's just you and me until noon."

"Okay. Put the call through."

"It's all yours." Oz got out of the chair. With lifts, he stood five foot two inches, the same height as Mimi. He also weighed the same, a fact Mimi loudly refuted. He peered sternly at her. "Don't call her an ectoplasm stalker like you did that guy last week. I had a bitch of a time refunding his credit card."

"He was an asshole."

"I don't doubt it, but don't do it again," he said and left.

Mimi stuck in the ear bud, adjusted the mike on the headset, and punched the lit button. "Hello"—she glanced down at the LCD panel where the caller's credit card information was listed—"Jessica. This is Miss Em, your friend on Straight Talk from Beyond. Shall we begin?"

"Sure. Let's hear what she has to say," came the reply. A young woman, Mimi guessed. Young and angry.

"I'm sensing some sort of conflict between you and one of the departed." When in doubt, go with the safe bet.

"Wow. I'm impressed," Jessica replied. "How many people do you think don't have some sort of 'conflict' with one of the 'departed'? I'm going to go out on a limb here and say none."

"Hey, Jessica," Mimi said. "You called me, right?"

"Yeah. We all make mistakes."

"Perhaps you should call back tomorrow—"

"I can't. I'm heading for Mexico tomorrow. I deserve a vacation. How come you didn't know that if you're a psychic? Huh?"

"I'm not a psychic," Mimi replied. "I'm a spiritualist. I make no claims about being able to tell you where you left your purse, how your Aunt Ida makes her world-famous brandy balls, or what tonight's lotto number will be."

"So, you're more or less useless except for a little celestial gossip, eh?" Jessica snickered.

Mimi stared disbelievingly at her phone. What the hell? "Look. Here's the deal. I sense the departed: their emotions, their wishes, their regrets, and, most important, their advice. Hence the name, Straight Talk from Beyond."

"So, sense away!" Jessica snapped. "I'll wait."

Mimi took a deep breath.

"Wow, again," Jessica said. "Was that the sound of you being possessed by my mother's spirit?"

"No," Mimi said. "That was me trying to figure out how to deal with you."

"I'm still waiting for that straight talk."

"That was straight talk," Mimi said. She'd dealt with Jessicas before, people with issues. Most of the time Mimi accommodated them. After all, listening to a rant was as good as a coffee break. But Jessica didn't sound merely angry. She sounded *bewildered* and angry. Mimi recalled the feeling. For those first few weeks after her dad had failed to show up and retrieve her from Chez Ducky when she was eleven, she'd felt that same throat-constricting anger and panicked bewilderment. Oh, she'd hidden it from the rest of the Olsons, but she'd felt it all right; until she'd finally let it go.

And everything else with it.

No, she mentally shook her head at the insidious notion, just the bad stuff. Just the stuff that could make you miserable. *Like thinking about the baby that didn't get born?* She took a deep breath. Exactly like thinking about the baby that didn't get born. Okay. Enough of this crap. She had a client on the phone who needed help.

"Here's some more advice. Seek counseling, Jessica."

"What?"

"Seek professional help. Your mother's spirit isn't going to tell you anything you don't already know. You need to get in touch with someone who can help you deal with this."

"Did my mother tell you to say that?" Jessica's voice rose. "She did, didn't she? Will she ever stop trying to tell me what to do? Even dead, she's nagging me!"

"I'm afraid I'm the—"

Jessica hung up.

Mimi sighed, realizing she'd just as good as signed a contract for a weekly shouting match with Jessica. It happened.

Contrary to popular belief, Mimi and her coworkers were not in the least reluctant to advise callers to seek professional help when the situation warranted. Depression, drug use, abusive relationships, alcoholism, talk about suicide, any of these would have Mimi giving out one of the dozen helpline numbers she kept posted on her bulletin board quicker than a rat leaps from a sinking ship.

Sadly, there were a lot of sinking ships out there; people sailing through life without rudders, pitched about by circumstance, their hulls punctured by disappointment. It was not Mimi's job to plug the holes, but if she could direct them to a likely harbor, all the better.

The private line light on her phone console lit up. It never lit up, unless . . . She punched the button. "Yah, mon?"

"Do you have to answer the phone in that hideous fake accent?"

Bingo. "Hi, Mom. I was channeling a Jamaican."

"Hello, Mignonette," Solange Charbonneau Olson Werner replied. "Are you busy?"

Why did she bother asking? Even if Mimi were to say yes, Solange wouldn't believe her. To say Solange disliked her career path was a gross understatement. Solange considered working for Straight Talk much akin to working a pyramid scheme. In short, her mother believed Mimi had "wasted her genius" bilking people of their hard-earned dollars.

Mimi had to allow that as a ringing denouncement of another's life path, that one's emotional decibels were off the chart and Mimi felt her mother's disappointment resonating in her very bones. Which is one of the reasons she didn't spend much time with Solange. Her bones didn't need the grief.

"Nope. Whaddup?"

"Please stop it. You're too old to use such affected language. I'm calling to remind you that next month is Tom and my anniversary party."

"What? Mom, I sent an RSVP with my regrets. Didn't you get it?"

"I know. I've chosen to ignore it. You must come, Mignonette. The only excuse I will accept is surgery. You miss too many of our family events. I insist you attend this one."

Mimi squirmed. The truth was her mother's parties were only marginally more interesting than watching paint peel. "I went to Sarah's graduation."

"Oh. Well, that makes all the difference."

Mimi ignored the sarcasm. "Besides, are you sure you want the reminder of an earlier marriage wandering around while you celebrate your anniversary to a Husband Number Two guy? It might make someone uncomfortable."

Ten years after the debacle of her first marriage, Solange had wed a proper power-brokering baby boomer. In quick order she produced Mary and Sarah, so named to give the world notice that Solange was through with dreamy-eyed nonsense like naming a kid "Mignonette" and that this time she meant business. This time, she meant to produce energetic overachievers. And she did. The baby, Sarah, had entered a doctorate program at twenty and Mary was fast-tracked in an Internet spyware development company. The pair of them had been cute enough as babies, but now that they were charter members of Young Overachievers of America, whenever Mimi spent any extended time in their company she was overcome with an extreme desire to nap.

"Don't be ridiculous," Solange said.

Solange was right. Tom was categorically uninterested in Solange's life before it included him. He'd never treated Mimi unkindly or ignored her. Actually, Mimi thought Tom liked her. He just didn't think of her as his wife's kid by another man. He seemed to think of her more as just another something Solange had brought with her to the marriage, like her vintage Chanel coat.

"I'll expect you," Solange stated, and then, surprisingly, "It will mean a great deal to me, Mignonette."

A command performance Mimi would have no trouble ignoring, but an emotional appeal from her categorically unemotional mother was interesting. Maybe even troubling. Was something wrong with her?

"Of course I'll be there. Wouldn't miss it for the world."

There was a short pause that lengthened, almost as if Solange was hesitating. Solange did not hesitate. She acted. Which was one of many reasons she and Mimi did not understand each other. Mimi considered action overrated and the root of many of the world's problems. Stand for something and you inevitably had to stand against something.

"Mom?"

"What are you going to wear?" her mother asked a little too casually.

Ah. All was explained. "I was thinking of clothes."

"Mignonette."

"A dress."

"Do you have something appropriate? There will be people there, Mignonette, who are connected."

Only strength of will kept Mimi from asking at what part of their anatomy. Her mother brought out her most juvenile impulses.

"*Very* connected."

"Um, ha. Mm."

"You're mumbling. Anyway, my dear, you might work the room a bit, try to engage in some serious discussions. Congressman Popitch and Bud Butter, our lawyer, are coming, as are various businesspeople, including the man Verity Brokerage is sending in preliminary to Tom's selling BioMedTech. Dr. Neidermeyer, the heart transplant specialist, will be there with her husband, who is a violinist, so there'll be artistic types, too."

"Sounds like fun," Mimi lied.

"Why don't you take this opportunity and make the best of it?"

"I just might do that."

"Mignonette, you have so much potential. You could still do something with your life."

No, she couldn't, and no, she didn't. Mimi didn't want to be a doctor or a lawyer or an Indian chief. It was an old argument begun soon after Solange had made the horrible discovery that Mimi had a higher-than-average IQ and decided Mimi was bound for great things and determined that she, Solange, would see that she got there. With or without Mimi's consent. Mimi, she was convinced, wanted to do *all* of these things; she just hadn't realized it.

Given the circumstances, as soon as she could, naturally Mimi had fled the Werner mansion and headed to the open arms of her father's family. Solange was horrified. She'd disowned the Olson family canon only to have her daughter throw herself right back into their midst and embrace it. Since Mimi was eighteen at the time, her mother had had no choice but to let her go. Especially since none of the threats or entreaties Solange employed to force her eldest to return had worked.

The primary of these was the threat of being cut off from the Charbonneau hair depilatory dynasty, an empire founded by Jacque Charbonneau, Canadian fur trapper, when he created a salve that not only did a first-class job of tanning hides but also dissolved the hair from his knuckles. However, Solange's threat had little effect on Mimi, whom nature had cunningly outfitted with a major disinterest in possessing things. Besides, Solange's father had already bequeathed a small annuity to all of his grandchildren, including Mimi— only, Solange insisted, because at the time of his death Mimi had not yet shown herself as a slacker.

As this sort of comment was an example of what Solange considered a winning emotional appeal, it, too, fell on deaf ears. And the devastation she claimed Mimi's half sisters had felt upon her leaving was equally unconvincing since Mimi knew for a fact—after all, she'd been there—that the day she'd left, Mary had lugged her Baby Brilliant Building

Modules trunk into Mimi's room, pushed back the furniture, and set about erecting a fifty-story skyscraper. All this passed through Mimi's mind's eye as she stared at her phone console.

"Mignonette?"

"Gee! My phone console just lit up like a Christmas tree!" she lied. "Gotta go, Mom. The dead wait for no man. And well you might ask why? Them being dead and all. But there you go. The dead call, I answer. Love you!"

"Wait!" Solange's commanding voice could have stopped a stampede.

"What?"

"Remember not to tell anyone about . . . *this.*"

"This" being her career. Job. Work. Whatever.

"It doesn't reflect well on you," Solange said.

Strangely, Mimi knew her mother meant it. She didn't really care how Mimi's profession reflected on her, Tom, or the little barracudas, also known as Mimi's half sisters. She sincerely wanted the best for Mimi. She loved Mimi. Mimi loved her. They were trapped by love. *Deliver me*, Mimi thought, but said, "You got it."

"Good. And I am going to send over your grandmother's pearls. We just had them reset and I expect you to wear them."

"Expect" had to be Solange's favorite word.

"Right. Gotta go, Mom. Bye." Before Solange barked out another command, Mimi gently depressed the END CALL button and wondered whether she could find a "suitable dress" at Nordstrom's Rack or whether she should just borrow one from the rich and powerful (and crossing-dressing) Ozzie.

She'd try Ozzie. He bought only the best.

"I think we achieved a lot this afternoon." Delia Bunn, a tall, athletic-looking woman in her early thirties casually reached across the corner of the conference table and let her hand drop over Joe's wrist. Delia was D&D's CIO, D&D

being the London-based company Joe was assessing for possible purchase.

"More than I'd planned," Joe said, smiling at her. Her accent was pure Sloan Street, and like her, well-bred, elegant, and smart. "At this rate I'll be able to wrap things up here in a week. I can't remember the last time I brought a project in ahead of schedule. I have to thank you for that. Thank you."

Delia smiled and crossed a spectacular pair of legs, angling herself sideways on the chair as she bent over the open file folder on the table and did some last-minute checking of figures. He watched her. He knew she knew he was watching her. They both pretended otherwise.

Delia wore a dark navy pencil skirt and a cream-colored shirt with gold cuff links. She'd coiled her thick honey-colored hair into a smooth knob at the nape of her neck. The masculine wear and severe hairstyle only accentuated her femininity. And she knew it. Here was a woman who understood image and its power to influence public opinion. From the height of her heels to the rims of her reclaimed tortoiseshell reading glasses, every element was designed to make a statement about her self-confidence, her sense of self-worth, her status.

Mimi Olson could have borrowed a few lessons from Delia's book, he thought in amusement. But then—his smile grew wry—why? It would probably never occur to Mimi Olson to make a statement via fashion. Except she had. Her clothing said uncategorically, "I don't give a damn what you think about me. I know who I am and that's enough."

He couldn't recall ever having met someone quite like Mimi Olson, and it wasn't just her career choice, though that was extremely off-putting; try as he might, he could not come up with any possible way to view telemarketing dead people's advice as anything more than a legitimate con game. *Unless* she actually believed she was talking to the dead. In which case, she was even more peculiar than he thought. Which only made the fact that he not only thought of her often, but wondered about her, and, in fact, *liked* her, all the stranger. She wasn't like anyone he liked. She was unique and uniquely her own person. All her own.

Which made it unfair to compare her to others. Her situation, like her, was unique. She didn't have to worry about what impression she made on strangers. Mimi Olson, up there in her odd little commune, didn't meet many strangers. She was surrounded by a vast and vastly odd conglomeration of relatives and friends who apparently knew her so well and had known her for so long that all her quirks and traits were comfortably familiar, not only tolerated but embraced.

What would it be like to be so open? To have all your idiosyncrasies, your vulnerabilities and peculiarities, exposed to the public? No, not the public, he reminded himself, your family. Who knew him so well he'd feel comfortable letting them see the chinks in his armor . . . ?

He frowned. What *chinks*? He didn't have any chinks. More important, he didn't have any armor. Christ. Next time he was channel surfing he was *not* stopping at *Dr. Phil.*

"It all looks good." Delia closed the file folder and straightened the edges by clicking it lightly on the counter. "I must say, I'm famished. You must be, too. What do you say we find ourselves a bite? There's excellent curry just down the street and a decent Thai just a bit farther on."

The way her warm gaze held Joe's telegraphed an interest in something more than a meal. He considered, but he had strict rules about mixing business and pleasure, at least until the business aspects were complete. Of course, she might simply be suggesting they share a meal, in which case he was being an egocentric ass. On the other hand, why test it and make both of them uncomfortable? True, she was lovely, but—and this was sadly the biggest factor—he felt not one iota of physical attraction. Appreciation? Yes, of course. You couldn't help but appreciate a lovely, elegant woman like Delia, like you would appreciate any fine work of art. But he didn't want to go to bed with Edward Hopper's *Nighthawks,* either.

Joe was forty-four years old and he hadn't been seriously involved with a woman since Karen. He didn't want to be involved. If it hadn't worked out with Karen, whose intelligence, work ethic, sense of purpose, and commitment reflected his own values so closely, how was it supposed to work out with someone who didn't, at least discernibly, share any of those traits? Except the intelligence thing. Mimi was undoubtedly intelligent. Joe always took the measure of a thing, weighed the pros and cons, and projected relative outcomes before acting. He'd given up impulsiveness when he'd found out Karen was pregnant. . . . And how had he gone from considering dining with Delia to why he didn't want to become involved with Mimi?

"I'd love to, but I have a phone conference in an hour and I'd like to prep for it," he lied.

"Oh." Her mouth puckered with disappointment. "Well, another time." She stood up and he followed suit. They discussed the next day's agenda as they walked to the elevator and from there down to the building's lofty marble-sheeted lobby and to the taxi stand outside, where he saw her into one and took the next for himself.

At the hotel, he greeted the desk clerk and made his way to his suite on the second floor. The rooms were lovely, the trio of small sofas surrounding an electric fireplace imbued the suite with a cozy feel, the black granite bar separating out a discreetly situated and well-stocked wine cooler and tiny refrigerator. The original artwork gracing the walls was excellent. In the large (at least by London standards) bathroom, thick towels toasted on a brass warmer rail, and thousand-count Egyptian cotton linens dressed the immense bed. The walls were soft sage, the furnishings a deeper hue of the same, only accented by a plummy color. It was distinct from any of the hundreds of other hotels in which Joe had spent the majority of his adult life, and in that, exactly the same. An expensive, well-planned poser, some outrageously expensive designers' ode to gracious home life.

It might almost pass, too, except for the lack of clutter, unpaid bills and half-read paperback novels, jewel cases carrying mismatched CDs, a brush with a few curls of dark hair in it, out-of-focus photographs, half-completed crossword puzzles, shoes hiding under sofas and stickie notes with intimate instructions about dry cleaning or grocery lists, the detritus of complicated and rich relationships.

He tossed his jacket over the back of one of the sofas and sat down, reaching for the universal remote on the coffee table in front of him, noting idly that the maids had replenished the perfectly fanned stack of glossy magazines this morning. He picked up the phone and punched room service's number.

"Good evening, Mr. Tierney," the voice on the other end, a voice he'd never matched to a face but to which he had spoken at least once daily over the last month, greeted him. "What can I get for you?"

"Oh, just a sandwich. Do you have . . . pastrami?"

"Of course."

"Great—no, wait. Do you have corned beef?"

"Yes, sir. A corned beef sandwich? How about a Reuben sandwich, sir? The chef makes a really stellar version."

Joe shrugged. "Fine."

"Right away, sir. Can I tempt you with dessert?"

"No, thank you, Ahmad."

"You're quite welcome, sir."

He ended the call and sank back into the cushions, feeling subtly unsettled. He probably should have hit the gym before ordering dinner. He hadn't gotten enough exercise lately. But logging mileage on a treadmill, or climbing a perpetual ladder, always with limited appeal, tonight had less. He found himself wishing he knew where they were playing a pickup game of basketball. Or no-contact football. He missed the camaraderie of team sports.

He probably should have gone to dinner with Delia. If for no other reason, he would have enjoyed the company. Most of the time he was perfectly content with his own company. He liked himself, he enjoyed his job, the travel, the people, the challenges. Probably, he admitted, because he was good at them. The only thing he wasn't good at was being Prescott's father.

And being Karen's husband.

No, he thought, slipping off his shoes and putting his feet on the coffee table. All in all, strict rules about mixing business and pleasure aside, it was a good thing he hadn't gone out with Delia . . .

There was a good reason Joe hadn't become seriously involved with anyone since Karen's death. He used to think that it was because no woman could match Karen in dedication, drive, and smarts and because all women paled in comparison. That was partially true. But as the years passed, he hadn't been able to ignore the objectivity that time allots, and that objectivity made it brutally clear that his marriage hadn't been a smashing success.

He and Karen hadn't been a team, as much as independent franchises of the same company, existing apart but under an umbrella of mutual benefice. He attributed this to the fact that they'd married without knowing each other very well and that soon afterward distance and different obligations kept them from getting to know each other better. He would not make that mistake again, and he didn't know when his life would allow for the time and proximity he would need to have before giving a committed relationship (let alone marriage) another shot. The career that had kept him from Karen and Prescott nine months out of the year still kept him from having adequate time to get to know a woman well enough to take the next step in any relationship.

Someday, maybe. But not now.

A discreet bell tone announced that room service was at the door. He swung his legs down from the table and went to open the door. A pleasant-faced young woman stood in the hall on the opposite side of a cart, a silver-domed plate in its center. "Good evening, Mr. Tierney," she said without her usual sparkle. Her dark hair was drawn into a bun so tight it stretched the skin back from her temples, lifting her eyes in an expression of faux surprise, but there were shadows under her wide-spaced eyes.

"Good evening, Esther." He stood aside and she wheeled the tray in.

"Where would you like to eat tonight? Fireplace or by the window overlooking the park?" She tipped her head toward the window and he could see the hair on her temples stretching with the motion. She winced.

"Everything all right?" he asked.

"I just have a bit of a headache is all," she said. Small wonder, with her hair being dragged back so ruthlessly like that. "Thank you for asking, though."

"Just leave it there and I'll decide later," he said, handing her a folded five-euro bill.

"Thank you, sir." She accepted the bill and turned and he noted that a coil of dark curls had somehow escaped the strict confines of her severe bun. It reminded him of something. . . . Mimi Olson's dark coils. He wondered whether her hair, like Mimi's, made tiny corkscrews when wet, and if dried under its own volition, would cloud about her shoulders like Mimi's. He bet Mimi never got a headache.

As soon as the door shut, he lifted the dome off the plate on the cart. A triple-decker sandwich sprouting all sorts of crisp-looking julienned vegetables and deep-fried, à la Monsieur Croquette in some fabulously fragrant batter, lay amidst a bed of matchstick potatoes. It looked unlike any Reuben he'd ever had. Quite unlike the corned-beef sandwich Mimi Olson had slapped together for him at Fowl Lake. It looked wonderful.

Unfortunately, his mouth had been set on a Fowl Lake rendition.

Chapter Seventeen

November

Mimi gazed longingly out the tall French doors of the Calhoun Beach Club's second-floor solarium at the beach across the street. Though the sun had set on Lake Calhoun, one of the most popular of the twenty-four lakes within Minneapolis's city limits, dozens of hearty individuals were still out, bent on squeezing every last minute outdoors before winter arrived. Dog walkers, runners, in-line skaters, and strollers emerged into the pools of light beneath the lampposts circling Calhoun and just as abruptly disappeared in the shadows between. Mimi wished she were one of them.

She turned back into the room. The solarium's cheesy white trellises had been hidden beneath midnight blue bunting that matched the imported slipcovers on the chairs. On long, linen-clad tables, florists and chefs had competed to see who could create the most sumptuous display. Tom and Solange's guests seemed to have a similar agenda: diamonds and gold, platinum and silver, crystal beads and lamé. Mimi's eyes hurt just looking at all the stuff winking at her from the crowd. It was too bad some of those necklaces couldn't speak because she was sure the stories they could tell would have been far more interesting than any she'd heard so far this evening.

Not that the Werner guest list was shy on wit, intelligence, or humor. It was just a very public party, attended by very powerful people who were very discreet, a combination that led to a lot of requests for club soda and innocuous chitchat. Any really interesting conversations—and Mimi had no doubt there were at least a few of those—would be taking place in more private venues: the parking ramp, or the restrooms, or the lobby downstairs.

Mimi spied her oldest half sister, Mary, making nice with another woman a short distance away. Mary, as short as Mimi and as dark and square as Solange, was smiling and sipping from a nearly empty highball glass, her gaze darting around the room. Mimi watched her, trying to dissect Mary's game plan for success, which apparently depended on looking dumpy, because though only twenty-eight, Mary looked like a Doric column, a squat, black, Doric column. A tube of stiff black brocade encased her from wrist to ankle without betraying any of the female curves beneath. Sensing her scrutiny, Mary glanced up and spied Mimi. She spoke a few more words to the woman and chugged purposefully toward Mimi.

"So, Mignonette," she said upon gaining Mimi's side. "Still seeing dead people? Or are you dating someone new?"

"Better watch out Mom doesn't hear you wrenching open the family's closet doors."

Even though she hadn't seen Mary in six months, nothing had changed. Mimi had hoped Mary's feelings might have slowly segued into the same sort of vague, distant affection toward her that Sarah, the youngest, had. But nope. Mary still disliked her.

It hadn't always been so. When Mimi had flown the coop, Mary had been five, just memorizing the periodic table when she wasn't following Mimi around, adoration in her dark little eyes. But Mary had deeper feelings, and not positive ones, either. At some time during junior high, Mary had taken up Solange's "Mimi must be saved from herself" banner. Over the years, as it became apparent that Mimi wasn't going to be saved from herself but instead live blissfully on just as she was, the crusade had become more acrimonious. Mimi thought she understood the source of her sister's animosity. Mimi was happy and Mary was not, and poor Mary, a clinical specimen of workaholism if ever there was one, could not figure out why.

"Why bother?" Mary said, patting her dark, spray-fixed helmet of hair. The flash of a giant sapphire ring on her finger nearly blinded Mimi. The gaudy rings were the only vulgar display Mary allowed herself. "Girl gifts," she called them, which made them seem sophisticated and clubby at the same time.

"New ring?" Mimi asked, pointing at the ring.

"Yes. Dishy Manfranke gave it to me when Sub-Surfer went public." Sub-Surfer was the cyber Peeping Tom company Mary had founded her senior year of high school. She'd made a fortune selling the means to spy on one's family members undetected.

"You're kidding. Someone's actually named Dishy Manfranke?" Mimi asked. The question was rhetorical: Mary did not kid.

Mary didn't deign to answer.

Mimi reached out and disconnected a green broccoli floret from an artfully constructed vegetable tree on the table beside them. "Well, from the looks of it, I'd say Dishy wants to go steady." She popped the floret into her mouth.

"What a wit," Mary said. She cleared her throat and looked Mimi dead in the eye. "Speaking of going steady, seeing anyone?"

"Mom asked you to ask that, didn't she?"

Mary didn't deny it.

"Tell her, 'nope.' I am an island unto myself."

"Then, you must have a gold mine on that island. I've never seen you wear anything like that before." Mary looked markedly at Grandmother Charbonneau's re-designed pearl necklace hanging around Mimi's neck.

Mimi did not for a minute think Mary's interest avaricious; whatever her faults, covetousness was not one of them, but she must be dying to know where Mimi had come by something like the borrowed necklace. Let her die.

"This? Lovely, isn't it," she said, then, "Hey! Truffle quiche. Yum." She used the little silver tongs to deposit a couple on her plate. "Mary, look behind you. What are those figs stuffed with?"

"I wouldn't know. I'm not the caterer."

"Well, try one and tell me."

"Forget it."

"Come on. Goat cheese makes me nauseous and I wouldn't want to spit something out at Mom's party."

"Oh, for God's sake—" Mary snatched up a fig and took a bite. "Roquefort. You are *such* a child."

Mimi smiled and rescued the fig from Mary's hand. Old habits die hard. When Mary was a little girl, Mimi had always been able to coerce her into doing her bidding. Mary had idolized her, following her around the Werner estate, just waiting to be asked to fetch her a soda. Ah, those were the good old days.

Mimi was still wallowing in nostalgia when Sarah arrived. Or, more accurately, backed into her. Sarah spun around, her toffee-colored blond hair swinging like a satin curtain. Mimi caught her by the arms to keep her from falling. In the four-inch stilettos she was wearing, Sarah, five foot nine without the heels, towered over Mimi. Mimi found herself staring into Sarah's exposed cleavage.

Now this, she thought, was different. Not that Sarah was tall, obviously, but that Sarah was exposing her bosom in a soft rose jersey dress. The last time Mimi had seen Sarah she'd been dressed in an ill-fitting navy blue, no-iron pantsuit, and sensible flats.

It must have been longer than she'd realized since she'd seen Baby Precocious—her pet name for the dour little automaton who, in all of Mimi's memories, was planted in an armchair in the Werner library reading a book. Mimi did a quick calculation. Almost a year. Before that she'd seen even less of her—not on purpose, but because Sarah had graduated from high school at sixteen, finished her undergraduate degree at Penn State by eighteen and her master's at Stanford at twenty. Now twenty-three, she was pursuing her doctorate in international economics at the University of Chicago. Sarah was not only a genius; she was an übergenius. Solange had finally hit the jackpot with her third daughter. *Boo-rah!* You'd think she'd be content with that, but nope.

"I'm sorry," Sarah hastily apologized, looking down at Mimi. "I was just— Oh, it's you. Hi, Mimi."

"Hi, Sarah," Mimi said. "You look great."

It was true. Sarah had shed the last bits of baby fat, exposing some pretty spectacular cheekbones. Also, the Accutane Sarah had reported using some years ago had worked big-time. Sarah's skin was creamy and smooth, a perfect foil for the honey blond hair. And speaking of foils . . . were those highlights in Sarah's golden tresses? Sarah, whose idea of fashion forward was Lands' End? Even more impressive, Sarah looked frankly happy. As in cheerful of mien and agreeable. The Sarah Mimi recalled had been a somber, earnest child with all the spice of an egg-white omelet.

"Thanks," Sarah said, smiling.

Unlike Mary, Sarah still retained a sliver of her bigsister worship. Even when she'd been taking double credit loads at Stanford, Sarah had dutifully e-mailed Mimi at least once a month, mostly about what she was studying.

"Still working for that, ah, you know, spirit thing?"

Spirit *thing*? What was this? Sarah always used exact terminology. The fact that she'd used such a nonspecific noun as "thing" was also new.

"Oh, yes," Mary answered for her. "Mimi's still whispering to ghosts."

"Actually, I often have to shout," Mimi said. She rolled her eyes. "They are *so* distracted by the whole wings and halo thing, you know? Ghosts. Can't live with 'em; can't live with 'em."

Mary scowled and drained the rest of her highball.

"That's ridiculous," Sarah said. "The common religious iconography of angels as human beings with wings can be traced back to ancient depictions of the ancient Assyrian sun god, Assur, within a winged disk. Besides, only certain orders of angels have wings. And halos, though currently denoting Christian holiness and divinity, were originally depicted in Roman art, particularly in reference to the god Mithras."

Ah. There was the Sarah Mimi knew. "My bad," she said.

She popped another fig in her mouth and glanced at Mary. "How's the cyber–Peeping Tom business going? Catch a lot of voyeurs this year?"

"Sub-Surfer is an important tool," Mary said stiffly. "We save people from financial and emotional devastation. Wouldn't you want to know where the money that you need to pay the bills was being spent? What your significant other was doing when they shut the door on you and spent the evening on the computer? Or would you rather live in ignorance, hoping the ax you don't even realize is hanging over your head doesn't fall?" Mary asked.

"I choose ignorance!" Mimi declared without hesitation.

Mary made a disparaging sound and motioned a nearby server over.

"You're kidding," Sarah said, her expression stunned. "You'd actually choose to live in a state of ignorance?"

"Information is overrated," Mimi answered. "Clutters the mind and muddies the priorities. Plans can be thwarted, blueprints lost, fast tracks derailed. It's better to just go with the flow and let things slide, because what you don't know can't hurt you."

"Like not knowing where certain family members are?" Mary asked.

The allusion to Mimi's father was as subtle as a jackhammer.

"Exactly," Mimi said, knowing insouciance would annoy Mary far more than a counterattack. "And the health benefits are fabulous." She gave Mary the once-over. "Are you getting enough sleep, Mary? You look peaked. Haven't you ever heard the old saw about stopping to smell the roses?"

"Like you? Mimi, you didn't stop, you laid down and rolled around in them, and you've never gotten up." The server arrived and Mary ordered a Scotch old-fashioned.

"I *am* blissful." Mimi nodded agreeably.

"Yeah, blissfully taking up space and little more."

"Maybe. But it's space no one else seems to want, so what's it to you?"

Sarah was scowling, not anxiously, but clinically, as if she was watching a debate and hadn't yet decided who was ahead on points.

"It's a waste." Uh-oh. Mary was channeling Solange again. More good-daughter points to Mary. "I used to look—"

"What are you all talking about?" Whatever Mary used to look at would remain unknown, as Solange emerged from a knot of nearby guests.

Drat. Mimi hadn't noticed her mother there. Not that her mother lacked presence; she just lacked inches. At a firm five feet nothing in heels, Solange Charbonneau Olson Werner looked like a plump little squab, all front-forward breasts and small ass and bright little eyes. She even walked like a pigeon, little forward-darting motions interrupted by abrupt pauses. Her coal black hair apologized to no one for its artifice, and the arch of her brows had been tattooed in place of the thick ones nature had bestowed and electrolysis had removed years ago.

"Nothing of importance," Mary said to their mother.

"Hi, Mom," Mimi said.

"Hello, Mignonette." Solange's gaze frankly assessed Mimi. "Good," she approved in a low voice. "Very nice."

Bless Ozzie's self-indulgence, and bless his hobby more, and bless his generosity in sharing his wardrobe with Mimi most of all. Of course, since they wore the same size, Mimi had been commandeered to act as his model–cum–stand-in on more than a few shopping trips.

"You've lost weight," Solange murmured, cocking her head.

"I wouldn't know. I don't own a scale."

Her sisters traded openly disbelieving looks. *They can't prove anything without a key to my apartment*, Mimi thought. "It's incredibly liberating. You should try it."

"There is more to life than liberation," Solange said, her small eyes aglitter. "Have you spoken with anyone?"

For a woman whose nationality prided itself on its sangfroid, her mother sometimes displayed an amazing lack of sensitivity. Mimi made a discreet gesture toward her sisters.

"I mean, anyone who might help you *professionally*?"

Mimi's eyes went round with feigned surprise. "You didn't tell me you had a palm reader lurking amongst the unsuspecting. Aren't you the mother to beat all mothers? Are they hiring?"

Sarah laughed and Mimi glanced at her in surprise. Maybe she had a sense of humor after all.

"Mignonette," Solange said, "would you please be serious? I know you don't really want to spend the rest of your life pretending to give strangers on the phone messages from their dead relatives."

The quip Mimi hoped would occur to her didn't arrive. Her easygoing smile gelled into something stiffer. Whatever else might be said to Solange's credit or discredit, her ability to cut to the very heart of the matter was never in doubt.

"*Am* I pretending?" she finally muttered.

Her mother ignored this, patting her arm. "It's not too late, you know. Forty's the new thirty."

"I thought fifty was the new thirty. And I'm forty-one."

Her mother, knowing full well her point had been made with surgical precision, didn't bother pushing the blade deeper. "Promise me you'll mingle. That's all I ask."

It would be so much easier if Mimi could convince herself that her mother was only interested in Mimi's success, or lack thereof, inasmuch as it reflected on her, but Mimi knew this wasn't true. Solange wanted the best for all her daughters. She just had a very specific definition of "best": challenging work, satisfaction in a lucrative career, social standing. She'd been waiting Mimi's entire life for her to "sort through things and find a purpose," and no matter how many times Mimi had told her mother she *had* a purpose (which was living with as few complications as possible), Solange refused to believe it.

Not my daughter. You have too much potential. I refuse to believe you intend to squander it. How many times had Mimi heard a variation on this theme? A thousand? Two?

Poor Solange. Still, if it would make her mother happy . . .

"Sure," Mimi said.

"Excellent." Solange nodded approvingly. "Sarah knows everyone here. So, if you want to know who anyone is, ask her." She turned to Mary. "Your father is in dire need of salvation. He's been tending to your grandmother for the last fifteen minutes. I'd go, but . . ."

But Mother Werner despised Solange, Mimi silently finished. Mimi had never met Solange's mother-in-law. For years, the old lady, a staunch Catholic as well as a second-generation German American, had not recognized her son's marriage to a divorcée, and a French one to boot, and so had never visited the Werner household while Mimi lived there. From the few remarks Sarah had let drop over the years, Mimi thought Solange had probably met her match in Mother Werner.

Mary lifted her chin like a soldier who'd been given a suicide mission and chugged off through the crowd, her gown swishing. Solange turned the laserlike focus of her gaze on her youngest. "Hm. You look awfully well, Sarah."

Sarah's smile held a hint of trepidation, and Mimi realized she was hiding something. Mistake. Solange could detect dissembling like a guard dog can sense fear. She had a similar reaction, too: attack. Mimi had long ago learned simply to tell the truth and mentally hum until the storm of words passed.

"You, too, Mom," Sarah said, tucking a lock of her blond hair behind her ear and leaning forward to kiss their mother's cheek. "Happy anniversary."

Solange was so startled by this unprecedented display of affection from the most undemonstrative of her very undemonstrative children that she became flustered and lost whatever train of thought she'd been pursuing. She blinked, opened her mouth, closed it, said, "Oh. Well. Thank you. Ah . . . Well . . . Be sure to introduce Mimi around," and disappeared back into the crowd.

Mimi eyed Sarah thoughtfully. *Sarah* handle Solange? Nah.

"What's up with Mary?" she asked when Solange had vanished. "She's reached new levels of bitchiness."

"Cankles," Sarah answered without preamble.

Cankles, the uninterrupted merging of the lower calf with the ankle resulting in a column effect, were the curse of the Werner women. Mary had them; Sarah had them to a degree. You could lose all the weight you wanted and do toe raises until you fainted; there was no cure for the Cankle Gene. Thankfully, Mimi did not carry any Werner genes.

"You may have noted the floor-sweeping dress," Sarah went on. "She's covering them up. She's become preoccupied with them."

"But she's always had cankles."

"I know, you know, but I'm not sure she did," Sarah said. "It's like she looked down one day, discovered them, and has been pissed off ever since."

She grieved for her sister's cankle tragedy for a few seconds before shaking it off and sweeping a champagne flute from the tray of a passing server. She lifted the glass in Mimi's direction and twinkled at her. "Here's to us, Big Sister."

This was unsettling in the extreme. In all the years Mimi had known her, Sarah had never, not even once, twinkled. It was like Sarah had had a personality transplant.

"You look pleased with life," Mimi said.

"I am." Sarah nodded eagerly as if she'd been waiting for an opening. "I'm seeing someone."

"Seeing *someone*?" Oh, poor Sarah. Mimi didn't know for a certainty, but she strongly suspected—and she was usually never far off mark in her strong suspicions—that Sarah had never had a serious relationship before. Mimi asked, "Female or male?"

"Male. Definitely, extravagantly male."

The twinkling, the laughter, the dress, the cleavage. All was explained. "So, you're in love, huh?"

Sarah's brow furrowed and she looked at Mimi like she hadn't understood her. "Love?"

Mimi was pretty sure her face wore a similarly confused expression. "Yeah. Love."

Sarah's face cleared. "Wow, Mimi, I didn't realize until now just how much older you are than me. I'm not in love. We hook up on weekends." She leaned forward, her voice lowering to a whisper. *"The sex is fantastic."*

"Oh," Mimi said because she didn't know what else to say. Good for you? Congratulations? Does he have an older brother?

"He's my first," Sarah said happily.

"But not last."

"Don't get me wrong, he's a nice guy," Sarah said with such casual insouciance Mimi was taken aback. "Smart, too. He's one of my—"

"Professors," Mimi said, feeling a stir of anger.

"No. One of the grad students I tutor." She giggled. *Sarah* giggled. "Isn't that naughty?"

"Yeah. My sister, the Ivy League Mary Kay Letourneau."

Sarah gave a ladylike snort. "Oh, he's older than me. But what makes it great is that neither of us wants a relationship. But we're not pathetic bedroom prowlers, either."

"Does Mary know?"

"Good lord, no! She'd go Judge Judy on my ass."

Ass? Sarah didn't use vulgar language. Did she?

"I knew I could tell you, though."

Mimi wondered why and was about to ask when Sarah grabbed her arm and pulled her into the crowd. "Mom at twelve o'clock high. She'll be over here in a few minutes unless she sees you talking to someone."

"I am talking to someone."

"Me? Thank you! Aren't you a honey?" Sarah said, tickled. "So, who do you want to meet?" She looked around the room, her eyes narrowed purposefully. "Aha! See that guy over there? Darn, he just turned. He's talking to Congressman Popitch. Dark hair, tallish?"

Mimi nodded.

"Dad just sold BioMedTech to an equity trading company and he's their ax man. Man, I bet he has stories to tell." Sarah was practically licking her lips.

"Ax man?"

"You know nothing about business, do you, Mimi?" Sarah asked pityingly.

"Nope."

"He's the scouting team and advance unit all rolled into one. When his company is deciding whether or not to buy a business, they send him in to scope out the situation, find the weak links, and determine the business's value. If his company goes ahead with the purchase, he makes recommendations about how to, ah, trim the fat." She made a cutting motion across her throat.

"Cold," Mimi said. Which is exactly why she never wanted to be in business. All the responsibility, all the cold-blooded decisions to be made, all the people depending on you to make a sound judgment. What if you had hay fever that day and your judgment was impaired? No, thank you.

"Growth, especially economic growth, is never painless." Sarah cast an appraising look at the tuxedo-clad back. "But if your head has to be on the chopping block, he's the guy I'd want swinging the ax."

"Oh?" Mimi asked.

"I met him a couple days ago. Sex appeal. He oozes it."

"Okay, I'm in," Mimi said in the spirit of cooperation.

"Great," Sarah said. "Just don't tell Mary I introduced you. Mary"—Sarah's grin was conspiratorial—"has a crush."

As opposed to Sarah, who had a boy toy.

Sarah led the way to where the two men stood in conversation. They were closing in for the kill—the Charbonneau tendency to see things in hunting terms must be catching—when their prey must have sensed their approach and turned.

Wow, was all Mimi could think. He'd been smooth before, but the tux and dress shirt had jettisoned him into the Rolls-Royce league. The Phantom line. His jawline shone, his eyes glittered, his white dress shirt glowed, even his manicured nails had a soft luster. And his hair, Mimi thought disbelievingly staring up at him, was perfect. Warren Zevon would have been proud.

"Hi, Mimi," Joe Tierney said. Yup. His voice was still the sexiest soft masculine purr she'd ever heard.

His gaze flickered over her, quickly, no more than a second of assessment, but she saw the surprise in his eyes. So she let her gaze drift over him, too, only in a much more speculative manner.

"Well, don't you clean up nice?" she said.

Chapter Eighteen

Joe burst out laughing. Mimi had said exactly what he'd been thinking and she knew it. She looked lovely, womanly and relaxed. A floaty peacock blue dress followed her curves as though made for her, the color turning her tanned skin amber while around her throat hung a magnificent pearl and diamond necklace.

Both the dress and the necklace surprised the hell out of him. He'd thought she was poor. Hadn't she said something about not being able to afford a replacement for one of those shacks neighboring Prescott's lake home? Maybe it was just the Olsons. Anyway, he'd still have pegged her as more of a madras caftan type, one who wore lots of handcrafted bead necklaces and parted her hair in the center for special occasions.

"Aren't you going to return the compliment?" she asked. Beside her, Sarah Werner and Congressman Popitch traded startled glances.

He tipped his head and gave her a slow once-over. "I don't know," he said thoughtfully, "I rather miss the seaweeds."

"No, you don't," she chided him without criticism.

Of course, she was right. Only for a minute there he'd forgotten. A chasm separated their lifestyles. His life was controlled, structured, and refined; hers was unstructured, unplanned, and messy. In fact . . . what was she doing here? The incongruity of seeing her at a party given by and for the Midwest's most successful and conservative citizens struck him broadside. He'd been so caught up in the pleasure he felt on seeing her again, he hadn't asked how it had occurred. And on closer inspection, she was simply a more polished version of the Fowl Lake bon vivant he'd met last September.

In spite of the designer dress, she hadn't bothered with high heels or stockings, and the only makeup she wore was lipstick. She'd wrestled her thick curly hair into a plait and coiled it at the nape of her neck, but a few mutinous tendrils, mostly silvery ones, had escaped and drifted like spider silk around her temples. He glanced at her hands, long fingered and light boned, the nails cut rather than filed, and unpolished. Maybe she was some sort of wacky trust-fund baby. He could look into the future and see her in another two decades; she'd be a full-fledged eccentric complete with waist-length gray hair and caftan, wearing a fortune in pearls around her neck as she Birkenstocked her way to the co-op.

"I forgot your phone number," he abruptly told her, though God alone knew why. She hadn't asked and in fact looked surprised he'd mentioned it. She hadn't expected him to call, he realized. This disconcerted him. Hadn't she wanted him to call?

"I tried looking you up in the phone book," he went on. "Do you know how many M. Olsons there are in Minneapolis?"

"Quite a few, I'd imagine," she said, her smile giving nothing away.

"You know Mimi, Mr. Tierney?" Sarah Werner, Tom Werner's pretty young daughter asked, recalling Joe to the fact that he and Mimi were not alone. It was unlike Joe to forget his social skills.

"I've had the pleasure. We met at a family gathering," Joe answered. At Sarah's inquisitive look he added, "Her family."

"Excuse me?" Sarah said.

"He said 'at her family gathering,' " Congressman Popitch repeated, pleased to be able to add something to the conversation.

"But *we're* Mimi's family," Sarah said. "She's my sister."

Joe couldn't disguise his surprise. He couldn't imagine anyone less likely to be associated with the conservative, slightly stuffy, socially prominent Werners.

"Half sister. Same mother. Hello, Walt," Mimi said, turning to Congressman Popitch.

Solange? Solange was the driving force behind Tom Werner. A woman with a mind like a steel trap and a will, Joe was convinced, that could be subverted only by black magic. It had been Solange who'd convinced Tom to sell BioMedTech. He couldn't see Mimi insisting on anything. She hadn't even raised her voice in protest when her beloved lake shacks were being put on the auction block. This was interesting—

What was he thinking? He didn't want to be interested in Mimi Olson. She was a Bohemian nutcase in a family of Bohemian nutcases, since she clearly hewed to her Olson relatives more than her mother's. What did he want with a nutcase? Besides the obvious, he admitted, as his gaze touched discreetly on the small, curvy figure the slippery-looking material slithered over. Besides, he added sanctimoniously, she was also Tom Werner's stepdaughter, which made her, by his own rules, off-limits. There, he thought, convinced.

Now the only question that remained was why he'd had to convince himself to stay away from Mimi Olson when he hadn't had to do so with Delia Bunn, a woman who in every respect fit his criteria for a "really attractive woman."

A sudden commotion on the other side of the room, near the big arched windows overlooking the lake, drew their attention. Sarah stretched herself on her tiptoes, looking over heads. "Oh, dear. Poor Mother."

"What's going on?" Mimi asked.

"It's Grandmother. She—she's dancing. Excuse me." She hurried into the press.

"So, you're Werner's stepdaughter," Joe said to Mimi. She'd been looking after Sarah but now returned her attention to him.

She gave a light guffaw. "No one has ever referred to me as Tom's stepdaughter. Even Tom. Do they, Walt?"

"I doubt it," Congressman Popitch agreed.

A muffled crash came from across the room. Mimi turned toward it. Around them, people had gone from interested to embarrassed and were now trying to cover up the sounds of whatever was happening with overanimated conversation, their eyes determinedly averted from the other side of the room.

"How do they refer to you, then?" Joe asked.

"Hm?" She wasn't paying attention. She bit her lower lip, clearly struggling with some dilemma. "Would you excuse me?" she abruptly asked.

"By all means," he said. "Promise you'll come back later?"

"Sure." She gave him an odd half smile, then nodded at the congressman. "Keep fighting the good fight, Walt," she said and headed into the crowd.

"You'd never guess she shared any of the same DNA with the other Werner women, would you? Couldn't be more unlike her half sisters," Congressman Popitch said, watching Mimi disappear. He shook his head. "Talk about a loose cannon."

Joe angled his head inquiringly. "You know Mimi Olson well?"

Popitch snorted. "Not really. But who does? Can you imagine? Here she's born with every advantage. She's cute, Solange claims she's a genius—and I use the word 'claims' advisedly—Tom's as connected as they come and unaccountably fond of her, Solange is rich in her own right—you've heard of Hair Today, Gone Tomorrow depilatory? That's

Solange's family"—here Walt leaned in and after a quick look around whispered—"and Mimi doesn't have those unfortunate Werner legs, if you know what I mean?"

Joe, even on brief acquaintance with the Werners, did.

"Yet what does she do for a living? Cons lonely folk into thinking she's talking to their dead loved ones. Course, Solange tries to keep that on the lowdown, but it's not a secret. What a waste." Popitch sighed.

Joe found himself nodding in agreement, but what he was really thinking was that he was intrigued. All over again.

Chapter Nineteen

Mimi wove her way through the people, her feelings mixed. Perhaps Sarah's subsonic sisterly SOS had been timely. Joe Tierney was entirely too attractive and Mimi might end up doing something impulsive. Mimi was not impulsive; she was laid-back. Indulging your impulses meant acting on them, and being laid-back meant acting on as little as possible, especially on those things that had high stakes. Which was why Mimi didn't have too many casual relationships with men (or any other sort, for that matter). The last time Mimi had allowed herself to scratch an itch in relation to a man, she'd scratched herself straight into pregnancy.

In short order, Life had once more alerted her of the need to keep her distance. Especially when it came to people who breezed in and out of her life. She preferred to do the breezing, a fact of which Mary's nasty little remark about her father's disappearance had reminded her. 'Twas better to breeze than to be breezed upon.

As soon as Mimi saw Grandmother Werner, she recognized the well from which the Werner cankles had sprung. She also recognized that Grandmother Werner was high. The woman, stout as a beer stein and with a froth of white hair to boot, slouched in her chair, her head thrown back, her eyes open but unfocused. A collar of diamonds dug deep into the fold of her neck, and her hands were laced across her round stomach, each finger cuffed by multitudinous rings.

Sarah sat in a chair pulled up next to her grandmother, smiling tremulously in answer to the sidelong glances shot in their direction. As soon as she saw Mimi, she went limp with relief as if she thought Mimi was an expert on stoned old ladies. Okay, Mimi thought, an image of Naomi Olson springing to mind, she did have some experience, but she was no expert.

"Where's your dad?" Mimi asked as she drew near. "Where's Mary?"

"She went to find Dad," Sarah whispered through her smile. "Grandmother thinks Mary is Mom. She called Mary a bad name."

"So?"

"Everyone was listening," Sarah said.

Poor Sarah, still young enough to feel like the cynosure of every eye. She sat down in the chair on the other side of the old woman, scooting it close so she and Sarah could talk over the old lady without being heard. "What happened?"

"Mary said Grandmother was acting oddly when she arrived but has just gotten steadily worse. She insisted on dancing with one of the servers."

"That's because she's as high as a kite, Sarah," Mimi said, casting an eloquent look at the glassy-eyed, smiling old woman.

Sarah paled visibly. "Oh, God."

"Don't tell me you didn't know she was using drugs," Mimi said disbelievingly. "You *did* occasionally look around all those years you spent in college, didn't you?"

"I swear I didn't know," Sarah denied hotly. "She's always been difficult about Mom. This summer she was diagnosed with diabetic neuropathy and in the hospital they gave her morphine. I know it's a terribly painful condition and since she's returned home she's complained about how the prescriptions don't work. And recently she started getting . . .

odd. I thought she had incipient Alzheimer's or some other form of dementia. I never put two and two together. Why would they give her those sorts of drugs?"

"I'd say she's doing her own pain management," Mimi said, not without kindness. She glanced at Grandmother Werner, who was chuckling quietly, muttering something to someone only she could see. Her fingertips drummed a rhythm on her plump knees.

"She's always been so aloof, and, well, a little superior. She detests 'scenes.' And now she creates them almost daily." Sarah gave a little hiccuped sob. "What do you think we should do?"

We? She should be on the other side of the room flirting shamelessly with Joe Tierney and deciding whether to make all his Fowl Lake beach fantasies come true. This was all plainly none of her business. For the love of God, she was meeting the old lady for the first time.

"What if she starts dancing again?" Sarah asked.

"Ask her if you can lead?"

"This isn't funny, Mimi," Sarah said. "When she came back from the bathroom, she accosted a server and insisted he dance with her. Everyone's looking at us. I don't know what to do."

Mimi glanced around. No one was watching them. Since Grandmother Werner had slipped happily into la-la land they'd returned to their conversations. "As far as anyone here knows, your grandmother was overcome with the joy of the occasion and now she's calmed down. So, why don't you just enjoy the rest of the—"

"Who're you?"

Both Mimi and Sarah, leaning forward so they could converse over Mother Werner's slouched form, turned their heads. Mother Werner peered blearily down at them.

"Who," she repeated, looking directly at Mimi, "are you?"

"Mimi."

"Mimi." Sarah's grandmother squinted, trying to place her.

A glint of recognition lightened her cloudy eyes. "The Frog's by-blow?"

On the other side, Sarah gasped. "Grandmother!"

Mimi looked askance at her. "Frog?"

"She's taken to calling Mother a Frog," Sarah said, casting anxious looks around.

"It's not an ethnic slur, simply a comment on her physical resemblance," the evil old lady purred.

"Gotcha."

Mother Werner's eyes narrowed to little slits. "I remember. You are the product of her first misalliance. The Frog *claims* it was a legal union. As if being a cheap divorcée was any better than simply being a cheap floozy."

At the mental image of Solange dressed in satin hot pants and a tube top and teetering atop four-inch Lucite stilettos, Mimi laughed.

The corners of Mother Werner's thin lips twitched upward and disappeared. "Your mother must have been wed at fifteen. How old are you? Fifty?"

Mimi stopped laughing. "Forty-one."

"You look older. You should use sunscreen. A good exfoliation might help. Try the spa. It's decent for a shipboard venture. My husband is there now. I should go find the old bastard before he starts pinching the poor masseuse's bum," she said, bracing her hands on the arms of the chair and preparing to heave upward.

"What's her name?" Mimi quickly asked Sarah.

"'Her' name," the old lady said darkly, "is Mrs. Werner."

Apparently, the old gal wasn't all *that* doped up.

"Christian name."

"Imogene," Sarah said softly. "And Grandfather has been dead for thirty years."

Imogene rewarded this betrayal by making a disgusted sound. "Bah."

"Thank you, Imogene—may I call you Imogene?" Mimi asked calmly. So the bum-pinching husband was dead, eh?

They were in her territory now. She mentally rubbed her hands together. "Your husband asked me to tell you he'd be with you soon enough."

Sarah shot Mimi a startled look.

Imogene studied Mimi sharply a moment before releasing her grip on the chair arms. "I suppose there's no hurry," she finally said. She settled like a bag of wet sand in the chair. "How long have we been on board now? I can't recall . . ." Her eyelids fluttered shut and she was out.

"Where would she get the sort of drugs that make you fantasize like that?" Sarah asked.

Maybe Baby Precocious wasn't so precocious after all.

"My stockbroker," Imogene said, eyes still closed, and chuckled. "At least he knows where his bread is buttered. The damn quack is too lily-livered to risk his precious medical license."

"I can't believe that," Sarah whispered helplessly. "Her stockbroker is almost as old as she is."

"I've got it!" Imogene's eyes had snapped open and she was staring with unconcealed relish at Mimi. "Why, you're that table-rapper, aren't you? I'm right, aren't I?"

"Got me," Mimi said without rancor.

"Ha! Well, I hope your little show is a bit more professional than that oily ciscebo," Imogene said, glowering at one of the male servers. "The lout stepped all over my feet. And he calls himself a dancer. Remind me to speak to the ship's purser about him. Insolent. Didn't even finish our dance." She closed her eyes once more.

"I'm sorry, Mimi," Sarah said miserably, her pale cheeks a tender blush shade Bobbi Brown would have died to re-create. "I haven't even thanked you for coming over. You've been so—" she looked up and Mimi was horrified to see unshed tears shimmering in her eyes—"so wonderfully uncritical."

Christ. What was with Sarah making with the maudlin? It was weird. Sarah wasn't emotional. At least, not that Mimi recalled. She wondered whether Sarah's new sex life could really account for such a drastic personality change. Maybe she'd hit her head recently. "Don't blubber."

"I'm sorry." She sniffed. "Dad or Mother should be back any second now. You should rejoin Joe Tierney. I think he likes you, and Grandmother's not your responsibility."

No. She wasn't. Which, Mimi well knew, made it easier for her than for Sarah. Because Sarah loved the old witch and seeing her like this was painful for her. It wasn't painful for Mimi.

Sarah had knit her fingers together and was studying them. Quickly, Mimi tallied her options here: Go and find Joe GQ or stay here with Granny Werner.

Sarah looked up and smiled bravely.

Ah, crap. Joe GQ had probably moved on to greener pastures by now, anyway.

"Look, Sarah," she said. "These are your parents' friends. You ought to be the one out there making nice on their behalf. I wasn't so keen on mingling, anyway, and you know I'm not self-sacrificing so I'm telling you the truth. So, go on. I'll stay here with Imogene. Besides, she's dying to expose me as a fraud."

"Did you read my mind?" Imogene asked, smiling smugly.

"Why can't people get this straight? I am a *medium*, not a *clairvoyant*," Mimi said.

"Isn't that convenient?" Imogene said, opening one sardonic eye.

"Yes."

Imogene laughed and Mimi gave Sarah a "get out of here" jerk of her chin.

Sarah rose, clearly relieved. "I'll be back as soon as I find Dad."

"No hurry," Mimi said.

"No hurry," Imogene echoed, both eyes now open. "Run along, Sarah, my dear. I might as well stay for this woman's act since the band isn't playing anymore." She leaned toward Mimi. "If you're any good, I'll tip you."

Chapter Twenty

Joe networked his way around the room, but his heart wasn't in it. The conversations seemed a little stale, a sense of déjà vu attending every exchange. When fifteen minutes had elapsed and Mimi hadn't returned, he assumed she'd found some friends—Congressman Popitch's comments about no one knowing her well notwithstanding.

He couldn't imagine Mimi was that much of an enigma. For him, yes, but she had a huge extended family and was obviously a fixture at Fowl Lake, so obviously she was well known to them. On the other hand, he knew this wasn't necessarily true. Like the neighborhood curmudgeon who never leaves his house, you could be somewhere without anyone knowing you.

He'd just decided to thank the Werners and take his leave when he spotted Mimi sitting next to a portly older woman against the far wall. They were engaged in a heated discussion. The old woman was shaking a finger a few inches under Mimi's nose, and Mimi, her expression obstinate, had crossed her arms over her chest. Both women looked like they were enjoying themselves immensely.

He stood back in the crowd, watching her, charmed. More of her hair, he noted absently, had come undone. She roused conflicting impulses in him: he wanted to personally place her in the hands of a good hairdresser, and at the same time being with her made him want to buy a pair of jeans. He hadn't had jeans since he was nineteen.

"Here. I remember you like Scotch. Single malt, right?" Mary Olson, the Werners' older daughter, appeared at his side with a highball in each hand. She pressed one of the glasses into his hand.

"Chin-chin!" She clinked the top of her glass to his with a little too much force, sloshing liquid over her hand. She frowned, traded her glass to her free hand, and shook the drops from the wet one, at which point he realized the young woman was blitzed. From what he knew of Mary Werner, she was normally fastidious in the extreme.

Joe glanced toward Mimi. Mary followed his gaze. Her coquettish smile overturned into a disapproving frown.

"Oh, Joe. Don't tell me you've succumbed to the charms of my loosey-goosey"—she drew out the vowels—"older sister." She took a swig of Scotch and smiled coyly. Oh, dear.

"Well, lookee there. She's even got Grandmother Werner twisted around her little finger. Ha!" Mary said, her eyes on Mimi and the old woman.

"Tell me about Sub-Surfer, Mary," Joe said, trying to divert her attention. "My company is always interested in software security applications—"

"She's not all that, you know," Mary said matter-of-factly.

"All what?"

"Anything." Mary ran her fingertip along the rim of her glass. Her cheeks were flushed. "That whole 'live for the moment' thing? *Pfbbt.* And her 'I don't want anything but my freedom'? Double *pfbbt.* I mean, that's fine as long as it isn't an out-and-out lie." A look of offended innocence turned Mary's cheeks an even brighter pink. "I never would have pegged Mimi as a liar."

"Liar?"

"Well, look at her. They don't wear designer dresses and pearls like that on Central Avenue. For someone who claims she doesn't care about worldly possessions, she sure has some nice ones."

Joe looked at Mimi. He'd noticed the dress and necklace earlier. And both did fly in the face of the impression she'd given him up at Fowl Lake.

"How can she afford a dress and jewelry like that?" Mary was muttering. She downed another swig of her drink. "Mom refuses to give her a cent. And she doesn't have a job. Not a real job."

Mimi had said that all of the Olsons—and she'd certainly given the impression she included herself in that category— were too poor to move the family compound from Chez Ducky. But when he'd seen the expensive way she was decked out tonight, he'd discounted that impression, thinking she had been talking about only the Olson side of her family, not herself. Apparently not.

"Mary, I'm not really comfortable discussing you—"

"Or maybe taking advantage of people pays better than I thought. I gotta say, from the looks of things, she must be pretty good at her job," Mary went on as if she hadn't heard him. She lifted her glass in Mimi's direction in a toast.

"Mom always said Mimi had more potential than anyone. She coulda been anything. Done anything. And *that's* what she chose to do with it."

Despite a certain sympathy for Mary's feelings—after all, her sister was a charlatan—he found himself wanting to defend Mimi, find excuses for her. Ridiculous. He didn't even know her. If her own sister thought she was a charlatan, chances were she was a charlatan.

"You really don't like her very much, do you?" Joe asked.

Mary looked at him, startled. "Huh?" she said, scanning his face as if she thought he'd been joking. Her surprise melted and she shook her head. "Nope. I'm just as big a sucker as the rest of you. I love her." She looked around. "I need a drink," she said and waded into the crowd.

Surprised, Joe watched her go before turning his attention

back to Mimi. She was still talking to the older Mrs. Werner, her unvarnished, piquant face animated, surrounded by more escaped tendrils of coiling black hair. She didn't look like a vulture, feeding on people's unhappiness. She looked like a handsome, humorous woman with no access to a beauty salon who, despite or because of this, and he really did not know which, was very appealing.

He wanted, very much, to figure out which image was closer to the truth. True, he was going to be in Minneapolis only another couple weeks. True, they'd likely never see each other after he left. Chances were he'd be halfway across the world for the next three to six months. It didn't matter. Until he left, he wanted . . . ah, hell. Did he always have to know exactly what he wanted or why he wanted it? No.

He made his way toward her. As he drew near he heard Mrs. Warner demand, "I insist you use a Ouija board."

"Fine," Mimi said, looking around. She spied an empty serving tray resting on the table next to her and moved it to her lap, then upended a clean glass ashtray from the same table. "Here," she said. "Rest your fingertips on the edge of the planchette."

• The old lady didn't move. "That's not a planchette; it's an ashtray. And that's a serving tray."

Mimi blew out a deep breath.

"You'll never get very far in your chosen profession with such obvious gimmickry." The old woman sniffed. Suddenly, her face contorted in pain.

At once, Mimi slid the tray from her lap. "Are you all right?"

Joe started forward.

"Mother?" Tom Werner came hurrying from the corridor, Sarah beside him. Joe stopped.

The old woman looked up at Tom. "Tom, I'd like to go to my cabin. Could you . . ."

"Of course." Tom turned and gestured to someone in the hall. "I'm sorry, Mother. This has been too much for you." He looked over his mother's head at Mimi. "Thank you, Mignonette."

There was sincere affection in his gaze. A fresh wave of pain contorted Mrs. Werner's face, but she still managed a tart smile. "What are you thanking her for, Tom? She tried to convince me that tray is a Ouija board. Whoever hires the acts for these ships ought to vet them more closely."

Mimi sighed. "No tip?"

The old lady's lips twitched with amusement, but she mastered the impulse, pinching her mouth into autocratic lines. "No tip."

Aided by Tom, she lumbered to her feet, wincing, and limped away supported on either side by her son and Sarah, her nose high with disapproval.

Mimi was still smiling when she saw Joe. She rose to her feet, her expression surprised and pleased, without the least trace of guile.

"I take it social disaster has been averted?" he asked, taking two wineglasses from the tray of a passing server and handing her one.

She shook her head. "No, thanks, and no disaster. Just keeping Tom's mom company for a little while."

He didn't believe her.

She looked around and her expression grew crafty. "But now would be a good time to make my exit. The dutiful daughters are all otherwise engaged, so I can slip out unnoticed. You may have to stay and mingle, but I don't. Do me a favor? If one of my sisters or my mother asks, tell her you saw me on the other side of the room. If I play this right—and *you* play this right—I can get brownie points for having been at the party for a three full hours rather than"—she craned her neck to see the Rolex on his wrist—"one and a half."

She was close enough so that he could smell her soap. He wondered whether her hair was as silky as it looked. The few other times he'd seen her it had been wet, either from a lake or from a shower. Now it looked unbelievably soft and lustrous. Maybe she didn't need a hair salon after all. He wondered whether she wore a lace bra beneath the expensive dress or if all the surface sophistication was just that. He wondered whether she would still seem such a cipher in his milieu, amongst the rich and powerful, as she had been in hers, amongst the odd and not so powerful. But most of all he wondered who she was. Really.

"I'd rather you let me come with you," he said before he realized it. *This,* he thought, *is a mistake.* He didn't mix business with his personal life. He wasn't going to. He was giving her a ride on his way to the Grand Hotel.

Her eyes widened with feigned shock. "But, Mr. Tierney, *your* absence will definitely be noted."

She was right.

"Do you have a car?" he asked.

"No, I took a taxi here."

"*I* have a car." He dangled the bait temptingly.

She laughed. "Let's go."

Chapter Twenty-one

While grappling with Joe in each others' arms in the hallway outside her apartment, their mouths locked in another passionate kiss, Mimi lost her balance and stumbled. Arms tight around her, Joe toppled backward, his shoulders hitting the wall with a bone-shaking jar. He didn't stop kissing her, however, and Mimi, impressed by his single-minded focus, laughed breathlessly against his lips.

Abruptly, he broke off their kiss and pushed her gently away, holding her at arm's length. He was breathing heavily. Unbelievably, he looked even better with his dark hair rumpled and his brilliant white shirt collar unbuttoned and the black silk tie loose around his throat. She liked his dazed expression even better. She had an inkling Joe Tierney was seldom dazed.

She felt a little wobbly herself. She melted toward him, linking her hands behind his neck to draw him down. He held her off, gripping her upper arms, crouching slightly so they were at eye level. He swallowed visibly. If it had been someone less sophisticated than Joe, she would have called it a gulp.

It was surprising, the effect she had on him. It was also a potent turn-on. Oh yeah, she'd been told often enough that power was the ultimate aphrodisiac—hell, it was practically the Werner family motto—but until this moment she'd never fully understood it. She tilted her face, inviting him to kiss her.

He blew out a gusty breath. "Stop it."

"Stop what?"

"That," he said and bent forward to kiss her, a favor she immediately returned.

Once more, he pulled back first. "This is not good business," he said, sounding a little shaky. "You're Tom Werner's stepdaughter and I'm in town to determine if one of his companies would be a good investment for my employers."

"Determine away. I won't stop you."

"I don't want to confuse the issue."

"I'm not confused," she whispered, ducking a shoulder and slipping within the circle of his arms. She flattened her hands against his chest. His heart hammered under her palms. He groaned. "I won't try to pry any state secrets out of you. Promise."

"It's not that."

"You *don't* think I've been sent to keep you occupied while Tom's CPA flunkies break into BioMedTech and cook the books? Dang."

Her hands followed a leisurely path over his tuxedo jacket, paying particular attention to the area covering his pectoral muscles. The material was warm with his body heat, supple and well cut and rich. Like him.

"Well?" she prompted, deftly trailing the tip of her tongue along his jaw. His skin carried the slightest fragrance of citrus and sandalwood. Her lips, sensitized by all the preceding kisses, not to mention all the hormones flooding their nerve endings, read the hint of his nascent beard like a blind woman reads Braille.

"I never allow business to overlap with my personal life. I always keep . . . ah . . . ." He tilted his head back so she could keep going down his neck to the hollow above his clavicle. She obliged. He looped one arm around her, swinging her around and pushing her against the wall, his arms cushioning the impact.

He pinned her, his forearms bracketing her face, his hands tangled in her hair, angling her head gently so he could kiss her more fully, more devastatingly, when she was already plenty devastated. She felt light-headed and primed with sexual anticipation.

"This is nuts," he said, breaking away. He stared down into her upturned face and looked like he might groan again. He bent forward until his forehead pressed against hers. He closed his eyes and took deep breaths, like a guy who'd just finished a marathon and might collapse. "Look at us."

Unwillingly, she glanced around. They were in a public hallway, and yes, it was a little smarmy, but they were alone. Mostly. She had a sudden image of the neighbors opposite her apartment with their eyes pressed to the peepholes. Critiquing.

"You're right." She came to a quick decision: she was in no state to pretend she had any outcome in mind other than that she and Joe end up horizontal and quickly. *Then* they could slow things down a bit. Or not.

Yes, yes, it was impulsive. Yes, yes, she had an object lesson in where such impulses could lead to. But right now hormones were doing the talking, and her body was willing to listen.

She disengaged herself with businesslike brusqueness, smoothing her dress and briefly touching her hair before digging into her purse and coming up with the key to her apartment. She jammed the key into the lock and flung the door open, reaching back and snagging Joe's sleeve—there had to be cashmere somewhere in there—and pulling him in after her. But he didn't pull. Startled, she looked around.

Joe stood in the open doorway, straight-arming himself against the jamb. He was *not* following her in. Was *not* scooping her up and storming around the apartment like a testosterone-maddened maniac looking for the bedroom. *Why* not?

She flashed on a sudden image of glum, plump, thirty-five-year-old Jennifer Beesing across the hall, one eye pressed to the peephole as she dolefully stirred the batter for some delicious caloric nightmare, unsurprised that Mimi Olson couldn't lure a man into her apartment. Jennifer might even call her tomorrow, brownies in tow, to commiserate. Mimi had seen her bring such presents to other single women on the floor. Mimi wasn't one of them. Sure it had been a while since a man had been here, but that had been her choice.

"Come in!" Mimi whispered urgently.

"I'm sorry, Mimi." He sounded a little frantic. "The rules work only if you abide by them."

She couldn't believe this. She didn't give a rat's right ass cheek about his wacked-out rules. Jennifer Beesing had been joined in her imagination by the Gertzes next door, trading spots at the peephole as they hurled invectives at each other (the happy couple were always sniping), yet thinking, "At least we have each other." Even the decrepit and evil Widow Dinwiddie had made it to the peephole by now and was clucking to herself, "Poor old Mimi Olson. Can't even get one to cross the threshold anymore. Not surprised. She's no spring chicken, after all."

"Get in here," she commanded in a low voice. Joe's rueful smile gelled. He took an awkward step back. She could read his thoughts: *Fatal Attraction* time.

She leaned back against the jamb in a retro-fifties siren slouch. She whispered through what she hoped was a sultry smile, "I promise you'll leave with your virtue intact in twenty minutes."

"Huh?"

"*My neighbors.* They've probably been watching me trying to drag you bodily inside my apartment and they've just as probably seen you resist. Strenuously. I have my dignity, you know. Or should I say, 'had'?"

Understanding dawned. "Oh, shit."

"My thoughts exactly." By now, all earlier thoughts of seduction had vanished. She was fighting for her pride here.

"It would really help me out if you would just enter my lair without being physically forced—"

He scooped her up in his arms, catching her so off guard she let out a whoop and flung her arms around his neck. He bent his head, bringing his mouth close to her ear. "Is this better?"

Her heart hammered in her chest. Her ebbing physical excitement rushed back in a tidal-wave surge. *Where's your pride, Mimi?* she chided herself. She wasn't going to be resisted twice in one night.

"Only if you don't drop me," she managed to grumble. "I would never live it down if your knees buckled under my weight."

"Oh, come on," he said. "I've managed it before."

"Let's face it, Joe. You're not exactly the Adventure Travel type, so there's a distinct possibility both of us will end up in a pile on the floor here if you don't get a move on."

"I work out." He bounced her up higher in his arms. He didn't seem to be straining and his heart against her side wasn't pounding too heavily and he wasn't all red in the face. So, he probably wasn't about to stroke out. That was good. Still—

"Come inside until the news is over; then you can go."

"The news?" he said. "Hey. I have my dignity, too. If I come in, I'm staying more than twenty minutes."

He had a point. Not a good one, however. He wouldn't ever have to face her neighbors. "We'll see," she allowed.

He dipped forward and planted a deep kiss on her mouth, twirled halfway around, and backed into her apartment, kicking the door closed behind them. Once inside, he stopped and looked around. She followed his gaze, trying to see the apartment through his eyes.

It would look cheap. Not cheap as in slatternly, but cheap as in warehouse-clearance-sale affordable. Unsurprising, since that's where she'd gotten the cranberry-colored, microfiber five-piece living room suite (sofa, chair, ottoman, coffee table, and lamp). A crocheted rug was heaped at one end of the bean bag chair a former tenant had left behind. It had some crumbs on it. Across the back of the armchair were strewn a half dozen of the couture dresses Ozzie had insisted she take and try on before making her final decision about what to wear tonight. The price tags still dangled from the sleeves of a few.

He'd also insisted she take the accessories that went with each dress, and these, shoes, jewelry, scarves, and even a faux fur shrug, were piled on the love seat. She hadn't worn any of them. After all, she'd been given orders to wear Grandmother Charbonneau's redesigned pearl and diamond necklace, which was just about as much glitz and glam as a woman could pull off in one sitting.

In the corner, Grandmother Olson's oak pedestal dining table acted as her desk, adorned with a laptop computer and a Bubble Jet printer. Writing tablets, magazines, and books overflowed the area next to it. Ceiling-tall twin bookcases she'd found at a garage sale flanked the single picture window. As well as books, they held useful things including a hair dryer, an unopened bag of tube socks, and a mini-microwave still redolent of last night's popcorn. Opposite the window was the crowning glory of the room, a forty-inch flat-screen plasma television.

Mimi loved television. It was her one vice, watching the drama surrounding a fictional cast of characters unroll on a weekly basis, their problems all tied up, their mysteries solved in an hour or, at most, a season. It was an extremely satisfying way of conducting life.

Of course, up at Chez Ducky she didn't need—wrong

word—didn't care to watch television. Aside from the fact that they wouldn't get any decent reception even if she did haul one up there, there were other things to do and a cast of real people who interested her every bit as much as those on *Heroes* or *House*.

"Nice," Joe said. He didn't sound like he meant it.

She looked again. It wasn't cluttered, it was comfy, she told herself. Sure, it needed vacuuming and dusting, but what home didn't? "You can put me down now."

"Thank God." He dipped and set her on her feet, straightening, with one hand going to the small of his back. "I gotta do more stretching in the morning."

"You didn't have to stand there holding me. You could have put me down as soon as the door was closed."

"After that smart-ass comment about my knees buckling? Are you kidding? I had to uphold the honor of men over forty everywhere. I couldn't suggest it. You had to."

"Men really are at the mercy of their testosterone, aren't they?" she asked wonderingly.

He nodded.

"Do you ever grow out of it?"

He shook his head. "Doubtful. I was thinking of trying to impress you by pounding my chest but realized I'd probably start hacking."

Nothing was guaranteed to make Mimi's pulse jump faster more than a handsome, masculine, self-effacing guy. "Poor old geezer. How about I get you—"

From inside her purse, her cell phone began playing a muffled version of "When the Saints Go Marching In." She had the cell programmed to play the song when she was receiving calls from Uff-Dead clients. "Dang."

She generally didn't work at home—Ozzie had tax reasons for keeping his employees on-site—but on occasion, when they were short staffed, she'd have calls forwarded to her cell. Assuming she'd be back early from tonight's party, she'd done so tonight in exchange for the loan of Ozzie's gown. Befuddled by spiking sexual hormone levels, she'd forgotten.

"Work. I usually don't do this from my home." She shrugged apologetically. She held a finger to her lips, signaling for him to stay mum, and opened the cell.

"Hello. This is Miss Em. Have you pre-entered your credit card information using your telephone's number pad?"

"Yeah, yeah. I wouldn't be talking to you if I hadn't already been approved, would I?" a young woman replied.

"Hello, Jess." This was Saturday. Jess called only on Mondays. Something must be up. "What can I do for you this evening?"

"You can tell me what Mom thinks I should do about Neil. He's my boyfriend."

Boyfriend? This was new. "Tell me about it."

"He might be moving in here with me. We've been going out for a while now."

"For how long?" she asked.

"Three weeks."

"That's not very long," Mimi cautioned.

"What the hell do you know about it?" Jessica exploded. In the weeks since Mimi had answered Jessica's first call, true to her prediction, Jessica had become her client-cum-problem. She'd play nice until Mimi, or rather Jessica's mom, said something she didn't like—which included pretty much everything—and hang up, only to call the next week.

"Nothing. Not a thing." She caught Joe's eye. He was regarding her a little oddly, but then it was an odd profession.

"Let me ask you something. Are you seeing the woman I told you about? Have you talked to her about this, too?"

Mimi—and Jess's mom—had been urging the girl to look for a good counselor. One who, they hoped, did not see any contraindication in letting Jessica have the occasional air-clearing talk with her mom's spirit.

"Yeah," came the sullen reply. "She's damn expensive! She says I got issues."

"Really?" Mimi tried to sound surprised. "Well, I'm glad you're willing to pay. Believe me, it's money well spent," Mimi said, anticipating a blissfully Jessica-less existence.

"Yeah, great, but I didn't call to talk about my . . . about *her*. I want you to ask Mom what she thinks about me and Neil moving in together. I think he's going to ask me soon, and while I really don't care what Mom thinks, I figured I ought to give her a chance to bitch, seeing as how she enjoys it so much. She must really miss that. Hold on."

Somewhere in the background Mimi heard a young man's voice calling, "Where are you, Jessie? You said you'd be right back and I'm lonely and the DVD is stuck again. Can you fix it?"

Mimi heard the distinctive sound of a hand covering a mouthpiece and, through it, Jessica replying in a voice Mimi had never heard her use before, "I'll be right there, Neilly!

"I gotta go," Jessica whispered into the phone. "Find out from Mom what she thinks about Neil."

"Okay."

"I'll call later." Jessica hung up.

"I can't wait," Mimi muttered, closing her cell. "Sorry," she said. "I forgot I was, ah, supposed to work tonight. I didn't think I'd be at the party long, so I signed up for the graveyard shift." She grinned at her own wit. He didn't. "Get it? Graveyard shift?"

"Maybe I should go."

"No," she said hastily. "Most calls don't start coming in until after two. You know. People can't sleep. They get themselves all twisted up with regret and recriminations. . . ." She shrugged in a "who can tell why people do what they do?" gesture.

He looked downright uneasy.

"Don't worry. I won't ask your dead aunt Nettie what you were like as a little boy."

"I don't have an aunt Nettie."

"It was a joke." Crap. He was definitely uneasy with her

profession. "How about something to drink? I have pop, water, beer . . ."

"Thanks. I could use a beer."

She started toward the kitchen.

"That's quite a television," he said as she entered the tiny kitchen. "You must like television. A lot."

"The picture's incredible. You have to see it to appreciate it. The control's on the dining room table. Try it out," she called as she opened the small refrigerator. She ducked down, peering over the stacked Tupperware containers for the last couple of bottles of Pete's Wicked Ale she'd stashed and wondered whether animal crackers went with beer.

Joe liked to think of himself as nonjudgmental. Spending two decades in international business working with cultural differences and personality types from across the spectrum, he'd had to be. But as he walked toward the oak table in Mimi's apartment, he wasn't so sure.

No two ways about it, Mimi's profession threw him off balance, and Mary Werner's comments about her sister's obvious—and apparently very recent—success at that job, especially in light of how Mimi didn't receive any money from her mother, kept picking away at his comfort level. Sure, he'd ignored the uneasiness when he'd offered to take Mimi home. He'd ignored it when he'd leaned down to kiss Mimi good night. And he'd ignored it when their kisses exploded into passion. But as soon as that phone had started playing, his misgivings had come rushing back.

The stack of couture dresses with their outrageous price tags, and boxes of shoes and other expensive accessories of similar quality, did nothing to diminish those misgivings. Neither did that incredible pearl and diamond necklace. None of it jibed with the bargain basement decor, unless she'd recently come into a windfall. Or somewhere earned a bonus. Maybe she'd channeled Bill Gates's grandpa. Maybe she had—what would she call it?—a live one on the hook.

He hated to entertain any such suspicions about her, but he was a realist, and everything he saw and had heard about her pointed to this as being the most reasonable explanation for what he saw. Except how much reason could enter into an explanation when you were talking about a mystic or ghost whisperer or psychic or whatever she was? Added to which, someone like her was completely out of his sphere of experience. He was floundering in his attempts to figure her out. Fraud? Or odd? Was there another choice?

"Having trouble?" she called from the kitchen.

"What?"

"With the television. Use the POWER button, not the ON button. The ON just toggles from cable to antenna. I'll be there in a jiff."

The remote. Oh, yeah. He bent over the dining room table but didn't see it, so he started moving some of the piles of papers and found it lying— He stared.

The remote was lying on top of a picture of Prescott holding a small moth-eaten-looking dog. Which made no sense. Prescott was horribly allergic to dogs along with ninety percent of everything else in the world.

He picked up the photograph and his gaze fell on the picture beneath it. It was another one of Prescott, in different clothing but with the same dog. He picked this up, too, and beneath it found another picture of his kid.

What the hell was going on here?

Mimi Olson had mocked Prescott's "lodge" and called Prescott pathetic. She'd pointed out his lack of friends and his isolation. She'd also pointed out how rich he was. And Prescott was infatuated with Mimi.

Who could be more easily taken advantage of than Prescott? And who would be a better candidate for the "live one" he'd already suspected was hanging from Mimi's hook? If there was a hook. Please, let there not be a hook.

Maybe there was another explanation for why Mimi had printed out a dozen pictures of a misanthropic millionaire who had a crush on her. He just couldn't think of any. He raked his hair back with one hand. He realized he was making a rush to judgment but . . . but Prescott was so damn naive in so many ways.

"Still can't figure out the remote?" Mimi backed into the room carrying a tray containing a couple bottles of beer, a box of Ritz crackers, and a plastic tub of something in a weird shade of orange with purple ripples running through it.

"Yup. That's right," she chirruped, noting the direction of his gaze. "Port wine cheddar spread."

He had no idea what that was. "Oh."

She set the tray on the table and handed him a bottle of Pete's Wicked Ale. She lifted her own. "Here's to"—she puzzled a second before her face cleared—"letting the good times roll."

When he didn't lift his beer bottle, she reached over and clinked the bottom of hers against his, then raised it to her lips.

"Whatcha got there?" Mimi asked, nodding at the papers in his hand.

He held them out and said in very measured, very careful tones, "Pictures of Prescott. What are you doing with them?"

She lowered her bottle and tilted her head to look sideways at the papers in his hand. Color washed up her throat and tinted her cheeks. "Oh. Those. Prescott sent them."

"Why?"

"I asked him to." Her gaze flitted away from meeting his. "I mean, I didn't ask him to send so many, but—"

"Why?" Years of self-control stood him in good stead. His voice sounded reasonable, calm, not much more than curious, if a little insistent.

"Why?" she echoed. She shrugged. "Because he wanted to. I think he's lonely. I printed them off the e-mails he sent. Some of them are sorta cute. I think he uses a self-timer to get into the shot."

She leaned over the table and spread out the remaining

pictures across the surface, selecting one and holding it up. "See? Kinda cute, right? Not the dog, of course. The dog is not cute. The way Prescott is holding the dog is cute. You can see he's trying not to look sappy about the mangy mutt, but he is. Your son, I'm afraid, is an easy mark."

Easy mark? "*Why* does Prescott want to send you pictures of himself?"

That got her full attention. She was standing close, bent over the table, and now she turned her head slowly. He could see every tiny line at the corners of her eyes, the way the curls in her hair spiraled, the skin across her breastbone where the sun had permanently stained it tan.

He could also see the moment she realized the implications of his questions. The muscles in her neck tensed. "Why do you think?"

He ignored the question, gesturing toward the dresses lying across the back of the chair and the boxes on the seat cushion. "Looks like you recently came into some money." He tried to sound nonchalant. He failed and he knew it. "You win the lottery or something? Win big at the casinos?"

"I don't gamble." Her voice was icy. "Why don't you put into words what you're thinking, Joe?"

"You know what I'm thinking."

She waited a long minute, her eyes never leaving his, before answering. "I found that dog before I left Fowl Lake this summer. I was going to drive it to a shelter, but Prescott showed up and said he'd take it. I asked him to send me a picture of it because"—for the first time, she looked sheepish—"because I didn't know if he'd take good care of the dog."

Joe looked at the pictures in his hand. Now that she'd drawn his attention to it, he realized that every single picture showed not only Prescott but the little mongrel. The tightness in his chest loosened incrementally. "Why would Prescott offer to take a dog? He's allergic to dogs."

She'd stepped back, her easy manner notably absent. "I don't know. He's *your* son. Why don't you ask him?" She picked up her cell phone and shoved it against his chest. "Do you need his number?"

If he was just sending her occasional pictures, why would she have Prescott's unlisted number? "You know his cell number?"

"You *don't*?" she countered.

He was floundering. He couldn't find his objectivity. He was used to forming quick but astute opinions. Not here. He didn't trust his own judgment. He was acting like a boor, a fool, a foolish boor. She wouldn't tell him to call Prescott if she had anything to hide. And who knew why Prescott kept the dog? Probably to impress her. After all, he seemed to think of her as a sort—

She'd put the bottle back down next to one of Prescott's pictures, and his gaze followed the motion. This picture had been taken in the lodge. In the background, on the fireplace mantle, Joe could clearly see a framed picture of Karen and Prescott. His unwilling gaze snapped to the stack of expensive clothing. She still hadn't told him how she was able to afford the expensive dresses and jewelry. He wanted to shut up but he wanted to know even more. *Had* to know.

"Did you tell Prescott you could get in touch with his mother's spirit? Are you pretending to receive messages for him from her?"

She'd been mopping up the sweat ring left by the beer bottle on Prescott's picture, but that stopped her. She straightened.

"I think you should go now." Though her expression was cool, her voice quiet, her eyes were filled with hurt.

"I have a right to know. I'm his father. He's vulnerable and I don't want him to be hurt."

"No, you don't have the right to know," she said. "And you're asking because you don't want him to be bilked by a fraud because that would make him look gullible, and in your book, that's worse than being hurt."

"That's not true," he said stiffly.

"Isn't it? Maybe *I* shouldn't be so quick to judge. But let me set your mind to rest. No. As far as I know, Prescott doesn't have any idea what I do or who I am. And that makes him leagues ahead of his father in what he does know."

"You can't be angry because I asked you if you offered your services to my son," Joe said, stung. She wasn't being rational.

"Yes, I can." Her lips were stiff, her skin ruddy. "You accused me of exploiting Prescott's love for his dead mother for cash. I didn't. I don't. Now, good night. Good-bye."

He didn't deny it, because she was right—that's exactly what he'd done. There was nothing left for him to do here now but leave. Because he still wasn't sure what to believe. He didn't know if she was a sincere wack-job who really believed she spoke to ghosts or a con artist. He wanted to believe her but he didn't.

"I'm sorry," he finally said.

"Bye."

She didn't see him to the door.

The tears caught Mimi off guard. For the love of God, she was weeping over a guy she barely knew when she hadn't shed tears for guys she'd dated for weeks. Certainly not the hot-air balloonist who'd donated half the genetic material to the baby who'd never be born . . . That must be it. This must be some sort of estrogen echo left over from her pregnancy, because this was not her usual behavior.

It didn't matter. She wept like a sixteen-year-old girl who got dumped the day before prom. She was still crying when someone knocked at the door five minutes later. She bounded to her feet, dashing the tears from her face, envisioning Joe Tierney kneeling outside, begging for her forgiveness and realized she was heading into emotional territory she'd never visited before. It didn't stop her from jerking open the door.

Jennifer Beesing stood outside in her housecoat, fluffy slippers on her feet, a china plate filled with pecan patties clutched between her hands. Pecan patties, Mimi knew, took an hour to make. Which meant Jennifer must have started them the minute she spied Mimi in the hall with Joe. It was as if Joe's leaving had been predestined.

Jennifer held out the plate, her doleful expression welcoming Mimi into the fold of those whose romances are doomed to fail.

"I made pecan patties," she said.

Chapter Twenty-two

.

Prescott popped open the Prius's hatchback and pulled the Sam's Club carton toward him, tallying the number of Kleenex boxes he'd bought. Twenty. Should be enough for the week. The shots from the allergist were finally beginning to show effects. Of course, the same allergist had also advised Prescott not to share quarters with any fur-bearing creature. As far as Prescott was concerned, that wasn't an option.

He'd told Mrs. Olson he would take Bill (he'd picked the name from *The Lord of the Rings*, hoping for the same sort of loyalty Sam's pony had shown him on the road to Mordor), and he wasn't going back on his promise. Without Bill, Prescott didn't have any excuse to contact Mimi Olson, to send her pictures, to write her notes about Bill's care and progress. His diligence had been rewarded. Every now and then she had found time amongst her many obligations to write back. Last week, she'd written four full paragraphs.

Prescott jerked the carton toward him. Besides Kleenex, it held groceries and a dozen fully digestible dog chews in various sizes and shapes. He swung the heavy carton to his shoulder and grappled one-handed to close the hatchback.

He could tell he was losing weight, maybe even getting some muscles. He'd discovered that dog ownership entailed long daily walks, because a dog filled with pent-up energy is a destructive dog. Several chairs and tables had fallen victim to this object lesson before Prescott had tumbled to it.

He didn't mind. Since the weather had turned cold and snow covered the ground, killing off many of the allergens afflicting him, he actually looked forward to their walks. In fact, as he'd anticipated, dog cohabitation (he decided he was morally opposed to the concept of owning another living being) had totally enriched his life. He liked being greeted whenever he entered a room, even a bathroom. He got a contact high from the mindless rapture a dog could find in an empty plastic water bottle. The weight of a dog's warm body draped over his legs like a bean bag filled him with contentment. He enjoyed taking care of a dog, the feeling that someone depended on him not only for the basic necessities, but to fulfill a deep inner need to be part of a pack. He enjoyed it so much he'd decided to add to his enjoyment.

At the door, he set the dog food down and searched in his coat pockets for the keys. The workmen he'd hired to put in an in-ground pool had disabled the security system. He didn't expect to use it much himself, but during the first week he and Bill had cohabited, many times when they went on their little walks, Bill went for swims and afterward the little guy stank of fish. Prescott did not like the fragrance, but Bill loved to swim, ergo the pool.

With the unexpectedly early arrival of winter, the crew had been forced to quit and had neglected to reconnect the system. Prescott didn't care; he didn't need it anymore. On cue, frantic barks and yaps from inside announced that his arrival had been noted.

"Just a minute! I'm coming!" he called, fumbling the keys. He grinned at the howl of canine protest in answer to what must have seemed like a cruel tease. As soon as he dumped this stuff in the kitchen, they'd go for a walk. They'd go east, following the footpath through the woods to the Chez Ducky compound, deserted now, as quaint and seedy and slumberous as the backmost shelf in a secondhand bookstore.

He pushed the door open. Three dogs blasted past him into the yard, barking and jumping and tumbling over one another. Three. He'd tripled his enjoyment of his new life as a rural iconoclast.

"Okay, okay! Just let me get this stuff inside." He picked up the carton.

They wiggled, bounded, darted, and, realizing he had something that smelled really good in the cardboard carton, created a log jam at the entrance in their haste to be first back inside. His family was growing.

Chapter Twenty-three

On the flat-paneled plasma screen hanging on the hotel's beige wall, Joan Wilder slipped over the muddy edge of a precipice and careened down the Peruvian rain forest's soggy hillside. She plummeted into a mosquito-infested pool and disappeared beneath its surface.

Joe, sitting in the middle of the hotel's king-sized bed, plumped the pillow behind his back and turned up the volume. As a veteran of thousands of "Free HBO!" hours in hundreds of extended-stay hotel suites, he'd seen *Romancing the Stone* at least five times. But as he'd been surfing through the channels he'd caught sight of the familiar mudslide scene (which invariably made his skin crawl) and put down the remote. Because something about the scene reminded him of something . . . or someone.

As soon as Joan erupted out of the stagnant pool of water, her hair streaming with muck, he realized who: Mimi Olson.

Except Joan Wilder looked confused, and then when Jack landed in her crotch, shocked, and finally surprised into laughter.

Mimi had looked . . . like Mimi. Comfortable in mud. Unshockable. And there'd be no need to *surprise* Mimi into laughter, because she'd already be laughing. Joan was vague, with an air of naïveté. Mimi was matter-of-fact, and if she was naive about anything, he'd have a hard time figuring out what that could be. Maybe that's why the whole ghost-talking thing seemed so out of place. . . .

Once again, it occurred to Joe that he spent too much time analyzing Mimi Olson. It had been almost a week since the Werners' anniversary party and he still kept seeing the expression on her face when she realized he was all but accusing her of conning Prescott. Of course, if she *was* conning Prescott, what was she going to say, "Gee whiz, busted. My bad. Want more crackers?"

No, she would react exactly like she had reacted, with insulted dignity and cold indignation. Which is also exactly how she'd react if she was innocent.

But which one was she?

There was one way he could find out. He could call Prescott and check up on her story. It was not a new idea. He'd toyed with it ever since leaving her apartment, but something held him back. As irrational as he knew it to be, he suspected he felt some misplaced sense of owing her his confidence because *he'd hurt her feelings.* This was such dopey reasoning that he wondered whether he was having some sort of midlife crisis. But in that case he'd be lusting after a cheerleader, not a slightly frumpy middle-aged Petra Pan. Not that he was exactly *lusting* after her. Not exactly. She simply . . . interested him as a type he'd rarely, if ever, encountered.

So, as the days passed, nondopey reasoning reasserted itself. If he had misjudged her, it was certainly understandable given the circumstances. And if it was only himself he was concerned was being taken for a ride, hell, he'd still be in the damn car. She was that appealing. But it wasn't; it was Prescott, and he'd be damned if he'd apologize for being concerned for his son's welfare. When you came right down to it, he didn't owe Mimi anything; he did owe Prescott.

In fact, he *still* owed it to Prescott to find out exactly what sort of relationship he and Mimi had. Sure, part of his desire to discover whether she'd told him the truth or a lie had a personal basis, but he was pretty damn sure it wasn't the greater part. He'd probably already been negligent by letting the questions he had about Mimi stew as long as they had.

He clicked the MUTE button on the remote and reached for his cell phone, scrolling to Prescott's number. He hit the SEND button and waited. On the television, Jane Wilder arrived at a cantina wrapped in a Mexican shawl and wowed Jack. Mimi wouldn't have bothered with the shawl and still would have wowed Jack. It was all a matter of attitude. And any woman who could carry off a starfish-bedecked terry beach robe could carry off damn near anything.

"Hello?" Prescott's voice answered on the fifth ring. He sounded guarded.

"Hello, Prescott. This is J— This is your dad."

A pause. "Yes?"

"I'll be leaving Minneapolis in a few days and I thought I'd, ah, give you a call before I took off."

Prescott didn't reply.

"I'm heading for Hong Kong."

"Oh," Prescott said. Then, "Why are you telling me that?"

"Why?"

"You've, ah, never told me your itinerary before. Why now?"

"I don't know. I thought you might be interested. They love Pi—*table tennis* in China. Do they have any, like, special paddles over there you'd like me to get you?"

Prescott sighed. "I'm not a little kid, Joe. You don't have to bring me presents from your trips abroad."

"I know. But when you were a kid, I never seemed to get a decent present for you, and now, I don't know . . ." Why did he have to explain something as simple as wanting to pick up a gift for his own son to his own son? "I guess I thought I might finally get you something you'd actually like. Instead of something stupid."

Another pause. "I thought you were mocking me with the

pet rock. Until I found out all the kids at public school had them. I'm sorry I threw it through the window."

"Forget it. It was stupid."

"No. You made an effort."

Wow. Prescott had never expressed any appreciation for Joe's intentions before, however far they fell from the mark. This was going better than he'd expected.

"It must have been like buying the kibble brand your vet recommends for your dog only to discover he hates it."

Huh? Was this empathy? Oh, that's right, Prescott had a dog. The dog Mimi had given him. A perfect opening. "That's right. I ran into Mimi Olson at a function I was attending here in Minneapolis last week. She said you were taking care of a dog."

This time the short silence was much more attentive. "You saw Mignonette Olson at some function? What function?"

"A party for some business associates."

"Mignonette Olson works for a company your company is interested in?" Prescott sounded incredulous.

"No. She's related to the owner of the business my company wants to buy."

"She is?" Prescott asked. "Huh. I didn't think the Olsons were that well off. I mean, they don't seem to have much . . . Oh. Wait. That *is* cool! You mean they choose to stay in those huts? On purpose? Like domicile vegans or something? That is—"

"No," Joe broke in before Prescott could wax even more poetic. "The Olsons are her father's family. She's related to this guy I'm working with through her mother's side."

"But she's not an engineer or a tax lawyer or an accountant or does anything like you?" Prescott didn't wait for an answer. He snorted. "Of course not."

"Nope," Joe confirmed. "Do you know what she does do? For a living?"

"No. But I wouldn't be surprised if she was a nurse or a teacher. Maybe a kindergarten teacher. Why?"

Joe almost broke out laughing. Luckily, he didn't. "You don't happen to have her phone number, do you? Or know of any way I might reach her?"

"Why?" Prescott asked again. His voice had grown distinctly chilly. He was too old for this Oedipal crap. Even if his interest in Mimi had been a romantic one, he wouldn't act on it. She was too far off in left field. Hell, if she really thought she talked to spooks, she might not even be playing in the same ballpark.

"Look, Pres," Joe said tiredly. "I'm not interested in dating Mimi Olson. She lent me twenty bucks for a taxi. You know how I hate carrying cash. I'd like to return it to her."

"Oh." He bought it. "Well, I don't have her number," he said; then, his voice sharpening a little, "Why didn't you just call this relative of hers?"

"Oh!" Joe said, not having to feign his pleasure. Mimi hadn't been lying. "That's a great idea. Why didn't I think of that? Thanks, Prescott."

"Sure," Prescott said doubtfully.

"So, I'll see if I can find you the latest thing in Ping-Pong paddles, okay?"

"It's called *table tennis*," Prescott said and hung up.

For a few seconds, he and Prescott had had something like a conversation going there. Maybe there was hope here after all. He set down the phone, feeling pleased. Prescott and he had been talking more or less amiably; his son was not being readied for a severe plucking; Mimi had been telling the truth. Wherever she'd gotten the wherewithal to purchase that necklace—or whatever admirer had given it to her—Prescott hadn't been involved. Joe supposed that meant he owed Mimi an apology.

Wait. No, he didn't. He'd done what any self-respecting father does who thinks he sees his son being ripped off; he'd spoken up. It would have been easier, not to mention a lot more satisfying, to have kept his mouth shut and forgotten his suspicions and let nature run its course that night. God knows, he'd wanted to. But he hadn't and now he was glad he hadn't.

He just wished he'd gone about the thing with a bit more subtlety and a lot more composure. It was unlike him to be precipitous and accusatory.

And he had been accusatory.

Fraud or not, he owed her an apology, if not for his suspicions, then for his manner. He considered calling her but decided against it. He still didn't know what to make of her. Just because she hadn't ripped off Prescott didn't mean she hadn't ripped off others. In fact, that's what she did. For a living. *Come on, Joe,* he told himself, *she works as a* medium *on a* spiritualist hotline. Which was pretty much the textbook definition of a scam.

No. He'd acted impulsively enough where Mimi Olson was concerned. He'd send her some flowers, get rid of his guilt, and that would be the end of it.

Now, if he could just stop wishing it wouldn't be.

Chapter Twenty-four

December

"So, if a minority of the heirs wanted to keep the land, they'd still have to buy out those who wanted to sell?" Mimi spoke into the little wand dangling in front of her mouth. Ozzie had lately sprung for new headsets.

"That's the sum of it, Mignonette. And vice versa. But first, the property would have to be assessed," the lawyer, Bud Butter, answered. "Could you excuse me for a minute?"

As she wasn't paying him for his minutes—he was answering her questions as a favor to his best client, Tom Werner—she couldn't very well say no. "Sure."

Mimi shuffled through the papers on her desk while she waited, hunting for the piece of paper where she'd doodled the information Vida had given her. Vida, still trying to make amends for the "pathetic" comment, was relaying to Mimi as much intelligence about Debbie's activities as she could ferret out. Which would have been great if Mimi had known what to do with this information but instead only served to forcibly remind Mimi why she didn't like information: it made you crazy. It was like watching an avalanche charging down the mountainside. There was nothing she could do to stop it, but now, thanks to Vida, she would spend her last minutes staring over her shoulder in horror rather than in blissful ignorance. She thought maybe Vida and her information were giving her an ulcer.

Yet, she couldn't bring herself to tell Vida not to bother reporting on Debbie's nefarious actions. So, here she was on the phone with Tom's lawyer, asking questions as if she was formulating a plan. She wasn't. Not really. She was simply . . . figuring out what someone else could do if they wanted to.

A few days ago, Vida had called up to tell her that Debbie was petitioning Oxlip County to rezone the land around Fowl Lake so she could sell it to a townhouse developer and that she and Bill had managed to talk Naomi into "providing for the little Olsons' academic future" by voting to sell the Chez. From a couple text messages Birgie had sent on the cell phone—and why would Birgie suddenly be sending her text messages, for God's sake?—Mimi knew Johanna was crumbling under the weight of her heirs' expectations—or rather, their lack of them—too.

From what Bud Butter had said, Mimi realized it didn't matter. They either all said yes to keeping Chez Ducky, or the place went up for sale. Unless someone or some ones could buy out the share of the person who wanted to sell.

"Sorry to keep you waiting." Bud had returned. "Where was I?"

"How you determine the value of the property."

"Oh, yes. Generally the executor hires an independent assessor. In this case, who is acting as executor?"

"Birgie," Mimi said. This was a point in favor of those who'd just as soon stall this whole selling process. Birgie wouldn't hire anyone without tons of pushing and prodding. However, something told Mimi that as soon as Debbie recognized this obstacle, she'd hire an assessor herself and Birgie wouldn't kick about it.

"Those who want to sell the land can't make those who don't want to do so, can they? For example, if I didn't want to sell the land, I would have first shot at buying out those who do want to sell it, by paying them whatever their share of the fair market value would be as determined by the assessor?"

"Well, there are always variables, but in general, yes."

As she'd thought. "Thanks, Bud."

"No problem. If I can answer any more questions, let me know. Tell Tom I said hi and that I expect him to give me a chance to beat him at racquetball soon."

"I sure will, Bud. Thanks again." She clicked off and slumped back in her chair. She had no idea what the Chez Ducky property would be valued at—had Debbie said something about three million?—but she knew it would be much more than she could come up with on her own.

Her gaze drifted to her bulletin board, where she'd tacked up the latest digital photo from Prescott. She did *not* think about Joe Tierney.

She was very proud of this. She'd been angry at Joe Tierney. Angry and hurt and, worse, frightened by the hollow feeling she'd discovered sometime in the days after he'd left. She wasn't angry anymore. Or hurt. Why, she had even laughed about Joe's paternal posturing while Jennifer Beesing was teaching her how to make pecan patties last weekend.

True, she might have spared a few dark thoughts for him when Prescott had sent a note soon after Solange's anniversary party. He'd said his father had mentioned in a phone call that he'd run into Mimi Olson in the city and wondered if Prescott knew her phone number or where she worked so he could get in touch with her again. Bullshit. Joe had been trying to scope out whether or not Prescott was calling her eight hundred number and to find out whether she'd been telling the truth or lying about her relationship with his son. What a good daddy.

But he *was* being a good daddy. He was doing what he could to see that his son wasn't—what had been his charming term for what she did?—*exploited*. Mimi hadn't replied to Prescott's e-mail and Prescott had not mentioned Joe since. Good. Because without someone bringing up Joe, there really was no reason to think about him.

Which she wasn't.

She fixed her attention firmly on the picture Prescott had sent. It showed three blurry canine images caught mid-dash on the beach at Chez Ducky. Prescott must have been standing on the frozen lake when he took the picture. It wasn't the dogs that held Mimi's eye; it was Chez Ducky. The beach was empty, the swimming raft tipped against the side of Cottage Six, the old flagpole simply a rusting pole surrounded by a crumbling concrete skirt.

She'd always thought of Chez Ducky as hibernating in the winter, patiently waiting for the Olsons to return. But in this picture Chez Ducky didn't appear to be sleeping; it seemed to be dying. Unless someone intervened.

Mimi steepled her fingers and tapped her chin with the tips of her index fingers, wondering why someone wasn't intervening. Someone like Birgie or Johanna. Someone commanding and wise should don the mantle of familial authority and go fight for Chez Ducky. Which meant not Birgie or Johanna. Certainly not Mimi.

There was another possibility. It was a long shot, but if Mimi could convince Solange that Chez Ducky presented a unique and possibly lucrative investment opportunity, her mother might lend her the money to buy out the others. Long shot? It would have to be a hole in one. But it was fast getting to the point where any shot was worth taking.

Mimi stood up and peered over the top of the cubicle. Brooke, the big blond soccer mom–cum–medium who occupied the cubicle next to Mimi's, was sitting on the edge of her desk, chatting with Ozzie. She saw Mimi and picked up two bottles of nail polish from the lineup on top of her file cabinet. "Carnation or Miami Sunrise? Ozzie says Carnation."

"Never doubt Ozzie's taste," Mimi advised. Ozzie gave

Brooke a superior smile. "I need to be gone a couple hours after lunch. Can I go? I'll take the phones Friday night."

"Lately, you always take the phones Friday nights. And most Saturdays," Ozzie said. "You need to get a life, Mimi. Seriously."

"I have a life."

"Ah-huh." Ozzie and Brooke compressed their lips in unison and exchanged telling looks. "How long have you been working here? Three years? Four?"

"Five."

"Right. And in all that time you've never had a serious boyfriend."

"So what?"

"You need a life."

"Life happens without boyfriends, Oz."

"Not so you'd notice," muttered Brooke, a three-time divorcée.

Mimi was not going to argue about this with Oz and Brooke, whom no one thought of as successful relationship experts. Except they did have them. Well, she did, too. Just not in the same way.

"Do you have the sort of great girlfriends you go on vacations with?" Oz asked, and then answered the question himself. "No."

"You don't even have a pet," Brooke said accusingly. "I don't think you even have a plant."

"Aha!" Mimi trilled, triumphant, and wheeled around to point at the century plant clinging tenaciously to life in its pot at the window. "I do so. And what is it with people thinking I need to have things to take care of in order to be happy? Methinks that Brooke and Oz," *and Vida,* she silently added, "doth protest too much."

They both gave her pitying looks.

She thought of voicing another protest but decided to forget it. "Can you guys handle it here for a while?"

"Sure. It's dead anyway." Brooke laughed uproariously at

her own wit. Ozzie raised his eyes heavenward. A light on Mimi's phone console came on. She tilted her head to read the LCD panel.

"Hold on. Gotta take this." She adjusted her headset and punched the line-in button. "Hi, Jessica. This is Miss Em."

Brooke appeared at the entrance to her cubicle, grinning with malicious delight. Behind her hovered Ozzie, bouncing up and down on his toes to see around his much taller and wider employee.

"I have to know if Mom approves," Jessica said without preamble.

"Of the boyfriend moving in?" Mimi waved Brooke and Ozzie away, and with one last roll of her eyes, Brooke went back to her cubicle and Ozzie returned to his office.

"Yes. Ask her."

"What if she says no?"

Jessica met this posit with silence.

"Have you talked to your counselor about this?"

"Duh. Yes," Jessica said and then added primly, "I don't feel comfortable discussing my therapy sessions with you."

Good. "Okay. Let me see if I can make contact." Mimi sat down in her chair and closed her eyes and concentrated. For once, Jessica didn't interrupt her. After a couple minutes she opened her eyes. "Your mom's not answering."

"You mean she's *gone*?"

"How can she be 'gone,' Jess? She's already 'gone,'" Mimi said reasonably. "I mean she's not making contact. I don't sense her."

"Well, where is she?"

"I don't know. They don't wear GPSs. It's heaven, not house arrest."

"But why isn't she answering?" Jessica asked, sounding pissy and, beneath it, worried.

"Let me try again," Mimi muttered.

It was Jessica's worry that had gill-hooked Mimi into taking the young woman on as a semipermanent client. Despite what she said, Jessica sincerely loved her mother. A lot of her anger seemed to be the result not so much of Jessica's mother's controlling her, but of the fact that she wasn't anymore. Jessica missed her mother and she was angry her mother wasn't interfering in her life anymore. She was like a fishing bobber suddenly cut loose from the line, unconnected and set adrift.

"Why isn't she answering?" Jessica demanded again.

"I don't know. Maybe she's thinking. Maybe she's busy. Maybe she just doesn't have anything to say." *Like my Dad.* The thought slipped in and out so quickly, she barely recognized it, certainly didn't pay any attention to it, because she had no idea whether or not her father was Beyond the Veil.

"Not my mom," Jessica scoffed.

"Death is a transforming experience, Jess."

"But . . . what about Neil? Should I let him move in?"

Oh, noooo. This was one trap she was not going to fall into. When someone's dead relative or friend or ancestor gave them advice, it was one thing, but she wasn't playing at being anyone's mother. Her one shot at messing with little people's heads was gone.

The thought brought an unfamiliar throb with it. She'd passed that opportunity up. How many others had she missed? Opportunities? When had mother duty become an opportunity?

March, closing in on a year ago.

She wished these thoughts would leave her alone. She'd expected to be back to her old fare-thee-well state months ago, not to still be pestered by thoughts of what might have been (or who, she thought with an inner smile at the Baby Not) and questions about her father and where he was (or wasn't). But she was.

"You there?" Jess prodded. "What should I do about Neil?"

Ditch him, Mimi almost said. From the many times he'd been in the background while Jess whispered her questions to her mother to Mimi, she'd gotten the image of a whiny, needy, passive-aggressive loser. Jess definitely did not need that sort of additional baggage weighing her down.

"Miss Em?"

Almost said. She didn't want that sort of responsibility hanging over her head. What if Neil really was the love of Jess's life? What right did Mimi have to interfere? It was one thing to relay advice from the dead, another to give it yourself.

"How should I know?" she finally murmured, oddly disappointed in herself.

"Mom'll never approve," Jessica said, suddenly doleful. "She never liked redheaded guys."

"There is no hair color in heaven, Jess."

Abruptly, Jess laughed. It gave Mimi hope for the girl that occasionally she could provoke an honest guffaw from her. Jess was coming around, no two ways about it. The counseling was working. Mimi wasn't going to mess with that. At times, Jess was even sort of likable.

"You do *not* know that," Jess said. "You always say you have no idea what heaven is like and that none of the deceased even tries to describe it."

"True, but I'm hopeful."

There was a second's pause, and when Jess spoke her voice had taken on a hint of wistfulness. "Yeah. Me, too."

Jessica hung up and Mimi jerked the headset off. She rescued her winter coat from the hook on the outside of her cubicle, shoving it on. "I'm going!" she called.

"Just a second. Hold on there, scout," Brooke said, appearing in the door of her cubicle, carnation-colored fingernails splayed wide and held in front of her. "You mean you hung around just for the joy of talking to *Jessica*? Jessica the Snide? Jessica of the Massive Mother Complex?"

"Yeah," Mimi said, buttoning her coat. "She calls every Monday at noon."

"And you're feeling some pressing need to make sure you're here for her?"

Brooke was staring at her oddly. "Well, would you rather take her calls?"

"No, no, no," Brooke shook her head. "I'll leave that pleasure to you. It's just, you know, you don't like getting involved with needy types, and I think we both can agree Jessica falls into that category."

"What can I say? I'm a people person. And here you and Oz were worried I didn't have anything to take care of so I could be as blissed out with obligations as you two. Well, there you go. I have Jess to take care of. Is this a happy face or what?" She framed her grimacing face with the thumbs and fingers of both hands.

"Yeah, yeah," Brooke snickered. "Don't you have somewhere you were going?"

"Yup," Mimi agreed, picking up her bag and swinging it over her shoulder. "Ciao."

It was only when she was moving down the staircase to the first-floor lobby that she realized that despite her mockery, she had in fact been telling Brooke the truth.

And it didn't scare her.

Chapter Twenty-five

"You know, my initial impulse is to use your request as leverage." Solange finished pouring the cream into her coffee mug and regarded Mimi across the solarium's wrought-iron table. Overhead, a dusting of snow had collected along the roof's glass panes, but inside palms and orchids scented the air.

"You go to work for one of Tom's companies; I buy the other heirs' shares of this swampland," Solange elaborated as though worried Mimi might not be familiar with the concept. "That sort of thing."

"There is a certain historical precedent," Mimi acknowledged, picking her way carefully. She wanted Solange's help badly, more than she could recall wanting anything from her mother in a long time. It made her nervous, as if she were holding the door open and ushering in disappointment. If you didn't ask things, expect things, then you might be able to keep that door locked.

Solange picked up the box of vanilla wafers from the table and shook it invitingly.

Mimi declined. "No, thanks."

Her mother dug out a fistful of wafers and pushed the box away. Solange might be all about appearances when appearances counted, but in the privacy of her home, she was not nearly as buttoned-down as her public persona suggested.

After all, she had once been married to John "Summer of Love" Olson.

Right now, swimming in an oversized pale blue sweater and loose-fitting corduroy slacks, most of her lipstick left on her coffee mug, she looked like a slightly frowsy suburban housewife. Her demeanor, however, was one hundred percent regal. Though how a plump woman in a baby blue sweater working her way through a handful of vanilla wafers still managed to exude a royal air was a mystery even to her daughter.

"Well, I'm not going to," she said. "Are you surprised?"

"Not really," Mimi answered truthfully. She'd never *really* expected her mom to rescue Chez Ducky.

"Do you want to know why?"

"Not really," Mimi repeated. She already knew why. Solange was fundamentally opposed to all things Olson.

"I consider your proposal ill considered and poorly thought out," Solange said anyway. "You arrive with some nebulous plan for me to buy a piece of property without knowing exactly who the heirs who want to get rid of it are, how many there are, and what price they are asking."

"I was sounding you out," Mimi said, trying to control the flutter of eagerness in her voice. "Why should I go through the trouble of pinning things down without first finding out if you'd even consider it? Should I come up with the particulars for you?"

Solange munched thoughtfully on another wafer. "No," she finally said. "I don't think so."

The bottom dropped out of Mimi's stomach. That was it, then. There was nothing more to be done. Nothing more to be said. "Oh."

"Let me explain myself," Solange said.

"Not necessary." Mimi started to push back from the table.

"But I want to," Solange protested. "In the last twenty years you have never asked me for any money or financial help of any sort. I know why. You don't want me to have any control over you or feel any sense of obligation, even a financial one. I appreciate that. Very wise of you, truth be told. I would take merciless advantage of it if you let me do things for you."

Mimi had to hand it to Solange; she never minced words.

"So, for you to show up on short notice and ask me for this kind of financial backing can only be an act of desperation. Which is very interesting, especially coming from you. Interesting enough"—Solange paused, not above extending a dramatic moment—"that it gives me hope for you. Desperation is a powerful motivator."

Mimi pulled herself together. Chez Ducky was a place, for God's sake. Third-rate lakeshore on a fourth-rate lake. Sure, it would be nice to have it. But them's the breaks. If people could disappear from your life, why the hell not places? She wasn't going to make a mountain out of the Chez Ducky molehill, and she wasn't going to let her mother think this was something it wasn't.

"For the love of God, Mom. I'm not experiencing an epiphany, a metamorphosis, or a come-to-Jesus moment. I'm just trying to continue enjoying free-rent summers at a lake."

"I don't believe it," Solange said calmly.

Damn it.

"I believe you are acting because you care profoundly about Chez Ducky. I might not understand why, but that doesn't mean I don't think it's great you're willing to work, actively work, for something you probably won't get."

"Wow," Mimi snapped, irritably, "I'm feeling better by the minute."

Solange smiled. "You try to save it, Mimi. Do whatever you can. Whether or not you succeed will be immaterial. The journey will be the making of you. I can just tell."

"Mom. I'm forty-one years old. I am not going on any journey, except home to my apartment, and I'm already as 'made' as I'll ever be."

Solange's eyelids had slid half closed and the sanguine expression she wore looked weirdly familiar. Mimi had it. She looked like Ozzie on the brink of a mystical pronouncement.

"Some people, Mignonette"—here it came—"some people experience their coming of age later than others."

Mimi threw up her hands in exasperation. "This is not my coming of age. I did that at eighteen with Jimmy—"

"Stop," Solange said, picking up another cookie. "I'm speaking metaphorically."

"Metaphorically or not."

"We'll see." Solange's smile was infuriating. "Go forth. Save Chez Ducky. You have my blessing. I'd say I was sorry I can't help, but we'd both know I'd be lying."

Mimi pushed back from the table and came around to her mother's side. She looked down at Solange's upturned face. Solange looked back up, munching happily away. "You don't *have* the wherewithal to buy a quarter of Chez Ducky, do you?" Mimi asked.

"No," Solange said. "At least, not by myself."

"You would have blackmailed me if you had, wouldn't you?"

"Probably," Solange agreed without the least bit of embarrassment.

"And all that other stuff?"

"Oh, I meant that. You are changing, Mimi. It's taken a while, granted, but you're finally coming into your own. You're going to be a force to be reckoned with someday. You'll finally achieve the promise of your youth."

"Oh, please." At the sound of Mary's voice, Mimi turned. Her half sister was standing in the doorway of the solarium, enveloped in a black cashmere coat.

Solange smiled at Mary and said, "Look who dropped in."

"Unfulfilled Potential?" Mary asked, one brow angling derisively.

"Hi, Mary," Mimi said. She was in no mood for Mary.

She'd always thought of herself as someone who accepted without flinching or whining those things she had no control over. Apparently not so much, because she was practically twitching and definitely on the cusp of a whine. "I was just heading out."

Her mother's face crumpled. "Oh? Why don't you stay? I've got another box of vanilla wafers in the kitchen."

"Thanks, but I gotta go. I have a destiny to fulfill, remember? A chrysalis to burst forth from. Eagle wings to grow. A mountain to climb. A river to cross." She said all this mostly to annoy Mary, and it worked.

"Yeah, yeah, so I just heard," Mary said. "You're on the brink of actually doing something. Or trying to. Let the angel chorus sound! Really. *No* one could be happier about it than me. I promise." Mary spoke with unsettling conviction.

Mimi, who'd been about to bend down to kiss Solange's cheek good-bye, checked instead, caught by Mary's forceful tone. Why would that make Mary happy? It wouldn't. Mary was just being sarcastic.

"Before you go, Mignonette," Solange said, dragging Mimi's attention from her half sister, "have you heard from Sarah lately?"

"Let me think . . . ," Mimi said. "Yup. I did last Saturday." Since the Grandmother Werner incident, Sarah had been e-mailing Mimi twice weekly. Mimi still wasn't sure what to make of this or even how she felt about it. They weren't girlish confidences, mostly just stuff about patent law and an occasional question about relationships that Mimi invariably answered, "I don't know," or, "I'd let matters take their own course." That Sarah apparently saw her as an expert on human relationships was a sad commentary on her baby sister's own experiences.

"Why?" Mimi asked. "Is everything all right?"

"We don't know where she is," Solange said and, seeing the expression on Mimi's face, hurried on. "She calls and she sounds fine. I mean, really *fine*," Solange emphasized. "But she hasn't been in her apartment for weeks and she won't say where she's staying. Or with whom. And I sometimes hear a voice in the background. It sounds male."

Bingo. The no-strings-attached sexcapades partner. "Have you asked her?"

"I don't want to pry," Solange said primly. Which meant she had asked and been rebuffed.

"She's probably got a boyfriend," Mimi said, wondering how much Sarah would or wouldn't like her to say. Mimi had always found it best to stay as close to the truth as possible with Solange. She had a positive gift for ferreting out untruths.

"Really?" Solange asked. "Do you know who?"

"No."

Her mother's laserlike truth-finding glare leveled on Mimi and she opened her mouth, but before she could speak, Mary did. "Speaking of boyfriends, seen Joe Tierney lately?" Mary asked.

How would Mary know about her and Joe Tierney? Not that there was anything to know about. Joe was a moment from her past. A couple moments. Three. Two good and one not so good. Or mostly good until he'd proven to be a jerk. Why was she thinking about him again?

"Is Mimi interested in Joe Tierney?" Solange asked, her eyes brightening, Sarah, for the moment, forgotten.

"No. I— We just— I met him at—" She was not going to do this. She was forty-one, for God's sake. "No."

Solange sighed. "Well, nothing much would have come of it anyway. The man was putting in eighteen hours a day in order to finish up here last week. As soon as he was done, he said he had another project to start, somewhere overseas. I suspect he's already left the state."

Gone? A gentleman would have apologized before blowing town. So maybe he wasn't such a gentleman after all. Looks could be so deceiving. The thought didn't bring her as much satisfaction as she thought it should. "Geez," she said, "look at the time. I'm late for work."

"Wait."

Mimi froze.

"You *are* coming for Christmas dinner, are you not?"

Mimi did some quick weighing of the pros and cons. On the con side was leaving her snug apartment to spend an evening answering snide Christmas-themed remarks about her occupation ("Ever run into someone named Ebenezer on the Other Side? Ha-ha! Ha! Ha! Ha!") and unwrap a bunch of expensive presents she didn't need as Solange blithely informed anyone who'd listen that her oldest daughter was simply a late bloomer and Mary muttered, not quite under her breath, "Like a century plant?" On the pro side, she would get an excellent free meal, make Solange happy, and . . . get an excellent free meal.

"I'll try, but you know Christmas is one of our biggest days at Straight Talk. I'll have to see if I can get two or three hours off." Whether they woke up missing a loved one or came home filled with Christmas spirits and regrets, more people tried to make contact on Christmas Eve and Christmas Day than any other day of the year.

"Oh, Mignonette. Please. As if taking advantage of those poor souls during a normal day isn't bad enough—"

The unfortunate choice of words brought ungentlemanly Joe Tierney back to mind, and she was *not* thinking about him. "Gotta go!" Mimi chirped, swooping down and planting a kiss on Solange's cheek. She snagged her jacket from the back of the wrought-iron chair and fled.

Mimi stopped at her apartment on the way back to work to grab a bite of lunch. She was letting herself in when she heard the door behind her open and Jennifer Beesing say, "Look what came for you!"

She turned around to see what appeared to be a rose shrub sprouting from a plump pair of jean-clad legs. Jennifer lowered the bouquet and peered over the top. "They smell good, too!"

"They're for me?" Mimi asked.

Jennifer nodded. "They came about an hour ago. There's a card."

"Hold on while I get the door," Mimi said, suiting action to words, then taking the flowers. "Thanks."

"No problem," Jennifer said. "Secret admirer?"

Mimi smiled at this absurdity. "I'll let you know," she promised and backed into her apartment, shoving the door closed with her hip. She set the vase on the table inside the door and opened the note dangling from a gold cord.

*Please accept my apologies for my inexcusable rude-
ness. I am sorry I am leaving Minneapolis having
given such a poor account of myself.*
   Joseph L. Tierney

That was supposed to be an apology? It was about as im-
personal a statement of culpability as she could imagine. And why now? Why after all these weeks?

Because *now* he was leaving, she realized. Had he sent flowers earlier, she might misconstrue his apology as an in-
vitation to reconnect. But if he left it as the last item on his Things to Do Before I Blow Town checklist, he wouldn't have to risk any awkward encounters or embarrassing phone calls from her.

Well, he didn't have to worry. He could pop off to wher-
ever it was he was popping off to secure in the knowledge that he'd acted the consummate gentleman. Bully for Joe.

She ripped the card in half and as she did so heard a scale of notes coming from her purse, signaling that a text message had been delivered to her cell phone. She dropped the torn card beside the vase and dug her cell phone out of her hand-
bag, flipping it open and reading the few short lines of text.

*D got realtor license. Hired guy to assess Chez.
Consensus seems 2 B 2 sell. Guess that's it. Having
lawyers in F.C. draw up paper. Get junk out of Chez by
spring. No 1 else around 2 do it. Shot 85 last week.
Birgie*

"Hey, Birgie, are you up for another nine holes?" her golf
partner, a woman from Bonita Springs who had skin like
shoe leather and whom Birgie had just met this morning,
called from the golf cart they were sharing.

"Hold on a minute, Mugsy," she shouted back. She waited
hopefully for Mimi to send back some reply.

She felt a little underhanded about sending that text message to her great-niece. No one had actually hired an assessor yet, and a firm date hadn't been set to meet at the
lawyers', but it was only a matter of time and Mimi would
have to get her ass in gear if she was going to lead the movement to save Chez Ducky. Debbie was rallying the younger
cousins to pressure the older family members to sell. Some
of Johanna's grandkids were talking about getting dirt bikes,
which meant that the die was almost cast.

Birgie had been doing what she could, staying in close
touch with Naomi to keep track of Debbie's movements and
then funneling the information through Vida to Mimi. She'd
have contacted Mimi herself, but then Mimi might get all
comfortable with the idea that since Birgie was interested she
was going to do something, and, well, she wasn't. She
couldn't. Despite Mimi's opinion otherwise, Birgie knew
she didn't have the sort of personality that could sway others.
She also didn't have force of will, and she was too old to start
acquiring it now.

"You ready, there, Birgie?" Mugsy called.

"I'm coming," Birgie said and flipped down the phone.

WINTER

Chapter Twenty-six

January

"Ms. Olson? This is Otell Weber."

"Who?"

"Otell Weber, the private investigator?" the man on the other end of the phone said patiently.

"Oh, yeah. Hi." He sounded, Mimi realized, just like he'd looked: gray, tired, and rumpled.

"Hi. I just got back into town and since I told you I'd get in touch, here I am."

"Oh. Well, thank you."

"Nothing to thank me for, Ms. Olson. I haven't been real successful for you."

"I didn't really expect you would be," Mimi answered, trying to keep the disappointment from her voice.

"It's not all bad news, though. Before I left I sent out inquiries to any motels operating along Interstate 2 between here and Bainsville, Montana, asking them to search any records they might still have for summer 1979 for a John Olson."

"Why?"

"Well, Bainsville, Montana, was the postmark on the postcard your father sent you, and that town is on Interstate 2, and since your dad didn't have a car, the chances are he was hitching a ride or taking a bus along that highway. He might have stayed at one of them."

"I see. Anyone answer?"

"Nope. But since I got back I've compiled a list of motels that were in operation during 'seventy-nine but have since closed."

"And why is that not bad news?"

"Well," said Otell, "there's quite a few of them. And most of them were cheap joints, the sort a guy with limited means might stay in. Better yet, they tended to be family owned and operated, so a lot of the folks that ran 'em are still around, not like the chains who have a different kid manning the front desk every season. They also tend to hold on to things. So, there's some slim hope we might find your dad's name there."

"That sounds promising," Mimi said.

"That's way overstating the case. It's better than nothing. Marginally." God love a stoic, honest-till-it-hurts Minnesotan.

"Anyway," Otell went on in his laconic voice, "that's what I got. It's a long shot, Ms. Olson. I wanta be perfectly fair here. But if you want, I can keep at it. Your call."

Another shot, thought Mimi, was better than no shot. What the hell?

"That'd be great, Mr. Weber."

It was another few weeks before Mimi rented a sturdy four-wheel-drive vehicle and drove up to Chez Ducky with promises to Oz that she'd be back in two weeks at the most. As post-holiday business tended to be slow anyway, he didn't kick up a fuss.

As soon as the headlights picked out the old wood-burned sign with its welcoming Daffy Duck–like character, she regretted having waited so long to come. Above, the starry river of the Milky Way coursed through the indigo sky, while below, a fresh blanket of snow unfurled like a luminous white banner along the drive. Moonlight turned the Big House's pale facade silvery and glinted in the upper-story windows, all the light-reflecting snow creating a faux day, a dusky hybrid of silver and blue. She got out of the car, taking her backpack with her and slinging it over her shoulders as she trudged to the doorway.

Beneath her boots the snow squeaked, a quality it took on only when the temperature dipped below zero. It didn't feel that cold, but then Mimi was dressed in worst-case-scenario clothing: an oversized Alaskan Bag Company down jacket, a layer of thermal underwear beneath her felt-lined pants, wool choppers, and Will Steger mukluks.

Inside, the electricity had been shut off, but the same moonlight that illuminated the outdoors had seeped in here, too. Her breath made phantasms in the chill air as she moved down the hall, the floorboards creaking underfoot as she made her way to the kitchen. There, she opened the battered gray fuse box, threw on the master lever, and then flipped on the kitchen's single ceiling light.

They were tasks she'd performed a half dozen times over the last decade during Ardis's infrequent and impromptu winter visits. Ardis would call from Sun City, exclaiming gleefully over some cheapo last-minute airfare she'd gotten. Mimi, who'd inherited the use of Ardis's old Pontiac LeBaron during the winter months, would pick her great-aunt up at the airport, and they'd head north, arriving at dawn.

Mimi would leave Ardis snoozing in the warm car while she got the place ready, just as she was doing now. Except when she looked out the window this time, she wouldn't see Ardis, roused by some arcane Olson sixth sense that told her that all the work had been done, crawling out of the car and blinking like a baby owl.

Mimi looked around the kitchen, noting the ice chest, the Formica-topped kitchen table, and the old corked floor. She could see Ardis in her ratty old chenille bathrobe, her bare feet calloused, hammer toes crooked, adding a single spoonful of new coffee grounds to yesterday's in the old percolator. God, that coffee had been vile, but Ardis wouldn't hear of getting a drip brewer, and any suggestion that they start with fresh grounds when making coffee earned a stern lecture on wasteful practices.

"Ardis?" She held her breath and listened, half hoping to hear a reply. But all she got was the pop and groan of the house protesting over being awoken, so she shoved open the back door, pushing against a drift of snow that had accumulated there. She squeezed through the opening and slogged over to the propane fuel tank squatting beneath the kitchen's back windows. She turned its knob, then went back inside to the parlor and crouched down before the old gas furnace in the corner. Like many old cottages, the Big House had no basement, so all its mechanical guts were in the public rooms for easy access. She reached into the little door on the side of the furnace, turned on the pilot light, and waited. The light flickered on and, with a little whoosh, the furnace started. Mimi stood up, wondering what to do next.

Experience told her it would take a couple hours for the lower rooms to warm up enough for her to shed her jacket and a couple more after that before she could start the pump and return water to the pipes. The antique water heater would take an additional two or three hours to warm up enough water to fill a shallow bath.

She looked out the front window toward the lake. It reminded her of a particularly sugary Christmas card, the kind with the shimmering snow made out of glitter that gets all over when you open it. She had always wanted to walk through a Christmas card. She was certainly dressed for it, and it beat the dickens out of shoveling the snow away from the back door.

Pulling the earflaps on her hat down, she headed back outside and trudged through the snow to the beach, where she

followed the icy heave along the shoreline to the edge of
Chez Ducky's border. She stopped and looked up at
Prescott's monolith. Not a light shone from it. Like the rest
of the Fowl Lake summer people, Prescott had undoubtedly
ditched the place for the winter. He and Bill were probably
sitting in some spectacular replica of a Moorish castle he'd
built on the Mexican riviera, staring down at some other
beach. Good. She had the lake to herself.

She stood without moving for long minutes, memories
awakening to fill her mind's eye. She remembered the last
winter her grandfather had been alive. Solange, housebound
in her eighth month of pregnancy with Mary, had agreed to
let Mimi's grandfather bring her up here during Christmas
break along with Naomi and Bill, who'd returned from college for Christmas vacation. Granddad had woken her up in
the middle of the night and made her get bundled up for a
walk. She'd been a sullen, moody teenager and definitely not
the best company, but he'd insisted.

They'd ended up just about here, Mimi thought, looking
around. Her grandfather had told her some wacky
Scandinavian fairy tale she didn't recall much about other
than there had been ice trolls and wolves and a snow
princess. She'd been thirteen, after all, so more or less
obliged to scoff. He hadn't minded. He'd only said, "So
you're too old for fairy tales?"

She'd rolled her eyes, not deigning to reply.

"And I suppose you're too old to make snow angels, too,
huh?"

Once more, she'd rolled her eyes.

Her grandfather had grinned at her. "Thank God I'm not,"
he said. "Because it would be a crime to waste perfect snow
like this."

Then he'd turned around, dropped flat on his back in the
snow, and made a snow angel.

When Bill and Naomi had woken the next morning and
looked out at the lake, they'd seen the entire shore lined with

snow angels, alternating tall and tiny. By noon, they'd vanished in the wind.

"You're right, Granddad," Mimi whispered. She crossed her arms over her chest, tipped her head face to the sky, and fell backward. She landed a lot harder at forty-one than she had at thirteen. A white puff of snow erupted around her and the wind was knocked out of her lungs. *"Ouch."*

For long minutes she lay there getting her breath back, staring up at the sky and listening to all the years, all the summers and falls, springs and winters, that had gone before.

The beach had seen a thousand campfires and the careful construction of thousands of s'mores, many made by Mimi and even more eaten by her. Most nights, she and her cousins were serenaded to sleep by her aunts' and uncles' singing, not because they had fancied themselves some sort of Minnesota Von Trapp family, but because there was nothing else to do— no television, no radio signal; even the lighting was too poor to read by for long. She still remembered every note of "Autumn Leaves" and "Misty" and "Don't Get Around Much Anymore."

How many rainy days had she and her cousins spent in one of the tip-tilted porches playing dominos or Cooties or Candyland, while the leaf-choked gutters overflowed and the rain carved deeper ruts in the driveway? How many paper sailboats had she launched at the top of the drive?

Somewhere near where she now lay, her father had taught her how to swim, bobbing along beside her on an inner tube, holding her long braid in one hand to keep her head above the water and a beer bottle in the other. Mimi twisted her head, squinting as she tried to make out the shape of the swimming raft that had floated here almost thirty years ago. There. There . . .

Her father had brought her up to Chez Ducky for the summer. She'd been eleven. Her mom hadn't been keen on the idea. There were so many better, more productive ways to spend a summer, but in the end she'd relented. It was going to be a wonderful summer, an endless summer, with all the Olsons and her dad and her and nothing to do but play. But her dad had only stayed the one night before taking off again, casually saying good-bye and warning her he didn't know when he'd be back. In the meantime, she had to promise him to enjoy every day and let go of all her worries and cares for the summer. She hadn't protested. Protesting never got her anywhere, not with her father, not with her mother.

After he'd left, she'd tried to go with the flow. She really had. Yeah, the days were relaxed and the faces pleasant and the sounds comfortable, but she kept wondering when he'd come back. The days turned into weeks turned into months. September arrived and her father didn't return. Then, one afternoon, her grandfather told her that Solange was coming to pick her up and take her back to the cities because school was going to start soon. And all of a sudden, just like that, she'd realized her dad wasn't coming back. Maybe not ev—

Just as she had when she'd been eleven, Mimi stopped the thought from fully forming, returning to her memory.

Late that night, like dozens before, she'd heard her aunts and great-aunts splashing and laughing out on the lake. Her summer was almost over and she and her dad hadn't spent more than a single day of it together. But out there, on that lake, the summer was still going on.

She'd slipped from her cot and down to the beach to find the Olson women skinny-dipping in the moonlight. When they saw her they waved at her to join them. Eagerly, she'd stripped off her nightshirt and slipped into the water. She'd gasped, amazed at the sensation of every inch of her skin enveloped in cool, silky water, and thought she'd never truly been swimming before. She'd never wanted to leave the lake, or for that night to end.

And in some ways, it hadn't. That night she'd finally learned the art of letting go.

Now Mimi closed her eyes, inhaling through her nostrils. She stretched out her arms and started sweeping them up and down by her sides. Her legs joined in the action, scissoring from side to side, her boot heels scraping the ice beneath. There. Now *that* would be a snow angel the wind would have a hard time erasing, she thought when she finally stopped.

The only problem now was how to get up without ruining her creation. She couldn't roll over, even to get to her knees. How had she and Granddad done this, anyway? She tried bending at the waist, but a few years and a lot of goose down made the whole sitting-up-without-using-your-hands thing nearly impossible. But if she'd done it when she was thirteen, she could do it now. She gathered her resolve and heaved upward, grunting. Almost . . . She fell back.

She tried again with the same lack of success. Okay, how about if she bent her legs, grabbed her knees, and used the leverage to rock upright? She gave it a try. She almost made it, but like a Tommee Tippee Cup, at the last moment she listed sideways. She pitched herself in the other direction so as not to ruin the angel and ended up on her back again. This was ridiculous. All she had to do was stick her feet under her butt and— Her boots slipped out from under her.

Damn. If only she could—

"Mrs. Olson! Mrs. Olson!" a young man shouted frantically.

She lifted her head off the snow and peered between her feet. Someone, a man—*Prescott?*—was lurching down the snow-covered steps of the lodge deck, his coat flapping open, hatless, gloveless, waving his arms wildly. "Stay there! Don't try to move!"

Huh? She lifted her head higher.

"It's all right! I'm coming!" he shouted. And now he had been joined by three dogs, who danced wildly around his legs as he stumbled off the last step.

Sonofabitch. He better not tromp out here and ruin her angel. She heard a sound, faint but growing louder. It took her a minute to place it. It was an ambulance siren. What the hell?

"You're going to be all right!" Prescott was screaming while the dogs barked furiously. "Don't try to move! The paramedics will be here any minute!"

The para— He'd called an ambulance? For *her*? Her eyes grew round with horror. Her face burned with mortification. He *had*! He thought she was having some sort of attack!

She rolled over and shot to her feet, snow angel be damned. Prescott was scrambling over heaps of snow piled under the deck, shouting, "Mrs. Olson, no! You should stay down!"

"Prescott, you *idiot*—" She stopped. Blinked.

Prescott had disappeared.

Chapter Twenty-seven

As it turned out, Prescott hadn't disappeared. He'd fallen into his half-finished swimming pool.

Just as Mimi made it to the edge of the pool, two paramedics trotted around the corner of the house, the guy in the lead hailing her. "Where's the lady with the heart attack?"

"In the pool!" Mimi called.

"Huh?"

She pointed emphatically at the pool. The ambulance crew members came to her side and together the three of them peered over the edge. Prescott lay motionless on the bottom, sunk a foot deep into the snow, his army surplus coat flung open, exposing his flannel pajamas. One of his legs was twisted under his body. A boot lay next to him.

"Is that the lady?" the guy next to her, a hefty young man with a pale, feathery mustache, asked.

"There is no lady." The sight of Prescott lying there scared the crap out of her. The stupid kid might have killed himself in his misguided effort to save her life. "Aren't you going to do something?"

"You bet. Claus, get the rope ladder and tell Artie to help with the gurney. Pronto!"

"You got it, Bob!" The other ambulance attendant hurried off.

"We got a call about ten minutes ago from someone at this address saying there was a middle-aged lady flopping around on the lake, having a heart attack," Bob said, his hands on his thigh as he peered down at Prescott. "I musta misunderstood. You're lucky we were heading back from a false alarm out this way and only a few miles away when we got the call."

Prescott moaned, and Mimi breathed a sigh of relief until he started to roll over and she saw the direction his right ankle was pointing, which was not the direction it should have been. Her vision swam. The paramedic caught her by the collar and steadied her.

About this time the sheriff, who'd been cruising the southern part of the county and monitoring calls, arrived. He, alongside the paramedics, clambered down into the pool and together they secured Prescott to the gurney, then attached it to the sheriff's come-along and winched him slowly up the side of the pool. From there it was a straight shot into the ambulance.

Inside the ambulance, Prescott rallied. "Where am I? What happened?"

"You've had an accident, kid," said Bob, the paramedic, as he stuck an IV into Prescott's arm. "You've hurt your ankle and banged your head pretty good."

"I did? Last thing I 'member is—" Prescott lifted his head, looking around anxiously. "Where's Mrs. Olson? Is she okay? Did you find her?"

"Easy, Bud." The paramedic pressed him back down. "Who's Mrs. Olson?"

"The lady on the lake!" Prescott said. "She must still be out there—"

Mimi started to sidle away from the ambulance. Bob pinned her to the spot with a hard glance.

"Calm down. She's just fine. Aren't you?" the paramedic prompted, waving her inside the ambulance.

Shit. She climbed in and smiled weakly down at Prescott.

Sweat glistened on his pale skin, and his eyes were glassy with pain.

"Yeah, I'm fine. You just worry about you."

Geez. Here this damn kid lay, stretched out with a busted ankle and a concussion, and he was worried about her, a stranger whose only interaction with him had been when she'd foisted a mangy dog off on him in order to keep from having to deal with it herself. She could almost forgive him for calling her middle-aged.

He blinked up at her. "You're sure? I thought you were having a heart attack. I saw you flailing around on the snow and—"

"I'm fine," she repeated, and then said primly, "By the way, I'm only thirty—thirty-five."

"Really?" Even through his obvious pain, he looked surprised. Behind her, Bob snickered.

"Really."

"But you were, like, having a seizure, though," Prescott insisted.

"I was making a snow angel."

At this, both paramedics, the driver, and the sheriff, a good-looking man with all the charm of a cabbage, stopped what they'd been doing. The sheriff's gaze shifted toward the Breathalyzer in the front seat of his car.

"You guys have a problem with that?" she demanded.

"No, ma'am."

"Not me, ma'am."

"Stop calling me 'ma'am.' "

Prescott's eyeballs rolled back in his head.

"Okay," Bob announced to his driver, "that's it. We're ready to roll. You want to come to the hospital with us, ma'am?"

"No. I'm just the neighbor." The little pissant paramedic couldn't be that much younger than she was. She started to back out of the ambulance.

"Wait." Prescott's hand shot out, grabbing her wrist. His eyes were lucid once more.

"What?"

"You've gotta get the dogs into the house. They're out here somewhere." He stared up at her imploringly. "It's cold. They're small." He reconsidered. "Smallish. Please."

"Dogs?"

"Three. Bill, Merry, and Sam. You remember Bill. I adopted the other two to keep Bill company."

"Look, we gotta get this guy to the hospital," Bob said, his gaze on a monitor attached to Prescott via little cables. "Get his dogs rounded up, will ya?"

"And stay with them in my house until I can find someone else to."

"What? Why don't I just take them down to Chez—"

"No. Please," Prescott pleaded. "They're pound dogs. They have abandonment issues. They hate change. They get nervous in new places. It makes them act out. There is no one else. Please."

"Come on, lady," the paramedic piped up. "It's not like spending a few days in a mansion would be doing hard time."

It wasn't the house she objected to; it was the dogs. She hadn't planned on spending her last few winter days at Chez Ducky playing nursemaid to a pack of mutts.

"I'll look in on them," she promised, backing out of the ambulance and dropping to the ground.

"No! I told you, they have abandonment issues. They *hate* being alone for more than a few hours! They'll howl!"

"So?"

Prescott emitted a strangled sound of despair.

"Geez. Nice payback," she heard someone mutter.

Mimi looked around. The other paramedic and the sheriff stood behind her, regarding her with profound disappointment. The sheriff had crossed his arms over his chest and was shaking his head. Normally, disapproval held little sway with

Mimi, and it didn't now, but Prescott did. He really had thought he'd been racing to her rescue.

"Okay. Fine, I'll stay with the dogs at your house. But only until you can make other arrangements," she grumbled gracelessly.

"Thank you!" Prescott breathed. "Their food is in the freezer. There's lots of it. And there's stuff in the refrigerator-freezer for you, too."

"Let's move!" The other paramedic elbowed her aside as he got in, and Bob pulled the ambulance's doors shut. They took off, the siren blaring.

The sheriff stuffed a piece of gum into his mouth, chewing as he eyed her thoughtfully. "You'd think a woman your age who makes snow angels would be more . . ."

"More what?" Mimi asked, putting her hands on her hips.

He shrugged. "Tenderhearted, I guess."

"You want tender? Buy veal," she snapped. "Are you going to help me find these dogs or not?"

He backed toward the open door of his car. "Not. Got a call about suspicious activity on the other side of the county."

"You're lying," she accused him.

"Maybe. But you'd never be able to prove it." He slid in behind the wheel. "Besides, seems to me you were enjoying playing in the snow. Now you got an excuse. Have fun!"

He slammed the door shut, raised a finger off the top of the steering wheel in farewell, and drove away.

They weren't big dogs, true, but Mimi wouldn't have called them "smallish," either. One, a plush-coated blond girl dog with dangling ears and a long plumed tail, had to be fifty pounds. The other was the color of dirty snow, a slack-flanked and long-legged male with upright ears and a long narrow snout that had a bump in it, giving him an uncanny resemblance to the cartoon character Wile E. Coyote.

Mimi made her initial mistake by diving after the fluffy blonde as she scooted past her. She landed on her hands and knees. Blondie thought this was a game and darted in to tug at her boots, then jumped back when Mimi grabbed for her collar. She compounded her mistake by batting ineffectually at Wiley when he joined in, thus providing further evidence to their collective canine mind that the monkey wanted to play. (Mimi assumed all animals thought of humans as particularly mean-spirited monkeys.)

It took her some time before she managed to stagger back to her feet and convince them she didn't. She faced them panting as they stood splay-legged in front of her, tongues lolling happily as they wondered what she was planning next for their amusement. Somewhere in the past she'd seen an episode of the *Dog Whisperer* and remembered the guy saying that dogs needed a strong leader.

"Come!" she commanded and began marching toward Prescott's house. She looked back. The dogs were chasing each other in circles. She'd already been forgotten.

"Come *now*!"

They didn't. She dug her hands into her pockets, pondering her next move. Her fingers closed on a PowerBar she'd stuck there sometime in October. Were PowerBars good for dogs? Did she care? She broke open the wrapper and waved the bar in the air.

"Hey, doggies! Look! Num-nums!" Incredibly, at the word "num-nums," the dogs stopped chasing each other. They looked at her questioningly. "It's no lie, guys. Come with me and the PowerBar is yours."

She headed for the lodge, and this time the dogs dashed after her. True to her word, as soon as she got the pair inside she split the bar in half and tossed it to them. Then she looked around.

Impressive. True, impressive mostly because the house wasn't decked out like the Bat Cave she would have expected Prescott's house to be, but impressive nonetheless. There wasn't a lot of furniture, but what she saw was colorful and modern and looked surprisingly comfortable. Particularly the red S-shaped sofa and a pair of big, squat modern club chairs upholstered in nubby electric blue. But for all its visual appeal, it still had that ineffable interior designer vibe about it, like someone else was trying to figure out what would suit you. No stacks of years-old *Smithsonian* magazines, no moth-eaten dish towels draped over the spotless trough sink sunk in the granite kitchen countertop, no chrysalis suspended inside a peanut butter jar with holes punched in its lid, no empty painted turtle shells or unusually shaped rocks, no paperback novels, no agonizingly produced Play-Doh ashtrays painted in garish colors. In other words, it was as unlike Cottage Six as she imagined two lake places could be.

The only things that indicated the interests or history of the person living here were dog related. Books about dogs and dog psychology lay in neat little stacks on the surface of a hammered-copper coffee table. Most had their corners gnawed off. The most notable feature of the room, however, were all the dog toys: balls, bones, stuffed toys, squeakers, pull-bars, chews, and some things Mimi couldn't even identify. She glanced at her charges.

"Spoiled mutts," she grumbled.

The pair, evidently tired from their little escapade, had hopped up onto the cushioned club chairs and curled up for a snooze. Good. If she was really lucky the two wouldn't move until— *Two. Pair.* Prescott had said there were *three* dogs.

Damn it, she thought, realizing which one was missing: Bill. Bill, the dog she'd foisted on Prescott, the foundation of this menagerie; Bill, the opportunist who'd masqueraded as an Olson dog all summer and grown fat on the impersonation; Bill, of whom Prescott had sent all those pictures that had led Joe to the conclusion that she was planning to con his son—and yes, she knew it wasn't the dog's fault, but she really didn't care about being fair right now. She was tired, her toes were cold, and now that she was finally warming up, her butt was damp from where the snow was melting into her

pants. Being fair wasn't on the radar. Going out after the little bugger wasn't on the radar, either. It wasn't her fault Bill
had run away.

She shrugged out of her jacket. Blondie lifted her head
and regarded her with limpid, reproachful brown eyes.

"Bill's fine," Mimi told her. "He's probably already found
another patsy to take him in."

Blondie laid her head down and heaved a mournful sigh.

"He's *fine*." Mimi marched into the kitchen and to the refrigerator, intent on getting something cool to drink. A number glowed reproachfully on the little LCD temperature
readout above the crushed ice dispenser. Interior temperature: thirty-eight. That was at least thirty degrees warmer
than it was outside.

"Damn it!"

She snatched up her parka and rammed her arms into the
sleeves, jerked up the zipper, shoved her feet into her mukluks, jammed her hat back on her head, and stomped outside
onto the deck. "Bill! Bill! Come here, you lousy mutt!"

Amazingly, Bill did not appear in the distance, tail wagging, ears streaming as he raced toward the dulcet sounds of
his name. So, Mimi clomped down the deck stairs, nearly
breaking her neck as she slipped on an icy patch, edged her
way along the swimming pool cavity, and started out onto the
lake. "Bill! Num-nums! Bill!"

Nuthin'.

She tucked her hands up her sleeves, burrowing her chin
into the collar of her jacket, and screeched Bill's name. Bill
didn't show and her frustration turned to concern. She had
expected the word "num-nums" to work the same magic it
had with the other two beasts. When it didn't, she cast about
uncertainly, wondering where a little dog like Bill would go.
She tried tracking him, thinking maybe his smaller prints
would be easy to mark in the snow. But all she found was a
set at the bottom of the deck stairs amongst the jumble of

prints left by dogs, Prescott, ambulance workers, the sheriff, and herself.

Finally, after searching for thirty minutes, her voice hoarse with yelling, she realized she wasn't going to find Bill. She climbed the deck stairs, hating the anxiety flooding her. She'd spent decades avoiding just such feelings. And even though she knew dwelling on Bill's being out there would benefit no one, least of all Bill, she couldn't keep terrible images from invading her imagination. Maybe he'd fallen into some hole like Prescott, or gotten lost chasing a rabbit, or simply grown too cold to go on.

She went inside for her car keys, already having made up her mind to drive along the highway. Blondie and Wiley were still snoozing in their respective chairs, completely unconcerned about their lost comrade. Blondie lay on her back, feet dangling in the air. Wiley was curled next to a brown stuffed toy . . .

Mimi cocked her head, drawing closer. The stuffed toy emitted a little sputtering sound and a big toxic smell.

"Bill?"

The toy opened one eye and regarded her in a bored manner. She reached down and touched his back. He was dry and warm. He'd been in here all the time she'd been wandering through the woods hollering his name.

"Couldn't you have barked or something when I was screaming for you?" she asked.

This time, he didn't even open an eye; he just made another smell.

Chapter Twenty-eight

Mimi rolled groggily to a sitting position on the S-shaped couch, put her feet on the ground, and stood up. Her legs buckled and she dropped like a sack of potatoes. Wiley leaned over the edge of the couch and looked down at her.

"My legs are asleep because *you* slept on them," she told him.

He yawned and disappeared back under the goose-down duvet she'd found in the guest bedroom on the main floor. She probably should have slept there but that would have meant washing bed linens and she didn't think it was worth the trouble for one or two nights' sleep. Despite her promise to Prescott to stay here, she'd briefly considered hauling the menagerie down to the Big House, but something in the way Prescott had said, "It makes them act out," had brought to mind piles of dog poop and puddles of urine on various surfaces, so she'd decided to go the safer course and stay.

She pounded on her thighs until the nerves started firing, then picked herself up and headed into the kitchen anticipating a decent cup of coffee. A place like this was bound to have an expensive brass espresso machine. Maybe one with a steamer. She started opening cupboards.

Ten minutes later, she still hadn't found an espresso machine, but she had hit the jackpot in the Sub-Zero's freezer section: individual serving portions of all sorts of expensive and healthful food. This is what these mutts ate? she thought incredulously. It must be, because she distinctly recalled Prescott saying that the dogs' food was in the freezer and there was a lot of it. And this was the freezer and there was a lot of food. Of course, when you took into account that Prescott was so worried about their little canine psyches that he'd begged her to stay here with them, the portion-controlled gourmet meals made sense. Oh, well. What did she know? She'd never had a dog.

Mimi peeled back the film on a tray of breakfast wraps and popped it in the microwave, humming as she waited. The timer beeped, and Mimi retrieved her breakfast, turned, and promptly stumbled over Bill, who nipped at her ankles but otherwise didn't move. Were they to spend a lot of time together, she suspected Bill and she were likely to have trouble. Luckily, their time together was bound to be short.

A few feet behind him, Blondie and Wiley wagged their tails hopefully.

"Monkeys first," Mimi said, heading for the couch. She didn't bother with utensils. It was incredibly tasty. No wonder Prescott was plump. She'd finished the first wrap with the dogs gathered around her like little furry supplicants at the foot of the throne. She tore the remaining wrap into thirds and tossed the pieces one by one to the dogs.

It turned out that fluffy, sweet Blondie was the athlete. She not only grabbed her piece out of midair but sailed up and over the end of the sofa to intercept the piece Mimi tossed to Wiley. She didn't try this trick with Bill, however. Both Wiley and Blondie seemed to hold the stocky, elongated, and much smaller little cur in awe.

"Okay," Mimi announced. "You guys need to go out. But before you do, let's get one thing straight: we have slept together, so trust has been established. If you don't come back, you're on your own. Call when you get work."

She stood back and opened the door. The dogs charged outside.

Within five minutes, they were back inside.

Mimi waited until nine o'clock to call Fawn Creek Hospital. Like a number of people who had summer homes, Prescott had never bothered to have a landline installed, relying instead on his trusty cell phone service to stay connected. Most people, as soon as they realized that their cell phone service was not trusty, corrected this oversight. Except for the Olsons, who didn't really care whether they were in touch with the outside world, anyway, or Prescott, who seemed to feel that being without a phone was the last word in roughing it. So, Mimi was stuck counting on the locally spotty cell phone reception. Luckily, today it was decent. Especially out on the deck. She stood shivering by the rail and asked for Prescott Tierney's room. A moment later a woman answered. "Hello? This is Doctor Youngstrum. May I ask who this is?"

"Mimi Olson."

"Are you a relative of Mr. Tierney's, Ms. Olson?"

"No. I'm the, er, dog-sitter," Mimi said. "How's Prescott doing? Can I speak to him?"

"That's not possible. He required orthopedic surgery and was airlifted to Duluth last night."

"Will he be okay?"

"His condition was stable when he left here and he should be fine."

Well, that was a relief. "When will he be able to come home? What are we talking about here, a couple days?"

"I think you should assume a while longer than that."

"A while?" Mimi's voice rose. "I can't stay here that long."

The doctor ignored this. "We're trying to get in touch with Joe Tierney. Prescott Tierney's insurance agency has him listed as next of kin, but we haven't had any luck so far. Do you have a number where he could be reached?"

"No. Can you give me the number of the hospital where Prescott is?"

"Of course," the doctor replied. "But I doubt he'll be taking calls until quite a bit later today."

The day crawled by while Mimi waited for nightfall so she could find out from Prescott just how he intended to handle his dog problem. She didn't spend it at Prescott's for the simple fact that if Joe called, which he might, she would feel obliged to answer the phone, and she did not want to talk to him and explain how Prescott had ended up in the hospital, thank you very much. Instead, she trekked over to Chez Ducky for the day. She let the dogs accompany her mostly because she couldn't think of any reason not to, and besides, she wanted to see how they'd react.

The Big House had warmed up by now, the expanding joints groaning and popping in the walls and ceilings. True to Prescott's warning, the dogs were not happy about the change of scene. All except Bill, whose savoir faire was unassailable. The other two followed on her heels from room to room, slinking and skulking, their nails tapping against the old floorboards, panting, their heads low as they looked around as though they expected the place to be haunted. Maybe it was.

Thinking it might be worth a shot, she closed her eyes and listened. She didn't hear anything. Not Ardis, not her grandfather, not Charlie's long-dead twin, Calvin. Certainly not her father. But she never had found him here. It was odd, she thought, that the only shadow left of John Olson was the one when he'd said good-bye. She opened her eyes to find two pairs of canine eyes regarding her worriedly. Blondie turned and ran to the front door, scratching frantically at it.

"Calm down," she told her. "You musta chased the big bad spooks away, 'cause we are alone here."

She lowered the temperature before leaving, the dogs crowding her. Outside, the two larger dogs at once reverted to happy-go-lucky idiots. She threw snowballs at the dogs, which pleased them to no end, and shoveled out the path through the woods between Chez Ducky's and Prescott's, thinking that if she was stuck watching the beasties for a few days, she might as well spend some of that time at Chez Ducky.

By the time she was finished, evening was closing in, so she went back to Prescott's to warm up and eat dinner. She got out the deep-dish pizza she'd spotted in the freezer that morning and stuck it in the oven. When it was done, she cut it into quarters and set each portion on one of the stoneware plates, placed three on the floor, and called, "Num-nums!"

The dogs appeared, looked at the plates on the floor, and looked back at her. If dog faces could look stunned, these did.

"Look. I want pizza, so pizza it is. Until you guys grow opposable thumbs, them's the rules. The biped gets to choose," she told them. "Eat."

Bill pushed past his two larger companions and picked up one of the pizza slabs. He gobbled it, his gaze hard on Mimi as though he expected her to change her mind at any minute. Blondie and Wiley, needing no further urging than Bill's example, dove toward the other two plates, feet skittering on the floor.

Good, Mimi thought. They liked pizza. There were three more in the freezer.

She finished her own piece, washing it down with a bottle of designer water, and then wrapped herself in the down-filled duvet she'd used the previous night before heading back outside onto the deck. Once again, she was in luck; her cell phone worked.

"Hello?" Prescott answered on the eighth ring. He sounded dopey.

"Prescott, this is Mimi Olson."

There was a long pause punctuated by throaty breathing. He was snoring.

"Prescott!" she yelled into the phone.

"Huh? Wha—?"

"Prescott, this is Mimi Olson. From Fowl Lake? I'm at your house with your dogs." She spoke each sentence loudly and clearly.

"Mrs. Olson!" Prescott cried. He really cried. She heard the sob. "You're all right? You're not dead?"

"No. Don't you remember? I was making a snow angel. You thought I was having a fit and called the ambulance."

He thought about this. "Yeah. You were dying. You were flopping around on the ice. Woman your age, flopping around outside in the middle of the night." His voice was slurred, the volume moving up and down at random. Stoned out of his mind. "Flopping."

"Yeah, yeah. I get the image. But I'm not dead or dying."

"Flopping like a fish."

"Prescott, I'm here with your dogs. You asked me to watch them while you were in the hospital."

"Billy? You're with Billy?" Prescott's voice filled with jubilation. "Kiss Billy for me. I miss Billy. I love Billy. Kiss Billy," he insisted.

Mimi looked through the glass doors into the lodge's interior. Billy was sitting in the center of the scarlet sofa, licking himself. "Okay. I kissed him."

"And Merry and Sammy? Kiss them, too."

"Yeah, yeah, okay. Kisses all around. We gotta talk, Prescott."

"Are they adorable?"

"The bee's knees. What are you going to do about them?"

"Love 'em," he slurred without hesitation. "Love 'em, lead 'em. That's all a dog wants. To know his place and be accepted in it. In't that what we all want?"

Great, a stoned agoraphobic was pontificating to her.

"That's fine, Prescott. But I was speaking in the specific here. I can't stay with your dogs. I got stuff to do." It was a small lie. So what? "What are you going to do about them, and when?"

"Huh?"

"I assume you do not want the dogs left alone," she said, speaking slowly. "What plans are you going to make for their care?"

He was silent for so long that Mimi thought he might have fallen asleep again, but then he said, "I dunno."

Mimi tried again. "Who is going to watch them?"

"I dunno!" he said, sounding harassed. "I don't know anyone up there. I don't know what I'm gonna do. Why can't you stay? I saved your life."

"You *did* not—" She let it slide. "I can't stay. I have things to do."

"Like what?"

"Things. Like enjoy being by myself."

Like she hadn't done enough of that in her life. The sarcastic internal came out of left field, catching her off guard. She frowned.

"Well, I can't help you. *I'm in the hospital*," he said. "But I got plenty of money, so I can pay you—"

"I don't want your money. I want to go back to Chez Ducky."

He sighed. "Okay. They won't like it, and Blondie will cry, and maybe wet a few times, but if you have to, you can take 'em with ya."

"I don't want them in Chez Ducky. I want to be *alone* in Chez Ducky." She paused, half expecting another nasty internal editorial comment. None came. "That is why I came up here *alone.*"

"Well, I can't help you," Prescott repeated in the tone of a salesman speaking to an unreasonable customer.

"What about your dad?" Mimi asked.

"What about him?"

"Did anyone get hold of him? Can he come and stay?"

"Are you kidding?" Prescott sounded irritable. "The dogs'd hate him. And he'd hate them. I don't even know where my father is."

"Join the club," Mimi murmured, thinking of John. "Didn't he call you? Does he know you've broken your leg?"

"Joe? Yeah, I think so. I sort of remember talking to him. Doesn't matter. I don't want him. . . ." Prescott trailed off then came back abruptly. "I know. Hire someone. I'll pay 'em. But make sure they like dogs."

Good idea, but it was too late to start calling people this evening. She gave up. Fate had apparently decreed that she would spend another night on Prescott's couch. "Okay. I'll see what I can do."

"Thanks . . . *Mignonette*," he slid her name in with a slyness that almost made her laugh.

"Sure, *Prescott*. I'll let you know if I arrange something."

"'Kay. I'm glad you're not dead."

Mimi glanced inside the lodge. All three dogs were now cleaning themselves. One of them would lick her face tonight while she slept. She just knew it.

"Thanks," she muttered.

"Get off me," Mimi said, shoving Wiley off her lap the next morning. Blondie appeared from under the blanket at the foot of the sofa. Somewhere, Bill made a smell.

By nine o'clock, when she figured most of the Fawn Creek businesses would open, she was wrapped in the down duvet, sitting on the deck overlooking the lake, the thin Fawn Creek phone book open on her lap. She started punching buttons.

By nine thirty she'd called every person who might possibly be willing to house-sit a trio of dogs or know of someone who would. The town boasted two kennels, but both were closed for the season. The veterinary clinic sometimes took in boarders, but its six in-house kennels were currently filled. From the community center to church offices, from the Fawn Creek Shopper Advertising Circular office to Smelka's restaurant to the VFW, nowhere was a dog-sitter to be found.

Mimi punched the END CALL button in a daze of disbelief.

Fawn Creek was not a rich community. It did okay in the
summer, but during the winters those locals who didn't light
out for warmer climes must be scraping by. Yet, she couldn't
find one responsible, honest, and dog-loving person willing
to compromise his or her independence for cold, hard cash.
And while in theory she applauded this stand-alone attitude,
practically, at least for her, it sucked.

She looked at the dogs. They had just returned from a
wilderness ramble. Wiley and Bill were curled in their chairs,
but Blondie was standing before her, looking expectant. Ice
balls drooped from her furry underbelly like heavy orna-
ments from the boughs of a weedy Christmas tree. The low-
est had begun to melt, leaving a puddle on the hardwood
floor. Blondie shivered and wagged her long tail.

With a sigh, Mimi went to get a towel.

"Look," she said as she rubbed Blondie dry and the dog
tried to lick her. "I'll check in on you, but you're all big,
brave dogs and you can spend the nights here without a
babysitter. Prescott will never know, and I'll be able to . . ."
To what? she found herself asking. *To sit in a cold, drafty old
house by myself?*

Yes. Because she'd come here to say good-bye to . . .
What? Her adolescence?

No! She willed away the sneering suggestion. If she didn't
know better, she'd suspect she was being pestered from
Beyond. Unfortunately, she recognized these thoughts as her
own. They'd been slowly building momentum for almost a
year now. But they were wrong. She had come to say good-
bye to Chez Ducky, and, by God, she was going to say good-
bye, and these dogs—she frowned as she worked a
particularly knotty tangle from Blondie's left ear—these
dogs were not going to stop her.

What was she doing here in the home of her enemy, anyway? Okay, maybe Prescott wasn't her actual enemy, but he
did represent everything she despised about the country's
economic top one percent, stomping in uninvited and pissing

all over everything they wanted, presumptuous and self-indulgent and worst of all, without one ounce of self-restraint. Just look at Prescott's piney palace! It was obscenely large for one man, who, she had no doubt, would end up spending only a few weekends a year in it.

Fine. Maybe Prescott had thought he was saving her life. Maybe he didn't realize what a cliché he was. Maybe he didn't understand the impact this house was having on Fowl Lake's middle-class society. Ignorance was no excuse. Besides, she felt better being righteously indignant about him—or rather his house—than uncomfortably obligated to him.

Nevertheless, she spent the rest of the day dutifully wearing her charges out before feeding them, hustling them outside to answer the call of nature, and then, once they were situated in what she now recognized as their usual places, slipping unnoticed out the back door. She stood in the dark listening. Not a peep.

Thus reassured, she followed the path back to the Big House, where she spent a very uneventful evening alone. Around ten o'clock, lured by the magical moonlight on the lake, she ventured outside. At once, a faint but unmistakable chorus of howls greeted her.

Horrified, she spun on her heels and rushed back into the Big House, slamming the door shut behind her. They'd survive. They were just spoiled. She stuck her ear buds in, cranked up *Disco Hits of the Eighties,* and flopped down on the big, lumpy sofa in the parlor.

Unhappily, her imagination insisted on providing what her ears didn't, because try as she might to concentrate on a nicely torrid romance novel she'd brought with her, she kept imagining she heard Blondie and Wiley and Bill, even above Donna Summer wailing "Last Dance." She knew this was ridiculous; she'd barely been able to hear them when she'd been outside. Besides, they'd probably given up long ago and were by now curled up snoozing—and in Bill's case, farting—contentedly. To prove it, she'd pop outside and listen.

She unplugged herself from her iPod and stuck her head out the back door. The dogs were howling. Their muffled canine misery acted on her like nails on a blackboard. Again, she slammed the door shut. This, she thought grimly, is why she'd never had kids: guilt. She could feel herself aging as she stood there, the process accelerated by guilt and worry.

So it went. Every half hour Mimi opened a window or a door and heard the pitiful keening of despairing dogs. Around two in the morning she realized she had two choices: She could drag them over here and listen to them be miserable or go back to Prescott's. Wrapping herself in a big old sleeping bag, she trudged back to Prescott's to be greeted by a short (*very* short, she thought suspiciously) burst of doggy rapture followed forthwith by her formerly wretched companions flopping down and falling instantly asleep.

She thought about finding the linens and making up the guest bed, but it was almost three o'clock and the sofa was comfortable and for one or two more nights (because that's what she had decided "a while" constituted), she'd just as soon not make herself at home here, in the Temple of Conspicuous (but ecologically friendly) Consumerism.

"Move over," she grumbled to Wiley, wedging herself between the back of the sofa and the sprawling dog.

Three days later, Mimi was still sleeping on Prescott's couch.

So was Wiley.

Chapter Twenty-nine

Mimi opened the door to the garage and looked inside. Last night, the fifth night she'd been holding down the fort at Prescott's, they'd run out of pizza. As pizza was the hands-down favorite amongst all those currently residing at Prescott's Piney Palace (a sobriquet she'd arrived at after deciding Prescott's Erection was simply not what she wanted to call a place in which she was living, no matter for how short a time), she needed to go to town. She was a teeny bit disappointed to discover all four stalls empty except for a hybrid Toyota Prius. Despite her unswerving disdain for Prescott's conspicuous consumptionism, just out of curiosity she'd have liked to know what it felt like to be behind the wheel of a Bentley or a DeLorean.

As soon as the garage door started sliding up the tracks, she heard the dogs scrambling across the living room floor. Then Blondie and Wiley bolted past her as she stood in the doorway leading into the garage, almost knocking her off her feet as they dashed headlong toward the Prius, clearly expecting to go for a ride. What the heck. She wasn't in the mood for a battle of wills. Besides, the dogs—or more specifically Bill—always won those.

"Okay," she'd said, flinging open the back door. "It's not my car. Be my guests."

Wiley and Blondie jumped in and settled as primly as little

debutantes on the backseat. They did not wrestle. They did not tear at the seat belts. They did not hop around. They simply waited, eyeing her expectantly. Bill, who'd wandered outside the garage, had taken up a position sitting on the snow-covered sidewalk leading to the front door, his dumpy little body askew, his stubby little back legs sticking out to one side.

"Get in, Bill. Get in there, or I swear to God I'll leave you. You know you want to come."

The little bastard. If she made any move toward him, he would just take off. That's the way it worked between them. Their relationship was defined by her failure to appreciate any of his charm and his complete disregard for her role as pack leader. She got into the car and closed the door, starting the motor. Bill yawned. She backed up. Bill scratched.

If it wasn't below zero, she'd have left him out there. But she couldn't. He'd die and thereby, in some inexplicable way, win the battle of wills raging between them. She flung open the door and got out of the car, stomping toward Bill. "Why you miserable little piece of—"

The sound of a car approaching cut short her tirade as a big black BMW 540i emerged from the woods and rolled to a stop in front of her. The driver turned off the engine. She eyed the car's shining, lacquered surface and knew at once who had to be in it.

Sure enough, Joe Tierney opened the door and stepped out, his long black cashmere coat rippling in the wind, a graphite-hued scarf tucked beneath the lapels. He glanced up at her, pulling on a pair of gloves.

"You must be the dog-sitter," he said. Yup. Same voice: smoky ice. "I'm Joe Tierney, the homeowner's father." His voice trailed off. Had he been one iota less self-contained, his mouth would have dropped open.

"You." For a few seconds she could have sworn his gaze warmed, but no, that wasn't warmth, it was suspicion. "What are you doing here?"

"Gold digging," she said. "What else?"

Chapter Thirty

"Very funny," Joe said.

The surge of warmth he'd felt upon realizing that the bag lady hollering at a small, despondent-looking mutt was Mimi Olson didn't fade even in the face of her obvious hostility. Her words simply added an element of sheepishness to the mix, which was, he told himself, flat-out stupid. As he'd reminded himself more than once, he had nothing to feel sheepish or guilty about. It was bizarre how this small, rumpled woman in her drab, lumpy coat and hideous fur-lined bomber's cap kept knocking him off balance and making him blurt out whatever was uppermost in his mind.

And what was she doing here? Why was she even up here? From the glances he'd had of it, Chez Ducky didn't look like the sort of place that was fit for subzero dwelling. Something else was going on.

"Why *are* you up here?"

One of her brows lifted. "Because," she said, "*I* am the dog-sitter."

So he'd gathered. "But how did you get the job?"

"How? Just call me lucky. I happened to be here during Prescott's time of need." Then she grudgingly added, "In case you have forgotten, the Olsons are selling Chez Ducky. I wanted to spend some time here before people like your son bulldoze it over and slap up their own monster erections ass cheek to ass cheek along the entire shore."

She had a way with words, he'd give her that. A vulgar way, but then she felt strongly about the subject. See? He could be objective where she was concerned. Obviously he was over whatever spell this small unkempt female had cast on him, a spell that had followed him to China and had had him thinking about her at odd and inconvenient moments throughout the last three months. But now, looking at her chapped lips and the dark smudges under her brilliant eyes and the straight-backed precision with which she held that small frame, he was thinking quite clearly. He was in command. He was himself again.

And this urge to reach out and tuck a wild and glossy coil of dark hair back under her hat? Not an excuse to touch her. He liked things tidy was all.

"What are *you* doing here?" Mimi asked.

Tit for tat. "Someone from the insurance agency called to tell me about Prescott's accident. I spoke to Prescott's physician and came as soon as I could. I was in China." He paused a second or two. "Did you get the roses?" he asked apropos of nothing.

"Roses? Oh. Yeah. I got 'em."

"From your tone, I guess there isn't any reason to ask if my apology was accepted?" He knew he sounded stiff.

"Was that an apology? I thought it was an excuse," she said, meeting his gaze.

Touché. He didn't have a riposte.

"So, why are you *here*?" she asked.

"The surgeon said Prescott will need someone to be with him for a while after he is released from the hospital."

"And you didn't just hire a nurse? I thought you said Prescott was a 'dick.' "

"He's still my son." Joe flushed. He *had* considered hiring a nurse, but after seeing Prescott in the hospital yesterday, still semi-gorked-out on pain meds, truculent, employing his usual winning ways with strangers and looking so damn un-happy, a brainstorm had seized Joe. He could help his kid in and out of a wheelchair, microwave some meals, let the little mutt out. For the first time since Karen's death, Joe had a role to perform in Prescott's life. A real role.

True, home aide wasn't a role he'd ever seen himself in, and he wasn't precisely sure what he could do that a paid worker couldn't do better, but he was a competent man. More important, he *wanted* to do this. It would give him and Prescott a chance to . . . do more than occupy different corners of the same room.

He'd suggested it to Prescott, but, again not unexpectedly, Prescott resisted the idea. Strenuously. Joe had thought it was because Prescott saw the offer as a sacrificial duty, which, again, made Joe feel like that was exactly what it was. But oddly, rather than making him back off, it only cemented Joe's resolve to do this for Prescott. He wasn't going to argue with him, though, so he'd just smiled, said good-bye, and rented a car and driven from Duluth, determined to have the place handicap ready for Prescott's arrival after they released him, which, owing to an elevation in his white blood count, and concerns of infection, would still be a few days. He would also pay the dog-sitter.

But now, realizing Mimi must be the person Prescott had assured Joe "was taking care of everything," Joe had a different take on Prescott's unwillingness to accept his help. And how the hell had he talked Mimi into doing this in the first place? Mimi Olson hated Prescott's house. "They're releasing Prescott from the hospital this weekend. I'm going to pick him up."

"Have you spoken to Prescott about this?" she said.

"No. I was going to . . . surprise him." *Because if my being here is a fait accompli, there's a better chance he'll let me stay*, he thought, but he did not say aloud. "Why? Do you have a problem with that?"

"You bet," she said. "You're thwarting my plot to infiltrate

Prescott's inner sanctum, using his weakened condition to make myself invaluable to him," she said. "Curses. Foiled again. I guess I'll just have to go home and think up some other way to get to him."

"I wasn't going to say that," he answered, honestly surprised that he really hadn't been thinking that and possibly should have been. Damn.

"Oh?" she said disbelievingly. "Gee. Sorry, I misjudged you."

"Ah," he said, refusing to let her goad him. "Irony. Very good."

"Thanks," she chirped. "Now, if you'll excuse me, I'll get my wallet out of Prescott's car and my stuff from Prescott's house and be on my way. That's right," she said as he glanced toward the Prius and the two mongrels sitting patiently in the backseat. "I've been making free with Prescott's hot wheels all week. Man, I'm gonna miss that bad boy. Cruising the strip, mackin' on the Frosties, picking up 'bilers. It's been sweet."

"You know, if you're going to mock someone, it's most effective if you do so in their native tongue. Would you care to translate?"

Unwillingly, her mouth curled into a smile. "Mackin' on, making out with. Frosties are people from the city who come north for winter sports. 'Bilers, as in snowmobilers. Man, you are old."

"What's the strip?"

"I made that up," she said unapologetically. "There is no strip." She swaggered past him and opened the Prius's door. A pair of dogs, one some sort of fluffy retriever mix and the other a gray, slat-sided cross, leapt out and started jumping around, biting at Mimi's mittens and the tassels on her oversized boots. She swatted at them ineffectively, like this was routine, then ducked into the car and rummaged around inside. She backed out hauling a sloppy-looking tote with her.

Then, slinging it over her shoulder, she headed up the walk toward the front door.

The dogs romped after her, except for Prescott's dog, the dumpy little creature who'd been sitting on the walk. He continued watching Joe with an unnervingly direct stare. Mimi started opening the door. The dogs started trying to push their way past her.

"You're not going to let your dogs inside Prescott's house, are you?" Joe asked.

She looked around and started to smile. Even from a distance it wasn't a nice smile. "You mean, you don't know?"

"Know what?"

"These"—she pointed at the two dogs wrestling at her feet—"are not my dogs. *These* are Prescott's dogs. And now they're yours."

"But Prescott is very allergic to dogs." Even as he spoke, he realized how absurd he sounded.

"If you don't believe me, and there's a lot of that going around, call him yourself."

"Are you ever going to let it go?" he asked. "I apologized. I wrote a note. Would you like me to say I'm sorry again?"

"Yes."

"I'm sorry."

"Not accepted."

"I was wrong."

"Well, that had to hurt," she said, eyeing him. Her chill expression seemed to thaw a little. "The dog in front of you is Bill. One of these"—she pointed at the two dogs rolling around at her feet—"is Merry. I can't remember the other one's name."

"Which one is Merry?" he asked.

"I don't know." She shrugged. "It was late at night, the ambulance guy was giving me heat, Prescott was moaning, and I was thinking about other things. I blanked out on the names. I call that one Blondie and that one Wiley. As in coyote. Like the cartoon?"

He really didn't care what she called the animals. He was more interested in something else she'd said. "You were here when Prescott had his accident?"

"Actually," she said, "I was down there." She indicated the lake. "I was . . . taking a walk when I saw Prescott come out and fall." Her cheeks turned pink but she met his eye defiantly.

She was clearly lying. She didn't even do it very well, either, which had the odd effect of both heartening and disturbing him. Heartening him because as a seasoned con artist she wouldn't have any trouble lying, so she obviously wasn't a seasoned con artist—further substantiating what he'd already guessed—and disturbing him because she was lying about something. What?

"I gotta get my things inside. Is that okay?" she said, flinging the front door open. The pack of dogs exploded inside and disappeared amongst a racket of clattering nails and growls.

Mimi kicked off her boots and padded down the hall. Joe followed her into the great room overlooking the lake, but the arresting view didn't attract his eye. He was too busy staring at the homeless shelter someone had set up in Prescott's living room. Lap rugs and blankets tangled together in the center of the scarlet sofa, and a pillow without a pillowcase had slipped off one end. Crumbs were sprinkled on the surface of the big copper coffee table, along with books, magazines, half-completed crossword puzzles, and an iPod.

Clutter surrounded the sofa: a pair of mauled rubber flip-flops, a shredded T-shirt, disemboweled stuffed animals, and, my God, it looked like there was a cow's bone under one of the club chairs. Make that *two* cows' bones.

He didn't want to look in the kitchen, but he couldn't help himself. It was more of the same, only with empty food wrappers. A backpack balanced precariously on the edge of the island's granite countertop right next to a pair of rubber-soled moccasins.

"There are shoes on the kitchen countertop," he said numbly.

"Oh? Oh," Mimi hustled past him and swept them up. "Yeah. I had to put them up there so the dogs wouldn't get them. You can see what they did to my T-shirt. Or rather Wiley did."

"Ah-huh." Okay, Mimi wasn't merely eccentrically and exotically tousled, she was a bona fide slob. Four stoneware plates lay in the sink. "You've had company?"

Mimi followed the direction of his gaze. "Huh? Oh." She gave a little laugh. "No, one of those is mine and the others are the dogs'. I didn't know where their dishes were and I didn't want them to have to eat off the floor."

"Why not? No, don't tell me. You just washed it."

"No, I . . ." His sarcasm found its mark. Her gaze narrowed. "Listen, Joe. I am not Prescott's maid. I am, *was*, here doing him a favor."

"That doesn't mean you have to live like a squatter."

"A squatter?" She made an encompassing gesture. "The place just looks lived in."

"No," Joe replied with commendable calm. "The couch looks lived in. As in, you slept on it, lounged on it, ate from it— Dear God. Is that a toothbrush on the coffee table?"

She scooted over and snatched up the toothbrush, shoving it into the pocket of her jacket. "People come up north, Joe, to escape the tyranny of vacuum cleaners, clothes dryers, and curling irons. I was supposed to be on vacation up here. And I *did* sleep on the couch."

"Why?"

"I didn't know what to do about the dogs. I didn't want to mess up a bedroom—"

He started to make some smart-ass comment, but her hard, swift glare stopped him.

"I didn't want to mess up another room," she repeated, "and since I'd already slept on the sofa once, I just kept sleeping there. Besides, the dogs don't like being locked out of rooms and I didn't know if Prescott would like them on the beds."

"Probably just as much as he likes them on the sofa," Joe muttered, noting with disapproval the dog fur on all the upholstered surfaces. He couldn't believe Prescott didn't have a vacuum cleaner somewhere.

He looked around. Bill and Blondie were racing each other around the room, skittering across the hardwood floor, leaping over the back of the sofa, and bouncing off the walls like pinballs. The one she called Wiley had fallen with near feral glee upon Mimi's T-shirt and was proceeding to shred it to pieces.

"Why didn't you just tell them to stay and shut the door?"

"Ha!" Mimi said. "That shows what you know about dogs. Look at them. Do they *look* like they'd obey a command like 'stay'?"

"Have you ever tried?"

"Plenty of times. As well as 'come,' 'come now,' 'please come,' 'damn it, come' and 'get the hell over here!' All with the same results. None." She turned her head and abruptly bellowed, "Stop that!"

The dogs ignored her. She gave Joe a "told ya so" look.

"You've completely lost control," Joe said.

"What?"

"You have lost control of the situation, the household, the dogs, quite possibly more than that." *Like your life.* He didn't say this, though; he had finally found a job for himself in Prescott's life, and one at which he excelled: putting order to chaos, cleaning up the mess, pulling the brake on this runaway train.

She raised one straight dark brow at him.

"I find that a calm, assertive tone produces better results than a stridently demanding one." As soon as the words were out, he regretted them. "I possibly should have couched that in different terms."

"No, no," she declared, sounding patently insincere. "I

appreciate your interest and I'm ready to sit at the foot of genius and learn." She crossed her arms over her chest. "Teach me, *sensei*."

"You're being truculent."

"No. Please. Give it your best shot, Joe." She adjusted the angle of her arms. The dogs ran amuck. Joe hated things running amuck.

"Bill. Blondie. Wiley." The dogs, hearing an unfamiliar voice speaking their names, slowed down enough to glance at him. Joe kept his gaze locked with Mimi's. "Nagging only confirms in the minds of those you are attempting to lead your lower status in the social hierarchy. You receive attention by expecting attention."

Mimi gave him a bored look.

The dogs, obviously unused to someone speaking and not screaming, stopped running and began milling uncertainly. Finally, Blondie, as though she could no longer stand the suspense, wandered over to him. Soon, the other two, curious, ventured nearer.

Joe looked at them, each in turn. "Sit."

The dogs sat. Even Bill.

Triumphant, Joe looked at Mimi and found her regarding the dogs with slack-jawed incredulity. Her mouth snapped into a bloodless line. Without a word, she stomped toward the front door, whipping her backpack off the island counter as she went by.

The dogs watched her go then looked up at Joe.

"Okay," he said.

Perhaps feeling the animosity in the atmosphere—Joe had heard that dogs were perceptive—they slunk toward the front door, peeking around the corner to find out what Mimi was doing. Joe followed. Mimi was hopping on one booted foot as she tugged on the other one. She finished and snatched her mittens off the ground.

"Mimi." He didn't want her to feel bad. He just wanted her to . . . to what? *Stay.*

He didn't understand himself.

Though she didn't glance at him, she did glare at the dogs. They cowered behind Joe. In all fairness, had he been one of them, he would have cowered, too.

She whipped open the front door, turning at the last instant before exiting.

"Traitors!" she breathed and slammed the door shut.

Chapter Thirty-one

Mimi relaxed back in the old claw-footed tub and crossed her ankles on the porcelain rim. Now, this *was* the way she'd envisioned her time at Fowl Lake. Little will-o'-the-wisps of steam rose from the water around her, and the soothing, rhythmic *plop* of the water dripping from the faucet lulled her into a pleasant state of inertia. Her natural state, she reminded herself.

The uncomfortable sensation that she ought to be doing something—heating a pizza, picking burrs out of Blondie's coat, wishing Bill ill, would pass. After all, she'd been released from canine servitude only yesterday. The dogs, the house, everything on the other side of the woods, were no longer her concern. The only one she had to worry about now was Mimi. Who cared about a bunch of opportunistic four-footed sycophants? Good riddance to them. They had Drill Sergeant Tierney monitoring their every move. Finally, she was free. Free, free, free!

And cold.

The Big House, never intended to be a year-round residence, wasn't well insulated. The will-o'-the-wisps disappeared in a matter of minutes, and those parts of Mimi's anatomy exposed above the tepid water soon sprouted goose bumps. She turned on the hot-water spigot with her toes. The system sputtered and choked, rust-colored water gushing into the tub. Within a few minutes she'd be shivering again. Prescott's water heater delivered really hot water.

She stood up, grabbed the towel off the forced-air heater, and dried off as quickly as she could. Downstairs, warmly dressed and refreshed from her bath, she wandered around appreciating the peace and quiet that permeated a house with no animals careening around disturbing it. At noon, she made a peanut butter sandwich and washed it down with an Orange Crush. She stared out the window. She didn't see anything. No dogs. No Joe.

And wasn't he a piece of work? Had he once said, "Thank you for watching the dogs, Mimi?" No. He'd followed her through the house, clucking at the various lived-in-looking areas where she'd spent the majority of her time. Then, to top it off, he'd informed her that she'd lost control of the situation when it was in-your-face obvious he'd meant to say "her life." Pontificating, germaphobic control freak. He could have his control.

The whole master-of-my-ship thing was overrated. She didn't want to be master of any ship, especially her own. If you were steering a ship, you were missing the view. Besides, captains ended up not only driving but driving people away. Like Solange had driven her off. Why had she ever wasted time thinking about Joe? Yeah, yeah, he had an unexpected sense of humor, he was pretty, he smelled good, and he kissed better. Dime a dozen. Okay, he apparently also cared enough about Prescott to drop whatever he'd been doing wherever he'd been doing it and come out here to take care of him. Again she was reminded of Solange. Her mother would have been out here in a heartbeat if she thought Mimi needed her. Yup, if nothing else, you had to give that to the control freaks of the world; they could always be counted on. Thank God she didn't have to count on anyone.

That settled—though she would have been hard-pressed to say exactly what "that" had been or why it had needed settling—Mimi found her romance novel and spent the next four hours curled in a corner of the lumpy chintz-covered sofa. At midafternoon, she tried to get up. She could barely straighten her legs. She limped to the kitchen and looked without success for a bottle of Tylenol. She briefly considered going over to Prescott's and asking Joe if she could borrow something but decided he was arrogant enough to think she was making excuses to see him. A nice walk would work out the cricks. . . . Dang. She'd left her Arctic Explorer silk-blend socks at Prescott's. You could not spend any time outside without the proper clothing. There was nothing for it. She'd have to go get them.

As she followed the footpath between the two houses, she rehearsed what she would say. She would be civil, of course. There was no sense being unnecessarily antagonistic. The simple truth was that she and Joe held such different views on life that they barely comprehended each other. They were like two space alien species trying to exchange recipes. Not only didn't they understand the instructions, they didn't have the same ingredients. Like her recipe called for some kind of mushroom and his planet didn't even have dirt.

Before she realized it, she had crossed the property line and was at Prescott's front door. She peered through the big glass door. She saw Joe on his knees at the end of the hall, just inside the kitchen, a plastic bucket beside him. He was scrubbing the floor tiles. Suave Joe Tierney, scullery maid. Ha!

She knocked. He turned his head at the sound and regarded her expressionlessly, then dropped the brush into the bucket. He rose with fluid grace and started toward the door, snapping off his yellow gloves with the same sexy proficiency with which George Clooney had taken off his OR gloves when he'd played that surgeon on television. How could a man with hand towels tied around his knees look sexy? Because he'd rolled the cuffs of his blue dress shirt-sleeves up over his forearms—and extremely nice forearms they were, too, muscled, tanned, and with a light covering of silky dark hair that ended at the wrist. Mimi was a sucker for manly forearms. He opened the door.

"Yes?" he asked.

"I forgot my socks," she said.

He nodded. "Right. Come in."

She sidled warily into the house.

"I'll be right back." He left her at the door and disappeared into the house.

"You're scrubbing the floor," she called after him.

"Yes," he said.

She had to give him credit for not saying something like, "God knows, it needed it."

"I didn't see I had much choice," he added from deeper in the house. So much for giving him credit.

She looked around for the dogs, expecting that at least Wiley, with whom she'd shared so many nights, would show up to greet her. She'd sort of looked forward to seeing him and Blondie. Not so much Bill. "Where are the dogs?"

"They're in the laundry room," he answered. "I gave them baths. They're drying out."

Poor dogs. Joe returned a minute later holding a paper bag. He handed it to her.

"You put my things in a paper bag?" she asked. For some reason, this offended her even more than the crack about the floor.

"I washed them first," he said, adding, "Your tampons are in there, too."

"Thanks."

By dusk, it had begun to snow. Mimi, wandering along the shoreline, found herself looking at Prescott's place. A warm golden hue illuminated the windows looking out over the deck. Poor Joe. She wondered what he and the dogs had eaten tonight. Not much, would be her guess.

Mimi returned to the Big House and a can of Hormel chili

and beans. She appreciated the fact that she wouldn't have to share her meal with anyone, particularly Bill, considering what the meal was. Afterward she considered calling Ozzie, but her cell phone service had been crappy all week. Instead, she wandered around the Big House, stopping now and again to close her eyes as she tried to populate the rooms with long-gone Olsons. She had no success. Her imagination refused to open the doors to the past, staying firmly fixed on Prescott's house and the man and dogs in it. Was Joe bored, too? Wait. She wasn't bored. Simply . . . inert.

She wandered some more, opening drawers and trunks and finding nothing until the pantry. On the floor beneath the bottom shelf, she found a box of old photo albums. She hadn't noticed them there and, in fact, only vaguely recognized them. The Olsons weren't much for looking back. Mimi couldn't recall the last time someone had dragged out the battered books with their rusty black pages to look through them. She wondered whether she could find the forebear responsible for Great-Uncle Charlie's six toes.

She lugged the box of albums into the parlor and started leafing through them. The Olson archivists had pasted pictures in whatever album was closest to hand on whatever page had room. Most of the pictures had names printed on the backs; some had dates. Many peeled off their moorings as she opened the pages, the glue holding them giving up after decades of service. Mimi began piling these loose photographs up, dividing them by families and eras. It was better than a Sudoku.

She had just started on a new decade when she heard a faint sound at the front door. Joe? No, Joe wouldn't be scratching. A raccoon? She went to the door and peered cautiously out the window. On the step below stood Bill.

She couldn't help the . . . the what? It wasn't pleasure exactly. Satisfaction? No. Certainly not happiness. Gratification. That was it. She couldn't help the *gratification* she felt at the sight of him.

He looked up at her. She opened the door and put her hand on her hip. He was all glossy and brushed and—she sniffed—he smelled like baby shampoo.

"So, Bill," she said, "you've come to beg me to take you in, have you? And just look at you now," she continued scathingly, "you're nothing but Joe Tierney's fancy-dog."

But Bill's indifference was supreme. He plodded past her and headed down the hall. She followed him. He took a leisurely saunter around the parlor. Here the moldy scent of albums generated a few seconds of interest; then that was over and he wandered out. Again Mimi followed.

He returned to the front door and stopped. He didn't even bother to turn and gaze beseechingly at her. She reached over his head and pulled open the door. Without a glance in her direction, he hopped down the steps. She shut the door, looking out in spite of herself to make sure that he was heading back to Prescott's. He was, but first he lifted his leg and peed on the bottom step.

She was cold that night and the next night after that. She kept reaching down by her feet to drag Wiley closer.

The next day Mimi moved the multiplying stacks of photographs and albums from the parlor to the dining room, and drove to Fawn Creek. Once in town, she collected some groceries, including a couple of frozen pizzas, should she just happen to have any other late-night callers, and headed to the drugstore for photo-album supplies.

The pleasant woman behind the counter, scanning her goods, asked her whether she was scrapbooking. Mimi, who had no real understanding of what that was, said she thought she might be. The woman's face bloomed with delight, and she declared that she was a scrapbooker, too. Mimi regarded her blankly as she took Mimi by the hand and led her to a section of goods at the back of the store. Fifteen minutes later, Mimi left with a sack filled with metallic ink pens, dozens of sheets of stickers, special border-cutting scissors, glitter, hundreds of little die-cut figures, stamps, ink pads, construction paper, and special glue.

She returned to the Big House and spread her booty on the dining table. She liked the looks of all the crap she'd bought. But first she had to take all the old pictures out and clean the old glue off in the manner in which the nice lady at the drugstore had told her it must be done. She plugged in her earbuds and began.

When Mimi finally stopped for a bathroom break, she was surprised to see it was two o'clock. She glanced outside the dining room window and at once felt her equilibrium waver. She'd been bending over the photo albums too long. She needed some fresh air.

She donned coat and gloves and headed down to the beach, taking deep breaths and stomping her feet to get the circulation running. Hearing the sound of barking, she looked around and spotted Prescott's dogs—and Prescott's father—heading toward her across the lake. The dogs were straining against some sort of tethers attaching them to Joe, who was on cross-country skis. The dogs were pulling him, barking their protests as they went.

Now that, Mimi thought in disgust, was laziness. The poor dogs. She wasn't even sure that wasn't cruel. Joe was no lightweight, and those dogs, even pitiful little Bill, were really working. The dogs spied her and, undoubtedly seeing her as their only hope of salvation, veered toward her, yelping and squealing and dragging Joe after them.

As they grew nearer, Joe lifted one of his ski poles in greeting. He looked like a REI sports advert dressed in a manly-looking oatmeal fisherman's sweater and heavy brown wool slacks. A close-fitting ski cap hugged his head, accentuating the handsome angles of his face.

When they got to her, the dogs began bounding about, nipping at her hands and legs. Except for Bill, who plopped his round little rump down in the snow and yawned. Joe smiled, his face ruddy with health. His blue eyes looked like he was wearing cerulean contacts, and his teeth gleamed as white as the snow.

Mimi felt dumpy.

"What are you doing to these poor dogs?"

"Hello, Mimi. Stay down, dogs." The dogs didn't exactly freeze in midstride, but they did stop trying to knock her over. As they settled down, Mimi saw each was wearing a harness.

"Aren't they doing well?" Joe asked. "I had the belt and harnesses overnighted yesterday before the storm. This is only the third time I've had them out, but they really seem to have caught the hang of it."

"The hang of hauling your butt around the lake?" she asked sarcastically.

He didn't take offense. He laughed. Obviously something had tickled him. "No, no. Well, yes, actually. We're *skijoring*."

He looked at her as though he expected something to click. It didn't. She waited expectantly.

"*Skijoring*," he repeated. "It's a sport invented by the Norwegians, a hybrid between cross-country skiing and mushing. The dogs love it."

Mimi seriously doubted this, but when she looked at the dogs, they were staring at Joe with adoring concentration. They'd never looked at her like that. Except the time she'd shared the quart of ice cream she'd found hidden in the back of the freezer.

"They look exhausted."

"Oh, no. They enjoy this. All animals thrive on performing the function for which they were bred." He sounded like Solange.

"I don't think Bill was bred to pull you around."

"No. But he was bred to do something more than eat and sleep. Just like humans, animals need a job. It gives their life purpose, makes them happy, relaxed, more content."

Definitely, he was channeling Solange. Could you channel the living? Maybe she'd better give her mother a call . . .

"How do you know?" she asked.

"I read it in several of the books Prescott has on dog psychology and pack dynamics."

She glanced at the dogs. No one was cringing. She didn't see any welts. "Hm."

"You're unconvinced. Let me show you. The dogs really eat this up, and the little buggers are fast. Watch."

He pulled his poles out of the snow and tipped forward. "Hie on!"

The dogs sprang to life, hurling themselves against the lines as Joe skated forward on his skis. He skated for about ten more yards before the momentum shifted to the dogs. Then they flew, and Joe flew right behind them.

Mimi watched in fascination. The dogs, tails whipping around like eggbeaters in a doggy delirium of joy, barked and scrabbled, pushing for more speed. She heard Joe laughing. And damn it, she couldn't help but like him for it. And just when she was so close to being able to write him off as a pompous, self-important demagogue. He probably still was, but he was a really nice demagogue.

She watched, smiling now, noticing idly that if they kept going the way they were, they'd be skirting awfully close to the big tanning rock near Chez Ducky's beach. Normally, it stood far enough out of the ice not to be a threat to snowmobilers, but the recent snow had covered it with— Oh, dear.

"Joe! Joe! Turn the dogs. Turn!"

Joe, hearing her shouts, turned to look at her. He raised one ski pole over his head and waved. The dogs veered to the side of the mound, but Joe didn't. He hit it dead center. Then he *really* flew.

Chapter Thirty-two

"Another Tierney?" Bob, the ambulance driver, asked, wheeling the gurney up the ramp toward the Oxlip Memorial Hospital emergency entrance. He hadn't been in the ambulance that had arrived at Fowl Lake to transport Joe, but he'd met them in the parking lot with the paperwork. Apparently Bob wore many hats.

He punched a code into the double-wide glass doors, regarding Mimi across Joe's prone form. "You got some sort of vendetta going against these guys? Gonna pick 'em off one by one?"

"I didn't do anything to this one or the last one," Mimi said, offended. She damn well ought to be getting brownie points for saintliness rather than listening to some would-be mystery writer with a lurid imagination cast doubt over her selfless act.

After thankfully being able to connect to 911 with her cell phone, she'd hustled back to stay with Joe, who, as well as having a goose egg on his head, had all too obviously dislocated his shoulder and God knew what else. She'd left his side only when the ambulance arrived. She'd then shepherded the dogs into the house and been on the cusp of going back to Chez Ducky when Joe had requested—actually it had been more of a beg—that she follow the ambulance in the

Prius so that as soon as they'd checked him out he could leave, a possibility made more likely if he had someone to drive him. He'd said "please" with nothing short of desperation.

It wasn't too hard to figure out why. No place on earth could be more psychologically torturous for a germaphobe than a hospital.

"How'd you lure this one out onto the ice?" Bob asked. "Pretending to have another fit?"

"What?" Joe roused himself to say. "She was pretending to have a fit? When was she having a fit?"

"She *says* she was just rolling around on the snow, a woman her age—"

"Hey!" Mimi interjected.

"—a woman her age," Bob repeated with satisfaction, "and that your son mistook her snow-angel making for a seizure and called us. *She* says your son just happened to fall into his own swimming pool in the process of racing down to the lake to help her."

Bob eyed Mimi dubiously. "*I* think the whole thing is fishy is what I think," he said. "Though I will admit she doesn't look much like a black widow. Sharon Stone, she ain't."

"Hey!" Mimi said again.

"How'd she get you?" Bob asked Joe.

"She didn't," Joe said. "I was showing off and I ran into a boulder."

"On an Arctic Cat?" Bob said, interested.

Joe looked at Mimi for translation.

"That's a snowmobile."

"No," Joe said. "Behind some dogs."

At this Bob shook his head, embarrassed for Joe. "Man your age playing with dogs. You guys growing something funny up there on Fowl Lake?"

"Hardly," Joe said.

"So, you were stone-cold sober and just showing off to

her," Bob said as the door finally swooshed open. "What sort of dark spell has she got over the men in your family?"

"You spend a lot of time watching cable, don't you, Bob?" Joe asked.

Bob flushed.

"Did Prescott say she'd 'lured' him out?" Joe demanded.

"Nah-uh," Bob said in disgust. "Fact, he couldn't stop moaning about how wonderful she was. I had to listen to a half an hour on what a perfect woman Mignonette Olson is."

"Really?" Mimi asked, preening a little. She hadn't realized Prescott had a crush on her. Oh, she knew Joe thought he did, but Joe had also thought she was scamming Prescott by delivering bogus messages from his dead mother. Prescott was obviously much more perceptive than his father.

"Course the kid was half delirious, but still," Bob said, "that's when I figured out something was not on the up 'n' up. Kid like that oughta be drooling over Angelina Jolie, not"—he must have read a budding threat in her narrowing eyes because he said only—"her."

"Watch it, fella," Joe said.

Mimi gave Bob an exultant smile. Joe, white knighting for her. Of course, she knew enough about Joe to realize he'd white knight for anyone. He was white-knight prone. Still, it felt nice to be championed. So she decided not to remind him that he had entertained equally unflattering notions about her.

Then they were in the hospital's emergency room. A girl with red-rimmed eyes and sweaty skin sat in a chair, and a green-nosed toddler ran around hurling picture books at the walls while his mother filled out some papers at the desk. Joe blanched as Bob wheeled him down a short open corridor with three curtained bays on one side. Two were open but the farthest one was occupied by someone doing heavy mouth breathing. Bob rolled him into the first bay.

A plump but pretty pediatric nurse—she had to be a pediatric nurse; no one else would wear little-yellow-ducky print scrubs—moseyed up with a clipboard. "This the guy from Fowl Lake?"

"Sure is, Karin," Bob declared like he'd just pulled in a trophy-sized fish.

"This the same woman that was out there last time?" the nurse asked, nodding at Mimi.

"Yup."

The nurse looked Mimi over. "Ah-huh."

"Look, do you think a doctor could see Mr. Tierney?" Mimi surprised herself by saying. But since no one else seemed to be willing to get this show on the road and Joe seemed to be stricken mute with germ dread, she didn't see she had much choice. It was almost the dogs' dinner time.

"He's not dying?" The nurse directed this laconic query at Bob.

"Nope."

"Then we got paperwork to do first. Now"—she leaned over Joe—"you got insurance?"

"Yes." He rolled to his side, gritting his teeth as he fumbled for his wallet in his back pocket. He thrust it at the nurse. "The card's in there. Can we please hurry?"

The nurse opened the wallet and retrieved the insurance card inside. "Hold on, there, sport. We'll get you patched up soon enough. First things first."

A grubby little hand reached over the side of the gurney and gripped the rail, followed by the top of a small round head sprouting tufts of wispy blond hair. Then came a pinched, red-cheeked face, the most predominant feature being a very snotty nose.

Wide brown eyes met even wider blue ones. "Oh, God," Joe breathed.

"Wha' wong wid yo?" the small creature asked.

"Justin Bjorkland, you get right back to your momma, you hear me?" the nurse said, plucking the child from his perch on Joe's gurney and swatting his baggy behind.

Mimi looked down at Joe. His eyes were closed. It looked
suspiciously like he was praying.

"Your shoulder was dislocated, Mr. Tierney," said Dr.
Youngstrum, a tired-looking woman in her fifties. "Your
wrist is not in good shape. You wrenched that knee pretty se-
verely. I don't care if you actually lost consciousness or not,
that's still a nasty bump on your head. You should stay
overnight for observation. Besides, I don't know how you're
going to get around without a wheelchair for the next few
days. You can't grip crutches with that hand and your opposite leg isn't going to bear weight for a while. The nursing
home—"

"No!" Joe surged forward, banged his bruised knee, and
yowled.

The doctor regarded him stoically. "I was going to say, the
nursing home attached to the hospital has an extremely good
physical therapist. A couple days there and you'd be—"

"No!"

"A couple days there," the doctor went on as if the inter-
ruption had never occurred, "and you'll be much further
along in your recovery than if you just go back to your son's
place."

"I don't care," Joe said, his head wagging back and forth
like a truculent child's.

Mimi supposed she shouldn't be amused, but she was. Joe
would have been aghast at his behavior if he was in his right
mind, but he wasn't. The Demerol they'd given him before
popping his shoulder back into place had sent him straight to
the land of no impulse control, where every thought is given
voice and the foremost thought in Joe Tierney's mind was
that he didn't want to spend one more minute than necessary
in what he'd a few minutes ago described as a "pestilence-
ridden heap of virulence," known to the rest of the world as
a hospital.

"Fawn Creek doesn't have any private nurses or home

care. We have a nursing home. You need someone with you for at least the next forty-eight hours."

"She'll stay with me!" Joe said.

Mimi, who'd been picking diligently at a hangnail, looked up to see whom Joe was pointing at. He was pointing at her.

"Huh?"

"If she'll stay with me, I can leave, right?"

The doctor shrugged. "Sure. I can't keep you here against your will. Well, actually I can, but—"

"Nuh-uh," Mimi said.

"Please, Mimi." Joe was gripping the bed rails with white knuckles and his eyes reminded her unpleasantly of the ones from Eduard Munch's *The Scream.* "You were already watching the dogs. Just for a couple days. Just until I can stand."

The dogs. She thought of Blondie's sweet face, and Wiley's clownish one, and Bill . . . She thought of Blondie and Wiley. Someone would have to take them for walks and feed them. Besides, it might be nice to watch Joe Tierney choke a little on his pride once he came out of his drug-induced panic.

"Please," he said, his panicked gaze shooting toward the sound of someone hacking in the waiting room.

"Okay," she said graciously.

Chapter Thirty-three

On the drive from Fowl Lake, Joe sat in the back of the Prius with his leg propped up over the back of the passenger seat. Crowding next to him was a folded wheelchair. He didn't say much. Mimi assumed he was dozing, but occasionally, when they hit a rut, he moaned.

When they arrived at Prescott's, Mimi got the wheelchair out and opened it on the drive. She then let the dogs out and returned to the passenger side to help Joe. She found him already halfway out the back, stuck.

"Let me help you," she said, reaching in to lift his leg down.

"Did you wash your hands when we left the hospital?" Joe asked.

"What?"

"You're touching me and you were touching things all over that hospital. I saw you touch the rail where that kid was. I just want to make sure you washed your hands when we left."

Telling herself to make allowances for his drug-addled state, she smiled reassuringly. "Of course I did. I don't want to get sick, either. Now, do you think you can swivel your legs out the door? Then all we have to do is stand you up, pivot you on your good leg, and dump you in the chair. Do you think you're up to that?"

He gave a manly snort of disdain.

"Okay, put your arms around my neck." She bent down and smiled invitingly.

"Can't. They strapped my left arm to my side."

"Right. Okay. Here's how we'll do this: first, stick your good leg out and put your foot on the ground. Thatta boy. Now, I'm going to get my shoulder under your good arm and then we'll stand up together."

Dutifully, Joe lifted his good arm, allowing Mimi to put her shoulder under it. She wrapped her arms tightly around his chest, tucking her head under his chin, and prepared to stand.

"Your hair smells good," Joe said.

"You know, if you didn't sound so surprised I could almost take that as a compliment. Now, on the count of three—"

"I mean, it's really nice."

"It's Jo Malone. Whenever you're ready." His body felt very solid and very warm pressed next to hers. Even drugged up and laid low he managed to exude polished masculinity.

"Really? You don't seem like the expensive-shampoo type," Joe said.

Of course he'd know who Jo Malone was. His girlfriends probably wore it.

"I got it on eBay," Mimi said. "Ready? One. Two. Three."

She heaved, pulling him toward her. Together, they wobbled upright. Joe's good arm shot out and he braced his hand on the Prius's roof, steadying them.

He looked down into her upturned face. "You also have spectacular eyes," he said, relevant of nothing.

"You do, too." And he did. Black Irish good looks were killer.

"I know you didn't try to con Prescott," he blurted out.

She hesitated a second, amused. This probably wasn't the

best time to have a heart-to-heart. She had all her wits about her, and Joe was wacked out on Demerol. On the other hand, too bad for Joe. She was interested in hearing what he thought without a safety net of good manners and cosmopolitan polish to fall back on.

"Really?" she said. "How do you know?"

"I called him and asked him about you. I was very crafty. He had no idea you were . . . what do you call it?"

"A spiritual conduit?"

"Bull." Joe didn't seem at all averse to standing on one leg, the two of them wrapped in each other's arms. He seemed quite content, in fact. But then, so was Mimi. It felt oddly comfortable chatting like this. She suspected it wouldn't have been nearly so comfortable if Joe had been more himself.

"That's what it says on our Web site."

"Sounds pretentious." Thus Ozzie's best commercial efforts were damned. Privately Mimi agreed, but loyalty kept her mouth shut. "Anyway, Prescott didn't have a clue that's what you do. He thinks you're a widow bravely facing destitution and fending off despair through sheer optimism and courage."

"Why am I despairing?" Mimi asked curiously.

"I dunno. The widow thing I suppose," Joe said. "You have to know he has a crush on you. Even the ambulance driver knows."

"Well"—Mimi lowered her eyes modestly—"it is kinda obvious. I suppose that worries you. I mean, just because I haven't taken advantage of him doesn't mean I won't." He didn't deny it. "And yet, it didn't keep you from asking me to stay with you for a few days while you recuperate. What does that tell you, Joe?"

He pondered this for a minute, and if he didn't realize how odd the circumstances of the conversation were, what with her arms tight around his chest and her head nested against his shoulder, her face tilted up to his like a lover's, well, she wasn't going to mention it.

"Either I really hate hospitals," he finally said, "or you have really, *really* pretty eyes."

She smiled. "You sound disheartened."

"I am. I can't figure you out. Most of the time you don't seem like a nut."

"Why, thank you, Joe," she said solemnly.

"But you are. You'd have to be to drop out of Brown a month before completing your undergraduate degree and with a 4.0 average—"

"Don't be too impressed. The degree was in English. And who told you that?"

"Your mother. She spoke about you a lot."

She did? Of course she did. Hope springs eternal in a Machiavellian heart. Solange had probably seen Mimi leave the anniversary party with Joe and saw in him an opportunity to influence her.

"Ah, she says that about all her kids," Mimi said. "Don't believe everything you hear."

He wasn't listening. "And rather than get a real job and do something, you prefer to live in a low-rent furnished rental—"

"It isn't a furnished rental," Mimi protested.

"You mean you paid *money* for that stuff?"

Okay, the honesty thing was getting old. "And I do have a real job."

Joe scoffed. "Right. Tell me, Mimi. Do you really think you're talking to ghosts?"

"Do you?" she countered.

"I don't know what to think. I only know that you are odd, eccentric."

"*I'm* eccentric?" she guffawed. "I'm not the one rushing to leave my hospital bed because of all the icky-bad germs, sport."

She felt him stiffen. As she'd hoped, that put an end to the uncomfortable direction of the conversation. If she wanted to be harangued about her life, she could call Solange or Mary. She didn't need a new voice added to the choir. Which reminded her; she hadn't heard from Baby Precocious in weeks. Next time she was in Fawn Creek she'd have to hit the Brewski Coffee Shoppe and use their free Internet service to check her e-mail.

"Come on, Joe," she said, pivoting him on his good leg and easing him down into the wheelchair. "Let's get you inside the nice hermetically sealed house."

She rolled Joe into the house, the dogs ambling in after them. Kicking the Navaho rug out of the way, she rolled him across the wood floors to the center of the living area.

She could tell Joe's pain meds were starting to wear off from the way he grimaced every time he shifted. The doctor had been very pointed in saying he should stay ahead of the pain.

She went into the kitchen and returned with a glass of water, then reached into her jacket pocket where she'd stashed his prescription and took out the bottle.

"Here," she said, twisting off the cap. She motioned for him to hold out his hand and then carefully shook two tablets into his palm. It probably said much about his level of discomfort that he didn't kick about her handling his pills but popped them into his mouth and took a swig of water.

"Tell me, Joe," she said, regarding him seriously. "Is it hard being perfect?"

That threw him. "Perfect? What are you talking about?"

"Perfect clothes, perfect haircut, perfectly groomed, perfectly *clean* . . ."

"Tell me, Mimi," he countered. "In the morning do you walk into your closet and say, 'Anyone who wants to go for a ride, hop on. 'Cause that's what it looks like."

She sat down on the sofa's arm and leaned forward. "I'm happy how I am.'

"I'm happy how I am," he countered.

Why did she get the sudden inkling that they were both lying? But to whom?

"Obsessing over perfection is a sure way to drive yourself crazy," she said. "Just ask my mom."

"I don't obsess," Joe declared.

Mimi regarded him silently, flatly disbelieving.

"I don't," he insisted. "A person's exterior is simply a reflection of how they see themselves and those around them. Making an effort over your personal appearance tells others that you value their good opinion as well as yourself."

Mimi looked down at her sweatpants, bagging at the knees, and the oversized flannel shirt hanging open over her faded pink T-shirt. "So, I'm guessing I hate myself and everyone else?"

He inspected her thoughtfully. "It would appear so."

She laughed. She couldn't help it. Even gorked-out Joe was fun to trade barbs with. In a perverse sort of way. "You're good, Joe Tierney."

"Aren't I though?" The drug must be taking effect again, because his eyelids were sliding to half-mast. He looked vulnerable sitting there, and Mimi felt a tug inside. He'd hate this, this dependence, yet he was trying to make the best he could of it. He was trying to do the right thing by Prescott. Why? And why did she care? She usually didn't pry into other people's lives.

"Why'd you come, Joe?" she asked, taking the glass from his hand. "Really."

"Whaddya mean?"

"You could have hired a private nurse. A busted leg isn't exactly life-threatening. You didn't need to come yourself, and I can't imagine your employers were too keen on it, either. So, why did you come?"

"I'm his dad," Joe said, looking at her like he was sure he hadn't understood the question because the answer was so ridiculously obvious.

"Not every dad shows up just because their kid is in a

bind," she said. Her pulse had started racing a little. It must have been harder work pushing him up here than she thought.

"Sure they do," he said with patent certainty. A shadow further clouded his already glassy eyes. "If they can. Sometimes you can't. Sometimes you don't know you're needed, but if you can and you know, you do."

It was a little convoluted, but she got what he meant. And he really did mean it. He wasn't right, not about every dad, but he was sincere. Well. She just looked at him a minute, growing all buttery feeling inside. "Come on, Dad. Nappy time."

As all the bedrooms were on the main floor in a separate wing, Mimi had no trouble wheeling him into one of five guest rooms. She positioned the wheelchair next to the bed, locked the brakes, and bent over him. But when she started to slip an arm around his waist, he recoiled.

"What?"

"Nuthin'." His face became a mask of manly endurance. "I'm ready."

She drew back. "Is this still about me washing my hands?"

"No. Let's go," he said.

She didn't believe him. She reached out and patted his knee. "Touch." She patted his other knee. "Touch."

He looked up at her, startled. "Stop that."

"Touch." She flicked her finger against the tip of his nose. "Touch." She touched the top of his head.

"You're being childish," he said.

"Touch, touch." Her hands darted out and tapped his cheek and his shoulder. "Touch, touch, touch." Hand, chest, arm.

"Are you done yet?" he asked with heavy patience.

"Maybe."

"Fine. I think I can make it into the bed myself."

"Now who's being childish?" she said, lifting a brow at

him. "You're drugged. You'll probably hurt yourself. But if you want to prove you're irresponsible—"

She had measured her words carefully and now got the desired effect.

"You're right," he said stiffly. "Would you please help me lie down?"

"Do you think you can bear having my unwashed hands on you?"

"I told you I didn't care about your unwashed hands. Well, I do, but that's not why I flinched."

"Really?" she said disbelievingly. "Why did you?"

"Because you banged into my knee when you leaned over me."

Mimi's cheeks grew warm. "Oh."

He saw her blush and smiled. "Did you misjudge the situation?" he said. "Don't worry, there's a lot of that going around."

Did he remember everything she'd said to him? She cleared her throat. "No. Not at all. So, let's get you onto that bed, shall we?"

Mimi leaned forward and he wrapped a long arm around her shoulders. With a groan, he pushed up and balanced on his good leg. She used her foot to shove the wheelchair out of the way and aimed him at the bed. Then, very carefully, she began easing him down. Unfortunately he was a large man and she wasn't unusually strong for her size. He eased three-quarters of the way and toppled the rest. She landed on top of him. He gasped.

She pushed herself up with a hand against his chest, looking down at him anxiously. "Are you okay?"

"No."

"Yes, you are," she insisted. "You landed on your good side."

"But you landed on my bad side."

"Did I?" She felt terrible. "I'm sorry. I am *so* sorry." She tried to wriggle upright but his arm held her in place.

"You know, I think I'm feeling better," he said. His body beneath hers felt rock hard and anything but vulnerable.

"Ah!" She planted her hand and shoved solidly against his chest, freeing herself. He laughed. "Mimi, I have so many drugs in me right now the Goodyear blimp could fall on me and it wouldn't hurt."

Had he just likened her to the Goodyear *blimp*? "Ah!" She scrambled off the bed.

Despite appearances, Mimi wasn't offended. In fact, she was a little flattered by the lascivious glint in Joe's murky gaze. If she could, er, awaken the interest of a man with that much Demerol in him, she obviously still had it. In spite of the baggy sweatpants and flannel shirt. Or maybe the "it" she had was Jo Malone bath gel. That stuff was like witchcraft. She was going to have to get more.

She peeked back in the bedroom. Joe was already conked out, stretched out on his back, one arm flung wide, snoring lightly. Good. Now she was free to enjoy an unwitnessed and generally antic reunion with the dogs.

She didn't want Joe getting the idea that she actually liked being with the dogs because then he'd think it was no big deal that she'd agreed to take care of them—and him—and that would pretty much destroy all the nice beholdenness going on, although she hadn't yet figured out exactly why she liked the idea of Joe owing her. There was nothing he had that she wanted and nothing he might do for her that she needed. Unlike Joe, who was a slave to *Forbes* and *GQ* and elite airline upgrades but mostly antibacterial soap, she was an island unto herself, completely, serenely independent.

Ten minutes later she sat contentedly flanked by Blondie and Wiley, their warm doggy heads resting on her lap. She was a rolling stone. *No direction. No home.*

She frowned. That wasn't how the song went. It was "no direction home." Oh, well. She slapped her thighs, rousing Blondie and Wiley. "Okay, who's up for pizza?"

Chapter Thirty-four

Joe heard the front door open and close. A few minutes later, Mimi came into the living area carrying a large padded envelope. She walked toward the couch, reaching out and absently tapping Joe on the head as she passed, murmuring, "Touch."

"Would you please stop that?"

"Nope," she said. "I should be charging you for this. I'm desensitizing you."

"I don't want to be desensitized."

"Sure you do. Look how far you've come in just a couple days. You barely flinch anymore."

"You're reading that book by Stephen King, the one with the wacko nurse taking care of the novelist, aren't you?" he asked morosely.

"*Misery?*" she asked, delighted. Mimi spent a lot of the time being delighted. Anything that struck her as quixotic or odd, which in Mimi's slanted worldview could be almost anything, tickled her sense of humor. "No. Why? Do you think I'm going to come at you with a baseball bat some night?"

"No. That would be too quick. You want to torture me."

Her brows rose.

"Besides," he went on, "unlike what's his face, I'm not killing off your favorite fantasy."

"I wouldn't be too sure."

"What's that supposed to mean?"

"I had this fantasy that you wore starched boxers and ironed your socks."

He raised his brows. "How do you know I don't?"

"I'm guessing."

"Well, if you are really curious, we could always check. Together."

Mimi laughed again. She had a great laugh, low and throaty. "And there goes my fantasy. Someone who starches their boxers would never make such an improper suggestion to his day nurse."

"So . . ." he said hopefully. "Do you wanta?"

His pulse drummed a little heavier in his chest as he saw the inadvertent speculation in her quick glance. Then it was gone.

"Men, eternally optimistic, aren't they?" she asked, shaking her head. "Here you are, trussed up tighter than a Thanksgiving turkey and still hoping for the best. And before you make any snide comments, yes, by 'best' I am referring to me."

"There's only one way to prove it," he replied solemnly.

She didn't bother answering this time, but sat down on the sofa and began peeling the strapping tape from the package. He wasn't entirely joking in his half-assed attempts at seduction. The reason he didn't refine his pitch was that he wasn't sure how it would be received and he wasn't yet at the place where he wanted to find out.

Besides, he didn't want to screw up with Mimi again. That first day here, Mimi had examined anything he said to her for a hidden subtext. She needn't have bothered; if he hadn't already decided that whatever Mimi was, she definitely was not out to drain Prescott of his hard-earned cash, one day in her company would have been all it took to convince him. He didn't surmise this because he thought her particularly moral or ethical, but because he didn't think she had the necessary motivation to follow through with a plan that would require as much work and organization as a scam.

It wasn't that he thought she was lazy, either. Mimi was categorically not lazy, at least not in the accepted sense of the term. It was simply that conning Prescott would not get her anything she considered worth the effort it would take to acquire. That included money. Joe had never known anyone less interested in material possessions.

She lived like a stowaway on the Good Ship Earth, someone who'd figured out a way to avoid paying her passage with blood, sweat, and tears like everyone else. Yet, that wasn't quite true, either, he thought, watching her give up trying to peel the tape off the package and resort to gnawing on the corner (he cringed thinking about where that corner might have been). She clearly cared for things. Things like the dogs and Chez Ducky. She cared for her family. She even cared for him to some degree. She just went to great lengths to keep a distance between her and the things she cared for, a physical as well as emotional distance that kept her from investing too much.

She was frowning now, looking through a thick stack of variously shaped and weighed papers, someone's records and files.

"Mimi?"

She looked up, her expression uncertain. "It's from this guy, Otell Weber. He's a private investigator I hired to try and find out what happened to my father."

"Your father? What happened to your father?" Joe vaguely recalled asking Mimi about her father during the picnic. He'd gotten the impression then that he was around somewhere, just not at Chez Ducky at the moment. If Mimi's father had recently disappeared, she certainly was casual about it. "When was the last time you saw him?"

"Thirty years ago."

"What?"

"Thirty years ago. He dropped me off at Chez Ducky for the summer and went off to wander the world." She tapped her finger on a stack of paper. "Turns out the world may have stopped in Montana."

"Back up. Now, details, please."

She looked surprised by his interest but obliged. "After my parents divorced when I was a baby, Dad got me for the entire summer, every summer, as part of the settlement. And that meant we spent every summer up here at Chez Ducky. Always. It was just like it is now, kids and adults stacked to the rafters in those cottages. You could go days without actually speaking to an adult. Don't get me wrong; there were plenty of people to keep an eye on things, they just didn't interfere with kids being kids. My dad, in particular, had a very relaxed parenting style."

"He also must have had some job to be able to take off entire summers like that," Joe said.

"Oh, he didn't really have a job," she said casually. "I mean, he worked. But not like . . . a career. He worked to live, not lived to work."

She was making excuses for the old man, Joe realized. And what better way to tell the world that you stand behind your dad than to adopt his lifestyle for yourself? The whole "let it slide till it slides right on by" philosophy was beginning to make a little more sense.

"Most of the time Dad hung around, but it wasn't unusual for him to take off for a week or even a month or two here and there. But usually not so long during the summers."

What kind of dad just dumps his kid and disappears for weeks on end?

Me.

The word popped unbidden into his mind. At once, Joe discounted it. It wasn't the same thing. Not at all. Mimi's father didn't have a career and responsibilities keeping him away from Mimi. John Olson had a choice; Joe didn't.

Or maybe the difference was that Joe had an excuse.

How different were he and Mimi's father really? Both had left the work of raising their children to women they were convinced were fundamentally more capable, who seemed to enjoy, no *need*, to raise them. Why had John done so? Had he truly been as footloose as Mimi evidently thought him, as cavalier and heedless, or had he been secretly relieved not to have to step up to the plate? Had he, too, been afraid? *Like Joe.*

Joe didn't flinch away from uncomfortable questions, and he didn't now. But he didn't have a definitive answer. Maybe the truth was somewhere in between. Maybe that was the reason behind Prescott's animosity. Not that he felt Joe had abandoned him, but that he'd sensed Joe's relief that Karen had given him dispensation from full-time fatherhood. Joe wasn't even certain how he felt about that. Only that whatever relief he'd initially felt had not lasted.

When had his relief begun to turn to resentment? When had he realized that it wasn't only Prescott he was failing but himself? Before Karen's death? He couldn't remember. He'd never asked himself the question so directly before. He felt vaguely disloyal, questioning the consequences of Karen's devotion to their son. At the same time, he wondered whether it might not be disloyalty but simply seeing things with a new objectivity.

"Hey," Mimi said. "No need to look so stricken. I've had plenty of time to get used to the idea."

Joe pulled himself back from thoughts of Karen and focused on Mimi. She wasn't as detached as she'd like to believe after all. In fact, reading behind the shuttered brightness of her eyes, he would say she was far from detached. "What happened then? To your dad?"

"I don't know. He called from Mount Rushmore and spoke to my granddad. He said he was having a great time and had lost track of the days and he didn't know when he'd be back."

"That's all he said to you?"

"I didn't talk to him," she said, again a little too pertly. Too nonchalant. "Busy playing capture the flag. That was the last time we heard from him. Far as I know, he's still out there somewhere, and time still hasn't caught up." She grinned and Joe realized how thoroughly her self-protective insouciance had been constructed.

"And after all this time, you're still looking? Still getting reports from this Otell Weber?"

"Still? Oh. No." She shook her head as if she was denying some unpleasant accusation. "No. I've left it all alone for decades. I just hired Otell Weber last spring because I got this postcard. It must have been lost in the mail and"—she gave an embarrassed little laugh—"and, ah, it finally made it to me. It was from my dad, written thirty years ago. It was sent from Montana and I knew the people Granddad had hired originally to look for him had looked in North Dakota, so I . . . I just . . . I really just shoulda let it slide. I mean. What did I think would happen?" She laughed again. She was talking too quickly. "I don't know what's gotten into me. None of this can be interesting to you. I usually don't babble about, you know—"

"Personal stuff?" he suggested quietly.

She snapped her fingers at him. "Bingo. Personal stuff. Sorry."

"No, please. It's interesting." He purposefully kept his tone cool and objective, guessing that sympathy or concern would send her running. "Did your private eye find something?" He nodded toward the papers in her hand.

She looked down as though she'd forgotten she held them. "Maybe. I don't know. He actually found a guy who remembers seeing Dad. What are the odds?" She shook her head ruefully.

"You must be eager to find out if anything comes of it."

She shook her head again. "I don't know. I have this feeling that I should have just—"

"Let things slide."

"Yeah."

"Why?" he asked curiously. "Why didn't you ever try to find him before this?"

And just like that, that simply, all the bright, fake nonchalance fell off, swept away like a magician's cape, revealing the truth beneath. Her gaze was frightened, anxious, and bleak.

"I was afraid I'd find him," she said so quietly he barely heard her. "You'd think I'd know better." Giving him a small sad smile that told him she thought he'd know exactly what she meant, she slapped the file lightly against her thighs and got up.

The odd thing was that he did. He understood perfectly; if her father was dead, that was the end, and if her father was alive, well, then, that, too, was the end. Because he'd never come back for her.

"I better take the dogs for a walk." She edged by him and brushed her fingertips against his shoulder. "Touch."

Chapter Thirty-five

"Could you set the wheelchair up inside the door? I'd appreciate it," Prescott asked, hanging between his crutches inside Bombadil House's front door. Prescott wasn't supposed to use the crutches except to transfer from one area to another. The rest of the time he was relegated to the wheelchair. "Thanks for driving me from the airstrip."

"No problem," said the pilot of the plane he'd hired—well, actually, Joe had hired—to fly him from Duluth. Nice of Joe, but Prescott didn't need his father's help. He had Mignonette.

"You'll be all right?" the pilot asked, returning with the wheelchair and deftly unfolding it.

"Yes. Someone's here. I'll be fine," Prescott said, smiling.

Thus assured, the driver clapped Prescott on the shoulder and took off. Since neither Mignonette nor the dogs had greeted him when he'd opened the front door, he guessed they must be out taking a walk.

Prescott gently lowered himself into the wheelchair and set his crutches against the wall. It had been eleven days since he'd fallen in the swimming pool, his stay in the hospital elongated by a second surgery on his ankle, but all had gone well and now he was home. He took a deep breath and looked around in delight, noticing that all the furniture had been pushed back and the rugs rolled up and stored against the wall in order to make using the wheelchair easier. She was so thoughtful. And the place looked beautiful. The tiles gleamed and the granite countertop in the kitchen sparkled. The hardwood floor had a deep luster. She'd really taken wonderful care of his home. He'd known she would.

He rolled the wheelchair down the hall and into the kitchen, turning toward the living—

"Hello, Prescott," Joe said quietly.

He started and looked around, spotting his father lurking in the shadows across the room. He was sitting in a wheelchair, one leg sticking straight out on the footrest, his hands folded in his lap, his expression pensive.

"What are you doing here?" Prescott blurted out.

"I came to take care of you. I arrived four days ago to get your home ready, but then this." Joe ruefully indicated his leg. "I could ask the same of you, you know. I didn't think you were supposed to be released until tomorrow."

"My blood work came back fine, so they let me go early," he said; then, "What happened to you?"

"I had an accident. I wrenched my knee and dislocated my shoulder. I should be out of this thing in a couple more days. Sorry about having had to rearrange the furniture. You'll find it more convenient, too, I hope."

"Where is Mi—Mrs. Olson? Where are the dogs? *Did you send her away?*"

Joe studied him a second. "Come with me, Prescott." He rolled across the floor with an adroitness that Prescott couldn't help but admire, stopping in front of the windows overlooking the lake. Prescott rolled his wheelchair up beside Joe's with a great deal less dexterity.

"There they are."

Prescott followed the direction Joe pointed. On the lake below he saw his dogs running away from a cross-country skier hot on their trail.

"What's going on? Who is that? Why is he chasing my

dogs? Where's Mrs. Olson? She's supposed to be here. Not you!" All of this came tumbling out of his mouth as he watched in horror as the demented cross-country skier pursued his frantic dogs.

Joe didn't even turn his head. "*That's* Mrs. Olson, and she's not a Mrs., she's a Ms."

"What?"

"And she's not chasing the dogs, they're pulling her. She's *skijoring*. They're attached to her by traces and they're pulling her. I taught them that," he said wistfully. "It's really fun. She's been out there for almost two hours. She left me here. Alone."

That was Mignonette Olson? Prescott stared disbelievingly. That careening skier on the lake was his placid, middle-aged, preeminently mellow neighbor? "You're kidding."

Joe might not have heard him. "Don't you think that shows a lack of human feeling? She must know I'm bored, that sitting here while she's out there—with the dogs," he hastily added, "is making me crazy. With envy. Of being out there. Not of being with her."

Joe apparently knew more about Mignonette than Prescott did. He *hated* that. "How do you know she's not a missus?" he demanded.

"She told me. She was here with the dogs when I arrived."

"*Why* did you arrive?"

"The physical therapist said you'd need help for a while and I know how difficult it is for you to be comfortable around strangers."

Prescott opened his mouth and then snapped it shut, unwillingly affected by Joe's concern for him. However, that didn't make up for the fact that he was here and Mignonette was not.

"If you saw that Mi—Ms. Olson was here, why didn't you just go home?" He didn't want Joe here. He wanted Mignonette Olson here. He'd imagined mornings eating oatmeal with her and afternoons napping while she moved around the house, tidying things. They'd spend the evenings playing chess (or checkers if chess was too difficult to teach her). He would help her research a health insurance provider and teach her how to set up an online retirement fund. They'd be a little family. Mignonette Olson, Bill, Merry, Sam, and him. Instead, he had Joe.

He looked over to find Joe regarding him pityingly. A familiar sight. "Well?" he demanded.

"She didn't want to stay here, Prescott. I did."

"I don't believe you," Prescott said angrily, his resolve to keep his voice as level and melodious as Joe's disappearing. "Why would she go to the trouble to take such good care of Bombadil House—and yes, Joe, I named it after a house in *The Lord of the Rings*. I don't care!—if she didn't want to stay?"

"She hasn't taken good care of the house. I've hired a Mrs. McGoldrick to come in every other day and clean, but with Mimi and the dogs around, I should have made it daily. She is *such* a slob." He shook his head. "And those dogs . . ."

No, she wasn't! Casual, maybe, but not . . . *unclean*. Prescott loathed grime. He refused to believe his paragon didn't share this view.

"If the house got a little untidy, it was only because it was too much work for her," Prescott said. "I should have realized. It wasn't fair to ask her to keep up a house and tend the dogs."

"No, that's not the problem," Joe said. "The problem is that Mimi is categorically opposed to expending effort that she considers unnecessary. And that pretty much covers eighty-five percent of everything. She is undisciplined and proud of it."

Where the hell did Joe get off calling Mignonette "Mimi"?

"Look at her, Prescott," Joe continued, tipping his head in Mignonette's direction. "She's vibrant, lovely, intelligent, and a world-class slacker."

Joe finished with a deep heartfelt sigh. In calmer moments, Prescott would have thought this an odd way to end disparaging someone. But as this character assassination was directed at the woman he revered, Prescott spun his chair around and faced Joe. "Take that back."

Joe looked at him, nonplussed. Amused, but nonplussed, nonetheless. "Or what? You're going to hit me?"

Prescott lurched forward, delivering a roundhouse blow. Unfortunately, it connected only with air. Joe, segueing from nonplussed to startled, had wheeled his chair back. "Cut it out, Pres. Watch it. You're going to hurt yourself."

"Take it back!" His jaw clenched, Prescott shot forward in his chair. This time when he swung, the force propelled him out of his chair and into Joe. With a crash, Joe's wheelchair fell over, sending them both sprawling.

"Ouch!" Joe yelped.

Prescott, saved the majority of the impact by the layers of gauze and plaster, lifted himself up on his forearms and began dragging himself—and his plasticine-encased lower limbs—toward his father. "You deserved it. And it's *Mignonette*, not Mimi!"

"Jesus, Pres! Have you lost your mind?" Joe asked, cradling his wrist against his chest. Then, seeing the look on his son's face, he backed away, pushing with his good leg and skidding on his good elbow.

"And don't call me 'Pres,' " Prescott ground out.

"Fine! Have you lost your mind, *Prescott*?"

"She's a warm, caring, wonderful woman, and you have no right to call her names. Apologize."

"Names?! So help me, Prescott, if you don't stop acting like a third grader with a crush on his teacher—*ow!*"

Chapter Thirty-six

"Whew! I'm sweatier than a used towel in a Turkish steam bath!" Mimi called up the stairs.

Pleased with the colorful analogy designed specifically to make Joe wince, Mimi slapped the snow from her jeans and toed off her cross-country boots. She'd entered through the walk-out level under the deck, currently beyond Joe's scope and therefore not subject to his housekeeperly criticism. She started shedding outerwear with little regard for where it fell. Outside, the dogs lay panting in the snow. Experience told her they wouldn't be asking to come in for at least half an hour.

"Yoo-hoo! Joe? You're not sulking again, are you? The doc said you could put weight on that knee tomorrow. Then maybe I'll let you lean on me and we'll walk around the garage."

It had been four days since Joe had gone aerial, and since then he was getting grumpier by the hour. Unused to being physically inert and even more unused to depending on anyone for anything, he was having a hard time adjusting. Well, he couldn't be any more unused to depending on someone than she was having someone depend on her. And now she had four beings looking to her for food, exercise, companionship, and conversation.

This last had the most unexpected outcome. Not because of how much she had learned about Joe—she was a tele-medium, for chrissakes; her stock-in-trade was listening—but because in the course of their conversations Mimi had revealed more about herself to Joe than she had revealed to any half dozen people in as many years. And it had begun with that stupid package from Otell Weber.

The contents had been mostly Xeroxes of handwritten notes, but the upshot was that Otell had discovered a very faint trail to pursue. He warned her not to get her hopes up and, surprisingly, they weren't. She wasn't reacting at all like she'd expected; she was too busy taking care of Mr. Clean and the Dustmops. She tugged off her ski pants, disconcerted by how much she looked forward to verbal sparring with Joe, suspecting it was just a substitute for another type of heated encounter.

Joe was dangerous. Sometimes she found her heart doing stupid little pitter-pats when he made some sly observation designed to make her laugh or she caught him watching her or when he rolled his shirtsleeves up over those fabulous forearms. There should—*would*, she corrected herself—be no romantic relationship in their future. Sadly, they knew each other too well now.

She could see how it would play out. They'd enjoy the affair but after it was over they'd wonder about each other, feel like maybe a follow-up affair would be polite. Worry that one or the other had become more attached or, worse, less attached. Make a terrible error in judgment and phone, get his voice mail, hang up, and later that night wake up wondering whether her own phone number had shown up on his caller ID and whether he'd seen it and thought, "Thank God I ducked that call!" It would be horrible.

But that was the future that wasn't going to happen. Right now was right now and she wondered why Joe wasn't ha-ranguing her about bringing snow into the house. Was he asleep? Was she waiting for her? Would he greet her with the

heart-stopping smile she got when she reappeared after even
a short absence?

By the time she'd finished tugging on her jeans, her heart
was doing a calypso of anticipation. She decided to take a
leaf from her own book and let it dance. No harm in a little
heart dance. Good for the cardio-vas system. She took the
stairs two at a time. "Tell you what, Joe. We'll lug your
wheelchair into Fawn Creek for dinner . . ."

Prescott Tierney sat in a wheelchair by the window overlooking the lake.

"Prescott! When did you get here? Why didn't you say
something . . . ?" She trailed off, becoming aware of his
sullen, guarded expression. His hands were crossed tightly in
his lap, his hair disheveled. The shoulder of his black T-shirt
was ripped. "Where's Joe?"

"Here."

She turned at a sound. Joe sat in his wheelchair at the
other end of the bank of windows, trying unsuccessfully to
look natural, his lack of success due in large part to the shiner
blooming around his left eye.

"Hello, Mimi," Joe said conversationally. "How was the
snow today?"

"Screw the snow. What the hell happened to you?"

"A little accident. Prescott and I had a slight disagreement
and—"

"You hit your father?" Mimi spun around and faced
Prescott again, ambushed by her own unexpected anger.

"No!" both Tierney males said in unison. Her anger re-
ceded.

"No," Joe repeated. "We fell out of our wheelchairs
and . . . ah, I grabbed a table leg. It teetered and the book on
it slid off and hit me in the eye."

"And yet, still I have questions," Mimi murmured dryly.

"I tried to hit him," Prescott put in abruptly. The anger
flared again, but this time Mimi was prepared for it.

Whatever happened between Joe and Prescott was no concern of hers.

"He did." Amazingly, Joe seemed proud of this.

"I could have, too, after the book hit him. But I didn't want to lower myself."

"*Why* did you try to hit your father?" Mimi asked Prescott.

"He said terrible things about you."

It probably said something about how her and Joe's relationship had progressed over the last few days that Mimi didn't at once suspect that Joe had warned Prescott she was out to take him for every penny. Not at once. It took a few seconds.

It probably said more about their relationship that, a few seconds later, she decided Joe wouldn't have warned Prescott of this because just yesterday Joe had admitted he'd misjudged her, saying that she was too lazy to try to con anyone. She suspected she was supposed to be embarrassed by his assessment. She wasn't.

"What did he say?" she asked Prescott.

"He said you were a slob. That you were irresponsible."

Mimi snorted. Prescott looked shocked. "Compared to him? Yeah, me and the rest of the world."

Prescott frowned. "He said you were undisciplined and stubborn."

"I did not say stubborn," Joe piped in. "One has to take a stand to be stubborn."

"Ouch," Mimi said. "To the rest I plead guilty as charged. Now, does anyone want some pop?"

She could see how disappointed Prescott was. He'd been expecting her to demand he and his father meet with pistols at dawn, and she was suggesting Diet Coke. *Poor* Prescott. He didn't know her at all. Not like Joe did.

"He said you were so mentally lazy you might as well be asleep," Prescott said, his voice rising.

Mimi, halfway to the kitchen, stopped. "Now, that stings,"

she admitted. "And it's unfair. I do the hardest Sudokus in *Sudoku Master Magazine without penciling in any numbers.*"

"Wow. Notify the Nobel Prize committee," Joe said.

"I think it's great," Prescott said. "Really great."

She shot Prescott a look. She knew when she was being patronized. "I do other stuff, too," she said primly. "I set up the interface for my plasma television, DVD recorder, and cable system myself."

Prescott attempted to look impressed. Joe made a point of studying the buff on his manicured nails.

She'd never had to convince anyone of her intelligence before. It felt very weird. "Look. I'm not going to argue about this. I'll get you guys some pop; then I'm going back to Chez Ducky to sit in my usual blissful stupor."

"Wait," Prescott said. "You mean you don't stay here?"

"Nope. No reason to." She didn't add that there were also some very good reasons *not* to, primary of those being that as Joe grew more physically comfortable, she grew more physically uncomfortable.

She'd never been so tempted to fall into bed with a guy, and never had her self-preservation warning signals been flashing so brightly. She didn't know why this should be. She'd had wonderful short-term affairs before and no one had gotten hurt. (Correction. No one that she knew of. As a rule, she didn't make follow-up calls.)

"But what about the dogs?" Prescott asked lamely.

"I come over in the morning, take care of the dogs, and at dinnertime I make sure everyone gets something to eat. Including Joe. An admittedly mindless way of spending the day, but the dogs seem to appreciate it."

"You're not really going to leave me here with him?" Prescott asked, giving her a gooey look of adulation.

Joe straightened up at this. "What's wrong with me?"

"What's right with you?" Prescott snapped back. "You're ruining everything by being here. Go away."

The hurt occasioning his words caused an unpleasant sensation to burrow toward Mimi's heart. She disliked this treacherous feeling. Prescott and his ilk were in large part responsible for Chez Ducky's looming end. If people like him didn't build monsters like this place on every splotch of land with water near it, the Chez Ducky property wouldn't be worth a fortune and the idea of selling it would never even have arisen. Things could go on forever just as they had.

On the other hand, he sounded so damn young.

Joe must have thought so, too, because he didn't take offense. "I was just trying to help."

The unpleasant sensation by her heart blossomed into an all-out ache. Joe sounded so damn sad.

"Stop trying. *It's too late*," Prescott declared and with a jerk of his hand twirled his wheelchair dramatically away from his father. Unfortunately he overshot the mark, sending the wheelchair into a spin that ended with him crashing into the wall.

"Are you okay?" Joe asked worriedly, wheeling closer.

"Screw you!" Prescott yelled, red faced with embarrassment.

More emotions spilled like some corrosive acid onto Mimi's Teflon-coated heart. She could damn near smell the thing smoking.

Mimi stared horrified, not at the yelling going on but at herself and what she realized she was going to do. She was going to insert herself square into the middle of this family drama, and she wasn't exactly sure why or how to keep herself from doing so. But she could not stand to see these two hurting each other so unnecessarily.

"Fine, Prescott," Joe said tightly. "I'll—"

"Both of you, shut up!" And there it was. She was in. As in "*in*volved." Both men looked at her dumbly. The jerks had forgotten she was there.

"Shut up and stay shut up until I get back."

"Where are you going?"

"First, to let the dogs in. Second, to the kitchen to get

some wine. Then you two are going to sit on opposite sides
of this room and talk or I am leaving you here alone, at the
mercy of the dogs. *And* Bill's lower gastrointestinal system."

They shut up.

Chapter Thirty-seven

As Mimi rummaged in the cupboards for something that went with wine, her cell phone rang, startling her into spilling a glass of the sublime Whitehall Lane cabernet sauvignon on the granite island. It dripped over the edge and onto the tiled floor. She swore. Whitehall Lane's 2002 was simply too good to spill, not to mention too good to be lapped up by the likes of Bill. She snatched up the phone. "Hello."

"Mimi? Is that you?"

"Well, it isn't your aunt Irene, Ozzie," Mimi said, kneeling down with a towel to wipe up the wine. Bill spied her and propelled himself across the living room at the towel, grabbing the end and jerking, growling deep in his throat. He was not playing. Bill did not play. For days, Bill had laid in wait for something to savage. Since Joe's arrival, towels, shoes, and other loose articles of clothing were in short supply. "Hold on a sec."

Mimi wrenched at the towel in Bill's mouth. Bill did not let go. The towel—another towel—ripped in half. She released her half and Bill shot away snarling in victory. No sense fighting over a torn rag. She got to her feet.

"You're not going to let him run around the house with that wine-soaked rag, are you?" Prescott asked in shock.

"She is," Joe answered with weary resignation.

"Do you mind? I am on the phone!" she said, holding her hand over the mouthpiece. She lifted the cell to her ear. "What's up, Ozzie?"

"Who's that?" Ozzie asked curiously.

"My neighbors."

"Neighbors? I thought you were going to Chez Ducky to commiserate with the spirits of your ancestors."

Actually she'd said, "to blow the stink off the place," but Ozzie, who staunchly believed in dressing things up, had edited. "Yes. I thought so, too. Plans changed."

"Since when do you *plan* anything?" he asked.

Ozzie was obviously stalling, and Mimi had to get back to Prescott and Joe, who, along with Bill, were doing a fair reenactment of the Pamplona Running of the Bulls. Prescott and Joe had taken on the roles of the bulls and were skittering around the hardwood floors in their wheelchairs pursuing Bill as the Intrepid Runner, whose rag seemed to be acting as a cape.

"True, Ozzie, but lately the small tributary that is my life has wandered into a little backwater. Until the tide comes up again, I'm stranded here. Now, again. What's up?"

He took a deep breath. "I know this is way out of line and that you are on vacation, but I figured since you were due back soon anyway—" Crap. She'd forgotten she'd told Oz she wouldn't be gone more than two weeks and she'd been up here—she did a quick mental count—eleven days.

"It's going to be a while longer, I'm afraid."

"What?" Ozzie exclaimed.

"Look, I've got things I have to stick around up here for."

"Like watching snow fall?" Ozzie asked sarcastically, clearly not believing her. "That's not why I called, but how long? Another week? Look, Mimi, I need to be able to count on you because of things like—"

A clattering sound drew her attention. She spun around. Prescott had nearly upended himself down the stairwell. She clamped the cell phone to her chest. "Watch it, you idiot! Do you want to break the other leg?"

She couldn't leave the two of them alone like this. Her gaze slew to Bill, hunkered down under the red sofa, his eyes alight with a feral gleam as he growled at Joe, who was attempting to get the rag from him. Crap. She returned the cell phone to her ear. "Yeah, Ozzie about that—"

But Ozzie had gone on. "—told her that we run a legitimate business and that you only work out of the office to ensure that every call is properly documented and billed. She doesn't buy it. So, I was wondering if you could just tell her when you'll be back and reassure her that Brooke or I are eminently capable of contacting her mother in your place."

Ozzie was talking about Jess. Mimi stilled. She'd forgotten about Jess, whom she'd also told she was going to be on vacation but not for how long. Jess was expecting her, and her mother, back.

"Okay, Ozzie," she said. "Give me her number and I'll call her."

"Weren't you listening? I've got her on hold. I can transfer her to you right now. I'd really appreciate it. She is a major pain in the ass."

Jess was, indeed. She was also scared. "Put her on."

She heard Ozzie's sigh of relief. "Thanks, Mimi. You're the best."

"I know. Bye, Ozzie."

There was a series of clicks and then Jess's voice, angry and sarcastic. "What? Speaking to spooks is so exhausting you have to take time off from it?"

"Actually it's not the spooks who are exhausting." Mimi let the inference hang a second, then said, "Hi, Jess. How are you doing?"

"Not that great," Jess bit out. "Neil's having second thoughts about moving in, and I am sure it's because of Mother."

"Your mother's haunting him?" Mimi asked, unable to keep the skepticism from her voice. "Did he tell you this?"

"No, but what other reason could there be? I mean, he tells me all the time that he couldn't live without me, so why would he want to? Live without me, that is."

Warning bells went off in Mimi's head. With all the neediness going on, someone was going to have to do the giving, and Mimi greatly feared old Neil had decided it would be Jess. Mimi saw a manipulation in the works.

"He says he has a *bad vibe* about moving in. He needs reassurance. So, there you go. It has to be Mom."

"What does your therapist think?"

"Oh, some bullshit about learning to be independent."

Mimi looked over her shoulder. Someone had finally gotten the wine-soaked rag from Bill. It hung from the fireplace mantel like a flag of victory, secured by a heavy book. Prescott was tipped halfway over the side of his chair scrubbing at some red drops on the floor. Joe was watching her. She tucked the cell phone under her chin and wandered toward the hallway.

"You think that's bullshit?" she asked Jess. "I mean, you lived with your mother until she died, right?"

"Did *she* tell you that?" Jess asked, "she" being Jess's mom. "Well, she forgot about the *entire semester* I spent living in the St. Cloud dorm my sophomore year."

In the living room Mimi heard Prescott shouting at Bill and then the crash of something heavy, like a book. Bill had gone for bonus points.

"Jess, living by yourself is great." Really great, she thought, imagining herself on her knees scrubbing up after Bill. "You get to do what you want, when you want it, without having to ask permission or jibe someone else's schedule with yours. You get to immerse yourself in whatever interests you."

"Yeah, that's fine if that's the sort of person you are and you like that being-alone shit." Jess bit the words out as if she had trouble saying them, as if she understood how revealing they were and did not want to sound pathetic. "Look. *I* don't want to be alone. There's all this . . . space around me. I just want it filled up."

"I understand, Jess," Mimi said. "But maybe you should take your time, fill in those empty places slowly. There's no hurry."

"You don't understand," Jess snapped back. "You *have* people. I can hear them in the background."

Mimi almost snorted. She had people? She would love to tell Jess that she didn't want to *have* people. Oh, sure, she was used to being *around* people; she was around dozens of people every summer she'd spent at Chez Ducky. But then she was more like one of the benevolent spirits that hovered around the living, there but not affecting much, not really necessary. But even if she told Jess this, she wouldn't believe her. In fact, Mimi wasn't altogether sure she'd believe herself.

She was definitely having an effect here, she realized, and she was definitely necessary. And . . . having fun. More than just being content and satisfied, her usual condition, she was actually having a rousing good time torturing Joe (and herself) and messing around with the dogs. Which was only a testament to how flexible she was, she assured herself, not an indication of any late-life change of character.

"Ms. Olson!" Prescott hollered from the living room. "Bill has that soggy towel again and it's dripping on the rug this time! Can you *please* get it away from him?"

Blondie appeared in the hall and trotted by Mimi. She sat down in front of the door and looked over her shoulder. She wanted to go out. Blondie was the only polite one in the bunch.

"Mimi! Prescott is going to crawl out of his chair if you don't hurry up," Joe called.

No doubt about it, there was a lot of needing Mimi going around.

"I don't want to be alone," Jess repeated. Her voice had lost all trace of aggression.

"You're not," Mimi said. "You have me."

Jess made an unladylike sound. "Yeah. Right. But I pay you."

Mimi took a deep breath. What difference did one more person make? It was only for a short while.

"Not anymore, Jess. Let me give you my cell phone number so you can call me direct."

Chapter Thirty-eight

"*Nothing* I have *ever* done has *ever* impressed him," Prescott said an hour later, stabbing a finger in Joe's direction. He then held out his empty wineglass, and Joe, ever the attentive host—even when it wasn't his damn house, thought Prescott—leaned forward and refilled it. Didn't the guy realize he'd just denounced him as a father? Didn't he *care*?

"He should care," Prescott muttered. "I'm a bona fide genius. I am the youngest professor ever to get tenured at MIT. I invented a—"

"I used to be a genius," Mimi interjected cheerfully.

Prescott, stymied midrant, raised his eyebrows. Mimi was lolling on the couch with Wiley while she fiddled with Blondie's ears. Bill, deprived of his rag, sat on the edge of the carpet and sulked.

"I was," she insisted.

"How'dya know?" Prescott asked suspiciously.

"My mom had me tested when I went into kindergarten."

"*My* mom had me tested when I was *two and a half*," Prescott said smugly. "She was very perceptive."

"Couldn't be more perceptive than Solange," Mimi disagreed equitably. "Solange has a radar for untapped potential that is frightening."

"So, what happened to you?" Prescott asked.

"Whatddya mean?" Mimi said.

"You said you *used* to be a genius."

"Oh. Yeah. I gave it up."

"You can't give up being a genius." He looked at Joe, sunk comfortably on the other end of the couch, his wine-glass balanced on his stomach, a content smile on his face, though what he had to be content about was beyond Prescott.

Joe opened his mouth as if to say something. Great, thought Prescott, now he would take over the conversation because people *lu-vved* listening to Joe's Velvet Voice. He wondered if they'd love listening to him so much if they knew "the velvet" was a result of having smoked in college. His mom had confided that little bit of info. Prescott prepared to watch Mimi be charmed right out of her shoes. Except she wasn't wearing any.

"You know how many kinds of germs the dogs have undoubtedly carried in on their paws?" he asked, nodding toward her bare feet. He vaguely noted that Joe wasn't talking; he was yawning. "There's probably all sorts of snow-borne parasites and bacteria and God knows what all on this floor."

"I think they'd be frozen solid, Pres," Mimi said, unconcerned.

"No. They are not. Why, do you realize that scientists have found viable bacteria in bore samples taken from Paleozoic ice pack— What are you doing?"

Mimi's smile had broadened into a Cheshire cat grin as she leaned over the coffee table, reached out to where Prescott's foot was propped up on the wheelchair footrest, and flicked his big toe with her finger. "Touch."

"What's she doing?" he squealed, recoiling in alarm as she proceeded to flick each of his toes in turn, chanting, "Touch, touch, touch, touch."

"Desensitizing you," Joe said calmly.

"Tell her to stop!" Prescott recoiled.

"She doesn't listen to me. You tell her. She might listen to you."

With a cackle of glee, Mimi went back to Prescott's big toe and gave it a final yank.

"Ow!"

She flopped back in her seat. "And touch again!"

"She's drunk," Prescott said.

Joe studied Mimi a second. "I think so."

His father had been right about Mimi, Prescott thought morosely. She was not the woman he'd thought she was. The woman he had idolized had been a font of Zen-like serenity, an Earth Mother, a Madonna of the snows, a Mignonette—not a Mimi. Someone who encouraged and supported you, someone diligent on your behalf, who had only your welfare in mind. Someone like his mom.

"You're *nothing* like my mom," he muttered disconsolately.

"He's drunk," Mimi informed Joe.

Joe looked at him. "I think so."

Mimi, her suspicion supported, turned back to Prescott. "I don't want to be like your mother."

Both Joe and him gaped.

Mimi whooped. "You should see yourselves! Both staring at me with the same poleaxed expression." She whooped again. "What? No one ever told you how much alike you two are?"

No. Never. In fact, his mother had always said it was amazing Joe had produced a son so dissimilar from himself. Prescott whipped his head around to see whether Joe took this as an insult. He didn't look insulted. And he hadn't even been drinking that much.

Since it appeared Joe wasn't going to say anything, he would. *Before* his father started laughing. "That's ridiculous. We don't look anything alike."

Mimi's drunken hilarity segued smoothly into drunken seriousness. "True. I didn't think you looked anything alike

when I first met you, but take away the black hair dye—
please," she snickered, "and the eye bolt ring, pare off a few
pounds, get a tan, and there is a definite resemblance. But
where you really see the similarity is your personalities.
Both germaphobes. Both control freaks. Both overplanners.
Both regimented—"

"You think I'm a germaphobe? You think I'm a control
freak?" he and Joe broke out in unison. They looked at one
another in startled recognition.

"What about our good qualities?" Joe asked Mimi.

Our? Prescott thought wonderingly.

"Those were the good qualities," she said.

Joe laughed. Prescott couldn't remember the last time
he'd heard Joe laugh spontaneously. Of course, he and Joe
didn't make much with the merry.

"You have the same expressions, too," Mimi went on.
"Same smile. Same look of disgust. Same look of shock.
Like just now when I said I didn't wanta be like Kathy."

"Her name was Karen," Prescott said, his thoughts jerked
back to Mimi's inexplicable comment about his mother.

"Whatever." Mimi waved her hand.

"Why wouldn't you want to be like my mom?" he demanded. "Anyone would. She was an amazing woman. A
genius. Smart, motivated, capable of anything she put her
mind to."

"She was valedictorian of her class. Won a full ride to
Miami of Ohio," Joe put in, nodding.

But Mimi wasn't attending Joe; she was looking at
Prescott. "I take it she put her mind to you."

She sounded scornful. Why would she sound scornful?
Prescott must have misinterpreted her tone.

"Yes," he said. "She dedicated herself to seeing that I had
every opportunity to excel. She wouldn't take a position
anywhere, choosing to homeschool me rather than have a
career. She was a brilliant teacher."

"She got a lot of job offers, did she?" Mimi asked. "But she turned down all of them?"

Prescott frowned. He didn't actually know the answer to this. He'd just assumed she had offers.

"No," Joe said. "She never finished college. She stayed at home with Prescott. But she was planning on going back to school when Prescott entered college himself."

"*Pffbt.*"

"*What* did you say?" Prescott asked.

"*Pffbt.*"

Mimi was *dissing* his mother.

"Is that what she told you guys?" Mimi asked. "That she sacrificed all for Prescott? God, I gotta call Solange and apologize. At least she never gave up her life for me. Thank God."

The sneer in her voice was unmistakable now. And who the hell was Solange?

Mimi chuckled. Slowly, her amusement faded, replaced by consternation and then all-out amazement as a thought occurred to her. "Hey. You guys didn't know, did you? Prescott, I can sort of understand. But, Joe, are you telling me you didn't know you were married to a nut?"

"I didn't say anything."

"Your expression is loud and clear. Oh, Joe"—her voice softened—"Joe. I'm sorry. I'm sure she was a perfectly lovely nut. She'd have to be to have you guys so thoroughly snowed."

"She had the best intentions," Joe said stiffly.

"I don't doubt it. So does Solange."

"My mother was not a nut job," Prescott said.

Mimi's gaze danced away from Joe, the unmistakable tenderness in her eyes shifting to empathy. "My mother is a head case, too. Not in the league of your mom, evidently, but definitely triple A team. That doesn't mean I don't love her. I do. But I'm not blind to her . . . less desirable qualities."

"My mother didn't *have* any less desirable qualities."

"Look, kid," she said, "I understand loving a parent and thinking they are the bee's knees. Believe me, I do. But you can't let pining after what you lost keep you from seeing what you got. In this case, that would be your dad. Yeah, yeah, yeah. He wasn't around much when you were a little kid, but he's here now."

She stared into the ruby contents of her wineglass. "You know, genius babies would scare the shit out of a lot of guys. Maybe you scared the shit out of your dad. Maybe he felt inadequate. Hell, I bet I scared the shit out of my . . ." Her eyes widened slightly as she trailed off.

Prescott's glance snapped to his father. Joe was looking out the window.

Prescott didn't know what to think. It had never occurred to him that the cosmopolitan, erudite Joe Tierney would ever feel inadequate about anything. "So he's here out of guilt?" he finally asked.

Mimi gave a drunken little snort. "Hell. Who cares why he's here, Pres? Maybe between his being out of the country most of the time and your mom's grand designs for you, things aren't all Walton's Mountain between you and your dad. But the point is, Joe is here. She's not."

Prescott started to open his mouth to say he didn't need Joe but shut it again. Joe was here. And he had been here, or wherever Prescott was, arriving every year like clockwork. He frowned uncertainly. He had come to a crossroads: he could continue defending his mother, who, to be blunt, was dead, or he could give Joe, who was not dead, and as Mimi had pointed out, was here, a chance. Joe would likely screw it up, but still . . . He twisted the silver bolt in his brow thoughtfully.

The doorbell rang, startling them all. Disentangling herself from Wi—Merry (Prescott refused to call his companion the name of a cartoon character), Mimi got up and headed to the front door. Curious, Prescott backed his wheelchair up so he could peer around the corner and through the front-door window. A pretty young woman with soft blondish hair and a perfect complexion stood outside, her hand raised to knock.

She spotted Mimi and waved. "Hey, Big Sis! Lemme in! I'm freezing my ass off out here!"

Chapter Thirty-nine

"You're pregnant," Mimi said, staring at Sarah's protruding stomach.

"Almost five months." Sarah shouldered her way past Mimi into the house, her gaze traveling appreciatively around the open-beamed ceiling, the carved stone fireplace mantle, and the pegged hardwood floors. "No wonder you love it up here. This is great!"

"This isn't Chez Ducky."

"Crap." Sarah's face fell, but she shrugged philosophically. "I didn't think so, but hope springs eternal."

"Where's the father?"

"Don't know. Wait. That's not true." Sarah corrected herself. It must be a burden, Mimi thought, being that scrupulously honest. "I know. It's just not relevant."

"Does *he* know it's not relevant?"

"If you're asking if he knows I'm pregnant, the answer is yes. If you're asking if he thinks I ought to keep the baby or give it up"—she looked down at her large stomach—"any other option no longer being on the table, he doesn't have strong opinions one way or the other."

"This would be the grad student?"

"Yup."

"Mimi? Who are you talking to?" Joe called. Even when

he shouted, he contrived to sound sexy . . . Man, she *had* had too much wine. "Is it Mrs. McGoldrick? Because if it is, tell her you've been running unattended in the lower level."

"Yeah, yeah," Mimi shouted back.

"Who's that?" Sarah said, giving her a look.

"Joe Tierney, but—"

"Joe *Tierney*?"

"Look, there's a perfectly reasonable and innocent explanation, the same of which cannot be said of your, er, situation."

"Why don't you show her the downstairs, then come back?" Prescott shouted. Like her, he simply sounded loud. "We haven't finished the conversation."

"In a minute." She felt for the kid, but right now she had more important things than his abandonment issues to deal with, especially since he hadn't been abandoned. Now, she— Nope. Not going there.

"And who is that?" Sarah asked, brows rising.

"Joe's son, Prescott. He just got here this afternoon."

"Really? My, my, my."

Mimi ignored this. "What does Mom say about your interesting condition?"

Sarah flushed slightly. "Mom doesn't know. Or Dad."

Mimi's eyes widened. "How did you keep it from them?"

"I avoided them as much as I could. Then, when I started to show, I told them I was taking a six-month internship in Singapore. I've done internships out of the country before, so I knew they'd buy it. They did. Clever, huh?"

"Positively weasel-like. What about Mary?"

"Mary doesn't know anything. And we're going to keep it that way."

"*We?*"

Abruptly, all Sarah's newfound sangfroid drained away. She lifted her eyes to Mimi's, looking the same as when she'd been five and Mimi had told her that despite what Sarah had called "empirical evidence to the contrary," there really was a Santa Claus. She'd looked so pitiful, like she expected to be disappointed but couldn't help from getting her hopes up. "You and me."

"Oh, Sarah," Mimi said, backing away, "I'm not the person you want to talk to about this sort of thing."

"I don't want advice," Sarah said quickly. "That's exactly *why* I came to you. I knew you wouldn't have any. I just need time, you know. To see how everything shakes out."

"That's a baby, Sarah," Mimi said, aghast. "It's not going to just 'shake out.' "

"Things'll work out one way or the other if you just let 'em. That's what you always do and it's always worked for you."

"It's *not* the same thing," Mimi said sternly. But isn't that exactly what she'd done regarding her own pregnancy? Just waited? What if she hadn't? Would she be holding a little mini-Mimi right now? Would she have handed the mini-Mimi over to another couple? She'd never know. In order not to make a mistake, she'd done nothing and it turned out that might have been the biggest mistake. Damn it. Why did Sarah have to show up here pregnant?

"Sure, it is," Sarah was prattling on. "Things haven't always necessarily worked out *well*, but they do work out. There's a certain security in assuming nothing. Expecting nothing is smarter than convincing yourself things will always work out for the best. I understand you a lot better now, Mimi, what with getting knocked up and everything. The whole 'let it slide' thing?" She nodded portentously. "Makes total sense."

Knocked up? Once again, as she was at Solange's anniversary party, Mimi was struck by the changes in her sister. Sarah didn't use words like "knocked up." She'd be more likely to say, "now that I have procreated and am midphase of my gestational period."

"You can't let this slide, Sarah. This is a human being

we're talking about. You have to make certain choices, decisions, plans for the baby's future."

Sarah was regarding her stonily. "This is such a disappointment. I cannot believe this is you speaking, Mimi."

"Me, either," Mimi said faintly.

"Look," Sarah said, "I caught you off guard and it's thrown you. You're not yourself. I understand." She patted Mimi's arm. "You haven't had time to adjust. I have. I've thought about this a lot and I've decided right now, I *don't* want to think about it, so, I'm not going to. Whaddya say, Mimi? You'll let me stay, won't you?"

Of course. "All right. But you aren't going to like Chez Ducky. It's cold and drafty and it smells sort of musty. There's no television or radio. Even the cell phone service is iffy at best."

"It sounds wonderful. I've never been camping. Besides, I brought along my doctoral thesis to work on if I get bored."

"Mimi?" Joe called again.

Mimi looked over her shoulder. "I suppose introductions are in order, since we'll be eating together for the next few days anyway."

"Why's that?" Sarah asked.

"Follow me." Mimi led the way into the living room, Sarah waddling behind her. "Sarah, you remember Joe Tierney? This is his son, Prescott. Prescott, my sister Sarah."

For a few seconds, Sarah just stood politely looking at the pair in their matching wheelchairs, bandaged, bruised, and definitely bowed. Then, as if she couldn't hold it in any longer, she burst out laughing.

"My God, Mimi!" she sobbed, holding her stomach. "What did you do to them?"

"These meatballs are great," Sarah said, happily digging into a mound of Smelka's Swedish meatballs Joe had returned with a few minutes ago. "You guys eat like this every day?"

"Unless we run out of frozen food," Joe said.

Sarah started to push herself away from the table.

"Where are you going?" Prescott asked.

"To get a piece of bread to sop up every drop of that gravy."

"You should let Mimi get it," Prescott said. "It's easier for her."

Mimi? In the matter of the few hours since Prescott had arrived she'd gone from Mrs. Olson to Mignonette to Mimi. Hm. Sarah slipped back into her chair and looked at Mimi expectantly.

Mimi grumbled, getting up. *How fickle and foul, a young man's fancy.* But, Mimi reminded herself, Prescott hadn't ever fancied her, he'd idolized her. But, *how fickle and foul, a young man's idolization* just didn't have the same ring.

"Thanks, Mimi," Sarah said around a mouthful of meat-ball before returning her attention to Prescott. "What was I saying before? Oh, yeah. It's really lousy being the sister of an unproven genius. You oughta talk to our sister Mary about it."

Mimi slid the bread in front of Sarah.

"Mimi's a genius? I mean, she said she was, but I didn't really . . ." He trailed off, cheeks flaming.

Sarah nodded sympathetically. "I know. Well, we only have Mom's word for it. And I did say *unproven* genius."

Sarah winked at Mimi. Mimi couldn't remember Sarah ever winking before, at her or anyone else. Pregnancy had not only inflated Sarah physically but it had inflated her already expanding personality, too. At this rate, Sarah would end up on stage at some local comedy club by the time she delivered.

"I like to tell people that my oldest sister is the most brilliant person currently doing nothing in the world," Sarah said.

"You what?" Mimi said.

Sarah popped another forkful of meat in her mouth,

chewed, swallowed, and said to Prescott, "Which is fine by me, but Mary? I think she would give an arm if Mimi would just *try* to do something, anything that required her supposed genius. Hell, I bet she'd be satisfied if Mimi did something that just took some raw talent." She speared another piece of meatball and swished it around in the gravy. "You know, I can see her point, too."

"Uneven race," Prescott piped in, nodding vigorously.

Sarah looked at him approvingly. She pointed her fork at him and winked again. Maybe she wasn't winking. Maybe she had a tic. "Exactly."

"I'm not in any race," Mimi said.

"Exactly. *You're not in the race*," Prescott pronounced with the same eager intensity as the kid in the front row who always had the right answer. "Do you know how frustrating it is trying to prove yourself when no one's looking?" He glanced at Joe. "Someone explain to her."

Joe reached across the table for the butter dish. Sarah shoved it toward him, chewing away rapaciously. She caught Mimi's glance. "Hey, I'm eating for two."

"Yeah, and apparently one of them is Orson Wells," Mimi said. "And no one has to 'explain to her.' I'm not an idiot. I get it." She folded her hands under her chin and looked appropriately forlorn. "Poor little Mary Werner has always felt herself measured by a yardstick without marks. Tested against a chimera. Racing against a phantom. *So* unfair."

Both Prescott and Sarah stopped chewing long enough to look at her with humiliating wonder.

"Oh, come on," Mimi said disgusted. "It's not exactly the most profound insight ever offered."

"Yeah, but it's so self-aware."

"You know, just because someone doesn't particularly *care* what others think about them doesn't mean she doesn't *know* what they think. It's not the same thing at all, and before any more stunning psychological revelations are made, let me say that there's a very simple reason why I don't care about Mary's late-blooming case of sibling rivalry, and it does not stem from mishandled potty-training or being forced to babysit her when she was little, and this is it: I think it's dumb."

Sarah was the first to speak. "When did you figure this out?"

"I'd like to say years ago, but it was actually at Mom's house this fall. Mary was all grim gauntlet throwing. She kept saying melodramatic things about me 'actually doing something—or trying,' and glaring like Snidely Whiplash. I would have had to be as dense as last year's fruitcake not to get it."

"Mary must feel the comparison keenly," Sarah said loyally.

"Oh, yeah?" Mimi asked. "How did you manage to escape feeling so put-upon?"

Sarah thoughtfully slathered butter over a piece of bread. "I've always assumed I'm smarter than you." She gave the Tierney men a diffident smile, then said to Mimi, "Besides, I escaped that whole cankle unpleasantness. I told you how much it affects her."

"Cankles?" Joe asked interestedly.

Sarah stuck her foot above the table and pointed. "Cankles. Heel to calf, no stops in between."

The men accepted this bit of information with the gravity it deserved.

Mimi continued. "If Mary needs a worthy opponent to measure herself against, I hear Stephen Hawking is a scrappy little fighter."

Joe laughed. "You have to admit, Mimi has a point. If Mary purposely chooses to pitch herself into a contest only she's entered, she can't gripe about the lack of competition."

"My hero." Mimi fluttered her eyelashes.

"What can I say? I'm a sucker for a damsel in distress," Joe said. "Besides, I look too good in designer Shining Armor to pass up any opportunity to wear it."

Mimi sputtered, almost losing the mashed potato in her mouth.

Prescott and Sarah looked from Joe to her, and then back again. Prescott set his fork down and slumped in his chair, reverting to surly mode once more.

"What do you do, Prescott?" Sarah asked, either advertently or inadvertently saving the day. Or at least the meal.

"Computer stuff."

"Like what?"

"I, ah, design stuff."

"While teaching and doing research at MIT, he created a host-to-host security protocol used by every major investment firm in the world. MIT patented it, but Prescott gets a percentage of the royalties," said Joe, then added with what could only be pride, "He is the youngest tenured professor there. He's on sabbatical."

"Really?" Sarah asked, wide-eyed.

"Yeah." Prescott wiggled in his wheelchair, looking massively embarrassed.

"I am in awe," Sarah declared sincerely.

"I . . . I . . . think the dogs are hungry," Prescott said and cast Mimi a pleading expression. Poor kid did not know how to handle compliments. Or maybe it was Joe's obvious pride he didn't know how to take.

Mimi pushed back from the table. The dogs, sensing dinnertime, roused themselves, emerging from under the table like wolves from their den. Mimi picked up the lone meatball she'd left on her plate and tossed it into the center of the pack. On cue, Blondie sailed up and plucked the meatball out of midair just before it entered Bill's open maw.

"Nice pick!" Sarah said.

"What are you doing?" Prescott asked.

"Oh, don't worry," Mimi said, reaching over and liberating a meatball from his plate. "They all end up getting the same amount. Except Bill. Who is fat. He gets half."

Bill lifted his lip at her, but more out of a sense of

obligation than any real animosity. At least that's what she told herself.

She divided the meatball in half with her fingers and dropped one portion into Bill's mouth and handed the other to Wiley, who took it delicately. She looked up, expecting Prescott to be regarding her with sappy approval. He was frowning at her.

"You're not supposed to feed dogs from the table," he said tightly. "And you're not supposed to feed them human food. It's bad for them. Onions can kill a dog."

"I told her not to feed them table scraps." Joe nodded sanctimoniously.

Mimi narrowed her eyes at him. "Men who rely on the kindness of strangers ought to remember not only on which side their bread is buttered but who is buttering it. Besides, they're not scraps. We share and you did *not* tell me not to feed them human food. You said their food was in the freezer and the only thing in the freezer is human food," Mimi rejoined.

"That's because their food is in the freezer chest in the garage," Prescott said heatedly. "Portion-controlled rations with each dog's name printed clearly on the labels. A balanced diet of chicken, lamb, rice, minerals, calcium, and vitamin supplements that I designed for them individually after studying canine nutrition."

"That's what you meant when you were taking off in the ambulance and you said, 'There's food in the freezer'? I thought you were talking about me and *this* freezer. How was I supposed to know you were feeding these mutts a special diet? Let me tell you, Pres, they weren't talking."

"You are." Prescott gasped as if just tumbling to some deep universal truth. *"You don't know anything about dogs at all, do you?"*

"No."

"I bet you didn't even bathe them."

"Right again. Joe did."

"Why, you probably don't even like dogs."

"Now, that's *not* true. I entered the relationship in good faith, without any bias one way or the other. I've never had a dog or lived with a dog. I will say, however," she admitted in the spirit of full disclosure, "had Bill been my sole interaction with the doggy world, then no, I probably would have said I don't like dogs. But he's not," she pointed out, "and I do."

"If you don't like Bill, why did you give him to me?"

"Because you said you'd take him." Now, why would that make him go red in the face?

"You mean you *didn't* sense the sort of person I was? That you could trust me? That I was caring and responsible? That I would take the charge you placed on me seriously—"

"No," Mimi said, her voice hard. Prescott had made her feel like she'd let him and Bill down. Worse, he'd made her care that she'd let them down. "Look," she said, deciding to be scrupulously honest. "I saw an opportunity to transfer a responsibility I did not want to a kid who was dying to have one and at the same time getting a little back from him for ruining my lake."

Prescott's mouth dropped open and he gaped at Mimi.

Joe, Mimi noted, was watching them closely. "Dying to have one?" he asked.

"Well, yes," she shot at him.

"*Ruining your lake?*" Prescott breathed, his face tight with indignation.

Mimi frowned. "Well, yeah."

Prescott drew himself up in the wheelchair, his lip quivering with suppressed emotion. "And just how am *I* ruining *your* lake?"

Was he kidding? How could he not know the established Fowl Lake community loathed his Piney Palace and him for building it?

"Take a look," she said, amazed. "You and the people like you, people with more money than they know how to spend, you decide to build yourself a 'getaway' and come up and take over. Have you ever given a thought to what sort of impact throwing up these monster houses has on anyone else? Like families who've been coming up here for generations?"

Prescott glared at her. "Yes. I increase the property value."

"You jack up the property prices and with it the property taxes until no one but your type can afford them. But worse, you make anyone who doesn't own a half dozen Jet Skis and three-tiered decks with outdoor sound systems feel like an outsider. On their own lake. In the cabins and cottages their families have been coming to for decades. You slap up your mansions and you loom over us until people like the Sbodas end up selling. *That's* how you're ruining my lake."

Prescott was bright red.

"That's hardly fair—" Joe started to say, but Prescott, his face a brilliant red, swung around toward him.

"You stay out of this. This is my business. My house." He turned to Mimi. "Do you have anything else you want to add?"

"Yeah. Why do you even bother?" Mimi went on. "You don't care about the lakes or your monster mansions. The turnover is like once every three years. You're squatters, only here until the next thing captures your imagination. You're tourists."

"Bullshit," Prescott snapped, his voice quavering. "You can't just judge me like that. You don't know what my intentions are here or what motivated me to build this place. You don't know anything about me at all. Just like I guess I don't know you."

"Bingo. You're finally getting it," she snapped back.

He ignored her. "You might not like the house, but you can't tell me I'm a tourist. You just don't want to share the lake. You're just a snob, you and your family. So caught up in making comparisons that you won't give a chance to anyone whose family hasn't been here for a hundred years and still pumps their water from a well."

He had a point, but she was still angry about his idolization, her guilt, and this place and all the places like it that
would be built and what they meant to the future of Chez
Ducky. But at the very core of her anger was a realization that
her place, Chez Ducky, was the only place in her life where
she wasn't a tourist, a passer-through, the only place where
she had a personal investment. And with that realization
came fear. "You're not interested in sharing," she said.
"You're confiscating."

"I am not. I'm staking a claim. Just like your great-great-
how-ever-many-great-grandparents who showed up here one
weekend and decided to claim a piece of the lake for themselves. They were tourists, too. How am I—" He stopped,
tightened his lips, and went on, "How can a person ever belong somewhere if he doesn't ever make the effort to go there
in the first place?"

Abruptly, Mimi's anger evaporated as understanding took
root. Prescott had thought he was buying a place he could belong to, not a place that belonged to him. If anyone should
understand that, she should.

Empathy flooded her. She looked up to find Prescott regarding her with a defensive jut to his jaw. Sarah and Joe
were sitting quietly, their eyes watchful. Something about
Joe's expression told her that Prescott's words had struck a
chord with him, too. Was Joe, too, looking for a place he belonged? Was Sarah?

"You're right, Prescott," Mimi said. "I don't have any
business making assumptions about you. I'm an ass. I'm jealous because you can afford to protect what you have and I
can't."

Prescott blinked and Joe's brows shot up in surprise. Even
Sarah looked shocked.

"What? Don't people in your family ever own up to being
wrong?" Mimi asked. "And why are you staring at me like
that, Sarah? I said I was an ass. I got carried away."

"I know you did," Sarah said. "I've never heard you sound

so vehement about anything before. Mom would have been stunned. Mary would have applauded."

"Oh, crap," Mimi said.

"I didn't think it was all that impressive," Joe said, protectiveness coloring his usually soothing voice. "She simply went on the offensive."

For whatever reason, he abruptly stopped and his skin reddened slightly. "But even the most level-headed person, especially in the throes of strong emotion, can say things they might later regret. Most of us take weeks to admit it, if we ever do. Mimi doesn't seem to have that problem."

"Well, she did make certain points," Prescott conceded. "I just didn't think of things in that light."

"I didn't think of things in your light, either," Mimi said. They regarded each other warily. Joe and Sarah nodded encouragingly to both of them.

"Look, Prescott. It's not that I disliked you. I disliked—and continue to dislike—your house. But the main, the primary, the overwhelming reason that I gave you Bill was that I wanted to leave and you said you'd take the dog. You said you'd send pictures. I thought you looked like an okay guy. End of story."

Prescott was still offended. "I can't believe you left a vulnerable, defenseless little animal with just anyone."

Put that way, it did sound despicable. "In fairness to myself—and I always try to be scrupulously fair to myself—I don't know that I would do the same today. I didn't know how dependent dogs are when I dumped Bill on you, Prescott." It was true, too. "Peace?"

He looked at Sarah and Joe. They nodded again, like benevolent bobble-head dolls. "Okay. I guess."

Suddenly, from the front hall, "When the Saints Go Marching In," started playing. Mimi would never have believed a call from Jessica could make her so happy. "Excuse me. I have a business call coming in."

She headed to the front closet and the jacket she'd left her cell phone in.

"What business? What's she talking about? Who's that?" she heard Prescott asking from the living room.

"She's a medium," Sarah replied in a casual voice. "She talks to dead people and reports the conversation to the living."

"Some dead person's calling here?" Prescott sounded torn between fascination and holding on to his grudge. "She's talking to ghosts in my front hall? Can I watch?"

"No!" Mimi shouted back, digging the cell phone out of her pocket and flipping it open. "Hello, Jess. We just talked. Why are you calling again?"

"I wanted to see if you gave me your real phone number."

"As you can see, I gave you the real thing."

"I got something else to say."

"Go for it."

She heard Jess take a deep breath, then another, like she was preparing for a pole vault. "I know you can't really talk to my mom. Neil thinks so, too. I just want you to know I know."

"Okay."

Another, even longer silence followed.

"Aren't you going to say anything?" Jessica finally burst out.

Mimi sighed. "What do you want me to say, Jess? That you're right, I'm a fraud? I've bilked you out of hundreds of dollars and I wish you hadn't seen through my chicanery?"

"What's 'chicanery'?" Jessica whispered.

"Trickery."

"Oh." Another pause. When Jessica spoke again her voice was subdued, a little forlorn. "No. I don't want you to say that. I want you to tell me you're real. That what you say Mom said is real."

Mimi leaned her shoulder against the wall, tucking the cell phone close. "What good would that do, Jess?" she asked

softly. "I can't prove it. It would just be the word of a suspected fraud telling her patsy what she wanted to hear. Be
reasonable, what else would I say?"

"I just want you to say it."

"Can't do, Jess. Some things you have to take on faith."

"What if you find out your faith was misplaced?"

Mimi's thoughts turned toward Prescott and how he'd assumed she'd had everyone's best interests at heart when
she'd left Bill with him and how he clearly felt betrayed
when he found out she hadn't. She should see this as
Prescott's problem, not hers. She hadn't purposely misrepre-
sented herself. But Prescott had thought her better than she
was and Jess was still waiting for an answer.

"You hope it won't be the next time."

"But you keep on taking things on faith? You keep on giving people a chance?" she asked.

"If those people are lucky," Mimi said.

Jess was quiet a moment. "I should let you go back to
your friends. I . . . I guess I shouldn't have called. I guess I
should have had a little faith in you. Bye."

She hung up, leaving Mimi glad she didn't have to
answer.

Chapter Forty

Even though they'd finished dinner, Mimi and Sarah were still foraging. Mimi stood in the open refrigerator door, eating something straight off the shelf, and Sarah was picking through the rest of the salad looking for garlic croutons. All the high emotions of the previous hour seemed to have been forgotten by everyone except Joe. Prescott had evidently decided that Mimi's vitriol wasn't personal, and Mimi's attitude toward Prescott had subtly changed. Joe thought she regretted offending Prescott. In fact, the two of them were getting along rather well, though Joe no longer detected even the slightest trace of Mimi-worship from Prescott.

It had been a revealing conversation, not only for Mimi and Prescott, but for Joe, too.

While Joe felt Mimi had done the right thing in telling Prescott what she thought of his building this house here (he appreciated candor, even if it wasn't always pleasant), he'd been surprised by the surge of protectiveness that had come over him when he'd seen how hurt Prescott had appeared. At the same time he'd realized that Mimi had spoken only because her emotions had been so strongly engaged. Just like his emotions had been strongly engaged when he'd accused her of conning Prescott. He'd wanted to say more, but

Prescott had dealt with her accusations himself and done so
well. Joe had been proud of his son.

"Whatever you're eating, don't give any to the dogs,"
Prescott said. "Some human food can make dogs ill. Like
chocolate. Don't feed them any chocolate cake."

"Don't worry," Mimi mumbled.

"Right," Prescott said, watching her like a hawk.

Joe noted Prescott's reaction. Though Mimi had clearly
been sacked from her role as Mommy Madonna, Joe suspected she was being recast as Retro-Hippie Spiritualist. She
obviously fascinated Prescott. He kept asking her about her
philosophy. Mimi kept eating, giving him throwaway answers that sounded interesting until you realized they were
all quotes printed on the outside of the Starbucks paper coffee cups. Prescott didn't drink coffee.

Joe kept quiet. God, he knew so little about his kid. He
hadn't had much opportunity to watch his son interact with
other people. He and Prescott had always gotten together in
a vacuum, separated from the rest of the world. Why had that
been, when it was so clear to Joe now that Prescott was not a
loner at all, but someone who was simply alone?

Mimi could be spouting bullshit or brilliance, pap or sincerity. Whether she knew the difference was open to speculation. Joe figured she did. She'd certainly shaken up his
relationship with Prescott. And with Karen. It wasn't that he
credited her with illuminating his relationships with lightning bolts of insight. She just said aloud things he'd known,
but the way she'd said them, without ascribing any particular
moral weight to them, had dissolved both the disloyalty he'd
felt toward Karen in questioning her motives and the guilt
he'd felt toward Prescott for not questioning them earlier.
Questioning Karen, he realized, didn't mean he didn't love
her. He had. She was, as Mimi had pointed out, an amazing
person. And also very possibly a head case.

It didn't matter.

Mimi hip-checked the refrigerator door closed. In each

hand she held pale roundish globs. The sparkle was back in her eye—there was no keeping Mimi Olson too long on the serious side of life. Whether it was of devilment or pleasure he couldn't tell. Mimi often gave the impression of knowing a delicious secret that she was dying to share but knew no one would believe. He'd believe.

"What do the dead sound like?" Prescott was asking.

"Don't encourage her," said Sarah.

"No," Prescott said. "I'm interested. What do they sound like?"

Mimi popped a ball into her mouth and munched pensively. "They don't have actual voices. Unsurprising, since they have no voice boxes. I don't really hear words. I more sense things."

"How do you tell one ghost from the other?"

"I dunno."

Prescott turned to Sarah. "Is she putting me on?"

Sarah shrugged. "I dunno."

Prescott looked at Joe.

"I dunno, either," Joe said.

"Nobody knows," Mimi pronounced.

"The trouble I've seen," Joe rejoined.

Mimi smiled in delight. She looked damn pretty. "What time it is? Pop songs count."

Prescott's eyes widened with discovery. "Which way the wind blows!"

Mimi laughed. "God only knows."

"The Shadow knows," Joe said.

"Who's the Shadow?" Prescott asked.

"What are you guys talking about?" Sarah asked a little anxiously. "Were there funny mushrooms in those meatballs? Is my baby okay?"

"The baby's fine. We were just playing," said Mimi, giving Prescott a conspiratorial grin.

"And Sarah calls herself a genius," Prescott said, surprising Mimi into laughter.

Joe leaned back smiling and looked around the table. The mockery between the sisters, Prescott's unexpected humor, the casual affection with which everyone treated the dogs, even the lack of a cohesive reason for all of them being here, contributed to his sense of well-being. It was different from anything he'd ever known. It was irresistible.

"What is that you're eating?" Prescott asked Mimi, pointing at the little beige balls studded with dark flecks in her hand.

"Cookie dough."

"That's disgusting," Prescott said.

"Gimme one," said Sarah.

"No," Joe said, leaning forward and trying to knock Mimi's hand away. She avoided him.

"Raw eggs. Salmonella." Prescott carried on the fight. "Sarah could get sick."

"Not to worry," Mimi said, handing Sarah a ball. "These are prepackaged, preformed, refrigerated cookies of a type that does not use raw eggs. Now"—she brushed her hands—"we gotta get going, Sarah."

"Where? Chez Ducky?" Prescott asked. "But it's still early."

"Yup," Mimi said. "Sarah hasn't even seen the place."

"You should record your first impressions," Joe told Sarah. "I'll bet they'll be interesting."

"What does he mean?" Sarah asked Mimi.

Mimi smiled serenely at him. "Ignore Bubble Boy. Unless it's sprayed daily with bleach, he's sure it's carrying typhus."

He smiled back, but he wanted to say, *Stay*.

Sarah pushed herself up from the table. "Don't worry, Mr. Tierney, I'm not high maintenance. Mimi says it'll be like camping. I think I'd like camping."

"That's nice, dear," Joe said amiably.

Mimi led her sister to the front door, where they bundled themselves into their coats and jackets. After short good-byes, they got into Sarah's Lexus and drove away. Prescott watched them disappear into the night.

"I wish they could have stayed," he murmured. He shot a self-conscious glance at Joe. "Bill liked Sarah."

Joe rolled back out of the front hall, settling his chair on one side of the bank of windows. Prescott wheeled himself to the other side. Both of them stared at the darkening sky.

"Do you think I should let Bill out again?" Joe asked.

"I think he's fine."

"Okay." They fell silent again, but this silence didn't have the same quality as past silences they'd shared. This silence was less silent. Cozier. Smaller.

"Good stargazing," Joe said. He felt Prescott's gaze on him.

"Thanks for not telling Mimi about how we ended up on the floor," Prescott said. "That I swung and missed."

"No problem."

"And thanks for coming here to, ah, help out with things," Prescott mumbled. "It couldn't have been easy with all your work."

"No big deal," Joe said. "I was glad to do it."

The silence tensed and as quickly relaxed again.

"You know much about astronomy?" Prescott asked after a bit.

"Not a thing," Joe said, feeling weirdly content. "You?"

"Some. A little."

"Hm. So, where's Orion's Belt?"

Prescott rolled his wheelchair closer to Joe's and pointed out into the darkness. "See the Big Dipper?"

"That's one I do know."

"Okay. Follow the handle—"

The front door banged open, startling Prescott. The dogs, likewise startled, blurted into a chorus of frightened howls. All except Bill. His lip curled back over his teeth and a deep rumble emanated from his little barrel chest as he swaggered into the hall like Popeye the Sailor.

Prescott and Joe waited expectantly.

Sarah appeared in the doorway, clutching a suitcase. She dropped it with a thud. "To hell with the camping. Can I stay here?"

Chapter Forty-one

February

Mimi set the short stack of mail on Prescott's kitchen island and pulled off her gloves. At the other end of the island, Prescott sat with his chin in his palms studying the newspaper's Sudoku. She doubted he'd even noticed she'd come in. In the nearly five weeks since Sarah and Prescott had both arrived, Prescott's social eagerness had quickly lapsed into relaxed casualness. He took her daily look-ins for granted. Rather than be insulted by his lack of ongoing gratitude, Mimi found it oddly endearing. She found the whole arrangement oddly . . . nice.

She felt important to the workings of this little commune, but not essential, and she liked the feeling. In part for the very reason that she wasn't essential; she knew that all of them were perfectly capable of functioning without her, that they did not depend on her for their ultimate happiness (except maybe Wiley), and that's exactly how it should be. Still, that she contributed greatly to it . . . pleased her. Without her, they wouldn't have gotten by so well.

Yup. Pretty much everything was perfect.

Except that Joe . . . Nope. Not going there. She would continue to ignore Joe and the physical attraction that was

escalating by leaps and bounds every time they were together. She knew Joe felt it, too. If she'd been of a more dramatic or egocentric bent, she might even have imagined that
Joe had gone skijoring yesterday—a full two weeks before
the doctor had said he could—with the express purpose of
making himself too sore to be able to act on that attraction in
the very short— Nope. She was not going there.

The happy mood in which she'd entered the Piney Palace
was disappearing, taken over by restlessness and discontent.
Where was Sarah anyway? She shed her coat and flung it
over a nearby stool and ripped open the end of an expensive-
looking envelope addressed to her. Inside was a single sheet.

She read. It didn't take long. When she was done, she
crumpled the paper into a ball and rammed it into the bottom
of the garbage can.

The Peterson, Peterson and Petersen law firm could go
screw themselves. Mimi didn't care that they were only
doing what the majority of heirs of Ardis Olson wanted by
"requesting" they all meet at their Fawn Creek offices to sign
the papers that would put Chez Ducky on the real estate market. She hated the law firm of Peterson, Peterson and
Petersen.

It was better than hating her family.

Yes. She'd known it was coming. Birgie's cell phone message some months before had been substantiated by an
apologetic phone message from Vida, which Mimi had
picked up a few weeks ago. In a nutshell, Vida had explained
what Mimi already knew: there were so many reasons to sell
Chez Ducky and so few to keep it. The decision had not been
made lightly. They felt terrible about it, but practically speaking, it only made sense, and the Olsons were an eminently
practical people.

It was out of her hands now. It had never been in her
hands, she reminded herself. The idea, rather than consoling
her as it would have in the past, for whatever reason, now just
pissed her off.

She dropped the lid on the garbage shut and, as she did so, spotted an expensive set of luggage in the front hall, which the lid had hidden. All hopes of not thinking about Joe vanished. The luggage was waiting for Joe because Joe was leaving tomorrow. He was returning to Singapore to handle negotiations because apparently *no one else* was capable of putting paid on the bill. That's what happened when you were essential to something. Today, Fate seemed intent on smacking her in the face with the inevitability of all good things coming to an end.

It was a good thing. She didn't want Joe to leave. Both facts further fouled her mood. She hadn't expressly *not* wanted someone to go away for years. Sure, she had experienced a couple moments of warm, vague "Gee, that was nice. Too bad it didn't last longer," but not this gaping ache. This panic in the base of her throat.

She was the absolute champion of letting go, of waving good-bye. But the thought of losing Joe—no, wait. That wasn't right. What a terrible choice of words. She didn't *have* Joe, so obviously she couldn't lose him. The thought of the absence of his company, his conversation, his understated sense of humor, hurt her more than she'd have believed possible. And it was more than that. She wouldn't be able to annoy him, challenge him, provoke and amuse him. She'd never felt so important to anyone before. And . . . he might be important to her. Really important. So important that if he disappeared—

Was it all in her imagination? She didn't know. She didn't even know how to ask him, or even if she should ask, a fact that befuddled and upset her. She supposed she should just let it slide until it slid away.

Behind her, Mimi heard Sarah's heavy footfalls and the opening of a cupboard door. She spun around, too ready to do battle, and spied Sarah pulling a carton of Little Debbie frosted minidonuts from the shelf. Mimi grabbed for them.

"Dr. Youngstrum said you should lose some of that

weight," Mimi snapped, giving voice to the first excuse she
could think of as she tried to wrest the box from Sarah. She'd
insisted that Sarah see the family practice physician in Fawn
Creek at least once if she were to remain up here, on the
threat of calling Solange.

"It's my choice!" Sarah growled. "And I haven't gained
any weight in two weeks."

"You *waddle*."

Abruptly, Sarah's eyes welled up with tears. Her breath
hitched in her throat.

"Oh, no. No, you don't," Mimi said. "Do *not* play the
pregnant-lady card. It's not working anymore. You've been
here four weeks and in that short time you've doubled your
size."

"I have not!"

"You are huge. It's not good for your blood pressure."
Feeling Sarah's grip on the box loosen, Mimi jerked the carton from her hands. The top popped open and Little Debbie
frosted minidonuts flew around the kitchen.

Prescott ducked, barely avoiding being hit by the flying
carton. "Hey," he said. "Watch it."

Dogs shot from out of nowhere, scooping donuts up like
humpback whales through a school of krill, then disappeared
again to await the next culinary windfall.

Sarah plopped down on her stool with a "now look what
you've done!" air and crossed her arms, resting them on her
Baby Bulge, expanded in the last month from the original
Baby Bump and now well on its way to Mount Baby stage.

"Mimi says I am fat, Prescott."

"Um." Prescott's initial giddiness over adding Sarah to the
household had detoured into nonchalance over the last
month. At first, Mimi had worried that he might have trans-
ferred his crush on her to a more romantic one on Sarah.
Deciding her usual course of letting things slide might not
best serve the situation this time, she'd confronted Prescott
and had asked point-blank if he had a thing for Sarah.

He'd turned bright red. "No! No, she's pregnant."

"Some men find that sexy."

"Ew."

Mimi hadn't felt it necessary to pursue the subject.

"Prescott! Defend me," Sarah commanded. "I'm not fat, am I?"

Prescott glanced up. "Not fat. Really big."

Mimi shot Sarah a triumphant look.

"That's because the baby is big," Sarah sniffed.

"The baby would have to be the size of a hay bale to account for all that weight. Look at your legs. You've got cankles."

Sarah recoiled at this charge, her gaze flying to Prescott for support. "Pres?"

He looked down at Sarah's legs. "Canklish," he pronounced sadly. The talk of legs must have reminded him of his own, because he lifted his left one in its new walking cast up on the stool beside him.

"Fine. I didn't want any donuts anyway. And, by the way, your cookie dough is gone." Sarah whirled around and stalked out of the room.

The night Sarah had arrived, Mimi had been delighted to wave good-bye to her as she drove her Lexus away from Chez Ducky on her way to the Piney Palace. In fact, she'd rubbed her hands together. Finally things were going to be the way she'd imagined them to be when she'd arrived.

As soon as the taillights were out of sight, she'd turned back into the parlor to wallow in nostalgic bliss, fully expecting to find her ancestors waiting for her. She'd turned to find an empty room. Surprised, unhappy, confused, she had nonetheless refused to give up. When she wasn't up at Prescott's taking care of things, she'd spent the last weeks puttering around with the albums, poking through the cottages, doing a little sketching, and being monumentally bored. She could have relocated to Prescott's, too. She had a good excuse in Sarah. But that would be admitting there was nothing here for her. And maybe it would be admitting to something being at Prescott's.

"Where's Joe?" she asked.

"Outside," Prescott said.

Mimi pounced on this bit of intel. "He's not skijoring again? That would be criminally stupid. With that knee, I can't believe he was dumb enough to go skijoring yesterday. He's lucky he didn't do more than bruise his other knee. He—"

"Calm down, Mimi." Prescott twisted on the stool and looked out the window. "He's just sitting on an overturned pail about fifty yards off shore. How weird is that? Joe Tierney sitting on a pail doing nothing." Prescott squinted thoughtfully out the window at his father. "I think there's an End of Days prophecy about that."

"Well . . . good," Mimi grumbled. She should just go back to Chez Ducky and not return until he was gone. That way she could avoid good-byes.

"It's hormones," Prescott said without looking up.

"What?"

"Sarah's moody because of hormones."

"Oh. I knew that."

"What's your excuse?" Prescott asked, setting down his pencil. "You've been as touchy as Bill Gates at an Apple convention. You're not a moody person. What's up?" His face reflected both puzzlement and concern.

He looked so earnest and young. A regime of fresh air and dog-induced exercise and dealing with an emotionally unpredictable pregnant woman had done wonders for Prescott. Mimi doubted he'd ever be the belle of the ball (he was still awkward and prickly), but he was certainly easier in his own skin these days. And his heart was good. And true . . . *Shit!* Why was she getting all maudlin over Prescott? *He* wasn't going anywhere.

"Well?" he asked.

She plopped down on the stool next to him. "I dunno," she said. "Stuff."

"Like what stuff?"

She considered whether or not to tell him. Blurting out her little frets and stews was decidedly not her way. In fact, she generally eschewed acknowledging them to herself. But . . . what the hell? She wasn't asking anything of him. She was just answering his question.

"Like Sarah. She won't call Mom, and I think she ought to." He still looked questioning, so she decided to elaborate. "But I don't feel it's my place to press the issue. And . . ."

"And?" Prescott prompted mildly.

"And I am really concerned about her. She won't make a decision about the baby. She won't even look into any options."

At this, Prescott looked appropriately taken aback.

"She won't take any birthing classes. Can you believe that? She's in this massive state of denial—not to mention a massive state in general. Do you think that's healthy? I don't. But she keeps saying, 'Just let it slide.' " Mimi's voice rose with irritation and worry. "I can't figure out if she's mocking me or if she's lost her mind. You can't let a baby 'slide'!"

"Have you told her that?"

"All the damn time! I really wish Mom was here."

Prescott nodded sympathetically.

"And Joe," Mimi went on, amazed at how cathartic all of this felt.

Prescott shot her an inquiring glance.

"His knee," she hastily explained. "It bugs me he was that dumb about it."

Before Prescott could ask why, she diverted his attention. "*And* I got a call from Ozzie yesterday asking me when I was coming back, and I told him I couldn't for at least another couple months, because I have to stay with Sarah until she delivers. He said he'd need to hire a replacement and he was sorry and I told him not to kick himself because, well, lately

Those Beyond the Veil have been staying there and not making with the chitchat."

Prescott's eyes alit with sly interest. He had the same blue eyes as Joe.

"Oh?" he said a little too casually. "The ghosts aren't talking to you anymore?"

"Good try, Pres. Do you want to know if I talk to ghosts?"

"Yeah."

"So do I," she said and smiled at his chagrin. She was starting to feel better. "And the wiring at Chez Ducky is falling apart. I was trying to put the albums together last night, and I blew five fuses. I had to drive all the way to Fawn Creek to get more. But I did."

"You're a tough woman," Prescott said. Something amused in his tone made Mimi regard him more closely. He returned her inspection with guileless wide eyes. Could he be mocking her? Nah. Prescott had come far, but he hadn't come that far yet.

"Better believe it." Tough and resilient. That was her.

"Anything else?"

Yes. Oh, yes. The runaway train of verbosity came to an abrupt end. Suddenly she simply felt deflated again. "I got a letter this morning."

"What is it?"

"It's a notice. Tells me when I have to be at the lawyers' office to sign the papers so they can sell Chez Ducky." There. She'd said it out loud. Chez Ducky was going to be sold. After this weekend Debbie would stick it on the market and that would be that.

She smiled at Prescott, hoping she didn't look as ill as she felt. "Sucks, doesn't it?"

Prescott, bless his soul, looked stricken.

"Have you ever seen a prettier day?" Joe asked, emerging from the lower level and stopping at the top of the stairs. He beamed at her and Prescott, content, at ease, satisfied with the world and his place in it. Which was *her* role, and she wanted it back. She was the one who was supposed to be gorging herself on raw cookie dough, doing Sudokus all afternoon, sitting on her butt in the middle of a frozen lake while time parted around her and flowed on by. Or just left her behind. She resented Joe at that moment more than she could have thought possible.

"I'm thinking of trying my hand at ice fishing," he announced. "Ever been ice fishing, Prescott? No? How about you, Mimi?"

"Yeah," she said. She flashed on an image of Joe and Prescott sometime next winter, sitting on overturned pails in companionable silence, fishing poles almost touching over a round hole cut in the ice between them, a thermos of hot chocolate at Prescott's feet while waiting in blissful nonanticipation for fish that weren't going to bite. And she wouldn't be there. Because her chapter in Fowl Lake's history would be over, done. Her chapter in *their* history, in *Joe's* history, would be over, done.

Her throat closed. Damn it, damn it, damn. This is what you got when you ventured out of the safe shallows and dared the deeper waters of relationships. You floundered. You sank. You'd think she would have learned by now.

"Really?" Joe's handsome head was tilted inquiringly. He looked so damnably . . . *friendly.*

"Of course I have," she said. "Whaddya think? That's *my* lake out there. My *family's* lake. I've been coming here all my life, spring, summer, winter, and fall. Of course I've been ice fishing: ice fishing, ice spearing, boat fishing, drift fishing, fishing with a bobber, fishing with a spinner, fishing with lures, fishing bait, bottom fishing, bass fishing—"

"Yo, Mimi!" Prescott intervened. "We get it. You're like Babe Winkelman of Fowl Lake."

Her rage left in a whoosh. The sting of tears started in her eyes. "When the Saints Go Marching In" began playing on her cell phone, saving her from making a scene. She grabbed the phone off the island and fled for the hallway.

She took a deep breath. "Hi, Jessica."

"Hi, Mimi." Mimi had long since gone from 'Miss Em' to 'Mimi.' There were no secrets between Jessica and her anymore. "Is Prescott there? And Sarah and Joe?"

"Yeah," she said. "The gang's all here."

"Put me on speakerphone for a second, will you?"

"Sure." Mimi pushed the appropriate button and held the phone through the door into the great room. "It's Jessica," she called. "Say hi."

"Hi," Jessica said.

"Hi, Jessica," Joe and Prescott said in unison.

"How's the class going?" Prescott asked. He'd discovered that Jess was taking night courses in Web site design at a local community college. He'd spent an hour one night on the phone with her, helping her pick her course load.

"Good. I wanted to thank you for your help."

"Glad to do it," Prescott mumbled, turning red.

"Okay, now you've embarrassed him, so I'm turning off speaker. Okay. How're things?"

"Ah," Jess gave a verbal shrug.

"Neil?"

"Not my soul mate."

Relief washed through Mimi along with a weird feeling of pride in Jess. "That happens."

"Thanks for not saying 'I'm sure it'll work out.' "

"You're welcome."

"I have a question."

"Shoot."

"I don't know if you can really talk to my mom or not."

"Okay."

"But I like thinking that you can. So I'm going to assume you do."

"Okay. So, what's the question?"

Jessica hesitated. "The thing is, I don't think Mom's really had any advice for me since she died. I've been thinking about it, and mostly she's just been . . . there. Like, I guess, she always was. Sometimes, like, too much."

"Yeah, moms are like that."

"Well, the thing is, I've been thinking and I'm not sure I really ought to be asking you what she says. I mean, it's not like I'm talking directly to her. And, well, I think it's probably good to do things without polling your mom all the time."

"Yeah."

Jess was quiet for a short time, then said softly, "I love her, you know."

"I know."

Jessica cleared her throat. "So, do you think Mom would be upset if I stopped contacting her through you?"

Oh, Jess. "Nah."

"Really?" she sounded surprised, but hopeful.

"Your mom doesn't need to talk to you either through me or directly. Jess, your mom doesn't *need* anything. She hasn't since she died."

She heard Jessica's slight sigh, one of tension being released.

"You have to remember, Jess, you're the one who called Straight Talk. You needed her, not vice versa."

"I miss her."

"Yeah." She understood. Right now, she missed Solange. Jess hesitated. "Can I still call, just to talk to you?"

"I'd be hurt if you didn't."

On the way back into the kitchen Mimi almost bumped into Joe.

"Prescott said Chez Ducky is being put up for sale soon," he said. "I'm sorry, Mimi."

Prescott, that informer. Mimi looked over Joe's shoulder. Sarah had emerged from her sulk—and her room—and was sitting next to Prescott on the sofa. They were discussing whether Bill was cinnamon brown or nutmeg brown.

"I'll just have to bow to the inevitable, I guess." She'd

tried to sound dismissive and knew she'd barely managed
flat. She didn't want a counseling session. She didn't want
anyone to tell her things would be all right.

He came closer, much closer than he'd been since she'd
helped him from the car that first day back from the hospital.
And this is why, she thought. She just wanted to melt into
him, trade breaths, soak up his warmth. And she would have,
too, with the slightest excuse, the least bit of encouragement.
And then this would have been even harder. This being-left-
behind crap. She couldn't believe she had acted like such a
histrionic hag.

"I'm sorry I went off like that," she said. "It's just that I
can't believe it's not going to belong to the Olsons anymore.
It's like they're pulling the plug on a family member. But
Chez Ducky doesn't *need* to die."

His eyes met hers. "Chez Ducky doesn't need anything,"
he said. "It never has."

She inhaled sharply. "You were eavesdropping!"

Joe nodded, unembarrassed. "You're acting as if that place
is a person. You know, Mimi, if you'd put half of all your
emotional energy into someone who could actually return
it . . ." He trailed off, his gaze locked on her face.

Her pulse started flip-flopping. She felt a rush of adrenaline, shooting her full of panic. Joe was leaving. Sarah was
going to have a baby, and both of them would vanish. Her father was gone.

"Nah-uh," she said, trying to laugh. "The thing about a
place is that you always know where it is. It can't just take
off. It always stays the same."

"*Nothing* stays the same."

She knew that was true about most things better than most
people did. Chez Ducky was different. It had to stay the
same. It had to be here for her. Something did. Panic shredded her self-assurance.

"Mimi, would you say Bill is ginger colored?" Prescott
called from the other side of the room.

"Mimi, while you're over there, could you bring me a glass of milk?" Sarah asked.

Wiley, slouching in from his midmorning nap, brushed by her, went to the front door, and scratched at it.

She wanted to run. She wanted to flee back to the sweet oblivious bliss she'd known last summer and all the summers before. But here she was, in the dead of winter, tied through Joe and Prescott and the damn dogs and even Sarah—people who were going to go away and go on—to a place she was going to lose.

So she ran.

Chapter Forty-two

Joe stomped along the path between Prescott's and Chez Ducky, every step jarring his knee. He figured it was as good a way as any to distract himself from the frustration that had been building inside over the course of an excruciatingly long month.

For four weeks he had lived in a state of acute physical discomfort. Some of this was due to his injured leg and shoulder. More often it was because he could not go to Mimi's room and finish what they'd started on this very same damn beach almost six months ago. And the reasons for this were various: he wanted his limbs to be fully healed because he didn't want to be groaning for any other reasons besides pleasant ones; he wanted his limbs to be fully functioning because he did not want to hear Mimi laughing for any other reasons besides pleasant ones; the proximity of his son's room to every other bedroom in the house; the presence of Sarah, whom Mimi fussed over like an overzealous mother hen (and really, every time she said something like, "I don't like being responsible for anyone or anything," which was often, he had to stop himself from bursting into laughter); and finally, he was willing to admit it, because he was afraid.

This, possibly more than any other factor, had rendered him an incompetent, ineffectual, undecided, waffling wreck.

Joe hated being a wreck. He did not waffle. He examined, assessed, organized, evaluated, and decided upon a course of action that benefited the most people for the greatest good.

But not this time. This time he was confounded by how high the stakes were. Nothing he could remember had ever been so important. To him. To them.

He hadn't been part of a "them" in decades. He wanted to be that with her so badly, it neutralized all his effectiveness. And just when he'd felt better, like his leg and arm and all the stars were beginning to align, Mimi had gone off the deep end. She'd become moody, combative, and emotional. His bright, laughing, serene Mimi.

It only made him love her more. Because it provided proof of what he already knew, that Mimi wasn't just drifting through life, detached and uninvolved— *Love her*? Joe stopped midstride. He tilted his head as though he heard something familiar and welcome and long overdue. Yes. He loved Mimi.

He found her in the parlor, sitting in the corner of a lumpy-looking sofa. She looked broody and rumpled, her shirt twisted around her waist, her bare feet curled under her. Her hair hung in a cloud of curls around her shoulders and her nose was red as though she'd been crying. She didn't look up but continued to stare—make that glare—out the window. "Mimi."

He moved toward her and banged his leg against a table. He strangled off a curse. "Would you look at me?"

"I'm busy."

Yes, he had to acknowledge that fear had started to dominate the quixotic mixture of emotions he had regarding Mimi. He was afraid he was going to lose everything he'd found here. He was afraid his relationship with Prescott would fall back into the same pattern of him trying to fix Prescott and in the process make Prescott feel broken. He was afraid he'd lose the time he'd found, the time to wonder about cosmic things like why nature would make dogs intolerant of chocolate and not humans. He was afraid he'd lose the home he'd found here. Wherever he went, he was never more than a charming transient, a cordial guest with the power to upset lives. But here he'd been part of a quirky quasi-family complex, and Mimi was at the center of it. And that was the bottom line: he was afraid of losing Mimi.

He couldn't lose her.

Just the thought made him feel desperate, and that feeling was so alien to Joe Tierney, he reacted badly to it.

"Would you please look at me?" he repeated tersely. "You're being childish."

She looked at him with exaggerated indifference, saw that he was limping, and shot up, disappearing into a back room.

"Walking out isn't going to help," he called after her. "I'll just limp after you. It'll be pathetic, ridiculous. Is that what you want?"

She returned with a glass of water and a small bottle of Tylenol. She set the glass down on the table with a bang and twisted open the bottle cap, tipping the bottle over her open palm without looking. Several capsules bounced into her hand. One bounced off her palm and onto the floor.

"Damn it," she muttered and swooped down to pick it up. She held it up to the window and blew something off of it. "Here." She held the glass and the pill out to him.

"You don't expect me to take that?"

"Why not?"

"It's been on the floor."

"Oh, for the love of— It's okay. I invoked the thirty-second rule." Her tone was patronizing. "If it's on the floor less than thirty seconds, no germs have time to get on it."

"Just give me a different pill," he demanded, holding out his hand. This was not how he'd envisioned this scene playing out. He was going to be charming, exude confidence, not whine about a damn pill. He had to be more masterful . . .

He knew snapping his fingers for the bottle of pills was a bad idea the minute they snapped.

Her eyes widened, then narrowed to dark slits that snapped every bit as loudly as his fingers had. "No."

"Come on, Mimi. Don't be absurd."

"*Me* be absurd? No. Forget it."

He was out of patience and out of his depth. He limped toward her. She held the contaminated pill over the open bottle.

"Don't put that pill in there," he warned.

She dropped the capsule in the bottle.

He lurched forward. She backed away, one brow climbing at a challenging angle, stuck her thumb over the top of the bottle, and shook.

He stared at her. "I cannot believe you just did that. Of all the petty . . . What am I supposed to do now?"

"Either take one of your pills like a normal, well-adjusted human being, or hobble back to the pharmacy and tell them the whole bottle was tainted by one that had fallen on the floor. I bet the pharmacist could use a good laugh."

She swaggered toward him, heading for the door with exaggerated indifference. He watched her, paralyzed by how incapable he felt, how inept he'd been. Her chin tipped up and just as she passed, she reached out and her fingertips skated along his chest, etching a trail of sensation. "Touch," she said defiantly.

He clasped her wrist and spun her around and into his embrace, not stopping until his mouth was on hers and her body was crushed against him. She made a sound deep in her throat, wrapped her arms around his neck, and kissed him back. Every shred of his uncertainty burned away. This was right. Perfect. Meant to be. Fate.

He held her face between his hands, his tongue tangling with hers as he moved them back toward the sofa, the pain in his knee numbed by the expectation of pleasure. She looped her arms around his waist and they fell back onto thick, soft, lumpy cushions.

This time, there was no prolonged torment of kisses and

tongue, of hands making tentative excursions along ribs and stomachs and thighs. This time, urgency took over. Deep-throated moans were punctuated by gasps as he stripped off her shirt, revealing her breasts. He bent his head to her nipple, sucking it into his mouth. She arched back and he coiled an arm under her hips, pulling her tight against his groin, and pushing himself against the V.

She grabbed his shoulders, holding him back. "Wait. Wait."

"Oh, God, no," he said, swallowing. "We're not going to talk, are we?"

She laughed. "No! No." She shook her head, lifting her hips up and pushing her jeans off, kicking them away. Then her fingers went to work on the buttons of his shirt.

"Touch." Her fingertips found his chest. He fell back, closing his eyes, bliss sheeting his skin at the feel of her hands on him, cool fingertips pushing open his shirt front.

"Touch." Warm lips settled with delicious possessiveness against his stomach muscles.

"Touch." Her tongue traced a damp trail down over his pectorals, down his abdomen and— He inhaled on a long, sweet hiss.

"Touch."

Too much. Too damn much. He caught her by the shoulders and rolled her beneath him. He needed to be in her, to feel her surround him. He entered in one long, slow thrust, and she settled around him, wiggling a little to seat him deeper, her thighs like a vise around his flanks. He moved. She moaned.

"Oh. Oh, Joe. Ohhhh . . . that's so . . ." She giggled but as soon as he started moving again the giggles turned into gasps, and then pleas and, finally, release.

A long time later—an impressively long time later, Joe thought—she lay spent in his arms. He moved the damp tendril away from her temple and kissed her gently. She turned her head toward him. Her dark eyes were dilated, her skin flushed and glistening, all that dark curly hair cushioning her head.

"You're leaving," she said softly.

"I'm coming back."

She didn't reply, but her gaze scanned his face, stopped at his eyes, looked at him with a mixture of despair and hope.

"I started the project and there are people in that company who deserve a second look."

"You don't let people down."

He hoped she would understand. "I could. This time."

She shook her head. "No. I like the way you are. That way." She touched his cheek. She would never ask him to stay, he realized. She'd built a life around having no expectations, making no demands. It didn't mean she didn't need them.

"Don't look like that."

"Like what?"

"Worried. Resigned. I'll be back."

"If you say so."

He kissed her once hard.

"You worry too much," he murmured. He doubted anyone had ever said those words to Mignonette Olson.

She understood the irony. It was one of the things he most appreciated about her.

"I should try to be more like you," she suggested. Her tone was amused.

"Definitely."

Her breath was growing shallower as the exploration of his lips moved lower. "Relax."

"Let it slide," he suggested.

"Oh," she said, "I intend to."

SPRING

Chapter Forty-three

May

Birgie stepped out into the chill, blinked into the morning light glaring off of Fowl Lake, and stretched, yawning hugely. She was still tired. Truth be told, she never got a great night's sleep at the Chez; the mattresses were too thin and she was too fat. Still, something about this place perked her up. She'd been feeling a little old down there on the Florida links these last few weeks.

She turned and looked up at the peeling facade of the house and wondered whether Chez Ducky would sell immediately or there would be time for a last summer visit. She turned back to the bright lake and wondered whether she'd ever go skinny-dipping again. She turned toward the long narrow strip of grass-tufted beach and wondered whether that kid with the splotchball realized she'd been practicing with her own sling-shot, pinging plastic golfballs at the crocs on the fairways. She turned and—stumbled over a flat FedEx envelope propped against the outside of Chez Ducky's front door.

"Shit!"

She stooped, grunting, and picked it up. It was addressed to Mimi, so she carried it into the house and tossed it onto the

dining hall table next to Mimi's backpack. Overhead she
could hear the sound of people stirring. Birgie and the heirs-
apparently-not to Chez Ducky had arrived last night in anticipation of their meeting with the lawyers tomorrow. Birgie
had expected to find Mimi, but she'd been nowhere in sight,
just this packed backpack, like Mimi was expecting to be
leaving here fast.

All that had sorta been explained a while later when Mimi
arrived. The backpack, she'd told them, was for when Mimi's
half sister Sarah went into labor. This news occasioned the
gape-mouthed puzzlement you'd expect. Mimi's half sister,
whom no one had ever met, was *here*? No member from
Mimi's mother's family had been up to Chez Ducky since . . .
well, Solange herself, and that had been the year John disappeared and Solange had come to collect Mimi. Why Mimi's
apparently very pregnant half sister had decided to carry out
her confinement at a stranger's house in the northernmost
part of the state only added to the mystery.

It had been even more of a shock to discover that Mimi
had been over in the enemy camp (aka Prescott's Erection)
making nice with the enemy—and the enemy's dogs. Oddest
of all, Mimi had acted as if her playing den mother to such a
household was normal. Mimi hated being depended on for
anything. It gave her the jim-jams, just like her great-aunt
Birgie. That's just the way they were. Or at least that's the
way Birgie was . . . Maybe Mimi hadn't ever really been that
way, only circumstances had made it seem so.

There were other changes in Mimi she'd noticed, too.
Mimi, the most carefree woman Birgie knew, worried about
her sister, fretted about those hounds, and dutifully fussed
about Prescott. Poor Mimi, it appeared that something had
woken her to all the worries and cares that assailed other people. But the burdens that had been dumped on poor Mimi
didn't seem to depress her as they would have Birgie. In fact,
she seemed energized. All bouncy and full of beans.

Birgie frowned, shoving up the lakeside window to let in

a little fresh air. It smelled unusually sweet for early May, carrying none of the dank spring mold smell that came with ordinarily wet, dank northern Minnesota springs. She wished it did. It would have been easier to think of this as the last May she'd spend at Chez Ducky if it were a crappy May. But the unusually warm and dry weeks had made the lake look and smell damnably lovely.

She turned back into the room, where Naomi, dressed in a dirndl skirt and buckskin shirt, was sitting on the floor in a semi-lotus position, eyes closed, humming softly.

"Getting anything?" Birgie asked.

Naomi opened her eyes. "No." She sounded deflated. "I'm afraid Mimi is the only one with the gift."

"You sure you want to sign those papers?" she asked Naomi.

"No," she said. "But Bill wants me to, and they've got those two boys to send to college, and believe me, neither of them is going to be getting any scholarships."

"I guess," Birgie said. "Do you think Gerald and Vida are thinking the same thing?"

"Yup. Plus there's Gerry's brothers. He'll split his share with them. When she drew up her will, I don't think Ardis ever imagined that she was deeding over anything besides the right to speak at the end of the summer powwow. I'm sure she never thought the people she named as her heirs were going to sell the place."

"Then she ought to have thought harder," Birgie grumbled. "Ardis was just like Mimi, thinking everything will go along the way it always has. Don't suppose I can blame her. I kinda thought so, too."

"How many grandkids does Johanna have now?" Naomi asked. "Eight? Ten?"

Birgie shrugged, deflated. She got the point. There was no way the Olsons and their offspring could allow this little gold vein to go unmined.

Naomi leaned forward and rolled to her knees, propping

herself up on the couch and lumbering to her feet. "What are we going to do for dinner? I could drive in to town and get meatballs from Smelka's. How many are there going to be?"

Birgie mentally tallied up their number. There were her and Naomi, plus Johanna and Charlie, who, having finally come clean about their decades-long affair, were shacking up in Cabin Six. Then there were Vida and Gerry, and Naomi's son, Bill, and Debbie, who, even though they weren't heirs per se, insisted on tagging along to "support" Naomi. Ha. Like Naomi needed support. They were here to make sure she didn't change her vote at the last minute. That made eight. Then there was Mimi and the people she'd adopted into the system, her sister Sarah and the kid, Prescott. She supposed she should see whether they wanted to be included, since Mimi had already included them.

She was still thinking about this when Mimi appeared.

"Hi, Mimi," Naomi said. "How's Sarah?"

"Fine, I guess." Mimi sounded testy. "I took her to Fawn Creek yesterday and Dr. Youngstrum said if she didn't return to Minneapolis soon to have this baby, she wasn't going to be leaving at all."

"So, is she leaving?" Naomi asked.

"She says not yet. I swear to God that pregnancy has interfered with her hearing because she is not tracking what either me or the doctor tells her."

Since when did Mimi tell anyone what to do? Birgie wondered.

The bang of the front door preceded Vida's arrival. "Well, if it isn't the resident ghost lisperer," she said, smiling at Mimi.

"Only Capote has managed to lisp from the Other Side," Mimi replied. "Besides, I've retired."

Naomi, Vida, and Birgie exchanged startled looks. "What? When? Why?"

"Forced out by my employer's unreasonable demand that I actually work more days than I take off."

"Really?" Vida asked.

"Really. Besides, I can't hear them anymore what with all the noise around here. When Prescott and Sarah aren't screaming at each other about who builds the better dedicated graphic accelerator, they're arguing about baby names—Prescott's current favorite being Galadriel for a girl and Faramir if it's a boy, Aragorn apparently being an impossible name to live up to."

Mimi must have misread Birgie's expression of confusion—what was she babbling about?—because she nodded.

"I know," Mimi said. "And Sarah hasn't even read *The Lord of the Rings.* She's leaning toward Beth or John, thereby proving my theory that every bit of her creativity has gone into the making of this kid. And before you ask, I have already gently pointed out that any naming rights get to go to the custodial parents of this kid, because Sarah still hasn't decided if she's going to give the baby up for adoption."

"Who can't you hear?" Birgie asked. She'd never been all that interested in kids, let alone kids' names.

The shift in subject caught Mimi off guard. "What?"

"You said you can't hear them anymore because of the noise."

"I told you. The ghosts. They've been shouted down by the living. Those two bicker like siblings. To top it off, Sarah has been teaching Bill to 'sing.'"

"Bill?" Vida asked, looking just as nonplussed as Birgie felt. Only Naomi seemed sanguine. She wore that all-knowing smirk of the cosmically connected.

"The mean little sausagelike dog with brown curly hair. The one we 'rescued' last summer? Sarah's actually got the little bastard to howl on command. Of course, the rest of them, not about to be shoved out of the spotlight, have started howling every time they hear Bill's reedy little wolf-speak."

"Does it make you mad?" Birgie asked, unable to leave Mimi's abandonment by the ghosts alone.

"Mad? No. I just leave. That's the beauty of being the neighbor."

"I meant about the ghosts."

"Nah. To everything there is a season."

What? Birgie thought in amazement. Who *was* this woman? Up here at Chez Ducky, regardless of the month or the weather, there was only one season due to the fact that nothing changed here. Things stayed the same. People might come and go, but the place was . . . timeless. If Mimi had said this once, she'd said it a thousand times.

Gerald came stomping in just then, his face glum. "Oh. Hi, Mimi. How come you look so happy? Oh, yeah. You're always happy. Does anything ever touch a nerve?"

"Nope," Mimi said. "Totally nerveless." But she *blushed.* "Why the long face, Ger?"

"You wouldn't understand."

"Gerald," Vida said warningly, putting her hand on his sleeve.

"Probably not," Mimi replied. "But what the hell, let me have a shot at it."

"Okay," he said gruffly defiant, "I'm going to miss this place. There. You have it. I'm getting all mawkish over a pricey length of swampy lakeshore. But, dammit, so many good parts of our lives have been spent here. Why, Carl was created right down on that beach—"

"Ger!" Vida yelped.

"I did *not* need to know that," said Birgie.

"I thought so," Naomi intoned.

"Anyways," Gerry picked up where he'd left off, "it makes me feel sort of blue. Knowing Chez Ducky won't be in the family anymore." He squared his shoulders. "Of course, selling it is the sensible thing to do."

Vida smiled at her husband and tucked her arm through his. "Come on, Ger. Let's take a walk on the beach."

"It's going to storm," he protested, still morose. "The

clouds have been building up on the horizon all day, and they're starting to move in."

"Oh, they've been doing that all spring," Mimi said. "Like a teenage boy with a condom, all show, no go. We haven't had rain in weeks. You may have noticed the lack of green?"

"See?" Vida batted her eyelashes at Gerry. "Maybe we could check out the vacant cottages on our way down to the beach. . . ." She snagged her sweater on the way out the door, Gerry lumbering after her like a suddenly eager Saint Bernard puppy.

They passed Johanna and Charlie on their way into the dining hall. "Well, look who's come down from the tower. Princess Mimi," Charlie said. He stopped by the table and the boxes of photographs Mimi had been sorting. "Hey. Look, Jo. Mimi's found the old photographs. What happened to the albums?"

They flanked Mimi, picking up and looking over the photographs she hadn't put away yet.

"They were falling apart so I started reorganizing them," Mimi said.

"Ha! Look, Jo. Here's you and the kids. And me. Gosh. I forgot about that tree house." He shook his head. "It's a wonder no one died in that thing."

"You know," he continued, looking up at Mimi, "this is a pretty clever way of organizing these things. You've got it sorted by family groupings rather than dates."

"This is just a start. Wait'll you see what I'm going to do with them," Mimi said. "Prescott and Sarah and I have been working on a digital search program. It uses a touch screen interface, and all you'll have to do to find more pictures of the same person is touch their face on the screen."

Mimi sounded surprisingly fired up at the prospect. *Why couldn't she have gotten all fired up about saving Chez Ducky?* Birgie wondered glumly. Birgie had set it all up. Sent Mimi up here with that bogus text message about wanting her to close the place up; left the albums in a convenient, but not too obvious, spot; gotten Vida to relay all sorts of provocative information, all in the hopes that it would get Mimi worked up enough, *passionate* enough, that she'd do something. Or at least try.

Johanna was shaking her head. "Inputting all that information will be a huge pain."

"Not if we have a face-recognition program associated with it."

"Come on. That's FBI stuff," Charlie scoffed.

"Interpol," Mimi said. "At least that's what Prescott claims. He says he helped develop it."

Suddenly, they heard the front door slam open and then the sound of barking dogs, nails clattering, and feet pounding, approaching the parlor. Prescott materialized in the doorway, doubled over, sucking wind and pointing over his shoulder. Dogs leapt around him.

"What? What is it?" Mimi demanded.

"Sarah . . ." Prescott gulped. His chest heaved. "Come . . . quick!"

Chapter Forty-four

Led by a panting Prescott, Mimi trotted up the footpath through the woods, followed doggedly behind by the rest in single file, even Debbie and Half-Uncle Bill, who'd spotted the commotion from their second-floor bedroom. All thoughts of Chez Ducky and lawyers and photographs and everything else she'd count as important faded in significance. Sarah was having the baby. "Why . . . didn't you . . . call the hospital?" she asked.

"I tried," Prescott gasped. "No . . . cell." He had been freshly delivered from his last walking cast ten days ago, and Mimi worried he was putting too much stress on his leg. "You . . . should stop."

He sucked wind. "Why?"

"Leg," she gasped.

He understood. "Fine," he gasped back.

They broke from the woods, chugged up to the lodge, shoved through the front door, and piled into the kitchen. Sarah was leaning against the granite island, one hip jacked up on a stool, calmly peeling a banana. On the floor by the refrigerator was a pool of fluid.

"Her water broke!" Johanna announced, looking back over her shoulder at the group jostling behind. This information was passed back through the group.

". . . her water broke."

". . . her water broke."

". . . her water broke."

"Who're they?" Sarah asked, her banana arrested halfway to her mouth.

"The Olsons," Mimi said, leaning forward with her hands on her knees and puffing.

"You're the Olsons? *Mimi's* Olsons?" Sarah asked, clearly delighted. "Cool. Hi."

"We've heard so much about you."

"Solange's youngest, imagine that."

"Nice to meet you."

"Here's my card." This last from Debbie, who'd handed Sarah her realtor's card.

"Yeah, yeah," Mimi said, her breath returning. "We can make with the nice later. For right now, Prescott says you—"

"Prescott freaked out," Sarah said flatly. "I told him it was perfectly natural. I told him I wasn't even in labor yet. I just think he didn't want to clean it up," she finished with a quelling gaze at the red-faced Prescott. She took a bite of banana.

"Would you?" Prescott asked. His black T-shirt had damp rings under the arms from his race to Chez Ducky, and his baggy black jeans looked like they were about to fall off his ass.

"You *gotta* get new jeans," Mimi said, eyeing him critically. "You're falling out of those."

"This young woman needs to go to the hospital," Johanna declared.

"I do not," Sarah said.

"We're half an hour away from Fawn Creek and we don't have any way to get hold of your doctor. Bad cell reception, remember? You need to go to the hospital. Now," Mimi said.

"I think I'm good for a while yet," Sarah said. She had that obstinate look on. "I appreciate the concern, really, and as soon as I feel a twinge, I promise I'll have Prescott take me—"

"You could go into labor at any minute," Vida said sternly. "You should go now."

Johanna and Naomi nodded in vigorous agreement. Even Debbie murmured, "She's right, you know."

"I can't."

"Why not?" Mimi asked, beginning to be seriously pissed off at Sarah. She'd spent the months deferring to Sarah's increasingly suspect judgment, decrees, whims, demands, etcetera, all under the auspices that this was Sarah's life and her decision and not really Mimi's business. Well, screw that. This was also that baby's life and *someone* needed to act responsibly. "Sarah Charbonneau Werner, if you don't—"

"Hell!" Half-Uncle Bill suddenly yelped from the living room. A growl followed. They all looked around to see Bill emerge from beneath a pile of lap rugs on the sofa, Half-Uncle Bill, standing in front of him, rubbing his bum.

"That dog bit me," Half-Uncle Bill said, seating himself gingerly on the end of the sofa as far from the blankets as he could. "It's a damn kennel around here."

"Yeah!" Sarah said, in the tone of one finding inspiration. "We can't go, because who'll watch the dogs?"

This was so stupid that for a second Mimi could only stare at her sister. Finally, Johanna spoke. "Honey, the dogs'll be fine," she said gently. "You need to get to the hospital. Staying here isn't going to keep the baby from coming."

Sarah looked like she might argue, but then her face crumpled. "She can't! I don't know what I'm going to do with her yet!"

She dropped the partially eaten banana to the floor, laid her head down on her arms, and sobbed. As one, the women in the kitchen surrounded her, clucking and shushing and making soft, reassuring noises. Mimi stroked the back of her head, Vida rubbed her back, Debbie picked up the fallen banana, Johanna got her a glass of water, and Naomi started an Indian birthing chant.

"Mimi?" Sarah's muffled voice sounded painfully young and uncertain.

"You'll figure it out, Sarah. Promise."

"I don't think I can."

Mimi's heart flopped over and melted. "Then *we* will, Sarah. We'll figure it out, I promise, but first you have to have her," Mimi said, brushing the hair away from her face. "Come on, Sarah. You don't really want Prescott to deliver your baby, do you?"

"Prescott is not delivering any babies!" Prescott said loudly.

In all the commotion, Prescott had disappeared. Now he emerged from the stairwell leading to the tower, his cell phone in one hand and his ultracompact notebook in the other. He held them up in the air as if to display their worthlessness. "I thought I might be able to get a connection if I was high enough, but I'm not getting satellite or microwave."

Good old Prescott. While the other men—and Birgie— were sitting on their butts doing nothing, at least he'd been *trying* to do something. "Thanks, Prescott," Mimi said.

His cheeks turned pink and he looked over at Sarah, all swollen of face and form, and said, "Okay, Sarah. You've had your Big Moment. Now get your ass off the stool and go to the hospital and have the baby."

Amazingly, she did. Without further protest, Sarah got off the stool, wiped her nose with the back of her hand, and began lumbering down the front hall. The Olson women fell in behind her, like nursery insects attending a queen termite.

Chapter Forty-five

The first hour wasn't bad; Sarah wasn't in active labor. Mimi and Sarah and Prescott sat in the Fawn Creek Hospital's "pre-birthing room," cozily lit with floor lamps and outfitted with overstuffed armchairs. They sucked on Popsicles and joked and watched television (Fawn Creek Hospital had a dedicated cable feed). Sarah told them about the new baby names she'd decided upon, Mignonette for a girl and Prescott for a boy. Both Prescott and Mimi declared themselves flattered, but while poor old Prescott actually seemed to believe Sarah was going to name her son Prescott, Mimi silently wondered how long Sarah's sentimental mood would last.

The answer was until Sarah had her first real contraction.

Sarah stopped in the middle of saying how much she liked Bill—another romantic exaggeration—cocked her head as one listening for the unwelcome arrival of an unpleasant relative, and said, *"What* was that?"

"What was what?" Prescott asked, looking around.

Sarah waited for long minutes, shrugged, and was in the middle of relaxing back against the pillows when she bolted up. *"That."* She pressed her hand to her stomach.

Mimi pushed the button to call the nurse. The woman swept in a minute later and hustled Mimi and Prescott out of the room while she examined Sarah. She called them back shortly thereafter and said, "She's gone into labor. Which is good. We'll just let nature take its course and see where things stand in a little while." She turned to Prescott and Mimi. "Did she attend any birth classes?"

Mimi looked at Sarah. "Tell her."

Sarah's mouth took on a mutinous tilt. "I didn't see the point," she said. "I read all about it. I went to the medical school and read the entire first-year curriculum on obstetrics."

"Attending a birth and giving birth is not the same thing," the nurse pronounced.

"Why would I need to go to—" Sarah's eyes widened in astonishment. "Now, *that* hurts!"

"And *that's* why you go to birthing classes, honey."

"Hey!" Mimi said. "That's my sister, and in case you haven't noticed, she's not having a great time, here."

"Down, Big Sister. She'll do fine. She just might have had a finer time if she knew what to expect." She turned to Sarah and redeemed herself a little by smiling. "You hang in there. As soon as you're a little further along, we'll give you an epidural. I'll be back to check on you a little later."

"How do you think she knew I was the big sister?" Mimi asked when she'd gone.

"I . . want . . . my . . . mother!"

Mimi's chin fell off her palm, jerking her awake. She looked around, dazed. She'd been dreaming she'd been skinny-dipping with a pod of singing whales. Instead, she was sitting at a round table in the hospital waiting room at the end of a long corridor, at the opposite end of which Sarah was shrieking. Not an "I'm terrified" shriek, but an "I will bring down the hospital with my bare hands if you don't get me what I want" shriek.

A virago had replaced the bewildered, amenable Sarah of some hours ago.

Mimi glanced at the wall clock. They'd been here ten hours.

She shoved herself to her feet and moaned. Her right arm was dead and her neck hurt. Prescott was sprawled over the green plastic-covered sofa, his mouth hanging open, snoring. She wanted to tiptoe over and remove the bolt from his eyebrow. She knew this was more a manufactured impulse rather than a true desire; she just didn't want to deal with Sarah.

She toyed with the idea of rousing Prescott and sending him in to Sarah, but that would be cowardly. Besides, Sarah had thrown things at Prescott the last time he'd been in to "cajol and hearten" her. She hadn't yet tried to physically assault Mimi. She trudged dutifully down the hallway.

"Mimi. Mimi!" Sarah called. "Is that you skulking around out there?"

"Yup!" Mimi answered, determinedly perky as she entered the room. She winced when she saw Sarah. Her face was pale and damp, her beautiful ash blond hair was all dull and matted up on the side, dark circles ringed her eyes, and her lips looked dry. An IV connected her to a bag suspended above the bed. They'd started her on Pitocin a few hours ago when her labor had begun petering out. The poor kid looked exhausted. But determined. God love her, you had to give her that. Sarah Charbonneau Werner had never known failure, and she wasn't going to start now.

"Hi, Sarah."

"You were sleeping, weren't you?" Sarah accused her.

"I'm sorry. How are you doing?"

"I don't have good labor. Whatever the hell that is supposed to be." She gave Mimi an angry look. "Let me tell you, Mimi, from where I'm sitting, there is no good labor."

"I'm sorry."

Abruptly, Sarah waved away her protest. "I want you to call Mother."

"What?"

"I want Mother. Call her."

"After all these months of routing your email through Singapore, getting Prescott to fake an international cell phone number for you to call from, and swearing the last thing you wanted was Solange involved, how can you lie there now and tell me you want me to call her?" Mimi asked, her hands on her hips.

"I changed my mind." Sarah didn't even have the grace to look sheepish. "Call her."

"As a matter—"

"Good Lord!" Sarah jerked straight up in the bed.

Mimi hurried to Sarah's side. "What is it?"

Sarah grimaced, froze, then blew out a long, unsteady breath, waited expectantly, and then eased herself back. "Just an extra-big jolt. Now, what were you saying?"

Mimi studied her closely. She seemed okay. "I already called Mom."

"What?"

"I called her this morning. She and your dad were in Cancún but they were going right to the airport and get a flight out, so they should be here anytime now."

Rather than going limp with gratitude, Sarah's expression turned thunderous. "*How dare you*? What gave you the right to interfere in my life?"

Mimi's jaw dropped. Literally dropped. "Me? Interfere in *your* life? You're the one who showed up on my doorstep."

Sarah sniffed. "Technically, I showed up on Prescott's doorstep."

"Semantics!" Mimi declared. "And *that's* what gave me the right to interfere. That and the fact that you're my sister, and she's our mother. An executive decision had to be made about allowing her to fulfill her role, and I made it since you were not in any state to do so and haven't been in any state for the last four months as far as I can tell," she said. "And, besides which, you just told me to call her. I simply did what you wanted a little earlier than you wanted it."

"Sophism!" cried Sarah.

"Deal with it," Mimi ground out.

"If you—*sweet Mary, Mother of God*!" Sarah seized Mimi's wrist, digging her nails into her skin.

"Ouch!" Mimi yelped, grabbing the buzzer from the bedside and ramming her thumb repeatedly into the call button. "What is it? What's wrong? Sarah? Sarah!"

Sarah's round-eyed gaze found hers. "I think I'm having good labor."

"Very good labor," the OB nurse declared approvingly. "The anesthetist is right down the hall. We'll get him in here, give you your epidural, and in a little while you'll be holding your baby. We'll be right back."

"You okay?" Mimi asked Sarah.

"Well, the nurse seems to think so," Sarah said sourly. Her face started to squeeze up in pain again. Mimi hated that.

"Pant," she said.

"What?"

"Pant. They always pant on the television."

Sarah started to say something but stopped and started panting. The anesthetist, a grandfatherly man with a mane of white hair, came in pushing a tray. "Ready for your epidural, Ms. Werner?"

"Yes! Oh, yes!"

"That's fine. Now, if you'd care to step out for a minute, Ms. . . . ." He glanced at the nurse.

"Olson," Mimi muttered.

"Olson," he finished, "I'll get her started, and then you can come back in."

"No!" Sarah said. "Please, can't she stay? Mimi, stay."

The anesthetist shrugged. Mimi stayed while they rolled Sarah to her side and opened the back of her gown. "Okay, I'm just going to swab the area, and then you'll— Oh. Oh, my." He closed the back of her gown.

Sarah, another contraction obviously coming on, twisted her head around. "What happened to that shot? Come on!

Let's get the lead out! I can feel another contraction starting!"

"I'm sorry, but I'm afraid I can't give you an epidural, Ms.
Olson."

"Why the hell not?"

"You have a pimple at the injection site."

"A pimple?" Mimi asked.

"So find another site!" Sarah said.

"It's not that easy, I'm afraid," he said sadly. "The area we
give the injection in is small and it's been compromised."

"Compromised?"

"By infection in the vicinity. The pimple."

"The pimple?" Mimi repeated.

The anesthetist nodded. "A pimple is an infection."

"You're not going to give me something for this pain because I have a *pimple*?" Sarah's voice rose on the last word.
"What am I supposed to do?"

"You'll have your baby without having an epidural."

"She'll be just fine," Dr. Youngstrum, the family physician
who'd admitted first Prescott, then Joe, said. "Yes, I wish she
wasn't retaining so much fluid, but I'm not too concerned.
She's young and healthy. And the baby's vitals are good."

"Prescott! Where the hell are you?" Sarah's voice thun-
dered from the room, reverberating down the hall.

"It takes some women that way," the doctor said. "Honest,
it's perfectly normal. She doesn't mean anything by it." She
tilted her head and regarded Mimi curiously. "You sort of end
up in the middle of a lot of things, don't you?"

"It's a recent curse," Mimi agreed dolefully.

Assured she'd be called as soon as it was time for Sarah
to push, Mimi decided to look for the computer the nurse had
said was set up in the family waiting room so friends could
get updates as they happened. She passed Prescott on his way
to Sarah's room. They traded glances but didn't bother
speaking, soldiers on the frontline of motherhood.

She found the ancient laptop as promised and typed in her e-mail address. She needed to tell Joe. She didn't overthink it. She didn't second-guess it. She wanted Joe to share the birth of Sarah's baby with her—even if it was from a distance. It wasn't a satisfying way to have a relationship. A year ago, Mimi would have seen only the benefits of having a lover who wasn't around making demands all the time. But now, it just didn't do the trick. It was unsatisfying. She wanted Joe. With her. All the time.

Her Hotmail inbox came up and she glanced through the messages, stopping when she saw Joe's address. She looked at the date. It had been sent yesterday. The subject line was simple: *On my way.*

She clicked open the message:

Dear Mimi,
The family that owns the company we were in the process of buying has decided not to sell. I'm out of a job. I'll be there by tomorrow. I love you. I can't wait to see me. You do, you know. Love me. Because, you do. Don't you?
Love, Joe

Mimi's pulse started to race. She doubted Joe—eloquent, sophisticated Joe—had ever written such a rattled, giddy, unsophisticated missive. The darling. Of course she loved him.

Chapter Forty-six

The elevator opened and disgorged the Olsons. Not some of the Olsons, but all of the Olsons. They milled around until they spied Mimi coming out of the family waiting room. She went to meet them. "Hey," she said, "what's up? It's only eleven. We aren't due at the lawyers' for another three hours."

"We came to see how Sarah is," Johanna said.

"Besides," Charlie said, "it looks like there's some real weather working itself up. There's tornado watches posted all over the north part of the state. You can see the lightning in the west. We didn't wanta take a chance we couldn't get in."

"Why?" Mimi asked, meeting her great-uncle's eye. "That eager to sign off on the place?"

"Don't see any point in delaying," he replied gruffly, his cheeks reddening. At least he had the grace to look sheepish.

"How's Sarah?" Johanna asked, frowning heavily at Mimi. *Mustn't upset Charlie.* "Is the baby a boy or girl?"

Mimi abandoned the Chez Ducky issue. It wasn't Charlie's fault they were selling. Only partially his fault. *And hers.* "We don't know yet. The baby hasn't been born."

"Poor Sarah. At least nowadays you don't have to go through the crap we did," Johanna said.

"Actually, she does. She has this huge pimple on her

back . . ." Mimi decided it wasn't important. "They can't give her anything for her contractions."

The Olson women commenced sympathetic clucking.

"I know some good Norwegian skulling songs that really make you wanta pull," Naomi suggested.

"Thanks, Naomi, but we want her to push, not pull," said Mimi. "I guess she's doing okay. Prescott's with her right now. I was just going to grab a snack. She swore if I brought food into the room, she'd get off the table and shove it—"

A bellow from down the hall brought the conversation to an abrupt halt.

"I remember that." Johanna murmured.

"Me, too," said Naomi, casting an accusing glance at Half-Uncle Bill.

"Not me," said Birgie. "And glad of it."

Mimi, who'd heard it all before, moved on. "What are you planning on doing until the meeting?"

"We thought we'd head to Buonfiglio's for pizza," Bill said. Buonfiglio's was new in town and had the distinction of being the first new establishment in Fawn Creek in the last five years.

The elevator doors chimed preparatory to opening, and the Olsons shuffled to the side of the foyer. When the doors slid open, half a dozen occupants were revealed. A small, top-heavy woman darted out, her head snapping right and left, like a pullet on the lookout for bugs.

"Hi, Mom," Mimi said.

Tom, Mary, and—good Lord, they'd brought Grandmother Werner—emerged from the elevator and stopped dead. Mary looked like she was considering slipping back into the elevator, but the doors closed behind her, trapping her. For a minute, no one said anything. The Olsons stood on one side of the vestibule, the Werners on the other, Mimi in between. It was weird standing between two families who had nothing in common except her. They eyed each other like two tribes of indigent people who'd heard rumors of the other's existence but until now had never quite believed it.

Solange was the first to move, walking past Mimi and up to Charlie. "Hello, Charles. It's been a long time."

"Solange, you're as pretty as ever," Charlie said, taking both her hands in his and beaming. Solange beamed back.

Mimi heard the collective unhinging of a dozen jaws. Including hers.

Solange apparently heard them, too. "Oh, for the love of heaven. Just because John and I divorced doesn't mean I wasn't fond of the Olsons. Some more than others." She smiled at Charlie again.

"I never did understand that divorcing a whole family bit," Charlie said. "Plenty of other Olson exes are still part of the family. Come to Chez Ducky every year . . ." He trailed off, his face falling.

"We saw things differently," Solange said.

"Very differently."

Now that Mimi thought about it, Solange had never said anything specifically negative about any Olsons. Except her dad. Johanna, who wasn't looking thrilled that Charlie was still gripping Solange's hands, shoved her way to Charlie's side.

Looking amused, and a little flattered, Solange disengaged with businesslike expedience and turned to Mimi. "Now, where's Sarah?"

"Is the baby here yet?" Tom asked anxiously.

At this, a chorus of questions and reassurances jumbled together into unintelligible chattering, interrupted by Imogene Werner's imperious voice. "Who are all these people?"

Mimi shot Solange a questioning look.

"She was in Cancún with us."

"Everyone's fine!" Mimi shouted. "Sarah is fine. The baby hasn't been born yet. Sarah's not pushing yet. Why don't I take Mom and Tom down to her room while you introduce yourselves to one another?"

Before anyone could protest, she grabbed her mother's arm and started towing her through the crowd and into the hall just as Prescott came trotting toward them, holding his pants up by the waistband, his eye bolt bouncing. "She's pushing!"

"Please tell me that's not the father," Solange said under her breath.

"Huh? Geez, no. That's Prescott." Mimi said, breaking into a brisk jog, Solange and Tom hard on her heels. She was about to lead the charge into the delivery room when the OB nurse stepped into the doorway and crossed her arms over her chest. The Werners skidded to a stop.

"This isn't a matinee, folks," the nurse said sternly. "There's a baby being born in there, and no one's going in unless they're approved by the mother and have the proper booties on."

"Mommy!"

Solange went right through the nurse.

"Let's go get a pizza and a pitcher of beer," Prescott suggested to Tom and Mary fifteen minutes later. The Olson clan had fled to Buonfiglio's at the last shriek, extending smiling if hurried invitations to anyone who got kicked out of the labor room to join them.

"What about Grandmother?" Mary asked, nodding to where Imogene lay eerily decorous on her back on the green sofa, her hands crossed at her waist like she was a body laid out at a morgue.

"You guys go ahead. I'll watch her," Mimi said. She glanced at Prescott, then looked tellingly at Mary. "But, ah, what if she wakes up and, ah, needs something?" Something like Demerol or whatever the old girl was using.

"Mom's got it covered," Mary replied blithely.

"Mom?" Mimi's voice rose. *Solange* was Imogene's . . . supplier?

Tom coughed. "I thought I saw a drinking fountain down the hall. I'll be back shortly."

"Look, Grandmother has diabetic neuropathy. She's never going to not have it. It is extremely painful—"

"I'm not judging," Mimi cut in. "I'm just surprised."

"Because he was taking into account her incipient dementia, her physician wouldn't prescribe enough meds to provide relief. He said he was worried about side effects, most notably that a delusion might lead to her getting hurt." Mary's mouth flattened. "That's what he said. Personally, I think he was worried about his medical license or being sued if she jumped off a roof because she thought she could fly. Not that I can wholly blame him."

"And Mom just . . . what? Went around him?" Mimi was still in a state of awe.

"Yes," Mary said. "Mom said, 'We can deal with the hallucinations. Not pain.'"

"How?" Mimi asked.

"I didn't ask," Mary replied primly.

"Wow," Mimi said. "Solange doesn't even like Imogene, and the feeling is mutual."

"Mom's not one to dodge responsibilities."

No, she wasn't. She never had been. "Maybe it was simple compassion," Mimi suggested.

"Maybe a combination," Mary countered.

"Anyone want me to get them a pop?" Prescott offered, looking desperately uncomfortable.

"No," both sisters replied, eyeing each other.

"Have you *really* been up here all this time taking care of Sarah?" Mary finally asked.

Oh, crap. Here it came. The expectations of a new, improved Mimi. She didn't like expectations. Granted, sometimes people couldn't help themselves. Like her expectation of something more for her and Joe. But they still made her uncomfortable.

Before she could answer, Prescott said, "Yes. And the dogs and me and Joe."

"Who's Joe—? Joe *Tierney?*" Mary had evidently put the last names together.

"My dad," he said.

"Never mind," Mimi said. "Don't get your panties in a bunch, Mary. I just . . . Sarah needed . . . and . . ."

"And you did what had to be done," Mary finished for her. "It's about time."

Mimi sighed. She had called that one, all right. "Look. Aren't you a little old for this 'proving yourself against your big sister' bit? Come on, Mar, let it go—"

"Oh, shut up," Mary said crossly. "Yeah, yeah, I know what everyone thinks—except Mom. That due to feelings of intense sibling rivalry little Mary is dying for Mimi to enter the race so she can go toe to toe and prove herself. Bullshit. Has it ever occurred to you the reason I'm so angry with you has nothing to do with sibling rivalry?"

No. Never, thought Mimi, but she didn't say so. She just looked askance at her sister.

"Are all geniuses so egocentric?" Mary asked the room at large.

"Yes," volunteered Prescott, obviously feeling that here was a subject he felt qualified to comment upon.

"I don't want to compete with you, Mimi. I want you to stop feeling sorry for yourself and start living. If that means using all those brains Mom claims you have—and just under the auspices of full disclosure, I have my doubts about that— or tap-dancing in a carnival sideshow, fine."

"Should I go?" Prescott asked again, squirming.

No one paid him any attention. "When I was a little girl, you were my hero, Mimi. Then your dad disappeared and so did you. You turned into some Lady of Shalott, living her life through ghosts. Only it isn't Shalott, it's Chez Ducky, and there's been no Galahad to draw you out."

She meant Lancelot, but Mimi didn't feel this was the right time to offer a correction.

"You're living at a distance. In stasis. It pisses me off. I want you to wake up. Not because I want to compete with you, but because I love you."

Huh? "You do?"

"What an idiot you are, Mimi."

"And the only reason you've been so angry at me for the last ten years is because of your concern for my happiness?" Mimi was trying very hard to buy this, and she could see from the look on Mary's face that she really wanted her to. Maybe it started out as sibling rivalry that had just grown into habit and now Mary was looking for a way out with a little dignity attached. Mimi could understand that.

Mary shifted a little like her underwear was binding but managed to meet Mimi's eye levelly. "Mostly."

There was possibly some truth in Mary's melodramatic analogy. Mimi had been living life at a distance. You didn't get messy at a distance. Things didn't have the same power at a distance. Mary wanted to reconcile; that was good enough for Mimi. Mimi's vision began to grow suspiciously shimmery.

Prescott pushed himself halfway up from his chair. "Should I maybe go now?"

Both she and Mary shot him identical looks of disbelief.

"Why?" Mary asked. "You've been here through the main event. Everything else is going to be a denouement, don't you think?"

Prescott lowered himself gingerly back onto the chair.

"So," Mimi said, "it turns out that all this time you've been the secure, well-adjusted one?"

"You bet your ass."

Happily, poor Prescott was saved from being subjected to any more Werner family secrets by Tom's return. He looked cautiously from Mimi to Mary and smiled when it was obvious that whatever was going to be said had been said. Men, Mimi thought, not for the first time, were basically cowards.

"Can we go now?" Prescott sounded like a grade-schooler begging for a bathroom pass.

"Sure."

Prescott jumped to his feet.

"Maybe I should stay," Tom said. He didn't look like he meant it, though.

"No, you go, too, Tom," Mimi said. "Sarah's been in a holding pattern for a couple hours. What are the chances of her going in the next forty-five minutes? I promise, if anything changes, I'll use the phone at the nurse's station and call. You're never more than five minutes away from anything else in Fawn Creek."

That's all it took. Tom, Mary, and Prescott headed toward the elevator looking every bit as tired as Mimi felt. She could only imagine what Sarah was going through. She looked at Imogene. She was snoring.

Mimi found an empty room right outside the waiting area, where she nabbed a folded blanket off the foot of the bed. She returned and spread it gently over Imogene, tucking it under her chin. There. Now she looked more like a snoozing old lady than a sarcophagus effigy.

That task taken care of, she sat down and put her feet up.

"I suppose I should be mad at you."

Mimi looked up to find Solange standing beside her chair. She looked exhausted. "Sarah asked me not to tell," she told her mother. "I would have called if there had been any trouble," she said, more tired than defensive.

Solange sat down beside her. "I know."

Mimi smiled at her. "Thanks. How is the little mother doing?"

"If she doesn't get a move on soon, she's having a C-section," Solange said. "I think the mention of knives has inspired her to try harder. I just came out to see how you were doing."

She looked around. "Where's Tom and Mary? And that odd young man with the hardware in his face?"

"Prescott. They went for pizza. I told them I'd call as soon as something happened."

Solange nodded, smiling wanly. "Poor Tom. He's no better at this than your father was."

"Dad?"

"He was a terrible mess. I think he threw up three times on the way to the hospital. We called a taxi, you know. I wouldn't have trusted him to drive across an empty parking lot, the state he was in."

"Dad?" Mimi asked in surprise. "But he was always so laid-back."

Solange gave her a funny look but said mildly, "Wasn't he, though?"

"Was he there? In the delivery room?"

"He tried," Solange said. "But he passed out as soon as my water broke, so the attendants dragged him off to the waiting room." She looked at Mimi. "You took *thirty-four* hours to make your appearance. Always were a strong-willed child."

Mimi flinched. "I bet you wish you could have left the room, too."

Solange shook her head. "No. Not at all. I wished you'd been a little quicker about the process, but we were in it together and I wouldn't have had it any other way. We made it just fine, too."

Solange had always seen her role as being there. Sometimes she'd been a little too much there, but Mimi had never doubted her mother's dedication.

"You never were quick to leave a room," Mimi said quietly. "I remember you used to read me to sleep every night."

"Didn't think you liked it that much," Solange said with a small self-deprecating laugh.

"Well, I might have preferred *The Boxcar Children* to the *Iliad*, but . . ."

"The classics are the classics," Solange said, rising to her feet. "I better get back to Sarah before she harms that nurse."

She patted Mimi absently on the head and headed back to the room.

Mimi stretched, glancing up at the clock. Sarah had better get a move on, or Mimi was going to have to take off for the lawyers' office without seeing Little Mignonette or the less popular Little Prescott. On the other hand, let the lawyers wait.

Still, she might as well be ready. She picked up her backpack and headed into the bathroom, where she stripped off her shirt and washed up as well as she could. She brushed her teeth and attempted to comb her hair with her fingers. She leaned over the sink, peering closely in the mirror. She was sure there was more gray in her hair today than there had been yesterday. Small wonder.

The door opened behind her. She glanced up in the mirror—

"Joe!" She spun around, her heart thudding like a snared rabbit's, dizzy with happiness.

He looked perfect. The sleeves of his white dress shirt were rolled up on those spectacular forearms, his collar was open, and his hair gleamed like polished carbon. He must have shaved in the parking lot. His jaw looked kissably smooth.

"Hello, Mimi." His voice. Her toes curled in her shoes.

"How did you know I was in here?"

"The desk nurse saw you go in," he answered, looking around. He saw a metal chair sitting at the end of the sinks and smiled. He picked it and tipped it backward, sliding the top under the door handle, saying conversationally, "I really would like us not to be interrupted."

"Oh," she said faintly.

"Did you get my e-mail?"

"Yes," she nodded.

"You haven't said 'I love you,'" he said. "I thought I was pretty clear on that."

Her heart was beating like a jackhammer. "Control freak," she said, only it came out in a breathy little rush.

"Absolutely." He walked over to her and, without breaking stride, cradled her face between his strong, beautifully manicured hands and proceeded to kiss the hell out of her. When he was done, his hands dropped to her waist, steadying her.

"I love you, Mimi," he said. "I want to be with you. And if I can't, as long as I know where to find you, I'll be okay with it. When I was in Singapore, thinking about you, I had this feeling of finally having reached some destination even though I was thousands of miles away from you. For the first time in my adult life, I have somewhere to go and someone to go to. You.

"You're my touchstone, Mimi."

"I think you mean lodestone," she said breathlessly. He smiled, his eyes crinkling up at the corners in an altogether sexy way.

She was having a hard time breathing and her hands seemed to keep reaching up to touch his face or smooth the material over his chest. Beneath her fingertips she could read the beat of his heart, and oops! She owed him a new shirt because his buttons were popping off and she was dragging his shirt from a very muscular pair of shoulders, her mouth nipping at the base of his throat, and—

"Come on, Mimi. Tell me."

"Yes!" She lashed her arms around his bare torso. He felt warm and dense and oh, man, she just wanted to crawl into him.

"Yes, what?" he insisted.

"I love you." He was looking at her and she realized that being half Scandinavian and therefore not prone to dramatic declaration had its drawbacks, because she couldn't think of any words that could describe the intensity of this feeling, the enormity, the wonder of it. So, she went with what she could. *"Unequivocally!"*

It seemed to satisfy him.

"Do you want to make love?" he asked, pulling her closer.

"Unequivocally."

"Where have you been?" Solange asked suspiciously as Mimi entered the hospital room. Joe had left to find Prescott while Mimi went in search of someone to tell her how the birthing process was going. She discovered that while she and Joe had been otherwise engaged, the birthing process had been completed and that Sarah was the mother of a healthy baby girl.

"I was trying to get hold of Tom and the others," she lied.

"And did you?"

"Yes," she said, relieved the nurse had already tracked down the crew by the time they'd exited the bathroom. "They're on their way. How are you doing, Sarah?"

She shouldn't have bothered asking. Sarah was rapt, gazing adoringly at a small puckered little creature in a pink blanket with a pink skullcap on. The baby's eyes were squished shut.

"Isn't she absolutely the most ravishing thing you've ever seen?" Sarah whispered without lifting her eyes from the baby.

"Yeah."

"Mom, does she look like any of us when we were babies?"

"Impossibly, she's even more beautiful," cooed Solange, reaching over and gently stroking the baby's cheek with the back of her finger.

"I think so, too!" gushed Sarah.

"You look good, Sarah," Mimi said. "Considering how long you were in labor." She did, too. It was as if someone had carved the fat from her face to find the cheekbones again.

"Yup," Sarah said. "The doctor said I was mostly carrying fluid." She giggled and stuck one leg out from under the blanket. "See? No more cankles."

Her leg was still a little canklish in Mimi's opinion, but in honor of the occasion, she kept it to herself.

"So, what did you name the little sweetheart?"

"Well," Sarah started. "You know how much I wanted to honor both you and Prescott for all the support you've given me and everything you've done for me for the past few months. But most especially for going behind my back and calling Mom so that she could be with me when the baby was born, because I don't think you would have been so good at that."

"Probably not," Mimi conceded.

"And Prescott," she sighed. "Such a doll. He cleaned up after me all the time. Did you know that?"

Again, Mimi kept to herself the fact that Prescott wasn't acting because of love, but because of a phobia.

"So what could I do? I couldn't name her after one of you and not the other!" Sarah chirped brightly. "And let's face it, Mimi, 'Mescott' or 'Pipi' just wasn't going to happen."

"So, what *did* you name her?" Mimi asked.

"Solange!"

Solange gave Mimi a complacent smile.

Mimi stared at Sarah a moment. "Okay. But you're telling Prescott."

"Oh, Mimi. Prescott won't mind. He'll be so giddy over being the godfather, he won't care."

"Prescott's going to be the godfather?"

"Well, who else?" Sarah said, her tone declaring *duh*. "He's family."

"Speaking of family, Mimi," said Solange, "aren't you supposed to be at the lawyers' office"—she glanced at the clock—"now?"

Mimi, hovering in the back of the room, barely heard this

last bit. Something Sarah had said reminded her of something Joe had said, and that reminded her—

That was it!

She got going.

Chapter Forty-seven

Mimi flung open the door to the lawyers' conference room. It banged against the inner wall and bounced back, nearly hitting her in the face. So much for her dramatic entrance. She pushed it open with a little less force this time and stepped into the room. Mike Peterson, the lawyer, Birgie, Charlie, Gerry, Johanna, Naomi, and Half-Uncle Bill sat around a pine table. In front of each were open file folders and pens. An empty chair and file folder waited for her.

"What's wrong, honey?" Naomi asked. "Is Sarah all right?"

"Sarah's fine. Has a baby girl. Healthy. Named her Solange," she said. "Too early yet to tell about the cankles . . . But that's not why I'm here."

"We know why you're here," Gerry said tiredly.

"No, you don't. I'm here because *we can't sell Chez Ducky*," she announced.

"You okay, honey?" Johanna asked. "It looked like that door hit you square in the nose."

"I'm fine," Mimi said, closing the door behind her. "Did you hear what I said about not selling Chez Ducky?"

"Yeah," Birgie said. She looked alert, interested. And well she ought to, thought Mimi. As matriarch of Chez Ducky, she should be the one doing this. "Why?"

"We can't sell because without Chez Ducky we'll fall apart. As a family. We'll disappear from one another's lives. Chez Ducky is the touchstone—or maybe it's a lodestone, I don't know—but it's the place we all keep coming back to," she said triumphantly. "*That* is the reason why we can't sell, why none of you have signed those papers yet!"

At this, Birgie glanced furtively around at the others' piles, and then casually covered up the bottom of her paper with her forearm.

"Oh, bull," Charlie said sourly. "You honestly think the bunch of us won't get together again?"

The lawyer stuck his legs straight out, slouched back down in his chair, rested his chin on his chest, and stared patiently at the toes of his wingtips.

"Okay," Mimi conceded, "maybe those of you here will, but what about the rest of the family?"

Her family traded confused glances. "Rest of the family?"

"Yeah," Mimi said. "When will they all get a chance to be together? To get to know one another? Not just blood relations and direct descendents, but all the other people who are part of Chez Ducky one way or the other? What about Frank and Carl?" Mimi spoke directly to Gerry. "What about Halverd? How is he going to know his half brothers?" she asked Johanna. "What about Emil and your ex-son-in-law Willy? Or the cousins three times removed?"

Johanna reached out and gave Gerry's hand a squeeze. Naomi dabbed at her eyes.

"How're we going to make sure they know the story about Great-Great-Aunt Ruth and the runaway Model T? Who's gonna tell Frank's kids that his great-grandfather's twin won a medal in World War II? Or that his great-great-uncle was a female impersonator during Prohibition?"

"If we're lucky, no one," said Charlie, and Johanna swatted him.

"And who's going to tell everyone where they get their eyes or their hair color or their six toes?" Mimi asked.

"What about that digital computer you're working on?" Gerry asked.

Mimi rounded on him. *"You are missing the point, Ger!"*

"Yeah, Ger." Amazingly, it was Half-Uncle Bill who'd spoken. He leaned forward. "You just keep on talking, Mimi."

Being championed from such an unexpected corner caught Mimi off guard, but she marshaled her thoughts. "If we sell Chez Ducky, all this stuff, who we are, who we were, is going to be forgotten. Because without all of us telling the stories, the threads will get lost and the connections will fade away. And don't make any mistake about it," she went on sternly. "This place isn't just about Olsons anymore; we're just the custodians."

Charlie chewed on the inside of his cheek. Gerry's eyes had gone suspiciously wide.

"What about my niece? What about little Solange?" Mimi whispered. "Where's she going to go to know about all the people who loved her and all the people *I* loved? And your granddaughters, Johanna. They live with their mother but they come up every summer. Where will they know us and where will we know them if it isn't here?"

She had their attention now. "This family is a convoluted mess. All families are. We don't have a homestead. We don't have a family Bible. We don't have a written genealogy or come from the same town or the same state. A lot of us don't have the same name, and if we do, that could change tomorrow. What we *do* have is Chez Ducky. All of us."

She started walking slowly around the conference table. "Like the swallows to Capistrano, the monarch butterflies to Michoacán, Mexico, and the college kids to Cancún, so are we drawn inexorably to the weedy shores of Fowl Lake."

She stopped, studying each face solemnly in turn. "Just as the salmon wander the oceans their entire lives only to return to the place from where they came—and I swear to God, Gerry, if you point out that no one was born at Chez Ducky,

I will come at you like your worst nightmare—we are drawn back to Chez Ducky."

Gerry didn't say a word.

"Like lemmings have their cliff and elephants have their graveyard, some places we are simply compelled to go to, to leave, and to return again."

She stopped. There was no more to say. She'd given it her best shot, and now it was up to them.

Charlie's face was unreadable; Gerry was blinking like the sentimental slob he was; Birgie was doodling over the bottom of her papers; Johanna twisted her braid, concentrating; Half-Uncle Bill had thrust out his lower lip and was scratching thoughtfully under his toupee; and Naomi's eyes were closed. She was chanting.

They were almost there. Mimi could feel that they wanted to keep Chez Ducky. But they were practical, unsentimental Minnesota stock, and they were considering passing up a great deal of money. They just needed something, something to tip the balance. Any excuse. *Anything* . . .

She took a deep breath. Closed her eyes.

"Ardis doesn't want us to sell," she said and opened her eyes.

For a full, pregnant thirty seconds no one said a word. Then Naomi cleared her throat.

"Really?" she asked.

"That's right," Mimi nodded. "If Chez Ducky is gone, then where does she go? Not you and I or just the kids . . . where do the *ghosts* go? Where will we go when we've shuffled off this mortal coil? Ardis is concerned. She thinks it's a bad idea."

"Huh? Are you talking about the dead, er, the deceased woman?" The lawyer had come out of his trance and was staring at Mimi as if she'd sprouted a second head. "You've got to be kidding."

"Nah-uh," said Charlie, a small smile starting at the corners of his mouth.

"If Mimi says Ardis doesn't want us to sell Chez Ducky, Ardis doesn't want us to sell. And that," Johanna said firmly, "is good enough for me."

"Me, too!" Birgie said, slamming her hand on the table and jumping to her feet. Quite a feat, considering how much there was to jump.

Half-Uncle Bill pushed himself back from the table. "Then I guess we're done?"

"Yup," Charlie said.

"Yup. Pretty much says it all," said Gerry.

"But . . . you can't be serious?" the lawyer said. "You don't really believe this woman talked to Ardis Olson?"

"Well, now, Mr. Peterson, Mimi here is a professional ghost whisperer," Gerry said with just a trace of what Mimi thought might be pride. Mimi blushed.

"Tele-medium," she mumbled.

"You can't argue with a professional, Mr. Peterson," Half-Uncle Bill said and, grabbing Mimi's arm, swept her out of the room along with the rest of the Olson clan.

Chapter Forty-eight

"Did you see your little niece?" Johanna asked as Mimi slid into the booth they'd commandeered at Buonfiglio's.

"I peeked," said Mimi. "But she and Sarah and Mom were asleep and the nurse said Tom and Mary had gone to get a couple rooms at the motel."

Mimi kept expecting someone to jump to their feet and yell, "What the hell are we thinking?" and dash back to the lawyers' office. No one did. Everyone seemed quite happy with their decision. No one had uttered a word about Ardis's Directives from Beyond the Grave. Even Debbie hadn't kicked up much of a fuss, capitulating with more grace than Mimi would have thought possible by saying, "It's not like the land's going anywhere."

They ate amongst contented chatter and after a pitcher or two of beer began trading stories about people who weren't even familiar to Mimi.

"Who's Olaf Junior?" she asked.

"You know," Gerry said. "The first Olson with six toes."

"Come on."

"It's true. I know I saw a picture of him *and* his toes on the dining hall table. All you have to do is look close to see 'em."

"You have pictures of Olaf Junior?" Charlie asked, interested.

"And his wife." Gerry nodded.

"I gotta see 'em," Charlie declared. "You gotta see 'em, too, Jo. Half your kids got six toes."

He stood up and started to sway. Mimi caught his arm and steadied him.

"Hold on," she said. "No one's driving anywhere except me."

"I want to see those pictures," Charlie said.

"Me, too," piped in Vida.

"Okay, look," Mimi said. "I'll go get the pictures, and you all head over to Smelka's— Don't look at me like that; I mean it. You guys stay here and you're just going to drink more. You need to get some good bland food into your stomachs. I'll get the pictures and by the time you're done with dinner, I'll be back. We'll look through them, and afterward you should be able to drive. Okay?"

"When did she become queen of the universe?" Gerry grumbled.

"Just be damn glad she is," Vida replied.

They split up on the sidewalk, where Mimi got into Sarah's Lexus and the others started walking to Smelka's. She could hardly wait to tell Joe and Prescott about the coup at the lawyers' office, but she had no idea where they'd gone. Maybe back to Fowl Lake. She started for Chez Ducky, smiling. The western sky lit up in an electrical light-show extravaganza. Dry lightning always put on the best spectacle, but this was a doozie. Despite earlier tornado warnings, it didn't overly concern her. All spring the weather and the weathermen had made a lot of noise that came to nothing. The ground was parched.

True to her suspicions, by the time she drove up to Chez Ducky, not a single drop had fallen. The lightning, on the other hand, had grown close. Booms of thunder shook the Chez's windowpanes and rattled the doors. Of course, a good sneeze produced much the same results.

She let her eyes play over the blistered gray surface of its clapboard siding, the multicolored roof, illuminated by the lightning, the soft, moss-covered foundations. She closed her eyes and heard the echoes of generations of children and adults hidden in the sound of the wind rushing through the pine tops, could almost see their shapes moving across the windows. Inside, she looked over the boxes of pictures, trying to decide which one to take. She finally decided she might as well take them all; Charlie had been more than a little tanked. She loaded them into the Lexus's trunk and returned for the last box. On her way out, she noticed the FedEx package lying on the table. She angled her head to read the return address label: Otell Weber. Her private investigator. Frowning, she ripped open the top and upended the contents onto the table. A small stack of paper slid out, held together by a paper clip. On the top was a typed letter from Otell:

Dear Ms. Olson,

I am very pleased to be able to report to you that my investigations have met with success. At the same time, I am saddened to inform you that those same investigations have led to incontrovertible proof of your father, John Henry Olson's, death. Enclosed you will find a Xerox and faxes and photocopies of the pertinent records.

To summarize, your father was hit by lightning in Bathgate, North Dakota, on June 26th, 1979, while attempting to cross a highway during a storm. He died without regaining consciousness en route to the nearest hospital in Minot. However, his possessions, including his identification, were damaged in the accident and when his body was admitted to the Minot morgue, he was mistakenly listed as "Henry Olson."

Enclosed you will find a copy of my bill. I accept no personal checks. Please issue a money order within thirty days to avoid late charges.

Thank you for allowing me the privilege of working

with you on this matter. Should you ever require my
services again, please do not hesitate to contact me. It
has been a pleasure doing business with you.
   Regards,
   Otell Weber

Mimi let the file slide back onto the tabletop. Her father
was dead. Gone. She lifted her head, staring around unsee-
ingly at the walls, the ceiling, the furniture, the floors. She
felt light-headed. Like the top of her skull was going to float
away and the rest of her would soon follow. She concentrated, trying to conjure up her dad's voice, his smile, the
way he'd ruffled her hair, the way he'd picked her up and set
her on his shoulders and galloped along the beach while she
shrieked with laughter, the way he'd winked at her every
night before he turned out the lights. Or left the house for
"an adventure."

He wasn't there . . . good.

Her eyes flew wide open at the thought. Good.

The thought was clearer now, firmer, more confident:
Good.

She didn't want to be a modern-day Lady of Shalott, experiencing life only through a reflection of what others had
been and done. But that's what she'd been doing, weaving
ghost stories because the living were just too hard to pin
down. But now she wanted out of the tower, she wanted to
take a ride in the boat down that cataract called Life, and she
did not want to go to Camelot. She wanted to go to
Minneapolis. Chicago. Maybe Rome.

And she wanted to go with Joe, not Lancelot. Their rela-
tionship was bound to be messy and convoluted and every-
thing but straightforward. There would be no guarantees.
But it wasn't just Joe's life she wanted hers meshed with.
She wanted it tangled with Prescott's and her mother's and
Tom's and Sarah's and Mary's and Ozzie's and all the

cousins and ex-wives and future wives and stepkids, and all the messy, tangled relationships that came with them.

That was the deal. Chez Ducky wasn't anything without all the people who came here, who'd found their own route to this odd, mismatched little community. Not a place, a tribe. An ever-shifting shoreline of faces and names, who kept coming back because here they belonged.

She'd always thought of Chez Ducky as being timeless, of never changing, of being a constant, but she'd been wrong. Chez Ducky was a revolving door of histories, changing from day to day so that you never knew who was going to be there or what their story would be or how they would be connected. Only that they were.

It didn't matter that she couldn't find her father's spirit. She knew it was here, and that was enough.

She was walking back to the car, still smiling softly, when the lightning hit, striking so close that the earth beneath her shook and she tripped and almost fell. She smelled burning ozone and then smoke.

She ran around to the front of the Chez to see what had happened. The Big House was fine, no fire anywhere— No. There was definitely fire somewhere. She loped back to the beach where the sightlines were more open. On the other side of Prescott's house, the Sbodas' cabin was on fire. Black smoke billowed and churned above the rooftop before being caught by the wind and pushed flat in a black pennant pointing straight at Prescott's house and, from there, Chez Ducky. And Fawn Creek and the fire engines were half an hour away.

For a second she could only stare. After all that. After all her angst and worry, and finally to go against decades of habit and make a stand and win . . . ? They were being screwed over by a storm. Shit. Shit, shit, shit. The woods was a tinderbox. There was no way the fire wasn't going to wipe out Chez Ducky before anyone got here. Not to mention Prescott's Palace and . . .

"Jesus!"

Lightning flashed again and she fled from the beach toward Prescott's house. Like most lake owners during the off season, Prescott didn't lock his door when he was going to be gone only a short while.

Inside, Blondie and Wiley hurled themselves anxiously at her, bouncing and pawing at her legs. She shushed them, fumbling in her jacket pocket for her cell phone. She flipped it open. None of the little black bars indicating signal strength appeared. Not one.

She stabbed 911 anyway and held the phone to her ear. Nothing. She headed into the great room, her eyes toward the north-facing windows. Through them, a hundred yards away, the Sbodas' cabin was a bonfire. Black snakes of smoke crawled out from the eaves and shot out toward Prescott's house, the fire leaping behind it, fed by the wind. A peal of lightning cracked open the sky overhead. Blondie howled.

She had to get the dogs out of here. She raced for the door, calling them by name. Blondie and Wiley were there ahead of her, leaping around like maniacs, their eyes ringed by white. Bill was nowhere to be seen.

"Bill!" she screamed. "Bill!"

Nothing. She looked down at Wiley and Blondie, realizing she couldn't get all three out at once. She couldn't just open the door, either. In their fright they might take off into the woods and be lost. Or worse. She wrenched open the front closet and got out their leashes, snapping them to their collars, her fingers stiff with terror. Then she opened the door and yanked.

The dogs didn't need any encouragement. As soon as the door was open, they bolted for the woods, dragging her with them. She barely kept up, stumbling after them along the footpath, heading pell-mell toward Chez Ducky.

They broke from the woods and dove for the Lexus. She yanked opened the car door and the dogs flung themselves in. She slammed it shut and spun, heading back for Prescott's on a dead run. Her legs ached and her lungs burned and she imagined she could hear the sound of the fire eating through the woods. All she could think was that Bill was somewhere inside the house, cowering or, knowing Bill, snapping angrily at the flames.

She saw the fire's light before she emerged from the woods. She stopped dead in her tracks, awed by the sight. Prescott's entire house was backlit in brilliance. But it was not on fire. Not yet.

The air was filled with the sound of things breaking, bursting, cracking, and behind it all the rushing roar of a runaway locomotive. The smell of burning pine and the noxious odor of smoldering rubber hit her nostrils at the same time. She dashed into the house, sweat streaming down her face, the salt stinging her eyes. "Bill! Bill!"

She sprinted down the stairs, racing madly from room to room, screaming like an idiot before heading back upstairs, looking to the north as she surfaced. Too late. The fire was at the windows. More than a glow now, she could see the flames clawing at the glass— Then it shattered inward, exploding in hundreds of glass pebbles across the floor.

"Bill!" She backed up into the front hall. "Bill!"

She turned and fled, tears streaming down her face, blinding her as she stumbled down the drive. Strong hands grabbed her.

"Mimi!" Joe shouted. "Get in the car!" He shoved her into the passenger seat of the Lexus and climbed over her, ramming it into gear and sending it squealing across the gravel drive. She craned her neck around and saw Wiley's head rise from the dark bottom beneath the backseat.

"How? Why are you here?" she asked Joe.

"I dropped Prescott off at the hospital," Joe said. "Gerry

told me you'd come out here. I didn't want to wait so I came looking for you. You weren't at Chez Ducky but I saw the Lexus. I looked inside and saw the dogs and that you'd left the key in the ignition so I got in to make sure they didn't hit a button and lock you out. Then I saw the fire." His gaze grew haunted.

"I didn't know where you were. I thought you might have gone up to warn Prescott. So I—" He broke off. "Thank God you're all right, Mimi." She was never to hear Joe Tierney sound like that again.

They were at the end of the drive now, a half mile between them and the fire. He slammed on the brakes and she flung her arms around his neck. He crushed her to him, sliding her onto his lap. "Everything will be all right. We'll be safe. The wind's pushing it straight south. As soon as we get a quarter mile away, we'll be out of its path."

"No," she gulped, shaking her head violently, her eyes riveted on the column of smoke rising from the shore. *Bill.*

"It's okay, Mimi."

She tucked her knees beneath her chin and held her legs tight against her chest, rocking herself on his lap. "No, it isn't all right," she sobbed. "I went back for Bill but I couldn't find him. Oh, Joe! I tried!"

She looked up, pleading for him to understand, to say she couldn't have done anything. He was looking at her oddly. "What is it? *What?*" she asked.

"When we came back from the hospital this afternoon, Prescott and I decided to go to Portia's and get a beer."

She watched him uncomprehendingly. Bill was dead and he was babbling about beer.

"Bill likes car rides, so . . ." He pointed behind him.

Mimi swung around and hauled herself over the back of the seat, peering into the darkness. There, flanked by Blondie and Wiley, lay Bill, staring up at her.

With a whoop of delight, she reached down, grabbed Bill,

and hauled him bodily to her, squishing him against her chest. "Oh, Bill!" she crooned. "Bill, you're alive! You're alive!"

She didn't know what she wanted to do more, kiss him or kill him.

Bill, being Bill, was not so conflicted.

He bit her.

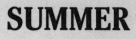

SUMMER

Chapter Forty-nine

August

Mignonette Charbonneau Olson was immersed in blue: the cobalt of evening sky up above, the silky indigo of the water beneath, the skeletal navy of the burnt trees abruptly turning to the blue-green smudges of darkness of living trees where the fire had been stopped. It was a perfect evening: the air warm, the bright chirrup of peepers a counterpoint to the sonorous lap of water against her float.

Lazily, Mimi studied the beach, where a huge bonfire was in the process of burning itself out. Scrawny backlit silhouettes, mostly adolescent Olson males, capered and gibbered about, joined by three similarly leaping canine shapes. The kids darted in and out of the light, poking the fire with sticks, and then jumping back when showers of embers erupted. The dogs barked wildly, except for the smallest one, who was making the rounds of the nearby tents, scavenging for s'mores.

Behind the bonfire glowed a cluster of tents and pop-up trailers, lit from within by Coleman lanterns and bobbing flashlights. At the near end of the beach, where the Big House had once stood, a battered old Aerodyne glinted silver in the moonlight, and next to it, a semi-new RV, dark except for the flicker of the television inside.

The only things left of Chez Ducky were the low log sauna squatting at the water's edge and the rusted old school-yard slide, looking somehow smug to Mimi, as if it had escaped the fire by fleeing into the water. Good for it.

That was the beauty of Chez Ducky; it changed, adapted. Time went forward and it moved with it. It survived.

As of now, there were no plans to rebuild Chez Ducky or any of the cabins, all of which had been lost in the fire. Hell, thought Mimi with a smile, there was no insurance money to rebuild anyway. Even if they'd wanted to, there was some doubt whether they could. The heirs to Ardis's estate had deeded the Chez Ducky property over to something called the Minnesota Land Trust in a conservation easement. It was a relatively new concept, the idea being that even though the land remained the Olsons', there could be no building or development of the property, thus ensuring that the native species and plant life and geographic features remained natural. All things considered, it was as close to a perfect arrangement as possible, and the financial benefits were pretty nice, too.

Of course, the next generation of Olsons could decide to just give the property outright to the trust or even the state. Frank and Carl were already displaying frightening tendencies toward having social consciences.

Mimi's gaze traveled the beach to Prescott's place.

He *had* rebuilt.

It wasn't the mega-monstrosity of his former digs, but Prescott's fascination with older architecture hadn't died in the fire. This was a replica Scandinavian farmhouse, a simple rectangular log construction with a steeply pitched gable roof, symmetrical lines of nine-paned, leaded glass windows across the back and side facades, a plain front, and a shed. After the fire, Prescott had approached the Sbodas and offered to buy their lot. He'd been more than generous.

Then he'd gone after the lot on the Sbodas' other side.

Mimi had the idea he was systematically planning on buying up everything he could. She had no illusions that he'd end up owning the whole lake, but still she missed no opportunity to say, "Thatta boy!" It wasn't as if he couldn't afford it. If what he assumed was true, and Mimi saw no reason to doubt him, he'd eventually be tripling or quadrupling his wealth with the software he'd developed in the process of helping her with her digital album. She was still a little surprised to find herself his partner. And not—possibly to Prescott's regret—a silent partner, either. She had ideas.

Besides, Prescott needed a partner, so he'd have time to devote to Jessica and their mutual online stalking. Jess and Prescott hadn't met yet. But Mimi saw the way things were heading. She wondered what Jess looked like . . .

Thoughtfully, she lowered one leg farther into the water and sent the inner tube on which she floated slowly spinning. Her feet drifted through wild celery and the soft, silky mass of algae floating just beneath Fowl Lake's surface and collided with another set of legs.

"Oops," she said. "Sorry, Mom."

Solange, whose butt had been dipping lower and lower in her own inner tube as she'd drifted to sleep, jerked back to wakefulness. "Huh?" She lifted her head and looked around.

Mimi followed her gaze. They'd drifted some distance from the raft, where Birgie, Johanna, Vida, and Naomi were lounging, having fallen silent some minutes ago as they scanned the night sky for the aurora borealis. They were also, Mimi suspected, waiting for Solange to leave so they could go skinny-dipping. They weren't quite comfortable enough to ask her to join them yet, but before Labor Day, Mimi expected Solange would be leading the cannonballs off the raft. They had time.

"For heaven's sake, Mignonette. Why didn't you wake me? It's night," Solange said.

"So?"

Solange made an exasperated sound. "I need to read Baby Solie her bedtime story. I hope Sarah hasn't put her to sleep yet."

"She's only five months old, Mom."

"Genius does not occur spontaneously, Mignonette. It must be teased from hiding."

"Or pried," Mimi muttered; then, "But as the howls of Baby Fury have not yet echoed along the lakeshore, I think it's safe to assume she's still up."

Solange laughed. "True." She rolled off the inner tube, her top-heavy body in its shiny black Lycra skin reminding Mimi of a harp seal vacating an iceberg.

"Sarah told me she's decided to finish her doctorate and start another," Mimi said. "And she and Solie are going to live with you and Tom."

"That's right," Solange said calmly, head bobbing above the water.

"That'll be a lot of work."

Even in the moonlight, Mimi could see Solange's superior look. "Mignonette. I have raised three children. It's what I do. I raise geniuses. I shall have plenty of help, too. Tom and Mary and all those Olsons. Plus there's you and Prescott and Joe to help raise her, too."

Mimi had even less to argue with this. She *liked* being Aunt Mimi. So far. And when she didn't like it, which simple common sense told her would be often because Baby Solie had already demonstrated the bullheaded Charbonneau personality, she'd focus on the good and anticipate the even better. Since she was stuck in the relationship for the duration, any other course would be stupid.

"You think Sarah will let me have Solie up here part of the summer?" Mimi asked.

"*Us,*" Solange said flatly. "I'll have to come in order to mitigate any untoward influences. I made a mistake in not coming up here after your father died and spending the summers here along with you. I thought it only fair that I let

John's family have you to themselves. Just look at how long it has taken to undo that. And the Olsons look eager to start the same process with little Solange."

Mimi couldn't argue, especially about the Olsons' involvement. Since they'd been there for the birth, they'd declared squatters' rights to her. That Solie was a baby girl, and no Olson had seen a baby girl since Mimi had held that rank, made her especially popular.

"Where is Joe?" Solange asked. "I thought you said he'd be here."

"He will," Mimi said, and now she really did feel stupid, because just the thought of Joe made her smile. "He's finishing up some work in the cities and driving up in the morning."

"I have to admit, Mignonette," Solange said, "when I realized you had a relationship with Joe Tierney, I was concerned. He has an extremely dominant personality. And far too charming."

"You forgot movie-star handsome," Mimi added happily.

"That, too. I thought possibly he would influence you too greatly, remake you closer to his own image."

"You mean like I'd be ironing my bathing suit?"

"Exactly," Solange declared. "But I'm glad to see you have held your own. In your own environs, you're still you."

"Thanks. I think."

"You're welcome, Mignonette." Solange began slowly backstroking away.

"Wait!"

Solange stopped.

"About Solie."

"Yes?"

"I brought *Goodnight Moon* with me. It's in the RV."

There was a short pause while Mimi held her breath, then she heard Solange laughing, a bell choir of honest amusement. Poor Solie. The *Iliad* it looked to be.

"Oh, Mimi," Solange said, still chuckling. "We read that last week. We're reading *Moo, Bah, La La La* tonight."

Well. Things do change.

Mimi watched Solange swim halfway to the shore before slipping off the inner tube and striking out for the raft, where Naomi was already peeling off her suit.

Dear Readers,

Since I was a kid I've been spending the odd week at northern Minnesota resorts and cabins and cottages. But the places I knew and know are disappearing, two-room cottages with the tiny screened-in porches perched on an outcrop of rocky ground, damp beach towels flying like pendants from clotheslines. On too many lakes, they are being replaced by five-thousand-square-foot houses with manicured lawns dumping fertilizer into once-clear lakes. The insistent roar of ATVs, wave runners, and stereo speakers has drowned out the subtler melodies of birdsong and wind and water. The night sky is no longer black and fathomless, but murky with yard lights. It's not the wilderness in the wilderness anymore. We haven't left the suburbs; we've taken them with us, and we have to start tallying up the price we are asking others to pay so we can have our boats and houses and lawns and toys. We have to be accountable for the impact we have on the lives of others. Not only human lives, but all life.

We are so enormously fortunate to have lakes and forests and silence and darkness. I want my children and grandchildren to be just as fortunate. As I am sure you do, too.

Finally, before I was married, I spent a summer weekend at a lake with my husband's extended family, the McKinleys. That lake provided a blueprint for Chez Ducky. In the years since, the extended family has kept extending and along with it the McKinleys' decidedly catholic notion of what constitutes a family, and with it the generosity of spirit that invests that singular splotch of shoreline. Long may it reign.

My best,
Connie Brockway

Also Available From

CONNIE BROCKWAY

HOT DISH

Here she is...

Years ago, Jenn Lind's family's dynasty crashed, forcing
them to move out of their Raleigh penthouse and into a
cabin in Fawn Creek, Minnesota. But Jenn saw a way
out: She'd win the Buttercup Pageant, grab the
scholarship, and run far, far away. The plan almost
worked too, until some conniving townspeople cheated
her out of her tiara. Still, she swore she'd make
it out someday...

Miss Minnesota?

Twenty years later, she's on the cusp of real stardom.
She's about to leave for New York to be crowned queen
of daytime TV when Fawn Creek asks her to be grand
marshal of the town's sesquicentennial. Her network
accepts, delighted over the potential PR, especially since
she'll be sharing the "honor" with international celebrity
Steve Jaax, a man she got tangled up with once long
ago. Between the all too attractive Steve, the
townspeople, and a hundred-pound butter sculpture,
Jenn may never escape Fawn Creek.
Or even worse, she might.

**Available wherever books are sold or at
penguin.com**